Shuttle Diplomacy

by

Mike Miller

AuthorHouse™
1663 Liberty Drive, Suite 200
Bloomington, IN 47403
www.authorhouse.com
Phone: 1-800-839-8640

First published by AuthorHouse 6/4/2008

ISBN: 978-1-4343-3132-8 (sc)

Printed in the United States of America
Bloomington, Indiana

This book is printed on acid-free paper.

Acknowledgements

Thank you Mom and Dad for letting me stay up as late as I wanted so long as I was reading a book. And, thank you for everything else.

For my wife and boys. Thank you for allowing me to sneak away to our attic on too many nights to write this novel. And, thank you for everything else.

Lastly, to my friend and colleague, Valerie, who helped me edit the manuscript. I will never forget the kind words of support and encouragement you always gave me, such as: "Does this make any sense?" "Why the hell would you write that?" and my favorite "Didn't they teach you punctuation?" If there are any remaining grammatical errors, they are, of course, the fault of my editor…just kidding Val.

Prologue

In compliance with Executive Order 12546 dated February 3, 1986, a Presidential Commission was formed to investigate the Space Shuttle Challenger Accident. On June 6, 1986, it made its report to the President. The report concluded, in part, a failure in the joint between the two lower segments of the right Solid Rocket Motor caused the loss of Challenger. Specifically, the seals intended to prevent hot gases from leaking through the joint during the Solid Rocket Motor burn failed. The commission stated that no other element of the space shuttle failed.

The commission further noted that "while assembly conditions had the potential of generating debris or damage that could cause O-ring seal failure, these were not considered factors" contributing to the cataclysmic failure.

Lastly, the Presidential Committee concluded, "sabotage was not a factor" with no further comment or justification for that statement.

Chapter 1

Tuesday, January 28, 1986
Briggs City, Utah

The dun colored western sky told Fire Chief Greg Zimmerman that the light flakes of snow falling on the scene of his investigation would soon come down heavier and faster. He'd already concluded that it appeared to be an open and shut case. Hell of a time to be out here, Zimmerman groaned looking at his watch. The whole town was shattered by the shuttle explosion and he wanted to watch the president's address to the nation in lieu of the scheduled State of the Union speech. His two younger brothers worked at the local plant that built components for the NASA rockets and he was hoping to stop by his mother's house to see how they were holding up. It looked like the blame game had already begun and he knew from his service days which way it would roll.

Chief Zimmerman had previously noted that the fire was contained to the dwelling structure spreading only to the sixty-eight Beetle parked by the side door, well, what used to be the side door. It was a makeshift home, typical of what you would find in the area. People out here just needed space and the type of dwelling didn't really matter. "Modern day pioneers" was Zimmerman's label for them. The victim's home was a trailer set up on cinder blocks for so long that the axles had rusted out and were lying on the ground; the bald tires had melted over the corroded wheel hubs and the factory paint, where it could still be seen, had long ago been bleached white by the summer mountain sun. At some point, the victim, or a prior owner, had built at least three add-ons that could still be discerned by the charred and smoldering wooden frames. The kitchen extension was where the explosion had taken place.

It had all of the earmarks of a propane leak ignited by the victim when he entered from the outside with a lit cigarette in his hand. The body wasn't badly burned; it must have been thrown right back out the door. The chief jotted down his observations on the report form that was rapidly becoming wet and shook his head thinking it was too bad the victim's head met the doorframe on the way out or he might still be alive. He cursed as his pen tore through the soggy paper.

"What do you think, Zim?" Sheriff Zane McDaniel asked coming back from the woods pulling up on his zipper.

"It appears to have been an accident." He clicked shut his pen, then stuck it through the top of the clipboard.

"How's that?" McDaniel asked turning up his collar and buttoning the front flap across his round face.

"See that?" Zimmerman pointed near the body's right hand. "There's a cigarette burned all the way down to the filter. He was smoking it when he entered. Look around, there are no butts anywhere else around here; he was a pretty neat fella. It's the same brand as the pack that's in his coat pocket. If you go around the side there," he said pointing. "You'll see that he had the kitchen stove jerry rigged to the outside tank - lots of duct tape. My guess is that he left it on after cooking something or maybe he left it on for the heat and the pilot went out. What do you know about him?"

"Not much at all. He bought this place last year and kept to himself according to his supervisor at the plant. The one neighbor down the road said she hardly ever saw him; she's the one that called us - saw the smoke but never heard the explosion. The vic came up clean in our call to the state police. Maybe your brothers knew him."

"I'll ask. Next of kin?" Zimmerman asked.

"No one local… I have his mother's address and phone number in Tennessee. I reckon I'll have to make that call soon.

Zimmerman gave his friend an understanding look. "I'm done. Tell the coroner he can take the body and have your guys mark off this whole area. I guess we'll all come back in the spring if we need to look around some more." The chief brushed off the accumulating snow from his report and headed back to the warmth of his county issued Chevy Caprice.

Chapter 2

Monday, January 13, 2003
Newark, New Jersey

"Newark, New Jersey…shit." Dan Gill lamented aloud darting off the highway and hitting the brakes as he pulled unto the litter strewn streets. Maneuvering the roadways was better now than when he was stuck in the city five days ago during a heavy snowfall, twelve inches recorded at the airport. Now, the only evidence of that was the soot covered lumps of snow delineating the parking spots on the side streets. Dan made his way to the law firm of Gotti and Murphy; fortunately, they had off street parking he recalled.

For the past four years, since his discharge from the United States Army, Dan Gill had been working as a claims investigator for Knight's Insurance Company; today, he was conducting a tape recorded statement of two of John Gotti's clients who claimed to be injured on a bus struck from behind by a young woman whom Knight's insured. Gotti did a lot of personal injury work and Dan was at his Newark office several times a year to meet the hapless accident victims who eagerly signed contingent fee retainer agreements as the price of admission for the tort lottery.

Dan found the one remaining parking spot and safely made his way to the front door despite the fact that the attorneys had nothing shoveled and a thin seam of ice remained on the pathway. The office was a converted one family home and last decorated in 1975 by the doctor who had sold them the building. Except for the computers and telephone system, Gotti and Murphy changed nothing, trusting, correctly, that the garish motif would be fashionable again. Gill thought Murphy did real estate work but wasn't sure; he'd never met the man.

"Hello, I'm Dan Gill with Knight's Insurance. I have a ten o'clock appointment with Mr. Gotti."

The big haired and top heavy receptionist pointed to the waiting area without looking up; she continued typing an address on an envelope.

"Thanks, I'll have a seat." Dan chose the least stained chair, opened his brief case and started perusing the file on Gotti's clients. He eyed the couple across the small waiting area.

"You from the insurance company?" The man asked loud enough to be heard across the boulevard.

Dan nodded.

"Good. Me and her been in two other accidents we got crap money for but this time we…"

"Mr. Gill!" boomed John Gotti's voice from around the corner. He appeared quickly saying, "Come on back and set your things up in the conference room. The coffee's hot."

Dan closed his briefcase; while walking towards the conference room he smiled at the attorney who replied by shaking his head in disbelief at - but out of view from - his clients.

Dan liked John Gotti, Esquire, who was known his whole life as Jack Gotti until the mid eighties when the more well known John Gotti became famous, or infamous. Then he changed his letterhead and billboard advertisements and insisted on being called John. Only in New Jersey could a lawyer have the same name as a mobster and increase his clientele. Anyway, Dan knew him to be a reasonable attorney and they settled a lot of personal injury cases together.

The conference room table was piled high with leftover courtroom exhibits. He cleared away a portion of the table and set up his tape recorder, then poured a cup of coffee. Gotti's muffled voice could be heard chastising his clients behind closed doors for speaking to the insurance "hack" without their attorney being present.

There were smashed up moped and car parts all over the floor and artificial limbs and crutches in the corner that Dan decided to check out as Gotti came into the conference room.

"Take a look at that statement and those photos." Dan said pointing to where he had set up shop on the table.

"Why? What's the problem?"

"I already took a statement from the bus driver and he claims that there were twelve passengers on board when he got hit in the rear."

"And?"

"To date, Knight's has received thirty seven separate claims for personal injuries stemming from this fender bender. In fact, that's too generous a description. The only damage to my lady's car is a cracked cornering light."

Gotti looked at the photos. After shuffling them around and then studying the bus driver's statement for a few minutes he said, "These photos don't impress me; in fact…they help my case."

Dan leaned back in the squeaky wooden armchair. "I'm waiting." He challenged.

"Did I ever tell you about my great closing argument where I compare for the jury the human spinal column with a diamond?"

"Enlighten me." Dan ghosted a smile.

Gotti started pacing back and forth, animated, as if a jury had suddenly materialized around his conference room table. "Well, you can take a sledgehammer to a diamond and it won't break. The way you cut open a very hard diamond is with a small tap from a tiny hammer." He held up a full sized anatomical skeleton that he seized from behind the door and made a slight tap with his index finger causing the nucleas pulposes to fall from its slot between the L4 and L5 vertebrae and land at Dan's foot.

"And this is done with a straight face?" Dan picked up the model part and wedged it back into place.

"Absolutely. It's a winner. Looks like the other twenty-five people committing fraud might have a problem, though."

"Did you read the second page of the bus driver's statement?" Dan flipped over the paper. "He's been on the same route for nine years; he knows by name or by face all of the passengers that night. Guess which two didn't make the list."

Gotti picked up the statement and flipped through it again and looked around the conference room imagining what a jury, even an Essex County jury, might think. "What do you want to do?"

"I'll take a general release from your clients stating that they won't sue my insured or Knight's and we won't refer this matter to the state fraud unit."

The lawyer drummed on the table and looked at the photographs again. "Sounds fair. What about the other case we settled, Kamel Kamel? My girl mailed you his release last week."

Dan fished out a fifteen thousand dollar settlement check from his briefcase and handed it to the attorney.

"Win some, lose some. Let me give my clients the bad news."

"Good coffee." Dan said downing the last of it and throwing the Styrofoam cup away.

"Thanks, I made it yesterday." Gotti said slipping back to his office with a copy of the bus driver's statement and the release forms.

Dan gathered up his materials and headed out. There was a full blown screaming match going on in Gotti's office by the time he reached the front door; he wondered if that ambulance chasing son of a bitch really heated up day old coffee.

Chapter 3

Later that day
Rosewood, New Jersey

Knight's Insurance Company maintained its north Jersey office in Rosewood, a well-to-do suburban community surprisingly not very far from Newark, but a miserably cold winter rain delayed Dan's trip back to the office. A heavy gray sky dumped inches of water in less than an hour immediately flooding the state highway and most of the side roads. Finally arriving back at the office, he parked near the entrance and ran towards the fifteen-story building as fast as he could; his old army raincoat kept him dry but his briefcase was poor protection for his head. It was time for his midday smoke.

Dan decided to walk up the five flights as penance for his tobacco habit, albeit diminishing, and made it to the office just in time to cast the last vote for lunch. The noon meal dilemma usually started around ten thirty but on really crappy weather days it started around nine since the choices were cut down to the places that promptly delivered. Today, they were ordering Mexican food from 'Tex-Mex-New Jersey!', formerly a Chinese take-out place called 'Lucky Food, USA' but still owned by the same Korean family. Somehow, it just didn't seem kosher, Dan thought.

Before wrapping up his report on Gotti's clients, Dan went to his on-line brokerage account to check his portfolio; it was more depressing than the weather, he murmured clicking off the screen.

"Still going on vacation?" Dave Rawlins asked, hovering over his cubicle wall.

Dan looked up. "Oh yeah. I should be in Miami by noon tomorrow and I plan on getting hammered and banging some broad who can't speak English by midnight," Dan said closing the New York Jets Official Web Site window that appeared on his monitor.

Rawlins, a transplanted Mormon from out west, ran the investigation unit for the Rosewood office and Dan knew he was wound pretty tight; the former paratrooper made a point to mention drinking and sex as much as possible to keep his boss from engaging him in *any* conversation. That's why God invented inter-office e-mail, Dan reasoned. Dave Rawlins unconsciously twisted his wedding band. "Going fishing, again?" He finally asked.

"Bone fishing." Dan gave a big grin.

Not familiar with the sport fish, Dave Rawlins feared asking any further angling questions. "I have an offer for you that would involve... well...it would involve beginning your vacation a little early."

"Boss, that's what my last commanding officer said to me when I told him that I was thinking of reenlisting past twenty."

Rawlins stepped into the cubicle, pulling a chair behind him. He sat down and opened the file he was carrying. "I see." He said taking out papers and photographs. "Well, nothing like that."

"Then it sounds good so far." Dan said finding a note pad.

"We received this file and senior management wants us to quickly... very quickly...nip it in the bud and get enough information to refer it to the fraud unit." Rawlins laid out a photo array on Dan's desk and continued. "We insure this car." He gave Dan a photograph.

"The accident happened on the southbound Jersey Turnpike just past exit three, at about two thirty in the morning this past Christmas. Apparently, our guy struck the claimant in the rear. The claimant thought he saw a deer, slammed on his brakes, and our guy couldn't stop in time. They pulled over to the side of the road, inspected their vehicles, and swapped insurance information. According to our insured, there was some minor damage to both cars. Apparently, it was very cold and neither driver wanted to wait for the police.

"Our insured called in the claim on the twenty-sixth and filled out an accident report for us. He mentioned that a witness briefly pulled over to see if he could help. No name, but the car had a Florida tag. A few days later, the insured called back. He received a summons to go to municipal court because he had been charged with a hit and run. That same day, we received a letter from the claimant's attorney claiming personal injury requiring immediate back surgery; major damage to the car; basically, the whole nine yards. I sent Marty Singer out and sure as day, the man's car had extensive rear end damage. Marty asked about the witness from Florida and the claimant said that he didn't remember one. He and his lawyer started making goo goo eyes at each other and the attorney ended the interview.

"What's our exposure?" Dan asked.

"Our insured has a one million, combined single limit automobile policy, plus homeowner's and umbrella coverage - all with us."

"That's a deep pocket."

"Right. The claimant has had numerous prior accidents that he sued on and some worker's compensation claims, too."

"What's the problemo? Did Marty talk to our insured yet?"

"No." Rawlins replied.

"Boss, you gotta be thinking of these things." Dan deadpanned.

"I did." Rawlins revealed a rare smile. "What is the chance that on the day Marty is scheduled to see him, our insured losses control of his car on ice and crashes head first into a tree. He's dead. Furthermore, his car is totaled and there is no way to determine what damage was there before he hit the tree. And, he lived alone and had a garage so none of the neighbors noticed his car between Christmas and the day he died. So, we need to prove what condition our insured's car was in after the accident on Christmas and before he chopped down a tree with his Caddy."

"Our witness in Florida." Dan said.

"Bingo. Marty found the man; Air Force Lieutenant Colonel Ben Ochoa stationed near Cape Canaveral. Unfortunately, he is a very hard man to get on the phone. Here's his work phone number." Rawlins handed Dan a slip of paper. "Try to get his statement as soon as you get to Florida. Submit your bills and we'll pay for your airfare and we'll pay for a rental, too. If he turns out to be a good witness, I'll see about picking up the tab on the rental for the whole time you're in Florida.

Otherwise, I would have to pay a per diem guy down there to do the work and you know what type of bill I'll get for services rendered."

Lunch arrived and everyone headed towards the conference room. Rawlins left the entire file with Dan who thumbed through it. He picked up the colonel's phone number and made the call. He spoke with a Sergeant Laura Smith who said that they were extremely busy; she rattled off a host of acronyms that meant nothing to Dan but he was able to divine that a space shuttle was being launched soon; hence, the urgency he surmised. Dan promised that he needed no more than twenty minutes and the sergeant said she could squeeze him in to the colonel's schedule. She told him to fax down photo identification and then gave him instructions for what he had to do when he showed up.

Sergeant Smith sounded cute but Dan was sure that she probably looked like Sergeant Snorkel's twin sister; he had been snookered by telephone voices before.

Chapter 4

Same day
Satellite Beach, Florida

Pavel Volkova enjoyed vigorous early morning exercising and a run on the beach was a particular favorite, reminding him of his youth as a military advisor in many such tropical climes. The former *Komiter Gosudarstvennos Bezopanosti* officer sat down by the edge of the water letting the final flow of each wave touch his bare feet. He finished the bottled water that he carried for the four mile run on the hard packed sand then walked back to the car to make another call.

Before his jog, he'd followed his quarry on her way to work at five thirty finally getting close enough for a better picture with his digital camera when she stopped for gas. The Cuban insisted that he needed a more defined photo - a good head shot; still, the bastard was being slow about it and Volkova had given him a final warning: this task should have been completed over a week ago and heads would roll if the Russian failed to meet his deadline. He hated having to rely on the Cuban but he needed to subcontract out the preliminary work to avoid as much involvement as possible since he could not afford to be discovered back on his old enemy's turf.

You have reached the office of... "Goddamn answering machine." Volkova bleated, ready to toss his phone onto the passenger seat.

"Hello!"

"Is that you, Raoul?"

"Yes."

"It's me. Can you talk?" The Russian asked.

"Yes." Raoul Viñals replied.

"I am sending you another picture of the lady; it's much better than the others you have."

Viñals acknowledged what he said while the Russian grabbed his towel, locked up the car and headed back towards the beach.

"What's taking so long, Raoul? You said he was ready."

"He is...was...I'll call him right now to find out what he's doing."

"I'll call you back in one hour and I'll e-mail the new photo this morning." Pavel Volkova barked and ended the call.

The sun was already hot, but comfortable; not burning like it would be in the coming months. He would go to the public library to access the internet after getting something to eat. The beach was empty except for some occasional beachcombers and a pair of older women power walking...he thought of Nicaragua. Beautiful beaches there, and beautiful women, he remembered. Better than here.

Nicaragua also reminded him of that piece of mule dung, Manuel Aquino of the Security Brigade. Major Aquino was an up and coming party man within the Security Brigade that was headed by one of President Daniel Ortega's corrupt and inept cronies. Well, corruption was to be expected but Volkova didn't have to tolerate a fool, the Russian schemed. Pavel Volkova had decided to fast track the young major's career in the hope that President Ortega would promote him to the top security position. This would have to be done without offending the old hard-line communists in Ortega's regime. The plan was relatively simple: get the Nicaraguan army off of its collective ass and kill as many *Contras* as possible. Surely, that would help draw the American cowboy president into another jungle conflict; a lovely little war to draw troops away from Europe and money from military research and development programs - like the Strategic Defense Initiative - *Star Wars.*

To that end, KGB Officer Pavel Volkova fed intelligence - soviet satellite imagery - to the aggressive and eager Aquino who soon became famous for his lightening swift and deadly accurate raids - of course, any dead peasant was counted as a *Contra.* Everyone knew that the agricultural equipment consultant from Moscow, who was traveling with the major on every strike, should not be asked any farming questions. The major's star was rising and he was even considered a possible successor to Danny Ortega. Within months, the chief of security had announced his retirement to make way for Aquino.

Then, the unthinkable happened: the American covert effort to help the *Contras* hit the proverbial fan splashing on to the front pages. It was soon apparent that the United States could not justify to its citizens a hot war in Central America when it had been lying about the covert war and its hostage release efforts with Iran for years. With all of the recriminations going on in Washington, the Central Intelligence Agency was having a hard enough time supplying the rebels with boots and socks never mind beans and bullets. So, Pavel Volkova cut off his flow of information to young Major Aquino. But like an addict, he was hooked and wanted more.

Major Aquino demanded a meeting with his soviet comrade and in the lobby of the Hotel de Managua, he calmly insisted that if Volkova were not more forthcoming then he would be forced to tell the journalists, in the luxury suites above, about the length and breadth of soviet expansionism in the western hemisphere. After that, he could work for Uncle Sam, he laughed.

Flying to Havana a few days later, stretching his legs in the first class section of the proletarian state owned airliner, Volkova read in the national paper about the brutal murder of Major Aquino, his pregnant wife and two young daughters by rebels in apparent retribution for the dozens of attacks he had commanded. Volkova folded the paper, sticking it behind the magazines in the seat pocket in front of him; as he looked out the window watching the broken clouds pass by below, a thin smile crept across his face.

Eager to wrap up his work in Florida and deciding to skip breakfast, the Russian went back to his car and sped off to the public library.

Chapter 5

Tuesday, January 14, 2003
Patrick Air Force Base & Cocoa Beach, Florida

Since Knight's Insurance Company was picking up the tab, Dan upgraded his airline ticket. If Rawlins questioned him about it then Dan planned on mentioning his admission into the Mile High Club with the stewardess…flight attendant, he mentally corrected himself. Pure fantasy of course, but Rawlins would stop the inquiry fearing the possibility of a sexual discussion in the workplace. Dan also rented a Mustang convertible. What the hell, he was saving his employer over a million bucks of exposure.

He checked in with Sergeant Smith and confirmed the appointment with Colonel Ochoa for fourteen hundred. Military time sounded out-of-place after being immersed in the civilian world for four years and he momentarily checked his watch to make sure it still meant 2:00 p.m.

Dan got a room in a two story beach front motel in Cocoa Beach and brought his bags up to his room on the upper floor. Before checking in, he bought a six pack of Red Stripe beer and placed the bottles in the unit's trash can, covering them with ice. They would taste good later on the beach, he knew for sure. Stepping out unto the balcony and looking northward, he could see the massive gangway towers used to launch the shuttle and America's other rockets. Since there was a launch scheduled for Saturday, he assumed the shuttle was already out there but couldn't see it.

The drive to the air base was shorter than it seemed on the map. Parking at the visitor's center, he got a day pass for his car and was informed by a young airman that Sergeant Smith was on the way to pick him up. He imagined a hulk of a woman tearing down the main drag in a Humvee mounted with a fifty caliber machine gun on top. Ten minutes later, a very trim and pretty blond wearing camouflage fatigues and sergeant's stripes stepped out of a yellow Camaro IROC-Z. Walking over, she crisply introduced herself as Sergeant Laura Smith and Dan mumbled something about insurance.

"Sir, why don't you ride with me? Parking is pretty tight and I have a reserved spot," she said going back to her car not waiting for a response.

Dan watched her walk away and remembered. *I need my briefcase.* He went back to his car and got it.

"Does this need to be checked or anything?" He asked stepping into the sergeant's car.

"No, sir." She started the Camaro, backing up and then accelerating forward onto the main road as if she were leaving a pit stop. "Colonel Ochoa confirmed that he was a witness to the accident you called about and I verified your employment with Knight's Insurance Company. So, you're what we would assess a low risk."

Dan looked out the window. Air Force bases always seemed foreign to him. For one thing, all the signs were blue instead of green. That sort of thing doesn't happen on an army base.

Mulling over the sergeant's statement, Dan offered. "What if I were a *Spetznaz* trained sleeper agent, here to damage the space center? I could have been waiting twenty years for this opportunity."

She looked over, lowering her head so she could see him over her wrap around shades. Shifting gears she remarked, "Good point. But, you're not at the space center. I suppose that you could blow up our squadron's admin building - that might not be such a bad thing - but, if you scratch this car, I'll make sure that this is your last mission, sir. It's a 1990, the last year for the IROC."

She clutched into fifth gear. "*Spetznaz*...I haven't heard that term in our security briefings for quite a while. Don't you know that the Russians are our buds now? They've had a cosmonaut on the last two shuttle missions."

Dan fiddled with the combination lock on his briefcase. "All right, I'm not really a sleeper agent. But, could you do me a favor?"

"Depends on the favor, sir."

She braked passing a twenty-five mile an hour speed limit sign and waved at the Department of Defense police car coming the other way. Both cops waved back.

"Don't ever refer to me as a low risk assessment again. It sounds so...unmasculine."

She laughed. "Yes, sir."

"And, please call me Dan. I work for a living."

"That sounds like former enlisted man talk."

"Army." Dan pointed towards her sleeve. "What rank of sergeant are you? All of those stripes are confusing."

"I'm a senior master sergeant, one up and six down. But, being army, I can understand how you would be confused."

"If I made fun of a civilian guest when I was on active duty, I would probably be court-martialed."

"If you're making a complaint, take a number. I'm fairly certain that I insulted every member of a visiting congressional committee last week." She downshifted and made a quick turn. "We're here."

There was a small sign indicating that they were at the administration building for the weather squadron. It was a one story cinder block structure painted white with brown trim. Dan followed his host inside and down a corridor lined with pictures of the unit's chain of command ultimately leading to a portrait of the president. She brought him to the top non-commissioned officer's office who was away on leave Sergeant Smith said.

"You can wait here. My office is right over there if you need anything. Do you want some coffee?"

"Sure."

"Okay, help yourself. There's a break room right down there," Sergeant Smith answered, pointing the way as she walked back to her office.

Dan followed her instructions and found the beverage table, impressed by the level of comfort in the break room. I should have joined the air force, he said aloud, going through the collection of

DVDs. He headed back, passing Sergeant Smith's office: she was at her computer furiously typing something on the keyboard.

"Thanks!" He said passing by and holding up his cup.

"Hey!" She shot back.

Dan stopped on a dime then back stepped. She looked up from her screen but still typed-but more slowly. "What did you do in the army?" She asked.

"Well, I started as an infantryman - eleven bush. That's slang for 'eleven bravo'...11B, the military occupational specialty designation for infantryman. Then, I transferred to the military police. I retired as an E-8. How long have you been in?"

She was about to answer when they heard someone call out "Attention!"

"Well, my boss is back." She said. "Get your briefcase; I'll bring you to his office."

*****

Sergeant Smith knocked on her commander's door. "Sir, Mr. Gill from Knight's Insurance." Then she left.

The colonel waved him in and then got up from his desk to shake Dan's hand. "Hello, Mr. Gill, hope you weren't waiting very long."

"No sir, you're right on time.

"Well, where do we start?" The colonel asked.

"I need to show you some photographs and take a tape recorded statement with your permission. I'll also need to take notes."

"Then have a seat there." The colonel pointed to an upholstered chair and began to clear off his coffee table. The colonel was in his mid forties and in excellent shape, filling out the top half of his uniform shirt and leaving a loose fit around the abdomen. Dan had expected some wussy air force meteorologist with thick black framed glasses and wearing a pocket protector. Maybe even a slide rule hanging off of his belt.

Dan laid out Marty Singer's photographs and set up his tape recorder, doing a test to make sure it worked. Rawlins could live with the first class tickets and the convertible but not if he brought back a blank tape.

"I was told this will only take about fifteen or twenty minutes."

"That's right, colonel."

"I don't mean to sound so self-important but with this STS mission we're very busy.

"STS?" Dan asked.

"Space Transportation System…the space shuttle."

"Is that a new name for it?"

"No, we've used it before." The colonel smiled. "We tend to use a lot of technical names and acronyms. It makes us feel better when we get paid."

Dan laughed. Pretty nice guy for a senior officer, he thought.

"This is about the accident on the Jersey Turnpike, right?" Colonel Ben Ochoa asked.

"On Christmas, that's right."

"Is it routine to do this for every accident?"

Dan explained that it wasn't and why he had come down to Florida on such short notice. Ochoa said that he had been visiting his parents when he'd had to end his leave early. After midnight mass, he'd headed back to Florida and he described what he had seen.

Sergeant Smith came back into the room with a Diet Coke for her boss. "More coffee?" She said to Dan, spotting his empty mug.

"I'll have one of those, please." He pointed to the soda.

"Don't talk too fast, sir; Mr. Gill is an old army man." She said leaving.

"I would have preferred she said *former* army man."

Ochoa grinned. "Sergeant Smith usually runs out of wise acre things to say by this time of day." He took a sip. "How long were you in?"

Dan briefly told him about his service with the Rangers. Sergeant Smith reappeared with his drink.

"Colonel, Mr. Gill told me that he used to eat bush." She said handing Dan his drink.

Dan's eyes pie plated as he looked at the senior officer.

"*Eleven bush*, it's slang for…" Dan said hurriedly.

"I know…infantry." The colonel interjected calmly.

"I must have been confused because of his accent." Laura said disappearing.

Dan noticed the colonel suppressing a smile and relaxed back in his seat.

"My older brother, Ray." The colonel said pointing to a picture on the wall. "He was an ALO…Air Liaison Officer…with the Americal Division in Vietnam. He was with an infantry battalion for about six months. From his letters, I know all about eleven bushes."

"He must tell some stories." Dan said looking at the wall.

"Yeah, well." The colonel halted then decided to speak some more. "Ray never made it home. A surface to air missile brought down his Republic F-105G Thunderchief in late seventy. He was in a wild weasel squadron flying a mission in support of the Son Tay Prison Raid when he got hit. The electronic warfare officer in the back seat was a confirmed KIA but Ray was listed as an MIA for twenty-five years until the Vietnamese government said that a farmer had found a helmet… with his skull inside. It was a serendipitous discovery because there was talk of growing trade relations at the time and his remains were miraculously found just days before our delegation arrived in Hanoi."

Lieutenant Colonel Ochoa got up and took his brother's picture off the wall handing it to Dan.

"I don't know what to say." Dan said.

"There's nothing to say."

Sergeant Smith came back into the room from where she'd been listening in the hallway. "I never heard you talk about your brother to anyone before, sir."

"Hey." The colonel said changing the subject. "We almost lost Sergeant Smith here a few years ago. She was working at a tactical weather station over in Kosovo. Driving back to headquarters, for the mail of all things, an A-10 appeared out of nowhere, then made a gun run right over her Humvee, wiping out a Serbian infantry squad half a click down the road waiting to ambush her."

"I didn't need that Warthog." She said. Silence followed.

"How about you colonel, any war stories?" Dan asked.

"A scud landed half a mile from my tent in the first Gulf War, that's about it." He looked at the clock on the wall. "Well, are we done here?"

"Just sign here and…one more thing. You said that the plate number for this car," He pointed to the photograph, "was CAP 51L. How did you know that? You can't see the tag from this picture."

"It stuck with me I guess. CAP reminded me of Cape Canaveral and 51L was the mission number for the last Challenger flight."

"I'll be a son of a gun." Dan said writing down the colonel's statement. "You'll make a great witness."

"I really have to go, now." The colonel stood up; shaking Dan's hand. He then grabbed his hat and some papers off his desk. Rushing out the door, he stopped.

"If you're going to be here for the launch, Sergeant Smith can arrange for you to watch it."

"Are you serious?"

"Sure."

"I was planning on doing some bone fishing down on the keys, but that can't beat watching a launch."

"Make it so, number one." The colonel said pointing to the sergeant, then left the building.

"He loves *Star Trek*." Laura said shaking her head. "More work for me, I guess. Good thing I had nothing else to do. I suppose you want a ride back."

"You could just give me the keys to your car."

"I don't think you could handle it. I saw your Ford."

Sergeant Smith made Dan wait almost twenty minutes, then drove him back to the visitor's center. She wasn't as talkative and Dan was feeling a sense of rejection - the same emotions from a dateless high school career came seeping back in to his belly.

"Not saying much." Dan finally broke the silence.

"I'm just thinking of what I have left to do."

"If it's a problem getting me a pass..."

"No, that's easy. I was only kidding back there."

The ride back seemed quicker and she pulled up next to his convertible.

Dan got out; then closing the door he leaned back in. "Thanks for all of your help and for the pass."

"No problem. Call me tomorrow so I can tell you how to pick it up." She said putting the car in reverse. "Bye."

Why do I feel like I just blew it on the first date, Dan thought as he tossed his brief case onto the Mustang's rear seat.

Chapter 6

Wednesday, January 15, 2003
Cocoa Beach

Instead of breakfast, former U.S. Army Ranger Dan Gill went running on the beach, heading north at first along the water line that was at dead low. After thirty minutes, he hoped for a better view of the structures jutting out on Cape Canaveral, but a morning haze had drifted in from the Atlantic totally obscuring the Cape. Dan Gill was in good shape having kept his army physical training regimen post discharge…for the most part. Now, to stay fit, he still ran as much but the bench press in the cellar was used more to hang up laundry than for keeping his pectorals and biceps pumped up. At six foot three and a touch over two hundred pounds, Dan was waiting for the day that one or both knees would blow out from all of his foot pounding. He had a road bike in his garage that he bought to keep some of the stress off his joints but riding in New Jersey scared him more than his two combat jumps.

After showering, he turned on the weather to catch the forecast for South Florida. While waiting, he heard about the blizzard hitting New York City. He couldn't help but laugh at his good fortune but soon realized how busy he would be when his vacation ended; he had visions of checking out all of the accident claims to be expected with the snowstorm.

Dan took his convertible for a ride up and down A1A; spotting a fishing pier, he parked and strolled out to see what was running.

He couldn't understand a word spoken by the heavy southern accents fishing the pier so he just poked his head down to see what was in their buckets - mostly spots, a good pan fish. Around eleven, he was too hungry to wait any longer and checked out a seafood restaurant just off the pier. After his second Jamaican beer, Dan decided to call Sergeant Smith about the VIP pass.

"Good morning, Weather Squadron, Airman Kranepool speaking, this is a non secure line. How may I help you?" The young airman briskly answered.

"May I speak with Sergeant Smith, my name is Dan Gill?"

"Wait one, sir."

After a few minutes, she answered tersely. "Sergeant Smith, here."

"Hi sergeant, this is Dan Gill."

"Yes?"

"Dan Gill from yesterday."

"Yesterday?"

"I'm with Knight's Insurance; I took a statement at Colonel Ochoa's office." He waited. "I was in your car and you insulted me several times."

"Yes, of course. Forgot the name, remembered the insults. What can I do for you?"

"I was supposed to call you today about making arrangements to view the space shuttle launch."

"Oh, we're all sold out."

"What?"

"Just kidding. Where are you calling from?"

"Sonny's Seaside Seafood, why?"

"There's a lot of background noise. Where are you…at the bar?"

"Yes."

"The sun isn't even over the yardarm yet."

"*I'm* on vacation." Dan said holding his empty bottle up to the bartender.

"Sonny's isn't the best place in town. Don't you have an expense account?"

"I did up until I finished your colonel's interview. I'm on my time, now."

"Didn't you tell the colonel you were going fishing?"

"I'm leaving after the launch."

"Okay, well I have your pass and instructions. Why don't you meet me at the visitor's center at seventeen hundred hours? That's five..."

"I know what time it is." Dan said cutting her off.

"That's right; you're an old navy guy."

"Army."

"Right. I'll see later. Out." The line went dead.

Very odd woman...I like that, Dan mused pouring his new beer into a fresh glass.

*****

Dan Gill arrived just moments before he spotted the yellow Camaro approaching from the opposite direction. The car sped up to beat the oncoming traffic, and then made a sharp left turn into the parking lot without the use of indicator lights. It was unfair that insurance premiums were higher for men, Dan opined.

She parked at the nearest available spot and Dan started walking over. Sergeant Smith got out of her car. He couldn't fully appreciate her proportions in yesterday's combat garb, but now she was wearing her service skirt and blouse. She was also wearing some make up that wasn't there yesterday, although she didn't need it at all, he reflected. Dan could visualize her walking into a board room or a courtroom as she approached him.

"Hello again, Dave." She said extending her hand.

"Dan." He took her hand.

"Right. Here are a few items I put together for you. Read the top sheet first: it's the launch itinerary.

They walked back to Dan's car and she placed the papers on the hood. She started explaining as Dan moved around and glanced at the outline of her breasts through the uniform. The lace on her bra was apparent, he observed, but if it weren't for the bright sunlight, it would be hidden by the heavy service blouse material.

"I highlighted these times." She said drawing his attention back to the car hood. "The launch is at 9:53 a.m., and you need to be here by eight. She showed him a map. "See, everything is in civilian time. The bus will leave promptly and take you to the viewing area about three miles away from the launch site."

"Three miles?"

"Believe me, that's as close as you'll want to get." She put the papers away and handed him a laminated day pass. "Don't lose this. There's nothing I can do for you if you show up without it. Here's my cell number." She wrote it down for him. "Call me if you decide not to come or are running late. Don't be late." She gave him the number.

"Will you be joining me?" Dan asked hoping it didn't sound so obvious.

"Yes, I will be escorting you and another gentleman." She looked at Dan apparently gauging whether the description applied.

"Who's the other guy?"

"Mike Muzikowski - a friend of Colonel Ochoa. He was in the area and wanted to see a launch, again.

"Again?"

"Mike was a mission specialist with NASA but left for health reasons a few years ago." Sergeant Smith peered into the convertible and noted Dan's compact disc holder. "Let me guess, Sinatra and Springsteen."

"I have a few others. Hank Williams and Elvis are in there, too."

She nodded her head in approval.

"What were his health reasons?" Dan asked.

"Does it make a difference?"

"Yeah, I want to know if I have to spend all morning with someone who's going to drool on me."

Sergeant Smith considered that possibility. "Fair enough, that's something that might run through my mind, as well. The colonel told me that Mike passed out at the gym several times and was finally diagnosed with an irregular heartbeat. I'm not certain of the medical term. He doesn't drool, I think. Anyway, the flight surgeons told him to find another career; he was three months away from his second STS mission. A good one, too; he was training for an EVA."

"EVA?"

"Extra Vehicle Activity…a space walk."

"What's a mission specialist?" Dan asked.

"Are we going to discuss the man's whole life, here?" Before Dan could say anything she added. "Let's go to Heffernan's. You can buy me a beer."

She marched back to her car instructing him to follow her.

Chapter 7

Later on, same day
Heffernan's Pub

The lot was filling as Dan parked and he ambled over towards Sergeant Smith's car. She stepped out and adjusted her uniform, placing her air force hat on. Dan was impressed by the way her rear end nicely filled out the matronly skirt; he couldn't believe that he was about to have drinks with the woman he was looking at. At last, he thought, I don't have to make up a story for the guys back at the office.

"This place looks popular, Sergeant . . ." Dan said, searching for conversation.

"Laura, please. It is, especially after work on Wednesdays and Fridays. They have a happy hour buffet that is to die for. Are you hungry?"

"I could eat." Dan replied.

"Good. I have to be back at work by nineteen hundred and didn't feel like going all the way home to eat."

Dan opened the door.

"My, I didn't think Yankees had such manners." She said in her very best Southern Belle.

"Of course, I can't let a broad open a door for me."

She smiled removing her hat.

"Why do you have to go back to work?" Dan asked while they waited for the hostess.

"Because, my boss is a type 'A' personality. Our squadron has its annual inspection next week and I need to brief him on what we are doing to get ready for it. He's been so busy with the launch, he's worried something might get overlooked."

The hostess came over and seated them followed by a waitress who took their drink order and quickly disappeared.

"What's the inspection for?" Dan asked.

"Everything - vehicles, equipment, training, maintenance. It's an annual readiness inspection."

"Oh, we called them I.G. inspections in the army - Inspector General."

The waitress brought them two beers and plates for the buffet. They visited the offerings returning to their table with peel and eat shrimp piled high on the small dishes.

"Don't you love ice cold beer in a frosted mug? Cheers." She said clinking their mugs. "We're not supposed to drink in uniform…but as you can see…it's really more of a guideline than a hard and fast rule." She indicated the young lieutenants at the bar. "Just don't embarrass the uniform."

"What is your military occupational specialty?" Dan asked after a few shrimps.

"I am the administration and personnel non-commissioned officer for the squadron. We've been without an officer for four months so I run the section all by myself and report directly to the boss."

"A file keeper." Dan said provoking her.

"A file keeper who can run a six minute mile and shoot expert with a Beretta nine millimeter semi automatic pistol." She said taking a sip.

Dan appreciated her ability. "Our human resources guy at Knight's can't do that. Although he might like wearing you're uniform on the weekends. Not that there's anything wrong with that." She smiled. Must be a *Seinfeld* fan, too, he surmised. A good sign. Dan eyed a plate of crab legs going by. "How long will your briefing be, tonight?"

"Depends. I would guess one to two hours. All of the staff officers are reporting their preparedness for the inspection and some of those dodo heads love to hear themselves talk."

They worked their way to the bottom of their buffet plates when the waitress appeared and took an order for two more beers.

"I really shouldn't since I'm still on duty. You said yesterday that you were an MP?"

"For about half of my military career."

"What was that other stuff you told the colonel about...bush whacking...or whatever?"

"That was for my first two enlistments."

"Why did you want to become a cop?"

"Long story." He said as the next round arrived. "Cops run in the family. My dad was a cop, my uncles - one on my Dad's side and one on my Mom's side, and I think nearly half my cousins are in law enforcement - cops, state troopers, corrections officers.

"I've known Colonel Ochoa since he was a lowly second lieutenant and I was still wearing my basic training hairdo and I've never known him to just mention his brother the way he did yesterday."

"I hope it didn't upset him."

"No. I don't think so. You two certainly hit it off, though, because Ben rarely bothers asking to get someone into the VIP viewing area. The last time was almost a year ago when his parents visited."

Dan took a long sip. "Ben?" His raised his eyebrows.

"Colonel Ochoa. We're friends; I can call him Ben when no one else is around."

"That familiarity doesn't happen much in the army."

"Well, we're not in the army." After a few moments, she said. "I need to get back on base."

The change in direction was palpable. "I didn't mean to imply anything, I just meant ... "

"What? That I'm sleeping around with the boss?"

"No." Dan shot back not venturing any further but the thought *had* immediately run through his mind like a freight train.

The waitress checked back and Dan handed her his credit card.

"The weather is going to be ideal for the launch. You're really lucky. Hopefully, there won't be any mechanical delays." Laura said after a while and Dan hoped that the squall had passed.

"Lately . . ." Dan looked at her. "I've been feeling lucky." Sure, it was lame, he knew. But he was hoping to wrap this up on better terms. He was already planning on some possibilities with the cute sergeant.

"Then you should play the Florida lottery." Laura said, getting up after the waitress brought back the receipt.

"I'll play your license plate number."

Going through the door she turned, "It will be the only luck you get from me. See you at the visitor's center." She headed towards her car.

Dan watched her get in. As she backed up, he jogged over and knocked on the window. She lowered the glass and George Strait on the stereo. "You're not going to ask me out for a date, are you?"

He had intended to, but said instead, "I was going to ask you what Mike Muza…whatever his name is…looks like."

"I tell you what. Just walk up to the guy wearing the 'Mike Muzikowski' name tag and ask if it's him."

"I suppose I have a 'Dan Gill' name tag in my folder." He said pointing to his Mustang where he left the folder she had given him.

"Uh huh. See ya."

Dan walked back to his car. "So, do you want to go out or do something tomorrow night? Real smooth Danny boy." He mumbled out loud getting into his rental.

Chapter 8

Thursday, January 16, 2003
Cape Canaveral

"Hi Mike." Dan said walking over to the angular figure resting against the side of the welcome center sign. "I'm Dan Gill."

"I see." The former astronaut straightened up and studying Dan's name tag replied, "Do I know you?"

"No, but we both know Colonel Ochoa."

"Really, Ben didn't say anything…"

"Actually, I just met him two days ago." Dan interjected offering his hand and then explained the relationship.

Mike leaned back against the sign. "Ben and I go back to the academy together but I haven't seen him in years. Does he still have all of his hair?" He pretended to comb his balding head with his fingers.

"It's all there."

"Damn him."

"But it's getting gray on the sides if that helps at all."

"It does, actually," he laughed.

A school bus painted air force blue pulled into the parking lot, turned and stopped near the visitor's center. The driver, a young airman in a rumpled uniform, informed the gathering assemblage that his bus for the VIPs going to the launch viewing area would be leaving in ten minutes then went back to his seat for some quick shut eye.

Dan and Mike got on the bus and sat down together. Dan, spotting Mike's bag filled with food and drinks, regretted his own lack of planning. Well, maybe there was a refreshment stand and souvenir shop out there, he thought.

"Do you know Sergeant Laura Smith? She helped getting me here this morning." Dan mentioned to Mike probing for some…any… background information on the woman.

"Only by reputation. She coordinated everything for me as well. I believe that she and Ben were a thing once but he never out-right told me so."

"Oh, wouldn't that be fraternization or something?" Dan asked as nonchalantly as he could muster as he turned to look the other way feigning even more indifference.

"It was a long time ago and I'm not sure if they were in the same chain of command at the time. Forget I said anything about it. Anyway, it's long over; Ben's been married for over ten years."

The bus filled up quickly. The driver closed the door in exactly ten minutes and cranked up the big bus, turning sharply to head north on A1A.

Mike looked out the window and then upwards checking the weather aloft. "You know," he said to no one in particular then turned to engage Dan, "studies show that most husbands and wives first meet each other at work or school. So, the military integrates women into just about every occupational specialty, then the brass gets disjointed when military men and military women are attracted to one another. For God's sake, where are folks supposed to meet?"

"I met my ex-wife in a bar outside of Fort Benning, Georgia."

"Well, I guess there are exceptions."

"No, you're right I think, for marriages that work out, anyway. We divorced after five years."

"Sorry, about that. Any kids?"

"No, fortunately, or I would still have to see the b…her once in a while for birthdays and weddings and crap like that."

The bus pulled onto a long stretch of straight roadway and started chugging loudly, picking up speed. "What went wrong?" Mike asked, feeling comfortable enough with his new acquaintance to make such a personal query.

"What went right? I was very young and we got married just after I got back from a tour in Korea. She was even younger than me and thought I would take her away from Bumphuck Georgia. I'll admit that I cheated on her…in my heart…as Jimmy Carter once said, but I found out she was cheating on me with Charlie Company. What about you? Married? Kids? Ex-wives?"

"Married, one baby girl. They were going to come but my daughter is getting over a double ear infection so my wife said to go and enjoy myself."

"That's what my ex said when I got alerted for Grenada. Where did you guys meet?"

"In the air force, of course, hence my lecture.

Mike took out a thermos. "Want some?"

"Sure, do you have an extra cup?"

"I have these cups I stole from my motel room." He reached into his bag taking one out and poured slowly. "Cream, no sugar." He finished and handed the cup to Dan. The road was well paved but the suspension on the old bus still made drinking a challenge.

"Sergeant Smith told me you were a mission specialist but I really don't know what that means."

"Well, a mission specialist is part of the shuttle crew. There is typically a seven member crew consisting of a commander who is also a pilot, the pilot, flight engineer, then mission specialists and payload specialists. I was responsible for the on-board maintenance of the orbiter, that's what we call the shuttle."

"What's the difference between a mission specialist and payload specialist?"

"It depends on the payload. For example, if we are going into orbit to conduct pharmaceutical experiments on rats in zero gravity, there may be a chemist or biologist on board trained to be an astronaut payload specialist. If we are launching a communications satellite then we may have an electrical engineer as a payload specialist. My job was to make sure that the shuttle was operating the way it was designed but I also had to understand each payload to make sure it was compatible with on-board systems."

"What kind of training do you need for that?"

"I'm a pilot first and foremost…and I happen to have a B.S. in aerospace engineering and an M.S. in engineering science."

"To think I was impressed with my community college degree in criminal justice. I'm not even going to mention all of the army schools I graduated from.

Mike asked, "Have you ever watched a shuttle launch?"

"Only on television. I remember doing the countdown out loud when I was a kid during the Apollo missions."

"Well, this countdown started around two and half hours ago. The final countdown, that is."

"I never gave it much thought beyond counting backwards from ten."

"It's a lot more complicated than that. At about four and half hours before launch, the external fuel tank, the big rust colored thing, gets partially filled with liquid oxygen. And, a few hours after that, it's filled with liquid hydrogen." Mike noticed the passengers around him listening in on his conversation and he started speaking louder.

"Is that the fuel for those side rockets?" Dan asked.

"No, the liquid hydrogen and liquid oxygen fuel the three engines at the back end of the orbiter. They are called SSME's for Space Shuttle Main Engines. The 'side rockets' are called SRBs for Solid Rocket Boosters and they have their own fuel. That fuel is solid and the SRBs are sort of like roman candles - once you light them, you can't shut the damn things off. The SRB fuel is a combination of ammonium perchlorate and powdered aluminum. The SRBs provide most of the thrust to get the shuttle off the pad. At this point in the final countdown, the crew is on board, tucked in, and performing tests with mission control."

"What kind of tests?" A nerdy looking teenager wearing a Star Wars Episode Three sweatshirt in the next seat over asked. His older, and much hipper, sister smacked him in the back of the head for the question.

"Depends, but definitely a communications check, cabin leak check, abort advisory check, inertial measurement unit preflight alignment…"

"What's that last thing?" The kid asked pinning his sister's arm down.

"To verify that the on board navigation system is precisely indicating that the shuttle is sitting on pad 39A. If that is wrong, then the whole trajectory and flight path is in jeopardy."

The bus was slowing down to pull into the viewing area. Dan noticed the shuttle for the first time and it certainly did not look three miles away. He spotted Laura in the parking lot and felt a warm aura of contentment creep over him knowing that the third wheel this morning was the balding married guy sitting next to him.

"Hello Mr. Muzikowski, I'm glad to finally meet you. And Mr. Gill, I'm surprised you made it."

"Ha ha. Can a civilian institute a court-martial?" Dan asked Mike.

"Come on over to my vehicle." Laura said. "I brought some breakfast and coffee."

They all walked the short distance to her Camaro. Laura was wearing her camouflage uniform again that Dan knew as BDUs, for Battle Dress Uniform, in the army. He didn't know what the air force called them but he assumed the word 'battle' was not in their lexicon. Dan watched Laura walking ahead of him and remembered one of his old army buddies telling him that if a woman could look good in BDUs then you know she had to look great naked. Sergeant Smith was looking pretty good, Dan thought.

Mike gave him a knowing nudge in the arm.

"What? Oh. Actually, I was thinking about the inertia test those guys are doing right now," Dan said, pointing to the shuttle.

"Yeah, right," the ex-astronaut smiled.

"I picked up some coffees and Krispy Kremes. Don't thank me; Colonel Ochoa stuck a twenty in my hand and I'm keeping the change."

They prepared their drinks and Laura put her two way radio on the car's roof, turning off the squelch. "If there is a delay, we'll know."

"So, Mr. Muzikowski, Colonel…" Laura started.

"Please call me Mike."

"Okay, Mike, Colonel Ochoa told me all about you; you're a shuttle veteran."

"A one mission veteran." Mike responded desultorily as he stared off at the shuttle.

Dan looked over. "When did you go into space?"

"For seven days in 1992. I was training for my second mission when I was diagnosed with my cardiac problem by the flight surgeons in early 1995."

"What's going on over there, now?" Dan asked looking over at the shuttle to change the subject. It was obvious that the man's change of career was not a happy topic.

Mike looked at his watch. "We're about T minus thirty minutes so all of the tests that I told you about have been done. The crew will continue with some additional cabin vent tests and voice checks. The commander and pilot will be given updated weather data to include the weather here in case of a return to launch site abort and weather at the other abort sites, like in Morocco. Ben's folks should be very busy this morning. Right about now, the ground crew will be falling back to their secure areas so they don't become crispy critters when the rockets ignite."

"Let's walk over to the stands and see if we can get a better view." Laura said. She gathered up the breakfast remains to throw away.

Dan asked, "What are the chances of a delay?"

"Pretty good, but a delay can be a few minutes to a few days. At least the weather conditions seem perfect here; but they have to be acceptable at the alternate landing sites, too."

They reached an area with bleacher seats and made a scan to see if there were any spots worth going to. Mike suggested that they just stay where they were since going up a few steps would not dramatically increase their view.

Looking at the giant countdown clock, Mike said, "They're coming to the twenty minute hold." Dan asked what that was and he explained that it was an administrative hold on the lift off clock in case there were any other scheduled activities that were running behind schedule. The hold allowed those activities to catch up.

"It looks so big even from here. It really is amazing that it can fly," Dan commented. He was getting as excited as the nerdy kid from the bus. From where they stood, Dan could clearly make out the orbiter, the SRBs, and the huge external tank. The entire space vehicle sat on a gangway that Dan knew rolled on railroad tracks out to the launch pad. The grayish colored launch structure designed to hold the weight of the space ship and withstand the temperatures involved at blast off was almost as impressive as the shuttle itself.

"It is an amazing machine," Mike finally replied. "Its origin goes back to the late sixties. When we were just about to land on the moon, NASA . . .really it was Werner Von Braun…was already planning for the post-Apollo world. Apollo was extremely expensive and, in a way, very wasteful. Everything was used only once. The NASA boys knew that they needed to trim their budget if they wanted to continue to get funding. So, their concept was to build a reusable space ship. The glider designs that the orbiter is based on actually go back to the late fifties. Right after the Russians put Sputnik…"

"Soviets; the Russians are our friends." Laura corrected.

"Okay, right after the Soviets put Sputnik into space, the U.S. Air Force developed a proposal for a manned space glider program. The idea was to launch a space vehicle on a Titan III rocket that would maneuver around in space to look for enemy satellites, destroy them, and then glide back to Earth. The glider was called the 'Dyna-Soar' and was later re-named the X-20."

"The big clock is going again." Dan pointed to the digital clock in front of the viewing area.

"T minus nineteen minutes. Well, we used to load the final flight plans into the computers. There will be some more testing done and then there will be another administrative hold at T minus ten minutes. That basically serves the same purpose as the hold at twenty minutes."

"Colonel Ochoa told me once that the shuttle is a dinosaur. Is that what you were saying before?" Laura said.

Mike laughingly explained the spelling of the X-20. "Ben is right though, the shuttle is a dinosaur. The average laptop has more memory capability than the computer systems that navigate that ship. Its computers were designed in the seventies. Remember, most people didn't even have pocket calculators or digital watches then.

"The final shuttle design, the masterpiece you are looking at, was finished around 1972. NASA wanted a fully reusable space ship but it was too expensive. So, they came up with that compromise design. Everything is reused except for the external tank."

"The big red thing?" Dan asked.

"Right, the big red thing is the ET, external tank. It is one hundred and fifty feet long, twenty seven and a half feet around and is made of aluminum. The orbiter and the SRBs are attached to it. At a little over two minutes into flight, the SRBs will separate and parachute down. They are recovered by special ships and reused. The ET is separated at just under nine minutes into the flight and it will burn up in the atmosphere upon reentry.

"What you're looking at is a combination rocket ship, airplane, spaceship and glider. It's basically a rocket ship until the SRBs separate, then it flies into space like an airplane using its own engines, then it becomes a spaceship and upon reentry, it's a glider. It's also home for the crew with a habitat to support human beings and it is also a truck that brings big things into space."

"Are we safe here if things don't go…as planned?" Dan quietly asked Mike.

"Is the army man scared of the big machine?" Laura teased.

Dan rolled his head towards her. "Just a matter of curiosity; how many times have you seen jets land into crowds at Ukrainian air shows?"

"This ain't the Ukraine," Mike retorted.

"I do recall an incident here back in 1986," replied Dan.

"January 28th, to be exact, and at about the same launch time as today." Mike turned to look at the shuttle on the pad. "The weather was very different though, extreme cold with strong wind gusts. The Challenger flight ended at about T plus seventy three seconds. She was eighteen miles downrange at an altitude of about ten miles.

"If we had been here then, we would be safe. This is still a safe distance even if something happened right on the pad, although I imagine we'd all be eating dirt as soon as we saw an explosion."

Mike noticed that his fans from the bus had found their way to him. He spoke up a little louder. "Okay, we're near T minus ten and the clock should stop. Hopefully, it'll get going again soon." The digital countdown clock stopped again at ten minutes and resumed after a three minute delay.

There were about a hundred spectators in the immediate area and there was a palpable rise in tension among the crowd. People were gearing up for the final countdown. Binoculars and cameras came back out and cups and food were put down. Mike pulled a camcorder out of his bag and handed a digital camera to Dan.

"Do you mind taking some pictures with this while I operate the camcorder?" Dan replied that he would and Mike set up the tripod legs and flipped open the flat screen monitor so he could watch the launch with his own eyes while glancing down to make sure the view was framed on the monitor.

"Do I get copies?" Dan asked.

"You bet. I'll e-mail them to you and send you a copy of this tape. Everything has fully charged batteries so we should be all right," Mike said then showed Dan how to take pictures on his digital camera. He said, with his voice getting louder, "T minus four minutes. The orbiter is now using its own internal power and the flight control surfaces are being moved to get the hydraulic systems in tune.

"T minus three minutes. The SSMEs will gimbal to their launch position."

"Gimbal?" Dan asked.

"Move, swivel, into their launch position. The ET O2, oxygen, vents are closing and the liquid oxygen tanks are pressurizing."

Dan took two pictures and was listening to Mike. "This is really fu...frigging exciting," he corrected, noticing the gaggle of young kids around the astronaut.

"Under two minutes," Mike continued. "The ET hydrogen vents are closing and the liquid hydrogen tank is building pressure for lift off. The orbiter will take over the controls of the SRB auxiliary power units and then the shuttle's on-board computers will be in control.

The noise of the crowd had swelled and Mike was shouting. "Okay, get ready. We're coming to T minus ten seconds, four seconds after that the first of the three SSMEs will ignite then at T minus zero the SRBs ignite."

The large digital clock struck T minus ten seconds and everyone joined in the countdown. Mike was yelling but no one could hear him any more. At T minus six seconds the first SSME ignited followed by the second engine point twelve seconds later and the third engine another point twelve seconds after that. Dan was planning to take a picture but just lowered the camera, caught up in the rapid expanse of the fiery ignitions. A tremendous amount of smoke billowed out from the shuttle, but he could still see most of the gangway and shuttle.

"Lift-off!" Mike yelled out.

"Ho…lee Shit!" Dan and the nerdy teenager yelled in unison.

The SRBs ignited shooting fire in all directions and at first Dan could see nothing but the inferno coming from the base of the gantry. He reflected back to the Challenger disaster and for a brief moment thought of hitting the ground. The shuttle seemed to hang in mid air but in reality took less then six seconds to lift clear of the launch pad. The rocket ship was just above the smoke and flames when Dan took two quick pictures and then went back to just watching. The noise and heat reached them. It seemed to physically press against their bodies. The last thing he heard before the noise became crushing was Laura and the crowd around them clapping and yelling "Go!"

Mike watched the shuttle rise while Dan alternately watched and took quick sets of photos, hoping he was following Mike's previous instructions. Once the shuttle rose above the brilliantly colored fire, it seemed to accelerate out of proportion to its initial rise off the pad. He remembered reading that the shuttle actually traveled faster than a bullet fired from a high powered rifle as it climbed into orbit. Being a former sharpshooter he knew that velocity was pretty damn fast. He couldn't quite believe that type of speed could be achieved but the space ship sure was going up in a hurry.

The shuttle rose rapidly executing a 120 degree roll so that the cabin was facing earthward. She then angled eastward over the warm Atlantic Gulf Stream with all five engines shooting flame for a distance that Dan could not calculate from his vantage point. Although the shuttle moved up and away the noise was still as loud. Much worse than the jet noise over the Jersey Turnpike near Newark Liberty Airport, Dan figured. Mike was yelling something to Laura and Dan moved closer to hear.

"What?" Laura yelled.

The noise subsided somewhat as if by her command. Mike repeated himself but not as loudly.

"At T plus two minutes, the SRBs will shut down and seven seconds after that they will both separate." Mike put a pair of binoculars up to his eyes then handed them off to Dan. "Give the camera to Laura and watch the SRBs separate. I'm going to try and catch it on this," he said pointing to his camcorder.

Dan handed Laura the camera and he tried to focus.

"There they go!" Mike shouted. Dan could not find the shuttle and focus in time to see the actual separation, but then caught the sight of the SRBs clearly away from the shuttle and external tank. They were fairly easy to spot once he focused in and he watched one go off to the left and the other to the right. He then looked back at the shuttle, which was getting further away and impossible to discern anymore except for its fiery trail. He tried to reacquire the SRBs but could not find them again.

The noise had further subsided, sounding simply like a large jet out over the ocean. Dan handed the binoculars to Laura. Mike was now watching the shuttle without checking his camcorder viewer to see if it was recording anything.

"That's about it," Mike said. "In about five minutes the SSMEs will throttle down so that the g-force inside the cabin is just under three gees. Then, shortly after that, the external tank will separate and at about T plus ten minutes, the shuttle will begin its orbital maneuvering system burn to get it into its programmed orbit."

"Are they in space, now?" Dan asked.

"They're just on the edge of space right now, I would say. Once they're at the point of separating from the ET, they are in space. After that, it's just a matter of maneuvering into the proper orbit. That could take about an hour."

The smoke from the launch slowly began to dissipate and drift slowly to the northeast and out to sea. The long column of smoke from the shuttle began to break up first at the higher altitudes but pretty much kept intact as it also drifted slowly away. The only noise now came from the spectators recounting the launch to one another. Dan noticed that the airman who brought them had watched the launch from the top of his bus. He was getting down now and Dan assumed he would soon be coming over to gather his flock.

Dan helped Mike put his gear away and said to Laura, "Please give Colonel Ochoa my thanks and maybe Mike can tell me what he likes to drink or smoke. I'll send him something."

Mike offered, "Good cigars, but not Cubans. At least not until 'The Beard' is dead. He likes bourbon. You know," he continued, "I always felt that NASA should pay to bring thousands of kids here for each launch to…spread the bug. Some day they'll all grow up to be taxpayers and I think they'll decide this is something worth spending money on. We really don't educate our children about our own space program. Kids in Taiwan know more than kids in Indiana about the International Space Station."

They moved along with the crowd. "Laura, where is a good place for lunch these days? I don't want a heavy meal because I'm meeting Ben for dinner and he said he'd treat," Mike laughed.

Laura gave him some choices.

"Would you two like to join me, later?"

"I can't but thank you. I'm still on duty and need to get back to Patrick. Why don't you let Dan treat since you promised him copies of your photographs and tapes?"

"Sounds fair to me." Dan said.

The airman had come over and said that he would be leaving in five minutes. Laura said that she had to be leaving as well. She shook Mike's hand, then Dan's and said it was a pleasure meeting them, then walked towards her car. Dan looked over at Mike and the astronaut motioned for him to go for it.

"I'll walk you to your car." Dan said.

Laura smiled without looking back and Dan caught up to her.

"Yes?" She asked.

"Just trying to be a gentleman."

"If that were the case, you would be back there with Mike."

"Maybe if Mike were a gentleman he would be here with us."

"Maybe if my aunt had balls, she would be my uncle."

"What?"

"Hemingway, For Whom the Bell Tolls."

"Am I being totally blown off?"

"No, walk me to my car."

They walked to the yellow IROC Camaro; she got in and closed the door. Taking a pen from her breast pocket, she wrote a phone number on the back of Dan's business card that he'd given her when they first met.

"That's my home phone. Call me after seventeen hundred, or you know, five o'clock, and we'll go out for dinner, if you're not leaving town. Do not…look at me. . . do not tell Mike about this because he'll blab to Ben when they're reliving their youth tonight and I do not want anyone I work with to know about my personal life. Got that?"

"Roger that ma'am." Dan palmed the card. Laura peeled out leaving a trail of dust, not quite as large as the shuttle's smoke.

Dan walked back towards Mike who had all of his gear stowed away and was walking towards the bus.

"What did she say?" Mike asked.

"I think your good buddy Ben turned her lesbo."

"Shot down?"

"In flames."

Chapter 9

Same day, afternoon
Orlando, Florida

Raoul Viñals was expecting another call at any minute. There were already three messages on his cell phone and he knew Volkova would soon be calling his office line next. Viñals wasn't necessarily ducking the calls: his real motivation was to stay ignorant for as long as possible about what he was being forced into by his former comrade.

Parking in the handicapped space closest to his office, the Cuban flipped his handicapped parking placard on the dashboard and stepped quickly towards his office while furtively scanning the busy parking lot for former agents of the late Soviet Union. He opened the glass door to his office and checked for messages at his secretary's desk - fortunately they were all business calls that his secretary would take care of when she got back. Damn the FBI, he said out loud as he made a pot of coffee and turned on his computer.

The phone rang. Knowing the machine would pick up on the fourth ring, he thought about letting it do so.

"Travel and Real Estate." He answered grabbing the handset during the last ring.

"Damn it. Where have you been?" Volkova growled.

The Cuban's answer was credible and the Russian let his anger drop, asking if it was a good time to talk. Viñals indicated that it was.

"Well?"

"He assures me today." Viñals said.

"You said that yesterday. I can wait no longer. The down payment has been delivered. What is the hold up?"

"He's probably under observation right now and his actions are certainly being scrutinized from the campus police to the federal government. You know who he's associated with and I can't afford to be seen with him again so soon. He left a message for me this morning apologizing and swearing that he was on the way to her house."

"What *is* his problem? This is a relatively simple task and his position at the university gives him the credibility to get the information I need from the sister."

"Pavel, he said he was on the way this morning. I am only your errand boy here; I never vouched for the son of a bitch."

Volkova grunted in acknowledgement and hung up.

Chapter 10

Thursday night, January 16, 2003
Near Melbourne Beach, Florida

Dan followed her directions to a seafood restaurant that was located just to the south of Melbourne Beach. The directions weren't very complicated: *go south on A1A for about ten miles, the restaurant will be on your left.* He offered to pick her up since she didn't volunteer to come by the motel to get him. *Meet me at seven thirty.* That wasn't a good sign, he judged. Two cars would mean that they would be parting company after dinner and in all likelihood, for the evening. He decided he would have to make up his own ending to this date for Rawlins and the Knight's Insurance boys back home.

The restaurant was just over ten miles from his motel, not bad for air force directions. He pulled in parking across the street from the restaurant and looked around for Laura's car. He strolled over to the entrance. The young hostess asked Dan how many for dinner.

"Two, me and you."

"Good! Then let's go somewhere nice." She answered quickly. Apparently he was not the first with that line, he thought.

"My date is late, so, maybe I'll just have a drink at the bar." Dan took a menu and was heading towards the tiki bar when he spotted Laura sitting outside at a table just off the beach. He turned around to tell the hostess, but she was already greeting new diners.

"Hey," Dan said walking over to her, "I didn't see your car."

"I took my pick-up. The Camaro is way over due for an oil change."

"How long have you been here?"

"Ten minutes, maybe."

"Whatcha got there?"

"A cosmopolitan. Do you want to try it?"

"No thanks, too strong for me." Dan looked around. "This is a nice place."

"Yeah, I like it. It's nothing fancy but I like sitting out here, and… it's away from the flagpole."

"I haven't heard that term in a while. What's good to eat here?"

She picked up her menu and started naming the appetizers and entrees that she'd had before. Dan started to follow along with his menu but then just watched her reading aloud from hers. It was the first time he had seen her out of uniform. She was wearing jeans but was already sitting down when he came over. Dan was looking forward to watching her walk away later on. However, from the waist up, he couldn't remember a more attractive date. Her blond hair, in uniform, was kept braided and pinned up but now was flowing past her shoulders; she was wearing lipstick but no other signs of make-up to take away from her soft hazel eyes. Definitely not a Jersey girl he thought. She was wearing a light cotton sweater over a collared lime shirt.

"Ready? What are you looking at?"

"The front of your menu. I think that's where today's specials are listed." Dan said quickly averting his eyes.

She flipped the menu over. "This is the story of Cap'n Jack, the original owner. You may need glasses."

"I might. What're you having?"

"I would suggest the crab cake appetizer. Rarely does one find crab cakes filled with crabs and not cake. For dinner, the pecan encrusted snapper with raspberry sauce is excellent if you've never had it before."

"Is that what you're getting? We should get different things so we can share."

"Sounds friendly enough. I'm going for the crab cakes and grilled mahi mahi."

"Then I'll get the fish chowder and the pecan snapper?"

"Chowder? How are we supposed to share that? We had a deal."

"Broiled scallops wrapped in bacon?"

"Better."

Dan gave the order to the waitress, who wasn't as pretty as the hostess, and ordered his beer and another drink for Laura.

"That's the last one. These things are potent."

"You should have let me pick you up," Dan said.

A wisp of a smile slowly appeared and she answered. "I did. That's why we're eating here."

He liked her last remark and let it hang for a moment. A nearly full deep orange moon was coming up over the water behind Laura's left shoulder and he gestured towards it.

"Where are you from, originally?" Dan asked her.

"Guess."

Dan took the opportunity to gaze at her without the burden of contrived conversation. He finally said, "Definitely not the New York metropolitan area. Not New England. I wouldn't put money on the west coast. I don't think southern: if so, you've lost most of your accent.

"Is this your military police training coming out?"

"You don't want to know all of my interrogation techniques." He smiled. "I would say Ohio or Pennsylvania, maybe Indiana but not any further west."

"Interesting."

"Was I close?"

"No cigar for you. I grew up in Lexington, Tennessee."

"Tennessee! No way."

"I do declare your Yankee belligerence on this issue is most unbecoming," Laura drawled. "My father moved us back to his parent's house when I was six. My grandparents, his parents, died in a car accident and my dad was laid off at about the same time. So, he inherited the house and we moved to Tennessee. He found work as a mechanic and my mother was a teacher."

"Where did you live before?"

"Cleveland." She murmured.

"Aha! So you *are* from Ohio."

"Actually, I was born in Michigan where my mother was from but I will give you partial credit."

"I deserve full credit, but thank you. Do *I* have an accent?"

"Are you kidding me?" She laughed, "Really, it's only thick when you get excited, like this morning. Otherwise, when you speak normally, it's a little hard to place. Anyway, my dad died a few years later and we stayed on in Lexington but I probably just picked up on the way my mother spoke. Then, of course, I've been in the air force since I was nineteen."

"How big is your family?"

"You're looking at it. My mom died in May of 1986 and I enlisted a little while later. My brother died earlier that same year. She never got over his death and when she got sick she had no will to go on. How about you?"

"Big Irish Catholic family. I have two brothers and two sisters and I still have my parents." He knocked on the wooden table. "During my whole childhood, there was always an uncle, a cousin or some other relative also living with us and I can't remember a holiday where everyone was on speaking terms."

"Where in New Jersey are you from?"

"Jersey City."

"I was near there once. When I came back from Germany, I had to pick my car up in Bayonne. I remember being told to get right on the turnpike and stay out of Jersey City."

"Sound advice. It's much better now; the waterfront area looks like lower Manhattan. I remember when that part of town was a trash dump, literally." Dan reflected a moment. "I have great memories of growing up there, though."

"Is that where you live?"

"No, I bought a house last year in Huntington County, about twenty miles from Pennsylvania. It's very rural. I have black bears trying to get into my garbage and the deer have eaten every attempt I've made to grow tomatoes and peppers."

The appetizers came along with the drinks and Laura placed one of her two crab cakes on a napkin for Dan and he slid some scallops onto her plate.

"How do you like what you're doing?" Laura asked.

"Well, honestly…I don't like what I'm doing. I complain a lot about how boring my job is and how lame my life has become. I used to serve in elite military units and now I drive around northern New Jersey doing accident investigations."

"What would you rather be doing?"

"I never thought about what I would do after the army and then, bada bing, you're wearing your old uniform to paint the house. But, I suppose I shouldn't complain. Between my pension and what I make at Knight's, I'm doing well. Plus, I saved a lot of money on active duty that I didn't blow on the stock market or a family. What are your plans?"

"Well, I have a few years to decide but I'm working on it."

The waitress gathered up their empty glasses. After she left, Laura said. "I started college but quit after my brother died and never went back until after I enlisted. I received a degree in political science when I was stationed at Seymour Johnson in North Carolina. Then I received an MA in international relations when I was in Germany at Rhein Main. Just about every major air force base has a university extension program but a lot of people just don't take advantage of what's available."

"Army bases, too. Point taken. What can you do with those degrees?"

"My master plan is to retire at twenty, and then spend some leisurely years working on a doctoral degree, probably in international relations, and then teach. Guess where?"

"Lexington, Tennessee?"

"Good try. No, the Air Force Academy."

"I wish I met you ten years ago to give me a kick in the pants on a post military strategy."

"You're doing okay. But if you're really not happy then go back to school for something."

Dinner arrived and they shared portions. "Have you thought of becoming a police officer?" Laura asked.

"No. I knew I would be too old after giving Uncle Sam my twenty to enter a police academy. You're right, though, about school. I could probably go to night school or on the weekends once I figure out what I want to be when I grow up."

"When are you leaving tomorrow for the keys?"

"I have to check out of my room by ten o'clock. I cancelled my bone fishing charter for tomorrow and figure I'll just see what's going on when I get there. Are you working tomorrow, too?"

"Our squadron is working a half day to prepare for the inspection. That means I'll be working a whole day."

They talked about places they had been stationed, current events, the war and before Dan realized, the waitress was asking if they wanted anything more. The moon was up higher now, fully white, and the night air was very comfortable. Dan surmised that Laura was interested in him or he wouldn't be sharing the last pieces of mahi mahi with her. He didn't think that he would be spending the night with her and wasn't sure where this date would ultimately lead. By morning he'd find he'd been wrong on his first assumption but still in the dark on the second.

*****

Dan paid for dinner and was glad that Laura did not insist on paying for her meal although she offered to leave the tip.

"I have to get up early," she said as they got up from the table. Dan recognized the comment for what it was. He would be following her tail lights up to the point where she went her way and he went his.

He signed the credit card receipt and left a twenty percent tip on the table. They headed for the exit together. "Then I suppose coffee somewhere is out of the question?" He asked.

"I'm afraid so. I had a better time than I expected, though." She waited for him to look at her then smiled.

"At the risk of sounding like we're in junior high, when can I see you again?"

She laughed. "I don't know; I'm in Florida, you're in Jersey."

"Why don't you come up and visit me? We can go over to Manhattan for dinner and a show or over to Pennsylvania for some cow tipping."

"I'll give it some thought; call me before you go back home. Where are you flying out of?"

"Orlando."

"That's reasonably close. Maybe we'll do something again before you leave."

They were outside and Dan took her hand and said he would walk her to her pick-up. She unlocked the door with the remote but Dan opened it for her.

"Thanks for everything. I had a great time today." Dan said.

She seemed distant, not replying. He leaned forward to kiss her but her response was tentative. "I'll call you during the week," he said, pulling back.

"Okay." She leaned forward and kissed him briefly, then got into her truck. Dan felt her moistness on his lips leaving the promise of another date. She started the engine and rolled down the window. "Don't wait; I have to make a phone call." She took her cell phone from under the front seat.

"Boyfriend?"

"Yeah, he wanted all the details. Seriously, I have to call the duty sergeant to see if there are any changes for tomorrow's schedule." She smiled and said good night.

"Good night, I'll call you during the week." Dan walked back to his car. He thought briefly of going back inside for a drink but concluded that the hostess would realize he struck out and was hence…a loser. Perhaps the waitress wouldn't give a crap, though. Instead, he got into his rental and lowered the top. The night air had become a little chilly but what the hell, he was renting a convertible. He fumbled around looking for Springsteen's *Greetings from Asbury Park.* Putting it on, he slowly backed up and headed out onto A1A. He turned to go north and looked for her pick-up to wave good-bye. He glanced over as he passed the restaurant and saw Laura's truck still there and a man waving his arms up and down at the driver's side window.

Dan pulled over and thought, at first, that the man might really be a boyfriend who had been following her. He looked over his shoulder while Springsteen affirmed that it's hard to be a saint in the city. He lowered the volume but couldn't hear what was happening. "If I go over there, I'll only make it worse," he said out loud as the man stopped flailing around. She *must* know him, he reasoned. Then the man struck the pick-up's hood with his fists.

"That's it," Dan growled, cutting off the engine. He shot out of the Mustang racing towards Laura's truck. "Get away from her!" he yelled. Before he could cross the street, the man turned, saw Dan and immediately raced off behind the restaurant towards the beach.

Laura flung open her door and sprang towards Dan grabbing his arm to stop him from pursuing the man. "Dan. Stop! Let him go. He's crazy."

"Who is he?"

"I don't know. I've never seen him before. There are homeless people that live on the beach."

"What was he so upset about?"

Laura leaned against her truck and put her hands up indicating that she needed to take a breath. Dan took out his pack of cigarettes and lit one up. Laura grabbed his smoke, taking several puffs before handing it back. After a minute, she answered, "I don't know. He kept asking me . . ."

A shot rang out from behind the restaurant. Dan broke away and ran to the corner of the restaurant, knelt down, then went prone - his muscle memory bringing him back to his urban warfare training. Laura followed and Dan looked back and motioned for her to move to the side of the building and get low. He peered around the corner and spotted a body on the cold sand. No one else was in the area but as he approached the downed figure other people from the restaurant started coming out onto the beach. A woman screamed when she realized the heap she was looking at was a man.

Dan reached the still body just as Laura caught up to him and put her hand on his shoulder. The body had a severe head wound: the entry hole was in the right temple and the exit wound was to the left side of the forehead.

"Everybody get back!" Dan yelled to the people coming closer. "This is a crime scene." The manager yelled to Dan saying that the police were called and then he invited his patrons back to the restaurant promising a bowl of ice cream for everyone - it was cheaper than a round on the house. Most of the crowd shuffled back toward the restaurant but continued to watch. Laura looked at the man and tightened up. She squeezed Dan's shoulders.

"That's the man from the parking lot," she whispered.

"Are you sure?" Dan asked considering the state of the man's face.

"Yes, that's his jacket - Harris Tweed. I never saw a gun, though. Thank God."

Dan stood up to turn her away.

"It's getting cold. Go back to your truck and wait for the police. I'll stay here to preserve the scene. I think I see the gun over there," Dan said, pointing to a revolver about ten feet away and just outside the light cast by the open door of the kitchen.

"Shouldn't it be in his hand if he shot himself?" Laura asked before leaving.

"We don't know if he shot himself, but no, actually with most suicides, the gun flies away from the firing hand because the hand loses its grip. The grip is a voluntary muscle control; the fatal head wound immediately ceases that function and the gun's recoil sends it flying," Dan said as a matter of fact going over to make sure that it was, indeed, a gun he had spotted.

*****

No more than five minutes passed before uniformed officers arrived. Dan showed them his driver's license and told them he was a former military policeman and that no one had been in the immediate area except himself and his date. One officer wrote down the information on a small pad and told Dan to wait until the detectives arrived. Dan told them he would be in the parking lot. As he was leaving, he pointed out the revolver to the second officer.

Laura was waiting at the edge of the parking lot just where the sand met the pavement.

"Who was it?"

"Don't know yet. We need to wait here for the detectives."

"Why? We didn't do anything."

"SOP, Standard Operating Procedure. We're witnesses, you especially. They'll need our statements. We were the last people, I think, to see him alive. Come with me while I move my car off the street."

They headed towards the convertible and Dan parked it next to Laura's truck. They sat together with the top down and the heater on. "What was he saying to you?" Dan asked.

"He started off by asking me if I was Laura Smith and then…"

"He knew your name?"

"Apparently."

"Then why did you think he was just some homeless guy living on the beach?"

"I don't know. He immediately started asking me for my brother's papers and when I told him to get away he started yelling louder. I rolled up my window and then he got really agitated. I started to back up and that's when he hit the car and you came running over. He seemed drunk and irrational and with his old clothes and crazy hair; my first thought was - crazy homeless person. By the time you got here I guess it slipped my mind that he said my name."

"Have you ever seen him before?"

"No."

"Any idea how he would know your name."

"I wear a name tag on my uniform."

"That's only your last name."

"Maybe someone called me Laura when I was in uniform."

"But you've never seen him before."

"I don't recall ever having seen him before. Maybe he's a stalker," Laura suggested.

"A stalker would want your panties, not your brother's papers."

"He sounded drunk and he had an accent. Maybe that's what he was trying to say."

"Not funny." Dan shook his head.

"What should I do?" She asked.

"Tell the detectives. When did your brother die?"

"January 1986. The same day that the Challenger blew up."

"Do you have any of your brother's belongings?"

"I have some old junk in storage. But most of it, whatever he owned, was burned in the explosion at his home in Utah. Whatever was at my mother's house was destroyed when her house burned to the ground a couple of month's later."

"Explosion?"

"Propane gas leak. He opened the front door to his house while smoking a cigarette."

"Smoking kills."

"I'm talking about my brother."

"Sorry."

"What do you have in storage?"

"I'm not entirely sure myself. I was at my first duty station in Alaska, and trying to sell my mother's house in Tennessee. She died in May, remember. Anyway, on leave, I moved some personal effects into storage but everything else…furniture, clothes, everything…was destroyed in the fire a couple of weeks later. I had some offers but my real estate agent told me to hold out. At least I got the insurance money."

Dan looked around and saw that no one was near them. He said quietly, "Tell the detectives that you don't know what he wanted. You couldn't understand him; then you rolled up the window."

"Why?"

"Because it will make your life a lot simpler."

"Why can't I just tell the truth? He was probably just crazy."

"But he *knew* your name. Just tell the detectives that you never saw him before. That's the truth. You thought you heard him ask for your brother's papers but you also believe that he was drunk and had an accent. So why be specific about your brother's papers. Just say you don't know what he wanted. In a way, that is the truth."

"What about him knowing my name?"

"Lie."

"What?"

"Well, skip that part. Don't tell that to the detectives . . .yet. If it comes up later for whatever reason, you can just say you forgot with all of the excitement. Remember, only two people had a conversation here and one of them is dead. Let's find out who the dead man is and see what the detectives can tell you before you open up a Pandora's Box about your brother's past."

Chapter 11

Later on that night

"Dan Gill!" Dan and Laura heard a shout from the crime scene area. They both turned around and saw a shadowed figure waving at them from the corner of the restaurant who then disappeared.

"Must be the detective," Dan said, getting out of the car.

"Should I come over with you or will they want to talk to us separately?"

"Let's stick together for now so our stories are consistent."

"Why are you making it sound like we have something to hide? We didn't have anything to do with that man being dead and we have nothing to hide," Laura said, catching up to Dan.

"Something isn't right here," Dan said stopping. He said softly, "*I* have nothing to hide. You *may* have something that you would prefer to keep in the family. As for that detective over there, no matter what he says, he will consider us suspects until that man's death is ruled a suicide by a medical examiner. He will act friendly because he probably has already concluded that it is a suicide, but remember, that detective is not your friend."

Dan clasped Laura's hand and pulled her closer until they were nose to nose. "He will want to know why a complete stranger knew your name. He will want to know why a complete stranger wanted your dead brother's effects or papers. He will want to know how a complete stranger knew to encounter you in this restaurant parking lot and at this time. And, he will want to know why that complete stranger had his brains blown out minutes after speaking with you."

"Dan, don't you think I have the same questions?"

"Of course you do and so do I. But, let the police work for you. Let them identify this guy and give you their theory."

"But if I don't tell them that he knew my name and wanted my brother's papers and they rule this death a suicide then...won't the case just close?"

Dan nodded in agreement.

"I'm not really a victim or anything so the police would never have to get back to me. Then, I may never know what happened here tonight."

"You're right. I'm just looking out for your privacy. You'll be under the microscope until this case clears and there is obviously some type of connection between the dead man on that beach and your brother who has been dead for almost twenty years. You have a military security clearance, right?"

"Top Secret. Why?"

"How would your career be affected if you lost your clearance?"

"You know how it would be affected."

"Mr. Gill!" The detective appeared again from around the corner and sounded even less friendly.

"Coming," Gill shouted.

As they approached, the officer opened his windbreaker to show Dan and Laura his gold shield attached to his belt next to his ten millimeter Glock semi-automatic pistol. The detective walked them over to a better lit area just on the edge of the beach where concessions were sold.

"I'm Detective Corey Leonard. Officer Quinn says that you initially secured the scene." He shook hands with Dan.

"That's right," Dan replied.

Laura extended her hand next. "My name is Sergeant Laura Smith, U.S. Air Force."

"Officer Hughes says that you're a former MP and the restaurant manager said that you kept the area clear and called it a crime scene. Why did you call it a crime scene?" Leonard sounded like he didn't appreciate former military policemen directing traffic in his neighborhood.

"I didn't see the gun at first and my first reaction was homicide. I later noticed the gun and assumed it was a suicide from the powder burns on the right temple but that was after I told everyone to keep back."

"Did you see him shoot himself?"

"No."

"So, it would be premature to call this a suicide, correct? Let's start at the beginning, shall we?"

Dan looked at Laura and began slowly, "Well, this past Christmas there was a car accident on the Jersey Turnpike and my tightwad boss..."

"Detective," Laura interjected, pulling on Dan's arm.

"Yes," Leonard replied.

"The beginning starts with me." Laura told the detective how she and Dan wound up together.

"So you were leaving, separately," Leonard asked.

"We came separately and we were leaving separately. That's my pick-up parked next to Dan's rental, the Mustang."

"Then what happened?"

"Dan left and I made a phone call to my unit. I was on the phone for maybe a minute...my bill will have the exact time...when I heard someone walking up to my car. I thought it was Dan coming back."

"I wouldn't do that on a first date. It's a definite sign of weakness," Dan inserted.

"If I may continue...I looked up and saw a man...that man." She pointed.

"Are you certain it's the same man?"

"Yes. I recognized the hair, what is left of his face and his jacket. Anyway..." She looked over at Dan and thought about his warning that the detective was not her friend and continued. "I couldn't understand what he was saying. He sounded drunk and he had an accent."

"What kind of accent?" Leonard was taking notes now.

"Russian, maybe. Eastern European. I don't know for sure."

"Okay, what next?"

"He startled me at first. I thought he wanted money. Then I thought I heard him ask about my brother, or my brother's papers. I'm not sure. I rolled up my window and then he started yelling louder but my window was up so I couldn't hear him clearly. I started to back up and he hit my car with his fists. That's when Dan showed up."

Dan took a step towards Leonard and Laura.

Leonard looked over at Dan and said coolly, "If you mention the New Jersey Turnpike we'll finish this at the station."

"Do you have fresh coffee, there?"

"Dan, just talk to the detective, please."

"Where were you when you first saw the dead man?" Leonard asked.

"Did you find any identification on him or do we have to keep calling him the dead man?" Dan asked.

"No wallet, identification or keys, just a twenty dollar bill and some pocket change."

Dan motioned back towards the street. "I looked over at the parking lot as I was driving back towards my motel and I saw the dead man, who wasn't dead yet, yelling at Laura; so, I pulled over and got out of my car. I couldn't hear what the guy was saying but my first thought was that it might be her boyfriend..."

"Good God! You thought *he* may have been *my* boyfriend?"

"Sure, my first thought was that he followed you here because you may have broken a date or something and when he discovered us eating together he had a fit."

"That was your first thought?" She replied. "Do you think I would go out with someone who looked like that?"

"You went out with him," Leonard pointed to Dan.

"Good point," Laura conceded.

"Can I continue now?" Dan said. "Anyway, when the soon to be dead man hit Laura's car as she was backing out of her space, that's when I yelled for him to stop and I ran over to Laura. He saw me coming and immediately ran behind the restaurant. I asked Laura if she was okay and we talked briefly until we heard the gunshot."

"Did you see anyone else?" Leonard asked.

"No."

"Did you move the body or the gun at all?"

"I moved his head until I saw the exit wound. I didn't bother checking for a pulse. I didn't move or touch the gun."

"Sergeant Smith, did you see the gun?"

"Only at the beach when Dan pointed it out. I didn't notice it when he was at my car."

"How about you, did you see the gun in his hand when he was running away?" Leonard asked Dan.

"He was facing away from me and running. I don't recall seeing a gun."

"Alright folks, it doesn't sound like an attempted robbery. Do you have a brother?"

"Yes. But, he died in 1986."

"And, you think he was asking about your brother?"

"I thought he was asking for my brother's papers at one point. Like I said, he startled me at first then I became a little anxious when he started yelling. I was busy rolling up my window and trying to back up my truck."

"Was your brother from around here?"

"No, we're from Tennessee, sort of. Anyway, he died in eighty-six. He worked in Utah but traveled to Cape Canaveral frequently because of his job."

"What did he do?" Detective Corey Leonard asked.

"He was an engineer and worked for one of the companies that make the shuttle rockets."

"So, if your brother spent time in this area, it's possible the dead man knew him. How would he know that you were his sister?"

"I have no idea," Laura replied

"I'm going to give you my card and if we ever identify the man, I'll try to get you a recent photograph, minus the head wound. It would help in our investigation if you could give this matter some thought and let me know if you ever saw him before tonight." Leonard pulled two business cards from his shirt pocket, writing a number on the back of each.

"That's my home number; I work 24/7."

Leonard left, saying goodnight, and walked back towards the beach. A crowd had formed in the parking lot as patrons had left the restaurant, they milled around trying to find out what had happened. A second news van had arrived and was jacking up its telescopic line of sight microwave antenna so the folks at home could get a live shot of the dead body just before bedtime.

"Let's get out of here before someone over there figures out we're witnesses," Dan said, pointing to the news vans.

"Well, I had a marvelous time, tonight. We must do this again sometime," Laura said, walking back towards their vehicles. "Follow me back to my house for a night cap. I won't be able to sleep, anyway."

Chapter 12

Early Friday morning, January 17, 2003
Laura's home

Dan followed Laura north along the highway. He knew that she must be upset from what happened because she obeyed the speed limit and most of the traffic signs, except for her California rolls through the stop signs. Dan turned the heat to full, zippered up his jacket and refused to raise the top on his car.

Just north of Satellite Beach, Laura made a left hand turn and went through two cross streets, pulling into a driveway just off the Intra Coastal Waterway. Dan pulled up along side and they got out.

"You must have frozen your butt off. Why didn't you put the top up?"

"Why? This isn't cold." He shivered.

"Whatever. Come on in."

"Nice place." Dan said looking towards the waterway. "We're paying sergeants too much these days."

"No we're not. I bought this place in 1990 in a foreclosure sale from some of the insurance proceeds from my mom's house. I had to finish the closing through the mail from Saudi Arabia; I would have personally killed Hussein if this deal had fallen through."

They entered the house. Laura turned on the lights and went into the kitchen.

"I'm going to put some coffee on and then I'm going to put something in my coffee as well. I keep the booze in that cabinet to your left. Can you bring me the Jameson's?

Dan stepped over to the cabinet at which she'd pointed. After opening the doors, he shifted his attention from the liquor bottles to the framed photographs that were displayed on the top of the cabinet. Some were definitely her parents and one must have been her brother. There was an older photograph of her in a sexy black slinky dress with a young man who had a striking resemblance to Colonel Ochoa. Dan grabbed the Irish whiskey for Laura and the Jack Daniels for himself. By rank alone, the photo had to be around ten years old. Laura looked great then, and now, too, Dan thought, studying the portrait some more.

"I'm making Irish coffee. Do you want one?"

"No thanks, I'll take this over ice." He handed her the JD.

Laura took two glasses from the shelf, dispensed cubed ice from the refrigerator and poured the Jack Daniels.

"Maybe I won't wait for the coffee. Here's mud in your eye," Laura said, clinking Dan's glass and sipping the Tennessee mash. "This has been a very interesting evening, Mr. Gill."

"Well, when you're from New Jersey, homicides and first dates aren't mutually exclusive," He deadpanned.

Laura moved over to the coffee machine that was in the final stages of brew and set out two oversized mugs and some half and half on the kitchen table.

"Interesting quip," Laura said.

"Why's that?"

"First, you called our evening - a date," Laura replied.

"It was a date. By any convention, this evening would be considered a date by ninety nine percent of the civilized world."

"And what do you consider the civilized world?"

"The eastern seaboard…not counting South Carolina or Georgia."

"You're very pedestrian, Dan."

"I own a Buick, back home."

"Pedestrian also means…"

"I know what it also means, smarty pants," Dan said, standing up to get the coffee. "Anyway, the point is that this was a date." He poured her drink and sat down again.

"The other interesting remark is that you said homicide. I think that has some significance coming from a former cop. Do you think it was a homicide?"

"I don't know what to think, yet. I would not be surprised to find out the guy was killed and the gun left behind to make it look like a suicide. Anything, at this point, is possible."

"Who would kill him and why would he be killed after talking to me?"

"He wasn't merely talking to you." Dan sipped his whiskey. "He demanded something from you, by name. Maybe he was sent by someone else."

"Jesus Christ, Dan. Don't you think I should call Detective Leonard?"

"I think I made a stupid remark and you're very upset about what happened. Let the police do their job. What would happen if you told Leonard that he called you by name and you clearly heard his demand? Do you think he will *protect* you? He will *suspect* you. Tell me about your brother."

Laura opened the Jameson's and poured a shot into her coffee, Dan offered his cup for the same.

"I didn't really know my brother very well. He was almost ten years older than me so we never really shared a childhood together. From my earliest memories, he was always away at school. I remember him the most around the holidays, Christmas and Thanksgiving, when he came home to visit or sometimes during the summer. By the time I was entering junior high he was already at Berkeley. Then, he went on for his masters in rocket propulsion engineering. I don't even remember when he graduated from his undergrad or graduate studies. He went from one right to the other and he was always interning somewhere or another. I remember when he went to work in Utah; it was about eighteen months before he died. Whenever my mother and I planned a visit, his business travels would interfere.

"He had a girlfriend, there. After he died, I met one of his co-workers at the memorial service and he told me that Ken rarely talked about her because he was very shy. In any event, she wasn't there for the service. I just assumed she was too upset to attend. I was told that she and Ken met in Chicago when he was studying for his masters; she was an exchange student from somewhere in Europe. That's all his friends at work knew about her."

Laura was getting tired and Dan could see that remembering her brother was painful for her. "Your brother, Ken, was a very smart guy. I can see that it runs in the family."

"Thanks," Laura said. She looked over at Dan and searched for the words to continue and Dan saw her eyes watering.

"Let it go, Laura. Don't be so tough, you've had a hell of an experience tonight."

She tried to hold in her emotions but couldn't. She got up to wipe her eyes at the sink but started crying. Dan rose and held her from behind. Laura felt his arms around her body and he held her hands in his. He spoke softly into her ear and she felt…safe.

She turned around and faced Dan. He let go of one hand to wipe the tears away and she kissed him.

"I'm sorry. I don't know why I did that," she said moving away and wiping her eyes.

"It's called post traumatic stress, don't worry about it, you're normal." Dan said. "For crying out loud, I sob when I watch *It's a Wonderful Life*."

Laura laughed. "But you don't do it in front of others."

"Whadda ya kidding me? When George Bailey is praying to get his life back, baby, the waterworks are on and I don't care who sees me."

Laura moved back to the table, bringing the coffee pot with her. She quickly ran her fingers through Dan's hair.

"Thanks for making me feel better." She topped off their mugs.

Dan waited for Laura to settle down and asked, "You never found out if your brother was engaged?"

"No. The fact is that he had a lot of colleagues but no friends, really. And because he was always going between Utah and Florida, even neighbors didn't know him well."

"I guess the sixty four thousand dollar question is do you have any of your brother's stuff left?"

"I have some of his things in storage like I told you before. I retrieved some of his effects from his office when we were in Utah for the service. His co-workers had already boxed everything up and I don't think I even looked inside the boxes. He also had some belongings at our mother's house. I moved some of it into storage but most everything was burned in the fire."

"Where do you keep it stored?"

"Our neighbors in Lexington converted a barn into a storage facility. I only rented about forty square feet or so and they send me a bill once a year. I haven't seen that stuff since the eighties."

"Maybe you should take a trip and see what's there. You'll probably wind up throwing most of it away. In any event, after you have inspected everything then you can make a decision about telling Leonard. Maybe it's nothing but maybe there is something…embarrassing. What if your brother and that man tonight had a…relationship?"

"I don't think Ken was gay," Laura laughed, spilling her coffee.

"Are you sure? He went to Berkeley."

"He had a girlfriend, maybe even a fiancée."

"You never saw her. Anyway, do you want the police to find out first and have some dickhead detectives laughing at photographs or love letters that show up?"

Laura looked at Dan and then poured more whiskey into her coffee. "I guess you're right in that I should check first for myself. After the inspection at work, I can probably take a short leave. What time are you leaving in the morning?"

"No particular time, I guess."

"How would you like a fishing buddy?"

"Who? Mike the astronaut?"

"No, me."

"I thought you had to work."

"I called Ben on the way home and told him what happened. I was starting to feel pretty tense on the drive home and was worried about not getting in on time in the morning. Anyway, he told me to take a couple of days off."

"Nice guy, that colonel of yours."

"Yes, he is. Anyway, I would like to get out of here for a few days to clear my head. Can I come?"

"Only if you don't cry the whole time."

She threw her rolled up napkin at him.

"I don't want to be alone. Sleep in my bed tonight," she said.

"Hot dog! Let's go!" Dan clapped his hands.

"Whoa cowboy. I'll be on the couch. I would let *you* sleep on the couch but you're too tall and I'm too nice of a person."

"Did you know, and I'm sure you've heard this being a smart college girl and all, that research studies show that it's dangerous to sleep alone after suffering from post traumatic stress?"

"I'll take my chances. We should leave early." Laura started to gather up the glasses and mugs. "I have to run by my unit in the morning. Do I need to bring anything besides clothes?"

"Do you have a salt water fly rod and reel?"

"No."

"Then just bring your clothes."

Laura left the kitchen to start packing and Dan ambled into the living room flopping out on the couch and turning on the television looking for the weather. He relaxed, slouching down while holding his JD on ice in both hands. He listened as Laura walked around upstairs, opening drawers and closing doors. The feel of her body and the warmth of her kiss were on his mind as he nodded off.

Chapter 13

Later that morning
On the road to Islamorada

Cruising past the last of the Miami exit signs just before noon, Laura finally fought off the last of her fatigue and massaged her face, vowing not to slip into another catnap. Her silence for most of the morning triggered Dan's disconcerting opinion that she was regretting her decision to come. He decided to keep listening to the sports station on the radio until Laura decided to converse - it was always a good idea to let suspects begin the Q&A, he recalled: it provided insight to further interrogation and...to what they were thinking. After all, there wasn't much difference in trying to discern the thoughts of a criminal suspect trying to avoid arrest and a woman trying to avoid further entanglement. Besides, the radio talk show was entertaining with all of the Dolphins fans bitching and moaning about their season.

"Where are we?" Laura finally broke her silence.

"Richmond."

"What? She jerked up and looked around. "Liar."

"I might fib a little but at least I don't snore."

"I do not snore," she protested.

"You snore a little...and drool; look at your shirt."

She felt her shirt and sleeves but they were all dry; she smacked Dan on the shoulder. Laura stretched in her seat and waited for the next road sign before saying anything. "Let's stop at Florida City for gas. It will be cheaper there than on the Keys."

"Do you need to stop now for anything?"

"I'm fine," she said, picking up the local newspaper from Cocoa Beach that she'd stuck between her seat and the console before leaving her driveway.

She unrolled the paper and folded the top half over.

"Are we in it?" Dan asked.

"Probably not, it happened late…here it is." Laura said.

"What does it say?"

"I'm reading it now, hold on." She started reading.

"Well?" Dan asked.

"Nothing we don't know. It says that the man is still unidentified. Here, it says that two witnesses saw him moments before he died. It says that the man may have tried to rob me, they withheld my name. It says you came to my aid, Donald Gill."

"Donald?"

"Donald."

"Leonard did that on purpose, he doesn't like me. Did you get that impression last night?

"You were a bit of a smart ass to him. Here, they suspect a suicide but a determination has not been made."

"That's it?"

"That's the whole story, no pictures; looks like a late edition insert, there'll probably be more tomorrow."

Laura folded the paper and stuck it in the pouch behind Dan's seat. She reached into her bag on the back seat, pulling out her sunglasses and an Atlanta Braves hat that looked like it had been around since they were in Milwaukee.

"You're not a Braves fan, are you?"

"America's team. I guess you're a Yankees fan."

"Mets."

"Sorry…too bad they choke whenever they play us."

"Tell me about it."

Dan spotted a Florida City sign and kept an eye out for a gas station. Laura turned her body towards Dan and lowered the radio. "Now that I have had some sleep and my adrenaline isn't running a hundred miles an hour, maybe we both overreacted last night."

"How's that?"

"Well, I know that you were trying to do what was best for me in light of your police experience, but I think I should just call Detective Leonard and lay everything out for him. I'll tell him that I am pretty sure the man called me by name and asked for my brother's papers. I'll tell him that there is very little left of Ken's life but I will bring him what I have in storage in Tennessee."

Dan digested what she said while he searched for a Bojangles, finally spotting one next to a gas station. He eased the Mustang over and came to a full stop for the light at the end of the exit ramp. "Well," he finally replied, "I guess you can never go wrong by telling the truth."

Chapter 14

Later on, that afternoon
Gainesville, Florida

Suppressing his ire on the telephone to the Cuban, Pavel Volkova relayed what happened at the restaurant the night before. "He's a drunk. Maybe you should have done this yourself," Raoul Viñals defended himself.

"In hindsight, it would have been less risky if I had," Volkova admitted, abruptly ending the call. The Russian was in Gainesville, on the hunt, looking for the professor's apartment. He stopped at a bodega and purchased a local street map along with a cola, chips, and cigarettes. The American trifecta, he smirked, paying the bill.

Pavel Volkova saw that he was less than a kilometer from the apartment and decided he would head there after his smoke. *Glasnost* and the utter collapse of his country robbed him of some of the really great contacts he'd had in America; otherwise, he never would have relied on that imbecile last night. Now, he had to do the clean up work himself.

He drove over towards the professor's house; spotting the bungalow style home that stood across the street from a strip mall. He coasted into the commercial lot, knowing that the homeowner would not be there…would never be there again… but the Russian needed to make sure that a friend or housekeeper wasn't inside. He settled in, lighting up; he gave no thought to quitting although he'd switched to filters a few years back. The rain stopped and the humidity spiked. He raised the windows and turned on the air conditioning.

Volkova checked his jacket looking for eye drops. He discovered as he read the label afterwards, that the product was made by a company he was very familiar with. The Russian's true forte was befriending American university students, not starting wars in Central America. Well, they had to be the right kind of students-post graduate with useful majors and membership in radical student organizations were the initial criteria for him in assessing his targets.

His last acquisition, before that drunken blowhard Boris Yeltsin ruined things, was pharmaceutical graduate student Richie Gallo, a member of a noble student movement looking to increase aid to African countries and to forgive their debts and Mr. Gallo was also a double major: microbiology and biochemistry - perfect. Volkova also learned that Richie Gallo was arrested for protesting against the Shah of Iran while in high school and used that knowledge as a pretext to gain his trust over a game of pool.

The Russian pretended to be a displaced Iranian whose family was mercilessly tortured by the Shah's CIA trained secret police. Richie was absorbed by the story and he and the Russian became close friends. Casually, Volkova mentioned that he was working for an international human rights organization that was helping to provide medication to sub-Saharan Africa. Richie revealed, against the confidentiality agreement he signed, that he was working as an intern on a new antibiotic compound at the university which was in partnership with a big drug company. They were about to successfully complete FDA phase III testing. No surprise to the Russian.

One Saturday night after a game of pool, Pavel Volkova feigned distress about the news he received from a Ugandan village-many children he knew were dying from simple infections, he sobbed to Richie Gallo. Filled with righteous indignation and several pitchers of tap beer, Richie agreed to help.

Within a year, Cuba was cranking out the ripped-off antibiotic to fight infections for her people on their isle and her soldiers in Africa... and her allies' soldiers in Afghanistan. The university received an anonymous call that its intellectual property had been stolen. Richie Gallo was found dead inside his garaged car, an apparent suicide - the engine had cut off after using up all of the oxygen in the enclosed space but long after Richie ceased needing it. A typewritten note expressed remorse about his embezzlement.

At midday, Pavel Volkova walked over to the professor's apartment. He looked around as he approached, threw his cigarette into the gutter, and stepped up to the front door.

Chapter 15

Friday afternoon
The Florida Keys

After lowering the convertible's top, Dan and Laura raced out of the gas station and merged back unto the interstate looking for the Overseas Highway signs. Quickly finding the way, they made it to Key Largo by mid afternoon. The near tropical sun warmed the salt scented air into the high eighties and cirrus clouds dotted the brilliant azure sky that blended into the dark blue water of the Gulf of Mexico.

Searching for a topic, Dan asked, "Are those sunglasses polarized?"

"No, why?"

"Polarized glasses make the fish easier to see?" He explained.

"Why don't we just bring along night vision goggles and hand grenades," Laura chided.

"I'm serious. You have to spot the fish and cast to them."

"Won't that scare them away?"

"Sometimes, but that's how you fly fish. I'll give you lessons on how to cast with a fly rod tonight."

"That's a new euphemism," she smiled.

Dan laughed. "Unintended…but I like the way your thinking."

Laura unfolded the Florida map she'd purchased at the gas station, letting the unexpected subject die off. "When are we going fishing?"

"Tomorrow with Captain Dave Sisk. This will be my fifth year in a row with Captain Dave and he hasn't let me down let yet."

Upon arriving at Key Largo the traffic swelled considerably, slowing them down, but a signpost indicated that they were only twenty miles away from Islamorada.

Dan continued, "I want to go for bonefish but Captain Dave will let us know what's running. If we come back in about a month, snook season is open. That's a great fish to catch and very good tasting, too."

Laura watched Dan, immersed in lecturing her on how to spot cast bonefish on the flats and under the mangrove trees, as he alternated his right hand between driving the convertible and simulating fly casts. Watching his boyish enthusiasm about fishing, she hid her enjoyment at his demonstration. It had been a long time since she could relax with someone, especially away from her military surroundings. Upon becoming a senior non-commissioned officer, Laura Smith had to project an image for her career; that image was basically who she really was except for the part of her that needed someone.

"You said you've been to the keys before, right?" Dan asked.

"I flew to Key West once for a weekend but that's it," she answered.

"I guess if you live in Florida, this is nothing special."

"No, it's special. I just never have the time. I have over sixty days of accumulated leave right now and I need to use it before I lose it. Where are we staying?"

"Look for signs for the place where you can swim with the dolphins, the motel is past it a few miles or so on the right."

"Have you ever done that?" Laura asked.

"Swim with dolphins? No, I would feel a little silly at my age swimming with Flipper. That's why I need to have kids so I can do things like that."

Laura savored his last comment, finding another reason to like him. "You know what's odd?" She asked. Dan looked over at her. "You haven't asked me any really personal questions. You know, like, do I have a boyfriend."

"After you flew off the handle at Heffernan's when I asked about the colonel, I figured I should keep my curiosity to myself...do you have a boyfriend?" Dan succumbed.

"It's really none of your business; and, I didn't fly off the handle."

"You're right. Why did you bring it up?"

"Because you should have asked by now." She paused. "Do you have a girlfriend?"

"In Florida?" He replied.

"Anywhere, wise guy," she said.

"None in Jersey, maybe one in Florida."

She lowered her glasses to look at him. "Ever married?"

"A long time ago. She left me for a dolphin trainer. I think we may run into them later."

He was ready for her next line but it didn't come. Dan saw that she was still looking at him and he continued, "I was married for about five years during the eighties. We got divorced and I have no kids. Why all of the sudden interest?"

"Just curious."

"Were you ever married?"

"Really, that's *also* none of your business," she kidded, but he waited for a response. "No." She lied. "There's a sign for the dolphin thing."

Dan wanted to ask about the photograph of the younger Ben and Laura he saw at her apartment but decided against it. Everything was sailing along smoothly, why bring up any angst over a former boyfriend, or current boyfriend, or whatever the colonel was to her. Laura started to clean up some of the litter in the car. Dan spotted the motel, braked, and turned off the highway.

*****

The motel was of a style built when the only north-south road on the east coast was Highway One. The old Spanish style inn was a one story white stucco building with pink trimmings where the registration office was located and a similar style row building angled ninety degrees from that, comprising twenty small rooms. The office faced the road and the apartments had water views with a path leading to a small sandy beach with white painted concrete benches and tables just a few feet off the high tide mark. Dan and Laura walked into the empty lobby and Dan rung the bell on the counter. The back door opened and an old woman came up to the counter.

"Vat can I do fur you?" The woman asked with a strong German accent that grew thicker with her advancing years.

"Hello Mrs. Harwood, Dan Gill…Danny boy from New Jersey. Remember me? I have a reservation."

"Velcome back, *Herr* Gill!" she replied exuberantly. "I don't see so vell anymore. How have you bin?"

"Very well, I'm here to fish with Captain Dave again and I've brought a friend. This is Laura Smith; she's in the Luftwaffe." Laura punched Dan in the side.

"*Gut Got*, so pretty. Are you a pilot?"

"No ma'am, I work in a weather squadron."

"In the American Air Force?"

"Yes, ma'am."

"*Got* be vit you, dear, *kommen sie* here." Mrs. Heike Harwood motioned for Laura to come to the side of the counter. The old lady whispered, "You know, dear, I kilt two of dem Russian sons a bitches vit a *panzerfaust* ven I vas a *fraulein* even younger den you. You be careful, child, in dis var."

"Yes, ma'am. I have a pretty safe job, though, *danke schoen,*" Laura replied.

The *danke* made the old lady give her a big hug. Laura looked over at Dan who turned away grinning.

"So, Mrs. Harwood, what room?" Dan finally asked, saving Laura.

Mrs. Harwood let go of her and walked back to her peg board. "Number eighteen; it is closest vacant room to vater."

"Ma'am, are there other vacancies?" Laura asked.

"For you?" The old lady's brow crinkled like she'd just swallowed spoiled rice pudding.

"Yes, Ma'am."

"Vat, no romance vit you two?" Mrs. Harwood gestured, holding her palms up and looking at Dan, who just shrugged his shoulders.

"We really just met, Ma'am." Laura replied not wanting to be rude to the woman she just finished embracing.

"Vell, the closest is twelve, but…" She checked her messages and shuffled some papers. "You take room sixteen, next door to Danny boy. I send reservation for sixteen to twelve. Here are *der* keys. How do you vant to pay?"

Dan first paid with his credit card, leaving Laura behind while he pulled the car to the end of the parking lot and unloaded everything into his room. The spartanly furnished units were all uniform, with a queen sized bed, small desk and a television set suspended from the corner near the window. The bathroom was tiny with no tub, just a small shower stall. Laura walked in while Dan was hanging up the phone.

"Thanks for leaving me," she said coming in the open door. "She showed me her Iron Cross – First Class."

"Leave her alone. She's a great old dame."

"I think she was Nazi." Laura protested.

"Probably, at least until May of 1945. Now she's an American citizen and widow of Staff Sergeant Ed Harwood whom she met during the Berlin Airlift in the U.S. Zone. He died about ten years ago and she runs this place all by herself."

"She probably has experience running things…like death camps."

"Now now, leave her alone. She's a nice old lady and she thinks you're very pretty, probably because you have Aryan features. What are you, anyway?"

"What?"

"Nationality?"

"American."

"You know what I mean; English, Irish?"

"I'm a mutt like everyone else. I'm part English, Irish, Scot and German. What about you?"

"Pure bred, Irish-American baby. Hey, there's your bag," he said, pointing behind the door. She took it and went to her own room, returning in ten minutes.

"Who was on the phone, before?" she asked.

"Captain Dave. I called him. He had a night charter that cancelled. Let's go down to his boat. Maybe we can go fishing tonight."

"Tonight *and* tomorrow morning?"

"Sure, why not? We'll see. Maybe he can't go out tonight but I want to see what's running. How's your room?"

"Just like this one."

"Do you want to share my room and we'll sublet yours?"

"No."

"Vat, no romance vit you?" Dan said, locking the door.

Chapter 16

Late afternoon
Sisk's Marina, Islamorada

Sisk's Marina consisted of a small shack next to a weather-worn wooden dock mooring two boats on either side. One was a twenty six foot sport boat with twin Johnsons and the other was a smaller flat skiff used for the back country. Dan parked in the lot and spotted Captain Dave putting a cooler on the bed of his pick-up truck.

"Captain Dave!" Dan shouted and waved. The Captain signaled back telling them to head towards the dock. Captain Dave Sisk was a large man pushing sixty, with a frame just under six feet carrying close to three hundred and fifty pounds. He was wearing a floppy green Vietnam-era jungle hat, aviator sunglasses, shorts, sandals and a tee shirt that was stretched to the limit, with holes made from his customer's mis-casts.

"Which boat are we going out on?" Laura asked as they neared the dock.

"The smaller one," Dan replied.

"With him?" she said looking over at the Captain who was reaching into get something out of his truck. "Can it hold all of us?"

"Of course. The man's a pro."

"Why can't we use the bigger boat?"

"Too big. We're going to fly cast to bonefish and they hang out in shallow water."

Laura picked up a 'Captain Sisk's Marina' brochure from a plastic bin screwed to the side of the shack and skimmed through it while Dan went out to look at the boats.

"Hello, Mr. Gill," Captain Dave said, shuffling towards them. He was carrying a laptop computer and an attaché case.

Dan returned the greeting, walking over to shake his hand. "Good to see you again. I brought a friend, Laura Smith, and she is a fly fishing novice."

"Great!" Captain Dave turned to shake her hand and introduced himself. "I can give you some no hassle instructions before we go out tomorrow."

"No trip tonight?" Dan asked.

"I made the mistake of telling my wife that my night charter cancelled and so she wants me home. God knows for what," the Captain said, shaking his head and sitting down on a bench near the dock. He turned on the laptop. "This is your fourth or fifth year with me, Dan?" he asked.

"This makes five years - four as a civilian."

"I have everything in here." Captain Dave said as the computer came to life and he started retrieving data. "I have your home address, phone numbers for work and home. These numbers still good?" he asked, showing Dan the screen and he replied "yep". "I have what we fished for and what we caught. Water temps…what tackle was used...the weather." He typed some more. "What you like to drink, my fee and your tip. You'll definitely see a link between the tip and the following year's catch," he chortled.

"How's the fishing been?" Laura asked.

"The fishing has been great; the catching has sucked, at least for bonefish. The water is warming up nicely but still a little too cool for bonefish on the flats. We've been slammin' snappers and jacks up in the mangrove. We've taken some barracudas that are fun to catch, too."

"I wouldn't mind some snappers," Dan said. "They're a good fish to grill."

"I have some good recipes in here," Captain Dave said tapping the laptop. "I'll print some out for you."

"What time tomorrow?" Dan asked.

"Be here at seven." The Captain made a few keystrokes. "Diet cola?"

"You're the man," Dan replied.

"What does the lady drink?"

"The same," Laura volunteered.

"I'll get your information tomorrow. Once you're in my data base, I have you hooked. Get it? Also, you'll get my quarterly newsletter. Don't forget, you can bring your own beer or wine, too, but no hard booze."

"Are you from Jersey, too?" Captain Dave asked Laura staring at his computer screen.

"No, Florida," she replied.

"Where abouts?"

Laura wasn't sure that she wanted to receive Captain Dave's quarterly newsletter about bonefish. "I work at Patrick Air Force Base."

"Are you in the air force?" he asked.

"Yes."

"Really! What do you do?"

She explained what she did at the weather squadron and Captain Dave put down his laptop.

"That's where we met," Dan interjected. "Her boss got me into the VIP viewing area for the shuttle launch yesterday. That's something you gotta see for yourself."

"I've seen my share of launches. I used to work for a subcontractor who made components for the shuttle," Captain Dave said, putting away his computer and closing his attaché case.

"That's interesting. My brother did the same work, too, between 1984 and 1986." Laura mentioned the name of her brother's employer and Captain Dave nodded in the affirmative.

"Yup, one in the same. What's his name?" The captain said.

"Ken Smith. He died in '86."

"Sorry to hear that. I was there then but I'm afraid I don't remember him."

"He was just out of school and spent a lot of time between the Utah plant and Cape Canaveral."

"What happened to him?"

"His house trailer had a propane gas leak and he died in an explosion."

"My goodness, that's awful. You know, I seem to recall reading about that in our company newsletter. When did it happen?

"The same day the Challenger exploded," Laura said.

"Yes, I do recall. He wasn't with us long," Captain Dave reflected. "I guess that's true on many levels." He started walking back to his truck. Captain Dave put the computer on the front seat and went back to the cooler. "You guys want a beer?"

"Sure," Dan said and walked over to the truck with Laura behind him.

"Are you retired?" Laura asked.

"I guess you could say I'm retired from the rocket business."

"What did you do before you retired?" Dan asked.

"Mr. Gill, I was once a steely eyed rocket man - I guess it doesn't show anymore." He laughed, patting his belly. But, that job was extremely stressful and I had…what you might call…an episode." He sat on the tailgate of the truck and it dropped a foot. "Anyway, my doctor said that I should find a new line of work. Although I should add that my bosses had made that same suggestion a few months before my doctor did."

Laura looked over at Dan who shook his head *no* but Laura asked anyway, "What happened?"

Captain Dave took a swing of beer. "Panic attacks so bad that I couldn't move. I was nervous about everything and couldn't make decisions anymore."

"You made a hell of a decision to be a charter boat captain in the Florida Keys," Dan offered.

"Fishing was my first love but it was replaced when I fired off my first model rocket with my dad. I don't miss it. Rockets, I mean. In fact, I don't even watch launches on television, anymore."

"Why's that?" Laura asked.

"Y'know there's an old saying that if you love the law or sausages, you should never be around to see either one of them made - the same is true for making rockets. I was involved in the booster rockets, the SRBs…"

"Solid Rocket Boosters, the two rockets on the side of the shuttle," Dan interjected, looking at Laura proudly.

"Right." The captain continued, "And knowing how every nut and bolt was put together on the shuttle I can easily envision fifty thousand parts that can possibly malfunction on every launch and after Challenger, I just couldn't take it anymore.

"They seemed to have made the right corrections," Dan said.

"I believe they have but my career is done. I guess I was a bit of a troublemaker back then; maybe today I would be called a whistleblower. Anyway, we had flaws in our systems that were ignored and I suppose that I feel personally responsible for not being more of a pain in the ass. If I had been, seven astronauts would be alive today.

Captain Dave told them about the company he and Ken Smith worked for and how it was awarded the contract to manufacture components for the SRB and other NASA projects. Dan wanted to tell the captain that they could talk about this tomorrow on the way out to the back country but Laura was keenly interested and so Dan kept quiet, realizing that she was learning something about her brother.

"Do you guys want another beer?" Captain Dave was already fishing around in the cooler.

He fumbled around the ice and came up with the beer he wanted; Dan took a second brew while Laura nursed her first.

"I never heard of this beer," Dan said, looking at the label.

"It's a micro brew that the folks on yesterday's charter left me."

"So, how could you have been more of a pain in the ass?" Laura asked.

"Well, I always had a bad feeling about the SRB O-rings and when the time to say something about the rings presented itself, I just went along with the party line."

"What are the SRB O-rings?" Laura asked, deciding to finish her beer and get another.

"The SRB O-rings are seals, just like the rubber washers on your kitchen faucet except that they are much bigger and a hell of a lot more expensive. The SRB is manufactured in sections. When the sections are bolted together, an O-ring is set in place between the sections - just like a washer is placed between pipe fittings. The rings are made of synthetic rubber and they're supposed to fill any gaps that might occur between the rocket segments after they are bolted together."

"Sounds pretty simple," Dan said.

"Sure, until you factor in all of the information you need to manufacture a seal that can withstand the type of pressure that occurs upon ignition and the torque involved with the rocket's trajectory and any wind shears that might develop at altitude.

"Anyway, prior to Challenger, the coldest launch we ever had was the year before, January 1985, and the temperature then only dropped to fifty three degrees Fahrenheit. The O-rings were never even tested in the laboratory below forty seven degrees Fahrenheit."

"Wasn't that the reason for the failure?" Laura asked. "The temperature dropped below freezing the night before Challenger's lift-off."

"That's the common answer, I suppose. But, whenever there is a catastrophic failure, there is seldom an easy answer. You see, as incredible a machine as the space shuttle is, so too are all of the safeguards that go into each launch. What happened on January 28, 1986 was a culmination of a lot of little errors that occurred in such a sequence that it would have been almost impossible to predict."

"Yet, you had doubts," Dan said.

"I did, but so did others at my company who did a hell of a lot more than I did to try and stop that launch. You see, some of us knew that the O-ring was the weak link in the chain. A few years before Challenger, we discovered that the SRB sections would actually bulge outward to some degree of measurement because it was under such incredible pressure upon burn." The captain demonstrated the bulging with his hands. "The exhaust vent at the tail of the rocket could not handle the volume of the thrust plume and this back pressure caused the rocket segments to bulge outward. We felt that this bulging could harm the primary seals within the rocket leaving the O-ring as the last line of defense against the rocket's solid fuel from shooting out between the rocket segments instead of out the tail. Did you know that the SRBs are re-usable?"

Dan and Laura both nodded in the affirmative.

"So," Captain Dave continued, "each time an SRB was used, there was some degradation of the seals because of the bulging and shifting of the rocket segments during flight and its return to earth. We fired off a memo to NASA and they replied saying to continue with the launch schedule. However, we were encouraged to find a solution in the meanwhile.

"In addition to this evolving wear and tear that we discovered, you have to factor in the weather. That's mainly why Laura has a job at Patrick," Captain Dave said, patting Laura's knee. "Launches are dependent on favorable wind and temperature conditions; but cold temperature wasn't the main problem with Challenger's original launch date. Again, it was a series of little mistakes all leading up to a big disaster. Challenger was scheduled to fly on January 26th, a Sunday morning, but rain was predicted and NASA made a midnight decision to delay for twenty-four hours. Guess what? Sunday, January 26th turned out to be a beautiful day." Captain Dave lowered his sunglasses and looked at Laura.

"Don't blame me; I was driving the boys crazy in Tennessee in 1986," Laura said.

"You were?" Dan shot back.

"Anyway," Captain Dave continued after taking a long sip of his microbrew, "the launch was rescheduled for early Monday morning, the 27th. The fuel was loaded during the night and the crew boarded the orbiter. The weather wasn't great but it was within tolerance for launch. It was predicted that the weather would improve as the day went on. Guess what? A little handle on a hatch door broke and it took a few hours to repair it. When the repair crew left, the weather did not clear up as predicted. In fact, strong winds developed, forcing another delay." He lowered his glasses to look at Laura again.

"The boys in Tennessee, remember?" She laughed.

"Right," Captain Dave said. "Do either of you remember the history or the politics of that shuttle launch?"

Dan and Laura looked at the captain and both said no.

"I'm having another beer; you folks have no idea what's waiting for me at home. Dan?"

"Not yet."

Laura got him his next round and he continued. "It was an incredibly important launch. First, it was the twenty-fifth space shuttle mission. NASA had been taking a lot of guff from Congress and the media about the program's expense. The twenty-fifth launch was a milestone event to demonstrate that the program was becoming more streamlined, reliable, and cost effective. Second, NASA wanted to launch fifteen shuttle missions in 1986. Challenger would be the first so they had to get her in space to keep on schedule. Before 1986, the most shuttle missions NASA launched in any one-year period was nine. So, this was a major increase in launches. Third, they were launching Challenger from a new pad and this was important because they needed two launch pads to fly fifteen missions in one calendar year. Fourth, the shuttle was our only vehicle to get big things, like spy satellites, into orbit and there were a lot of classified missions...black ops...on the launch schedule. Fifth, the president already had a paragraph in his State of the Union address to be given that week praising NASA on its twenty-fifth successful shuttle launch. And, finally, NASA wanted to prove that the shuttle was so safe and reliable that regular folks could go up for a ride. Christa McAuliffe, God rest her soul, was lucky enough to be selected from a nation-wide 'teacher in space' contest to go into orbit. Every school child in America was looking forward to that launch. So, layered on top of mechanical and weather problems, Challenger was plagued by all of this political bullshit, too. Pardon my French."

"I've been known to curse once in a while myself," Laura answered.

"Okay, well, the shit really hit the fan the night before the launch. The temperature started dropping fast once the sun went down on Monday. That would be the last sunset for Challenger and her crew. The weather boys finally got it right this time."

"And weather girls." Laura added.

"And weather girls," the Captain acknowledged. "They predicted below freezing temperatures throughout the night going down into the twenties and maybe the teens with temperatures at launch somewhere at the freezing point. When we got this news we immediately got NASA on the horn. My bosses made a recommendation not to launch if temperatures got below fifty three degrees, the previous low record. They said that the extreme cold would increase the chance of an O-ring failure because the synthetic rubber would become less elastic, in fact it would become hard and contract. There were furious conversations going on among the NASA folks at Canaveral, at the Space Flight Center in Huntsville, with the SRB manufacturer and with us at the factory.

"Our folks held pretty firm, but then, for some reason, the company reversed itself…typical 'go-fever' mindset, and ultimately gave clearance for a launch, although some company men, me included, sent memos warning of an O-ring failure under such extreme weather conditions."

"Why would they reverse themselves? Wouldn't they be liable if something happened?" Dan asked.

"Good question. Oh that's right; you work for an insurance company. Of course they would be liable. But, I think you can add two plus two. All of those bull cocky political factors were driving the train at that point. The politicians were running space operations, not the astronauts or mission control. Besides, what's the harm if the company gets sued for an accident? Settle any claims and drive on. Who else is Uncle Sam going to get to build his rockets? Add the cost of the settlement to the next rocket.

"Believe it or not, even more things went wrong. On the morning of the launch, there was so much ice hanging over everything that NASA delayed lift-off so the sun could do its job. Well, the NASA boys were worried about ice falling off the external tank and doing damage to the orbiter's tiles. Do you know what they are?"

Laura offered that she knew the tiles were important for reentry as they deflected the extreme heat caused when descending through the atmosphere at high speed. The captain continued. "NASA sent an ice team out to look for damage. They had infrared recording instruments. During the investigation after the explosion, the investigators discovered that the external temperature in the right SRB, the one that failed, was in the single digits. Well, that could have been because of the winds affecting only that side of the vehicle, or, it could have been a warning that there was a leak in the external tank venting its super cold fuel onto the right side SRB where the O-ring is located. Guess what? Nobody at the time paid any particular attention to the temperature recordings because they were only looking for visible ice damage."

"Finally," Captain Dave said, "the last nail in the coffin, I suppose, was a wind shear that Challenger flew through at about 35 seconds into her flight. That may have been the straw that broke the O-ring's back. Who knows?" Captain Dave stopped talking, concentrating on flipping the beer bottle tops into a waste can ten feet from the truck. He missed every shot.

"Thanks for sharing that with us. I can only imagine what it must have been like to be involved back then," Laura said, getting off the tailgate and shaking the captain's hand.

"I don't talk about it much, so thank you both for listening to my old war stories. Besides, it's good to remember why I changed professions every so often." He chuckled. "I'll see you folks tomorrow - and no more war stories, I promise."

"Just tall fish tales?" Laura joked.

"Plenty." Captain Dave got into his truck and drove out of the parking lot.

"Nice guy," Dan said.

"He's still haunted by it," Laura replied.

"It's all ancient history, now. Let's go somewhere nice to eat - I have an idea."

Laura reached down to pick up her purse and checked her cell phone. "Got a message," she said.

Chapter 17

Early evening
Overland Highway on the Florida Keys

Dan turned north on the Overland Highway gaining speed and intending to drive to a restaurant whose specialty was turtle soup. He remembered it was located somewhere between Key Largo and the mainland. Meanwhile Laura lowered the volume on the radio and put her free hand to her ear so she could hear the message over the wind rushing past the convertible.

"It was Detective Leonard and he said to call him, it's urgent."

"They all say that," Dan replied. "When did he call?"

"About an hour ago. Pull over."

"Is that a Florida law? The driver has to pull over when the front seat passenger is on a cell phone?"

"I want to call Detective Leonard and I don't want to lose my signal in the middle of what he wants to urgently tell me," she said, taking from her bag a pen and a small blue pocket sized note pad with the air force logo on the cover.

"He probably wants to tell you not to leave town." Dan eased the Mustang onto the shoulder then turned into the parking lot of a closed hardware store. "I suppose he told you to call him at home, too."

"Jealous?" She teased.

As she started talking to the detective, Dan realized that there was a small bodega behind the closed shop where they had stopped. He pointed it out to Laura then walked over. After hitting the head he bought some sodas, returning to see Laura still on the phone.

"Okay," She said into the cell. "I will…as soon as I get back home…thank-you very much…good-bye."

"I need something stronger than this." She said taking the diet cola from Dan.

"What's up?"

Laura looked over the notes she'd made during the conversation with Leonard. "I need to see the detective to help him figure out what's going on. He said my life may be in danger."

"Really? Did they ID the dead guy yet?"

She went back a few pages in her notes. "Vasily Bera…Professor Vasily Bera…he's an economics professor and lives, I should say, lived in Gainesville. I've never even been to Gainesville."

"Why are you in danger? Wait a minute, does Leonard want to meet you at his place?"

"Stop it, I'm serious. After we left, they ran the plates of all the cars in the restaurant parking lot and a couple of blocks each way from the restaurant. They figured he didn't walk to the restaurant. Well by mid morning, all but four cars had moved and the police followed up and found out that one of the cars was registered to this professor and they got his photograph from his driver's license on file with the DMV and it matched up."

"You gotta love living in a police state," Dan griped.

"I thought you would appreciate their work? Anyway, when they searched the car, guess what they found?"

"Porno?"

"No."

"What, then?"

"A photo of me," Laura said putting down her notes.

"I was close. He was a pervert."

"Dan!"

"What? I'm serious. He probably was a perv. What kind of photograph did he have?" Dan asked.

"I don't know, the detective didn't tell me. Why?"

"Well, the police may be able to place the circumstances of how he knew you. For example, if it's a distance shot then he was stalking you at some point with a telephoto lens. Where were you when the photo was taken? Was the photo just of your head or a body shot? What were you wearing in the photograph?" He took a sip of his soda. "Did you tell the detective that he called you by name?"

"I told him that I thought he did. The detective doesn't think he was a pervert, though."

"Why is that?"

"Detective Leonard ran his name on a police computer and he is on some FBI thing called an OC list-that stands for…," she checked her notes.

"I know, Organized Crime; was he in the Russian mob or something?"

"He didn't say that but the FBI is interested in the case. He's spoken with an Agent Rowles, already."

"What about the connection with your brother?" Dan asked.

"We talked about that. I said that I am pretty sure now that he was only asking about Ken."

"What did Leonard say to that?"

"That there must be a connection between Professor Bera and Ken and whatever the connection is, or was, it may have led to the professor's death."

"Suicide?" Dan asked.

"He said death, not suicide or murder."

"Did he say whether any prints on the gun matched the professor?"

"He didn't say anything about finger prints."

"What were you saying about 'as soon as you get back home' to Leonard?"

"I told him I was fishing with you here on the Keys and that I would call him when I got back home."

"What did he say?"

"He said it was good that I was not in the area and I should call him as soon as I get home. By then he may have more information about Bera. He also wanted to know how long I've known you."

"I'm sorry he asked you that. Now I must kill you," Dan intoned a very bad Russian accent.

"Ha ha. I told him about the accident Ben witnessed and that I verified you work for an insurance company in New Jersey."

"He probably asked just to know if you're available. Did you tell him you're already madly in love with me?"

"No, I didn't want to lie or make him laugh."

"Smart thinking. Did you tell him that you may have some of your brother's stuff in storage?"

"No."

"Why not?"

"He didn't ask, besides…I want to look at what's there first. Are you tired?"

"I'll sleep well tonight. Why?"

"I was hoping you would drive me home," Laura flashed a toothy grin.

"Home! Why?"

"Because I don't have to report to my unit until Tuesday…and Ben will let me stretch it to Wednesday. I can drive out to Lexington and back by then. I can look at what I have left that belonged to Ken and let Detective Leonard have whatever isn't too personal or embarrassing. Then, I want to know why a Russian mobster had my picture in his car, yelled at me, and then got his brains blown out on the beach."

Dan slouched down a bit in his seat and rubbed his eyes. He looked over at Laura and said, "Going home is out of the way if you want to go to Tennessee from here. It would be easier to head west when we get back on the mainland then take Interstate 75. It will cut a few hours off the trip."

"We?" Laura raised her eyebrows.

"Well, where is Lexington, exactly?"

"It's in the western part of the state a few hours past Nashville off I-40."

"So we're talking about twenty plus hours to get there from here and about eighteen hours from there to Cape Canaveral."

"That's about right," she said.

"What about flying?" Dan asked.

"Well, since I didn't make reservations six years in advance it will cost a fortune. Plus, there are no direct flights and driving probably won't take that much longer."

"I can help with the driving. We can go in shifts."

"What about your vacation? Captain Dave?" Laura asked.

"The fish will be there next year. Besides, nobody back in the office will believe this."

"You really don't have to come with me. I'm good at driving long distances. I take quick naps when I feel tired and I take in black coffee intravenously. I'll be fine, honestly."

"I have no doubt, but I want to go with you," Dan said, turning toward her and taking her hand.

"Thank you," she said, kissing him briefly and pulling back. "Let's check out of the Eva Braun Inn and you better call Captain Dave."

Chapter 18

Friday night
Orlando

Katenka Tiverzin was just shy of the half century mark yet she routinely attracted men nearly half her age. Her physical conditioning began when she was just four years old as a student at the Kirov Theatre in Leningrad. By her twelfth birthday, it was apparent that she was growing too much to ever dance a Balanchine arrangement on that famous stage. Her mother was told that her daughter would no longer be attending the ballet school and young Katenka's dream of finishing a performance as adoring fans tossed red roses at her feet were abruptly and permanently dashed.

However, while in her late teens and still involved with ballet and gymnastics, she was recruited as an athletic trainer and surrogate big sister for the Soviet Union's 1980 Olympic gymnastic team and, in Moscow, she proved her value to the state well beyond the team's gold medals that were won that year. The officers of the *Komiter Gosudarstvennoi Bezopanosti*, whose job was to prevent Soviet Olympians from becoming friendly with western athletes and especially reporters, noted that she was exceptionally loyal to Leninist principles. The agent's reports included her verbatim statements of the misdeeds of her comrades and they also footnoted her striking beauty. After a year in training at the KGB Institute of Foreign Languages, where she learned much more than English, she was fast tracked by the Soviet embassy to receive a student visa to the United States of America.

Katenka sat up on the cheap motel bed for a moment and then went into the bathroom where she peed and washed up. Looking at her face for a long time in the mirror, she finally lit a cigarette and stepped over to the curtained window, pulling back the fabric to peek out onto the half empty parking lot.

"Really Pavel, this motel is so...clandestine," she said, standing naked and scanning the view.

"I'm on a clandestine mission." Volkova replied.

"You could have visited me in my home. Do you think my neighbors would report you to the FBI?" She laughed, letting go of the curtain and sitting on an upholstered chair across from the bed.

Volkova reached over to the nightstand on Katenka's side of the bed and took one of her cigarettes. He lit up, took a long drag and sat up to rest against the headboard.

The room was lit only by the escaping bathroom light and through the smoke, Volkova gazed at Katenka who was leaning back in her chair with her legs crossed at the ankles, arms resting on the chair and her head back. Katenka's rich black hair was still pulled back in a ponytail from her workout at the motel's sorry excuse for a health and fitness room. Her breasts were athletically compact and her pubic area wasn't shaved down to a wisp like most of the recent women he had been with. Pavel Volkova could sense her penetrating light blue eyes even in the darkness. He thought of her as she had looked almost twenty-five years ago and still felt the same desire. It was a testament to his loyalty to the motherland that he could orchestrate her romances to men more desirous than himself. He was certain that she had let herself fall in love with some of the targets he had selected; she was after all, an artist. And, artists could never be fully trusted not to fall in love.

"I think I will always be in love with you, Katenka Tiverzin," he offered.

"I think you were never in love with me, Pavel Volkova. But, I often wished you were," she replied not moving in the chair.

"Why is that?"

She paused. "Because I didn't want to feel like a...whore."

"You were not a whore: you were a soldier and you defended the motherland."

"That motherland doesn't exist anymore and my new motherland, Russia, would never condone what I have done." She looked at him to gauge his reaction.

"Perhaps you are right, but what's done is done."

"I've done awful things," she said softly.

Pavel took the ashtray from the nightstand and harshly stubbed his cigarette out. "Then see a priest and confess but get over what you have done. It can only cause you trouble."

She remained in her stretched position, confessing to her former mentor. "I have caused death to people who believed, right up to the moment they died, that I loved them."

"You served the motherland. The cold war...fucking euphemisms... you and I both know it was a real war with real people dying everyday on missions and in training for missions. Americans killed our agents and we killed theirs..."

"Now we are all friends," she replied.

"Yes, now we are all friends. And, Americans drive Japanese cars and rich Russians want a Mercedes after those bastards killed twenty five million of us in the Patriotic War."

"I am an American now, Pavel," she said, getting comfortable again in the chair.

"I heard. Congratulations."

"You don't sound sincere."

"I'm not. But I was sincere when I said that I still love you. I never heard you say that you love me."

She groaned, "We just *made* love, Pavel, what more do you want from me?"

Volkova kicked the bed sheet off his legs and moved to the edge of the bed. He leaned over, picked up Katenka's right foot, brought it to his mouth, kissing each toe. "I always wanted you to say that you love me." He said.

"I was afraid of you," she purred, enjoying his attention.

"Are you afraid, now?" He placed her right foot down and brought her other foot up to kiss.

"A little," she teased and pulled her foot back but did not resist when he took it again.

"You should be," he said and gently bit her big toe.

"What is my mission this time?"

Volkova let her foot down gently, got on the floor and moved so that he was on his knees between her legs. He kissed gently between her breasts and she slid down the chair onto him.

"I will brief you later, my love." he said.

She sat on the floor wrapping her strong legs around him as they embraced. Katenka knew that he wanted to make love again but felt there was more on his mind this time.

"What's wrong, Pavel?" she asked.

Volkova moved back then turned her around so that she was resting against him as he leaned back against the side of the bed. He put his arms around her pressing on her trim waist.

"My life is in danger," he finally said.

"More so than normal?" she laughed, slightly turning her head.

"I'm afraid so."

"What has happened?"

"Former comrades are blackmailing me," he replied.

"Over what?" she asked.

"Over what was done in 1986."

Katenka moved away from Volkova, got up, found her cigarettes and sat back down on the chair. She offered one to Volkova and lit up.

"Then I am being blackmailed, too," she said.

"No. I don't think so. Anyway, you're name wasn't mentioned."

"Who are 'they'?"

"I don't know. It could just be one person, but I was led to believe it was more than one," Volkova said, getting up and sitting back down on the bed holding his cigarette and ashtray.

"Well, what does he, or they, want?"

"Hard evidence of what we did so they can use it for blackmail."

"How did they find out?" Katenka asked.

"That I do not know. It was a tightly controlled operation and so my name should not appear. I would very much like to tell my blackmailers to screw off. But, I am concerned that, somehow, they were able to link that operation to me so their threat must be real. Since you are the only other operational member still alive, I need to ask if anyone has contacted you."

"No! Of course not!" she replied sternly. "I would have told you first thing, tonight."

"Then, my blackmailers must have some evidence. Are you sure nothing was left behind by your…lover?" Volkova asked moving towards her.

"Pavel, we went over this a hundred times, back then."

"I remember, but you know he kept that journal and there were also the technical drawings I gave him. Let's go over this one more time," he demanded, then nibbled on the nape of her neck.

"He left nothing behind. I met him at work Sunday, two days before he…*died*." She stopped, absorbing the denial contained in her own words. "When he went to the bathroom, I went through his desk. Afterwards, he was called to a meeting and I went through his computer files. I am sure he had no damaging evidence on his work computer.

"I deleted every file on his computer at the trailer in case the files could somehow be recovered after the fire. You know there was nothing left of the trailer after the explosion. I took everything from his car before the police and fire department arrived. We went through that material together. I visited his hometown. His mother had recently passed away and his sister had joined the air force. There was a 'For Sale' sign on the house. I called the real estate agent and scheduled a visit to look at the property. I broke in later. If he did leave anything there, it burned in the fire. Pavel, he left nothing behind."

"What about his sister?" Volkova asked.

"I never met her. But, if Ken told her anything, wouldn't she have acted on it long before now?"

"Yes, I suppose you are right. I just wanted to make sure that my blackmailers could not blackmail you, as well."

Volkova put out his cigarette. "Come to bed with me, my beautiful ballerina."

She got up, walked over with Volkova to the bed.

"What will you do, now?" Katenka asked.

"What will *we* do now?" he corrected her. "I need to find out from his sister what, if anything, she knows."

Volkova rolled Katenka over so that he was on top and then began making love once again.

"You will protect me, Pavel?"

"Haven't I always?" Pavel Volkova said between kisses. He was protecting her right now, he thought. She didn't need to be told any more.

Chapter 19

Friday night
On the road to Lexington

They merged onto the Dixie Highway south of Miami just after eight o'clock. While filling up the gas tank back on the keys, Dan purchased road maps, a small cooler that he filled with ice and caffeinated energy drinks, some snacks, and two fat cigars that he would enjoy when it was his turn to drive and Laura was sleeping. He calculated from the maps that the trip to Laura's home town would take just about eighteen hours. That would place them in Lexington on Saturday afternoon and, assuming that they spent about six hours there, they could be back on the road to Laura's house by ten o'clock that night. The trip back to Florida would take about fifteen hours, so they would arrive early Sunday afternoon, giving Laura enough time to recover before going to work.

And, Dan calculated, he could still make it back to the keys during the week to get some fishing done, although he was thinking about asking Laura if he could just stay with her for the rest of his vacation. He could do some party boat and surf fishing during the day near her place and keep her company at night, he plotted. He decided to hold that thought until the road trip was nearly over. Reminding himself of his track record with women, he thought she would probably kick him out of the car by the time they got to Atlanta.

"Did you calculate bathroom stops?" Laura asked.

"I fudged. I assumed that we would be traveling over the speed limit so that should wash out the downtime for bathroom stops."

"Boy bathroom stops or girl bathroom stops."

"I didn't discriminate," he replied.

"You should have but I'll do my best to keep to the flight schedule. I left a message for the Kurkes to let them know we're coming. I would hate to find the place locked up when we get there."

"I thought it was a storage facility," Dan commented.

"It is, but it's not quite like a regular commercial establishment. I think I told you, it's a converted barn and the Kurkes are on a first name basis with everyone they rent space to. Mr. Kurke has to unlock the main barn door and there are individual stalls inside. I don't even have the key to my stall anymore. I left my cell phone number on their answering machine. You got unlimited mileage with this car, didn't you?" she asked.

"Beats me, our admin assistant made the reservations," he replied.

"You should lie down in the backseat," Laura said after a few minutes.

"I haven't heard that line since high school."

"I bet you didn't hear it then, either," Laura laughed.

Dan reached behind, grabbed his sweatshirt, rolled it into a pillow and leaned against the window, slouching down in his seat. "I'm fine here, for now. I can sleep anywhere. I used to fall asleep on airplanes before jumping."

"When *were* you in the army and *what exactly* did you do?" She asked after a while.

Dan took his *NY Jets* hat from the dashboard and put it on, pulling it down over his eyes to shield them from the oncoming headlights. "I enlisted in 1978. How old were you then?"

"Nice try. Go on, you enlisted in '78." Laura smiled in the darkness.

"Let me tell you, joining the army in 1978 was not a popular thing to do. America was at the height of the disco craze and everyone had long hair - the dry look was in back then. I took a lot of abuse from my friends when I came home on leave with my shaved head. Vietnam veterans were still looked down upon as immoral baby killers and Hollywood movies or television shows always had some Vietnam vet going psycho and killing people. By extension, I suppose, any one in the military at that time was considered aberrant. I remember going back to my high school in uniform to see my old teachers before going overseas to Korea and a senior called me an asshole for enlisting and the students in the hallway were all laughing at me.

"Anyway, I was in the infantry for the first ten years and then, on my third re-enlistment, I transferred to military police. There was a shortage in that field and the army was offering choice of assignment."

"Are you glad you did that?"

"Oh, yeah. I come from a long line of cops and thought I might like to be one as well. But, it wasn't as exciting as what I was doing before and it hurt my career. I probably would have made E-9 if I stayed infantry. On the other hand, if I stayed infantry, I might be dead by now."

"Are you serious?" she said as he pulled his hat down even further.

"I think so. I have two purple hearts and didn't want a third," Dan said after a few moments.

"Two? For what?" she asked.

"My left calf and my left shoulder," he replied. "But my whole right side is still virgin territory to enemy gunfire."

"No. Where? The Gulf War? Somalia?"

"I was an MP during the Gulf War and I wasn't in Somalia," he continued after a while. "I got my first purple heart and a bronze star with a 'V' device…for valor…in Grenada. Remember that one?"

"Not much. We invaded the island and rescued some medical students."

"That's about it. Wake me up when you get tired."

"Come on Dan, I want to know," she reached over and shoved him.

He raised his hat and looked out the window. "Do you know what the difference is between a war story and a fairy tale?" He didn't wait for an answer. "A fairy tale starts off with *once upon a time* and a war story starts off with *no shit guys, this really happened.* Anyway, I used to like telling people what I went through because I was so proud of my unit and what we did, but you know what? Nobody really gives a crap."

"I wear a uniform, Dan," she replied indignantly. "I'm not some airhead on the street that doesn't have a clue as to what we do everyday. My whole career hasn't been as a personnel and administration sergeant in a weather squadron. I've slept in the woods, froze my butt off on mountaintops in Alaska; I'm a veteran of the Gulf War and was almost KIAed in Kosovo."

Dan let her vent a little more, knowing that he caused it. He recognized that he had that innate ability to fire up a woman's temper. "I apologize." He readjusted his make-shift pillow and stretched his legs. "The Serbs were lucky they got hit with the Warthog instead of you."

"Apology accepted. Why don't you go in the back and rest?"

"Because I'm comfortable here," he said, reclining the seat even further. After a commercial came on the radio Dan continued. "I went to airborne and ranger school after coming back from the Republic of Korea. Did you know that was considered a combat tour of duty back then?"

"What was?" she asked.

"Serving on the demilitarized zone, the DMZ in Korea. Only politicians can come up with a name like 'demilitarized zone' to describe a geographic area where two armies are standing off against each other and shooting at anything that moves - it should be called the VMZ for Very Militarized Zone.

"Anyway, a few years before I got there, the North Koreans butchered two of our officers with machetes in the DMZ. They were there to cut down a tree to clear a field of fire. It's a very dangerous place to go to work. While I was there, another squad in my platoon got into a fire fight on a night patrol and killed some NKs and they killed one of our KATUSAs, but fortunately, I don't have any war stories from the Land of the Morning Calm."

"What's a KATUSA?"

"Korean Augmentation To the United States Army…rich kids whose parents got them into our units because the ROK units were too tough for them. Anyway, after ranger school - sounds quaint - like the army sent us to a campus, I was assigned to the 1st Battalion of the 75th Ranger Regiment in Fort Stewart Georgia. I spent a few years there training for war everyday, and that was just with my wife," he laughed.

"Is that where you met her?"

"I actually met her in Columbus, Georgia. I had three weeks to kill between Airborne and Ranger school so I partied a lot and met her in town.

"Back to my war story. We'd had been getting briefings that there might be something for us to do in Grenada. Believe me; no one in the outfit had a clue where Grenada was before we went there. Even the officers were looking at the world atlas trying to find the damn place and we knew even less about its history.

"This guy Bishop took over the country back in the late seventies and he was very friendly with the Soviets and Cubans. They started to build runways to handle the Soviet Backfire and Bear bombers and I think they were building submarine pens, too, for the soviet navy. Bishop, Maurice Bishop, however, wasn't communist enough and a radical Marxist gang took over the government. At that time, there were American medical students on the island along with American and western tourists.

"Reagan didn't want a hostage crisis on his watch, that's why Carter got bounced from office, and he also wanted to rid the island of Marxists, to boot, since their presence had been a thorn in our side."

"It sounds like you should go back to school; you know more of international relations than most of my professors."

"Well, I have on-the-job experience."

She laughed and raised the speed on the cruise control. "When did this all happen?"

"On October 24, 1983, we were alerted and the balloon went up the next day - less than twenty fours between the initial alert and our combat jump. We had an eighteen hour schedule between the time an alert was ordered and a battalion of killers went wheels up in C-130s. There was no time to reflect or write letters or anything. You picked up your equipment, received a briefing, put on your parachute and waddled onto the airplane.

"We marshaled at Hunter Army Airfield, next door to Fort Stewart. Our battalion was ordered to make a combat jump onto the runway located at Point Salinas at the southern tip of the island. Our job was to secure the runway for the boys in the 82nd Airborne Division who would land and conduct combat operations against the Marxists from our airhead. The Marines conducted their own helicopter airborne assault north of us. The Marines and the Airborne also had the mission to get the students safely out of the country.

"The original plan called for my battalion to make the combat jump and the second battalion of Rangers to land like the 82nd. It doesn't make much sense to risk a combat jump when you can safely land an airplane.

"Once we were airborne, the operation got fouled up by all kinds of conflicting intelligence we were receiving from our army special operations guys and Navy SEALs who were already in place and from our U2 and spy satellite imagery.

"We were told that the runway was cleared of obstacles so a decision was made that we would land the planes. On our bird, we were told to take our parachutes off, which we did. Then, we received more intelligence that the runway was cluttered with obstacles so the jump was back on. We had to in-flight rig with combat loads and live ammo bouncing around all over the place - the jumpmasters earned their pay that day. The boys in the second battalion learned that they were going to jump their asses in, too.

"On the way down to Point Salinas, the air force navigation system malfunctioned and our flight of C-130's had to be re-aligned. We were supposed to jump in darkness at zero five hundred but that was pushed back to after zero five thirty because of the navigation screw up. Since it would be light outside, our commander ordered the jump altitude lowered to five hundred feet to give the enemy less of a target as we parachuted in; however, at that altitude, our reserve parachutes would be useless if needed. Some guys just left the damn things on their seats.

"On the final run to the drop zone, our C-130 came under fire. I couldn't hear anything because the plane itself is so loud and the jump doors were open. But the plane's crew and the jumpmasters knew we were taking fire because they were hanging outside the aircraft doing their pre-jump inspections and could see the tracers coming up and going past us. When the green light came on, we jumped. I never saw a dirty Herc empty out that fast before.

"Once we hit the silk, the noise abated as the flight kept on going and, for some reason, we didn't come under fire on the drop zone. I hit the ground pretty hard and at that point it was just like a training jump. We assembled with our units and went off on our mission. I was on the team to clear obstacles from the runway while the rest of the unit was pushing the perimeter out and running patrols. I heard gunfire but nothing near me. Ninety minutes later, the second battalion jumped in and by ten hundred hours, approximately twenty-four hours after being alerted, we'd secured our objective in enemy held territory.

Laura thought that he needed to get some sleep but couldn't help asking, "When were you wounded?"

"On the second day. I was assigned to go with our communication guys to run wire from our company headquarters down to the platoon command posts. They needed extra security because there were Grenadian and Cuban patrols in the AO…Area of Operations…and it was hard to lay down wire and keep a lookout at the same time. We were in between our company headquarters and the first platoon when we ran into a Cuban patrol and were outnumbered by about four to one. We spotted them first and hunkered down. I was afraid that they might be point for a larger unit so I didn't want to start a fight. But it was soon apparent that they were headed right for us. So we hit them first with grenades and opened up with our M-16s on full automatic. They hit the ground and threw grenades back at us. Me and the two commo guys all got hit by shrapnel; I got hit in the left calf. Frank Bolles got hit in the chest and Joey Babcock in the arm. I told Babcock to follow the wire back and carry Bolles to headquarters and let them know what's going on and I would cover their withdrawal. They left me all of their ammo except for what they had in their M-16s.

"The Cubans tried to come at me head on but I fired on automatic and they stopped cold in their tracks. I'm not sure if I even hit anyone. About ten minutes later, they tried to come up on my left. By that time I had started moving back following the wire. I hit one Cuban square in the chest, he went down and the others dove for cover. I tossed another grenade and ran about thirty meters following the wire. I waited there for about ten minutes and then started moving again. By that time my leg was killing me but I wasn't about to stop and dress it. Anyway, they stopped pursuing me; I made it back and my leg was treated."

"Was it a bad wound?" Laura asked.

"The wound was small, the piece they took out was the size of a finger nail clipping, but it dug into bone and my leg became infected and ballooned up to almost twice the normal size. I was in the hospital for weeks."

"I was in high school while you were in the hospital," Laura commented.

Dan wanted to just fall asleep but felt the need to add, "We lost five rangers and fourteen other servicemen and we had over one hundred casualties. And I remember reading when I was in the hospital that the press was upset because they didn't get to go along and editorials and political cartoons were mocking the operation as an uneven fight…I don't know, Laura."

"What don't you know?"

"Is any of this worth dying for?"

"You mean our country?"

"Yes."

"*I* think so but I've never had to knowingly put my life right on the edge like you did, but I believe it is. I've been to lots of places in the world and I think we're doing something right."

"I guess I'm just tired of seeing talking heads on television tell how the military should be used and you know none of those people ever served a day. I mean…they have no idea. Sometimes, I think of that day when I went back to high school in my uniform-all bright eyed and bushy tailed. Maybe I *was* an asshole for joining the army. The kid that said that to me was one of the biggest pot dealers in school and never got into any trouble for it. He made a fortune in real estate in the eighties and quadrupled it during the nineties doing pump and dumps with dot com IPOs. Now he's a state senator, owns a mansion and a second five thousand square foot home down the Jersey shore and a condo in Stowe, Vermont. Maybe that could have been me."

"But it's not you and that life wasn't for you, either," she tendered.

"Why not?"

"Because he may be rich…but you're special. What about the other purple heart?"

"That story will have to wait; I'm really tired. Wake me when you want to sleep. Good night," Dan said, turning on his side in the reclined seat and mulling over what Laura had said until he drifted off.

"Good night, soldier boy." Laura said.

Chapter 20

Saturday morning, January 18, 2003
Pancake House near Orlando

Raoul Viñals waited at the counter of the pancake house just off the main highway leading into Orlando. He ordered coffee and unfolded a courtesy copy of *USA Today* to kill time. It was nine o'clock and the place was filled with locals and tourists. He kept his jacket on the seat next to him hoping to save the spot but wouldn't put up an argument if asked. He'd learned early in his career to remain anonymous and nondescript.

He spotted his old associate approaching from the parking lot but didn't see what car he had arrived in. Volkova entered the restaurant and waived to Viñals, smiling at the hostess.

"Hello, John, how's the family?" Viñals said.

"Terrific, Bill, how's Ann?" Volkova replied.

They spoke about the family packages they got for Disneyworld and Universal. Viñals picked a spot where the waitresses placed their orders with the cooks so the ambient noise level was high. The counter had small jukeboxes along its length and Viñals picked three dollars worth of blues to add to the cover.

While searching the menu for breakfast, Volkova surveyed the premises for anything unusual. They each ordered the 'he-man' breakfast special - four eggs, pancakes, sausage and grits. The pair next to the Russian left and were replaced by an elderly couple. Finally, Pavel Volkova asked Viñals, "What did you find out about the Mustang?"

Viñals nodded. "The car is a rental, obviously, and the reservation was made by Knight's Insurance Company in New Jersey. The car was rented at the airport, here in Orlando. I had a woman acquaintance go to the rental agency and tell them that the man driving the car had an argument with her in the parking lot, threatened her, and called her a racial name. She demanded to know who the car was rented to because she was going to the police. The manager finally gave her the information when she said she was going to sue him, the rental agency, and also tell her story to the newspapers." The Cuban mixed the truth with lies effectively.

"It is to our benefit that this is such a litigious society. In Moscow, the manager would have told her to screw off," the Russian commented.

"Cuba, too. Anyway, the man with…what was her name, again?"

"Smith, Laura Smith. She's an air force non commissioned officer."

"Right, the man with her is named Dan Gill. I called Knight's Insurance Company in New Jersey. When you call their main number, their automated answering system lets you select an extension if you know the party's last name. I typed in Gill and got a voicemail message stating that he would be on vacation until next week but I could call his supervisor if there was an urgent matter. What is the connection between him and Smith?" Viñals asked.

"I don't know; romantic I suppose." Volkova answered. "I went by her house on Saturday night and they were both there. He stayed the night. I went back in the morning and her car was gone but his car and the truck were in the driveway. I drove by a little while latter and saw them backing out of the driveway in the convertible. She was in civilian clothes but I called her unit, nevertheless, later in the day and asked for her but was told she wasn't available and the airman wouldn't give me any more information. I went by her place again before going to Gainesville and her vehicles were still there."

"Sounds like Smith and Gill are enjoying each other's company somewhere. He probably has a room somewhere or maybe they're enjoying Mickey Mouse down the road." Viñals grinned at the waitress who had appeared and was waiting for her order from the kitchen.

"Do you still have your hacker friends at the university?" The Russian asked.

"The best have already graduated but I know how to get in touch. Why?"

The Russian said softly, "When I went by Smith's house, I grabbed her trash bag from the curb. She had recently paid all of her monthly bills and I have some credit card numbers for you." Volkova handed the Cuban an envelope. "Here are the discount tickets for you and Ann." He said louder in case the waitress was ever called upon to remember anything.

They offered their cups for refills as their breakfast specials arrived.

"You usually give me some idea of what you are up to when you ask me for a favor," Viñals said.

The Russian finished buttering his grits. "You arrived in Miami in 1980, correct?" Volkova asked.

"You know I did. Your partner Lasky placed me."

"And he put you right to work in the Cocoa Beach area?"

"I was trying to recruit my fellow refugees working in sensitive locations."

"And, you had no luck," The Russian said.

"My fellow countrymen became patriotic Americans: I found no one I could rely on to bring on board and found no good blackmail targets."

"Were you told what we had in mind if you found a candidate?" Volkova asked.

"Nothing in particular," Viñals replied, "but I always assumed it was to slow down the pace a bit at the cape. Most of the Cubans were only in entry level positions back then so I concluded that little acts of mischief from the maintenance crew would satisfy the objective."

"Well, my old friend," Volkova said mixing cream and sugar into his coffee, "with *my* recruitment efforts, we succeeded at more than *little* acts of mischief."

Viñals reflected on what he said. "Does this air force sergeant have any connection to what we did so long ago? And, from her rank, she must have been very young back then."

"Her connection is…tangential. I gave Bera enough information for his task. Did he not tell you after receiving my message?"

"Bera has been walking on eggshells for years. With the threats to his family back home by the Brighton Beach crew, the feds looking into his consulting company for money laundering and his drinking, he was a walking nervous breakdown. He was actually avoiding me the past few months."

The Russian looked around. "Smith's dead brother played a part. I wanted that idiot Bera to go to Smith's house and say that he was writing a book about the economic impact of the 1986 shuttle explosion on the telecommunication industry. He was to say that in his research, he had discovered that her brother worked on the shuttle project and was killed the same day and that it would be an interesting footnote to an otherwise tedious thesis. He was to ask for any of her brother's belongings that she or her family might still have that he could borrow for his book. Instead, for some reason he followed her to the restaurant and acted like a maniac."

"Was he paid in full? Viñals asked.

"I wired him two thousand up front and promised him eight thousand if he came through. Why?"

"He owed money. A lot of money and I heard he was getting desperate."

"I would have appreciated that information sooner," Volkova said stiffly.

"Well, you didn't ask what you needed him for and I told you he was a drunk," Viñals defended himself.

"I can work with drunks. Okay, you're right, never mind." Volkova relaxed. "What's done is done. Unfortunately, I still need to know."

"Why can't you just approach her with the same line about writing a book?" Viñals asked.

"Because Bera was shouting at her about her brother. She would be suspicious about someone else asking about him and she might go to the police."

"So, you were there with Bera?" the Cuban asked and Volkova nodded. Viñals continued. "Did you…end it for Bera?"

"He finally left a message on my cell phone Saturday night saying that he was following her to a restaurant. That wasn't what he should have done and I tried calling him back but he had his phone turned off. I got to the restaurant just as he was following Smith and her date back to their cars. By the time I parked and got out, Smith's friend,

Gill, had already chased him off and I caught up with him behind the restaurant. Bera was very upset."

"And?" Raoul Viñal wanted to know.

Two waitresses stood near by and Volkova started talking about the traffic on Highway 258 being snarled by recent construction. He stopped talking for a while to finish the last of his eggs and changed the subject to the Yankees' shortstop. When the waitresses finally moved off, he continued. "And, now the professor has no more concerns about his debts." Volkova picked up the tab. "My treat."

Volkova took out his wallet and placed enough cash on the counter for both meals and a reasonable tip. "Let's finish our coffee," he said.

Viñals watched the waitresses working along the counter. "Why now? So many years later?" he asked.

Volkova leaned forward and said softly, "my friend, I have created many enemies in my service to the motherland. These enemies are a ruthless lot divided between those who want to expose what I once did and those who want to forever forget my accomplishments. I want no evidence that will deliver me to the bottom of the Caspian Sea or to the World Court for crimes against humanity. Laura Smith is the last link that could connect me with any of that." He kept his eyes on the Cuban to assess whether this was believed.

"What about me? You just admitted . . ."

"A fairy tale. You have no physical proof."

Their waitress came and took away the empty plates. The Russian handed her his money and they both got up to leave. Volkova and Viñals parted ways at the front door of the restaurant. Raoul Viñals walked over to his car while keeping the Russian in the corner of his eye to spot the vehicle he was walking towards. Volkova backed out of his space and sped past the Cuban who also backed up and followed his old colleague out of the parking lot. Viñals turned to head west and watched Volkova's car disappearing in his rear view mirror going the other way. He lowered the volume on the car radio, took his cell phone out and dialed the FBI number from memory. As the call went through, he nervously scanned the road ahead.

"Agent Rowles," the voice on the other end answered gruffly.

Chapter 21

Same morning
Lexington

Dan drove from Atlanta to Chattanooga where Laura picked up the duty, persevering with it even after several stops for gas, food and bathroom breaks. She had not driven through Tennessee in several years, lacking a reason to even visit for over a decade. Now she relished the memories it brought back, including some she had completely forgotten over the years. Dan slept most of the way; she wanted to talk but knew it was better to let him sleep. He would be driving tonight on the same roads on the return trip and he would need to be rested and alert.

Low clouds had colored the sky dark gunmetal gray as they passed over the hills near Nashville. The radio news announced that it was snowing just to the north of the interstate but an hour later, west of the capitol city, the sun broke through and lit up the otherwise drab landscape.

The Kurkes, Laura recalled, threw nickels around like manhole covers, and Laura thought they may not be returning her phone call because it would be long distance. So, she called again, to her relief Mrs. Kurke answered saying she had just returned from the hospital. Mr. Kurke had fallen, broken his hip, and subsequently caught pneumonia; she would be going back to the hospital until visiting hours ended at eight o'clock. Mrs. Kurke made arrangements to leave the barn door and stall keys, telling Laura that they would be hidden under a flower pot by the front door of their house.

The tedious interstate highway drive left Laura feeling uncomfortable, exhausted, and unclean. They had been on the road almost continually since the day before when they left her house for Islamorada. That trip seemed like eons ago. She was tempted to ask Mrs. Kurke if she could take a shower before getting back on the road to Florida but didn't want to impose.

For the past hour, she had only thought of the man sleeping next to her. She was certainly attracted to him. Even when she had first driven him to interview the colonel, she had quickly noted that he was tall, athletic-looking, handsome, funny, about the right age and…not wearing a ring. The latter raised some questions for her, however. She could understand his marriage at a young age not working out but wondered why he didn't marry again, or have a girlfriend. The thought bounced around in her mind, of course, that he might not be telling the truth about not having someone waiting for him back home.

Laura knew that she could have Dan wrapped around her finger but had a feeling he would not let himself be wrapped for very long. She recalled a friend's evaluation once, saying that her problem with men was that she liked to dominate her relationships and then grew disappointed when the men became wimps. Dan offered the prospect of not becoming a wimp and she considered taking him up on his offer to see a Broadway show and dinner in Manhattan; maybe it could work for a while despite the mileage between their homes.

Laura turned off Interstate 40 and entered the outskirts of Lexington at half past three. She knew the rest of the way to the Kurke's farm by heart.

"Wake up, Danny boy, we're almost there." She nudged him but he was already half awake.

He returned his seat to its upright position and stretched as best he could.

"Where are we?" Dan asked.

"About five miles from the Kurke's farm."

"Did they call you back?'

"No, but I called. Mr. Kurke is in the hospital and Mrs. Kurke is with him but she'll leave the keys for us."

"What happened to Mr. Kurke?"

"He broke his hip and has pneumonia."

"Too bad. This is nice country. Where was your house?" Dan asked, looking around."Another five miles past the Kurke's on this same road. I sold the lot after the fire and the buyer, a developer, built a coin operated laundry place."

"I guess you can never go home again."

"Not unless I want to wash my clothes. Have you ever been to Tennessee before?"

"I was stationed at Fort Campbell and went to Nashville with some buddies pretty often."

"Isn't Fort Campbell in Kentucky?"

"Some of it is but most of the maneuver areas and drop zones are in Tennessee. What did you do in Lexington for fun when you were a kid?" Dan asked, looking at the barns, silos and barren fields.

"It was a nice place to grow up. I remember fishing with my brother in the summertime and helping out on a farm owned by my mother's friend. Ken and I would bicycle there and help feed the chickens, collect the eggs, and clean out the hen houses. I made twenty dollars a week doing that.

"My mother was sort of a church lady so Sundays always remind me of bible school and prayer service and then afternoon picnics in the field behind the church. I can still smell the barbeque cooking and hear kids playing and parents gossiping. An older man who lived next door to the church had an old appaloosa, named Trixie, and he would saddle her up and let the kids take turns riding her up and down the fence line."

She came to a stop sign and pushed the button to roll down the convertible top. "I know it's a little chilly, but we're almost there. I just want to breathe the air for a little while." She started moving slowly forward then picked up speed as the top folded down into its compartment. "What did you do for fun in New Jersey when you were a kid?"

"Well, me and my friend, Billy, formed a gang called the 'Hudson Hoods' and to become a member, you had to sneak into the cemetery that was a few blocks away from Hudson Street, find a good hiding spot, then throw berries into the open windows of cars passing by,"

Dan said, rolling the brim of his *Jets* hat, tossing it up on the dashboard and running his fingers through his hair.

"Sounds quaint. Is that why you joined the army? You know, jail or the army?"

"No, I was a good kid. Our gang was short-lived. Billy's cousin Georgie, who always had snot running down his nose…"

"Ugh! That's disgusting. You could have omitted that," Laura said.

"Georgie is a chiropractor, now. Anyway, Georgie threw these red berries into a car and hit the driver right in the face. The driver chased us all over the cemetery until Georgie decided to make a break for it and headed back toward Hudson Street where the driver caught him right in front of his parent's house. Georgie ratted us out and our parents slapped the crap out of us."

"That's a lovely childhood memory, Dan." Laura looked over at him.

"Let me tell you about the time we made a mortar out of an aluminum fence post behind our school..."

"A mortar?" Laura asked.

"Uh huh. We capped off one end of the pipe, carved an aiming notch at the other end, dropped an M-80 down the pipe, threw in the frog…"

"Threw in the frog?"

"Well, we didn't have real shells," Dan explained.

"Do you have any *nice* memories from your childhood that you can tell me about?

Laura asked him.

"Those *were* my nice memories. You want to hear some bad ones?"

"Not while I'm sober. There's the Kurke's property." She pointed out a two story farmhouse set back from the road. The faded white house was speckled with peeling paint chips with a dull green wrap-around porch. The barn was set back two hundred yards from the house and a half dozen smaller out buildings dotted the property. The trees were all bare and the grass was brown, creating a feeling of desolation.

Laura pulled up to the house. "The key is supposed to be in one of those flower pots." Laura got out of the car and walked to the porch while Dan walked around the car checking the tires. Laura saw an envelope with her name on it stuck in between the jamb of the torn screen door.

"Dan!" Laura waved at Dan. He jogged over and she said, "This is from Mrs. Kurke, she made us something to eat and said to make ourselves at home. Do you want to eat first?" she asked.

"Let's get what we need from the barn while it's still light outside. Do you think Mrs. Kurke would mind if I used the bathroom?"

"She said 'make yourselves at home'." Laura looked in the flower pots and found three keys in the fourth pot she checked. She tried them on the front door; finding the right key, she opened the door, shoving Dan to the side. "I'm going first!" she yelled running inside, having the advantage of knowing where the bathroom was located.

Dan went in and looked around the house thinking that he hadn't seen similar furnishings since he was a kid at his grandmother's apartment. The house had that 'old lady' feel about it which he found warming. The kitchen was tidy and immaculate with appliances that were at least thirty years old. He spotted a note and read Mrs. Kurke's invitation to enjoy the turkey sandwiches that were in the icebox.

"Your turn," Laura said, walking into the kitchen. "Isn't this a great old house?" she said.

"I was just thinking that myself. There are some sandwiches in the fridge; I think I'll take mine with me to the barn," Dan said heading for the bathroom.

Laura opened the refrigerator and took out the turkey sandwiches made on plain white bread with mayonnaise and she added a couple of sodas; then, looked around the kitchen. Her parent's house suddenly flooded her memory - the way it looked when they first moved in and before they modernized it with a new kitchen and bathrooms.

"Ready?" Dan asked coming back and going for the sandwich. "This was very nice of her to do especially with her husband in the hospital."

"It's called being neighborly. It's a lost art."

*****

They drove over to the barn and Laura carefully parked the car far enough back to allow the barn doors to swing fully open.

"When was the last time this was used as a barn?" Dan asked as Laura opened up the lock and slid the chain out of the handles. Dan heaved open the large doors.

"Twenty years at least. They stopped farming themselves and sublet their land to soybean and cotton growers. The tenants brought their own equipment for storage and processing so the barn wasn't being used. It was a pretty good idea to build these stalls and rent them out."

The barn was subdivided into fenced off areas varying in size. Everything from automobiles to children's toys was strewn about the inside of the stalls. Laura walked through the barn to the far end. Dan followed, looking at the collection of stored property.

"I remember bringing the boxes over there," Laura said, walking up to the place she was pointing to. "Here it is." She opened the lock of her stall.

Twenty boxes were stacked in the far end, blocked by small end tables, lamps and wooden chairs at the front.

"I should have taken this stuff a long time ago," she said, starting to move the furniture back towards Dan who moved it further away so they could get to the boxes. "I guess I felt that as long as this stuff remained here, then I had roots somewhere. Every January, I send Mr. and Mrs. Kurke one hundred and twenty five dollars."

"That's not a bad price; this size would cost you at least fifty dollars a month at a regular storage place," Dan commented. "I used to rent storage space."

"They only raised the price once since I've been here and they sent me a handwritten letter along with the bill apologizing for the increase." They made their way back to the boxes. "I think I'll take some leave when it gets warmer and cart everything home with me; it's silly to keep this place." Laura pointed at the chairs. "My mother and father would sit in those chairs every night at the kitchen while Ken did his homework and I drew in my coloring books. I should have them refinished."

She grabbed the top box and heaved it over to Dan.

"Let me do that!" Dan said, taking the box and placing it outside the fence and then switching places with her. Laura stepped out of the stall and opened the first box.

"China. Look at this. Isn't it beautiful? Laura held up a patterned plate. "My Uncle Marcellus sent eight place settings to my grandparents as an anniversary gift when he was stationed in West Germany right after World War II."

Dan kept bringing boxes out and laying them in a row for Laura to inspect. She found china in the first four boxes. "I should have labeled all these boxes," Laura said at one point. The next boxes she opened were filled with yellowed linens and fabrics that she had intended to make into curtains a long time ago.

"What exactly are we looking for? Dan inquired.

"I remember packing Ken's old school papers, report cards, and things like that from his room along with what I received from his friend at work. Essentially, that's all that remains of his life on earth.

She continued to open boxes. "I remember this box. I'll take it with me now." She picked up a blue metal box the size of a tool kit. "This had all of my family's important papers." She opened the box. "Here's my parent's wedding license…my mother's birth certificate… my father's high school diploma." She looked at a few more papers, then repacked them and set the box off to the side.

Dan carried the rest of the boxes out. "You've been quiet," he said, realizing Laura had become subdued. She was at the far end of the line of boxes, with her back to him. "What's the matter?"

"Nothing," she replied, but her voice betrayed her.

He walked over to her and saw that she was holding a framed photograph. He put a hand on her shoulder. "Can I see it?"

She handed Dan the frame containing a faded color photograph of her family at a lakeside beach. They were all wearing bathing suits and her parents were exaggerating a romantic kiss with young Laura pushing her big brother.

"Everybody looks so happy." Dan commented. He felt her shoulder tense up.

She stood up and fought the swelling emotion. Laura had not had a good cry for as long as she could recall, yet she cried in front of Dan the other night. She was not about to do so, again. Dan handed the picture back and she felt the emotional wave subside.

"That picture was taken when we went to visit my grandmother, my mom's mom, in Michigan. My mother said it was my favorite picture when I was small and I would show it to everyone who came to the house. It used to be in my room; I don't know why I left it here." She pointed at herself. "I was four in this picture and I had never seen a beach or so much water before. It's one of my earliest memories. I'm now about the same age as my mother was in this picture. I forgot, or maybe never even realized, how much she loved my father. You can tell they are in love with each other even with two bratty kids running around all of the time."

"Ken doesn't look bratty," Dan observed tauntingly.

"Well, he teased me a lot," Laura said, touching her brother's head with her thumb. She walked over and placed the photograph on top of the blue metal box.

"Do you want me to start putting things back?" Dan asked.

"Sure."

Dan had returned more than half the boxes that had been inspected when he heard Laura say that she'd found Ken's boxes. Dan turned to her.

"Here they are," she said, holding the lids of the boxes open for Dan to look at the contents. "Four boxes, but I think we can combine these two boxes to save room in the car."

Laura combined the two half filled boxes into one while Dan finished repacking the stall. He returned the last of the furniture and placed the empty box Laura gave him on the outside of the stall for someone else to use and then locked her storage area. They carried the boxes to the car and Dan locked up the barn and gave the keys back to Laura.

"How do you want to do this?" he asked.

"These two boxes are mainly some old textbooks and school papers. Let's put them in the trunk. This box is the one I combined and has Ken's belongings from work and what I took from his desk at the house before the fire. They should go in the back seat.

Dan followed her instructions and also put the family lock box and Michigan photograph in the trunk.

"Now what, boss?" he asked.

"I think there are two more turkey sandwiches with our names on them."

*****

Back at the house, Dan took out the remaining sandwiches while Laura wrote out a thank you note to Mrs. Kurke at the dining room table where she found a writing tablet.

"I see a cable box on the television. Let's find out what the weather's going to be tonight," Dan said, carrying his soda into the living room and turning on the set. Laura ran upstairs to take a quick shower.

"It's going to be cold tonight but no rain," Dan reported but Laura didn't answer.

"Laura!" he said a little louder.

"Up here." She replied.

"What are you doing?" Dan asked

"Looking around right now. Come on up."

Dan found a coaster for his drink and walked upstairs.

"Isn't this house gorgeous?" she asked him. "Look at the furniture in these rooms. It's like an antique store." Laura took Dan's hand and gave him a tour. In one room she picked up a bowl and pitcher. "Do you know what this was used for?" she asked.

"I don't know; a bowl to wash in?" He replied.

"That's right. Originally there wasn't a bathroom on the second floor. You had to go down to the kitchen to the well pump, fill this pitcher with water, carry it to your bedroom, pour the water in this bowl and then wash up. Afterwards, I think they just threw the dirty water out the window," She explained simulating all of the pouring and washing motions.

"Why didn't they just wash up in the kitchen?" Dan inquired.

"Because that would be impolite. Let's look in this room." She led Dan into a spare bedroom that was now Mr. Kurke's den.

"Do you think it's real?" Dan wondered looking at the bear skin rug.

"Probably. We do have bears in Tennessee." She started to sing. "*'Raised in the woods so's he knew every tree, killed him a bear when he was only three. Davy, Davy Crockett, king of the wild frontier.'* Remember that from the old television show?"

"Yes, but what's shocking is that you do." Dan knelt down and petted the bear's head.

Laura put her hand on Dan's head and stroked his hair.

Dan reached up and took her hand. He pulled her gently until she took a knee beside him. He thought to say something but decided to kiss her instead. He brought her body closer to his and then fell backwards, landing on his rear end with Laura falling with him. Dan guided her legs to the sides of his waist so she could sit on his lap. They started kissing again and Dan explored one breast and then the other. He started over her clothes until she lifted off her sweatshirt. She unhooked her bra inviting him to explore further. Dan pulled the drawstring on her pants. Laura started kissing his mouth then his face. She moved down to kiss his neck and then his chest.

Dan held Laura's face to stop her from kissing him any further and rose up slowly to lay her down onto the bear skin rug. He stopped to visually consume Laura's anxious body contrasted so beautifully against the hideously erotic rug. Dan moved to kiss her belly and started to probe further below until he felt her indicate that she wanted him inside of her.

They lay on the rug afterwards, holding and stroking one another. Laura finally checked her watch and said that Mrs. Kurke would be coming home from the hospital in an hour. She got up and went into the bathroom

*****

Laura turned on the shower and waited for the water to turn hot. She looked at herself in the mirror. After a moment, she smiled and stepped under the water.

"Danny boy," she called out to Dan still lying down and using the bear's head as a pillow.

"Wake me up in three days," he pleaded.

"Can't do that. Come in and take a shower with me." She said.

If Laura Smith had made that offer to Dan four days ago, he would have flown to her. Now, he struggled to get off the grizzly bear. He turned onto his stomach, did a push up, and stood up. He carried all of their clothes into the bathroom.

"We should shower together. These old houses sometimes have very small hot water tanks and I don't want to leave you with only cold water," she said soaping up a wash cloth.

"Okay," he said, "but that's the *only* reason." He opened up the shower curtain and joined her.

Laura took the bar of soap and started washing Dan's back and then turned him around.

Laura kissed him on the chest and said, "Do you remember the photograph in the barn?" He nodded and she continued, "I want to be as happy as my mother was with my father."

"They were in love," he replied.

"I know," she said softly.

Chapter 22

Saturday night
Raoul Viñal's office, Orlando

Raoul Viñals decided to catch up on his real estate files and possibly return some business calls while waiting for Special Agent Dennis Rowles to arrive. His travel agency in Orlando had been threatened in the nineties by internet reservations made directly with the airlines. He had adjusted by studying for and receiving his real estate agent and broker's licenses. He next formed his business, which was soon thriving, matching Orlando bound tourists with available time-share condo units in the area.

Viñal's office was located in an older strip mall where every store advertised its trade or wares in Spanish. Except for the supermarket and Caribbean restaurant, Viñals was the only proprietor whose lights were still glowing.

The Cuban heard a knock on the front door, recognized Rowles through the dirty plate glass window, and let him in. Special Agent Dennis Rowles of the Federal Bureau of Investigation, whose former assignment was with the counter intelligence unit, was in his late forties and wearing khaki pants and a red windbreaker over a golf shirt. His family could trace its roots back to England, Wales, and France where he claimed some nexus to nobility. He wasn't as light skinned as his forefathers and could pass for an upper crust old world Spaniard, especially when he spoke in a perfect Castilian dialect learned at the Defense Language Course at the Presidio.

The FBI man unzipped his jacket and walked over to the coffee pot and doughnut box next to the sink on the back wall of the office. "How fresh are these, Raoul?"

"They're good! My secretary bought them this morning. She's always hungry."

"Carmela?" Rowles took a glazed one.

"Ay, no, I had to let her go, *mi esposa* insisted," Viñals laughed, taking a doughnut. "My new girl is Linda and she is very fat."

"That never stopped you before," Rowles smiled, jabbing him in the stomach with his index finger.

"I know that but *mi esposa* does not."

"Well, what's Mr. Volkova up to?" Rowles asked.

"I believe he is trying to clean up a mess that he made a long time ago. I know what he told me but I don't know if he told me the truth. He likes to mix the truth, half-truths, and lies."

"As do you, Raoul."

"And, so do you Denny." Viñals smiled.

The Special Agent acknowledged that truth with a grunt. "Fair enough, go on." Rowles sat down in Viñals's chair and leaned back.

"As you know, I put him in touch with Bera…"

"And Bera's dead," Rowles completed. "Did Volkova kill him?"

"Either directly or Bera felt he had no other choice. Anyway, Volkova was present when Bera died."

Rowles said, "I spoke with the lead detective and they were leaning towards suicide until they figured out that there were no fingerprints anywhere on the gun or the cartridges. They also want to know what his connection was to an air force sergeant that he accosted."

"Did you have your people on Volkova and Bera Saturday night?" Viñals asked.

"Are you kidding me? They can't be bothered, that's why I'm still on special assignment with you whenever you make contact. The counter intelligence unit is a skeleton of what it once was, and they don't think the presence of a former KGB officer, even Pavel Volkova, is as important as tracking down A-rab terrorists. He's yesterday's news as the saying goes. Besides, Pavel Volkova has not been on the radar scope for almost ten years and his only contact has been with you and Bera. The unit's theory is that Volkova is somehow connected to the

Russian mafia, because we know Bera was. The Russian mob is a low priority these days as well."

Viñals went over to a beat up old upholstered sofa a few feet from his desk, propped up a pillow, and laid back. "Our Russian friend is very interested in an air force sergeant named Laura Smith because of her late brother. Do you know what that is about?" Viñals asked.

"That's what the detective told me as well. I'm looking into it. Sergeant Smith has an impeccable service record and she has a top secret clearance. Unless the Russian mafia is trying to steal a Doppler radar unit from Patrick Air Force Base, which you can buy over-the-counter, I don't think she has any direct involvement."

"It's only what she may know about her brother, I believe." Viñals said.

"I know. He died almost twenty years ago, but I don't know much more. I'm working on getting his school transcripts and any work history."

"What does your gut tell you, Denny?"

"Well, considering Volkova's *modus operendi*, then perhaps Ken Smith was honey for the campus bear," The FBI special agent said. "Campus Bear" had been Volkova's nickname, given to him by Rowle's former partner, Albert Garcia, during his fruitless investigation of a series of intellectual property thefts throughout the eighties. Honey referred to students, mostly post-graduate, ready, willing, and able to share their knowledge and access for a worthwhile cause. Garcia was a lone wolf, pursuing the cases from his counter intelligence unit when the white-collar crime agents had long ceased making any headway and had surrendered the investigations to the cold case vault.

Rowles slowly swiveled his chair from side to side. "He mainly exploited drug research and development projects. Those we knew about, six episodes of stealing intellectual property, new formulas, from university and small cap company laboratories that cost the pharmaceutical industry billions of dollars. Foreign companies were making a fortune selling ripped-off drugs that were still in clinical trials here. Sales of those drugs funded our enemies. And, we know some of what he did in Central America."

"You know that Gregor Lasky was working with me to slow down the space program?" Viñals said.

"Of course, but we weren't aware of any connection between Volkova and Lasky. You were very helpful in working with us; it led to new security measures for everyone working anywhere near the space center."

"I think, perhaps, Lasky turned Volkova onto Smith somehow. Start off by checking into how much Mr. Smith's education cost him and what the balance of his student loans were when he died," Viñals suggested.

"What are you saying? That Volkova recruited Smith to sell out the space program?" Rowles stopped swiveling.

"Sure, maybe Smith did it for money or maybe he was some kind of ideologue." Viñals put his coffee down and placed his hands behind his head. "It had to be something important for Volkova to surface again and even risk being pinched for murdering Bera."

"There's no proof of murder."

"It was still a major risk for him to be there when Bera died." Viñals paused. "I believe that Volkova may be concerned about retribution."

"From whom?" Rowles asked.

"From his old bosses…from former comrades…from you, who knows? He's paranoid, too, just like the rest of us."

"Why do *you* think he's resurfaced?" Special Agent Rowles asked.

"I think his recruit, Ken Smith, had a hand in destroying the space shuttle Challenger and I think he wants to hide any evidence of his connection to it," Viñals said sitting up and leaning forward. "At least, that's my best guess."

Rowles got up and walked over to the plate glass window and looked outside at the nearly empty parking lot while he considered Viñals theory and his continued importance as an informant. He looked down at the butt end of his Glock automatic strapped under his windbreaker in its shoulder holster, turned around to look at the Cuban and said, "Your plants need watering."

"My secretary was supposed to do that today but she was too busy."

"I can only imagine what you had that poor girl doing. Look, the Challenger wasn't blown up, it blew up. And the cause is well known."

"Perhaps, but what if you are wrong, Denny? What if evidence surfaced and tomorrow's *Miami Herald* had a front page story stating that the Soviet Union duped some kid out of college to sabotage the shuttle and that sabotage led to the death of seven astronauts."

Rowles moved some papers around on the secretary's desk and picked up a pen with Viñal's name on it as proprietor of his business. "Can I keep this?" He said putting the pen in his jacket pocket. "I don't know about that. What kind of evidence could there be? Certainly Volkova wouldn't leave anything behind and these kids that he recruited all thought they were James Bond. In the pharmaceutical cases, Garcia never found any direct evidence, just dead bodies after the thefts were discovered and Pavel Volkova's description as a recent friend to the decedent."

"What kind of evidence?" Viñals thought out loud. "He may have told others."

"So what? A twenty-year old memory is not very reliable. But it does warrant looking into, I suppose although you'd think someone would have come forward by now. Sergeant Smith needs to be questioned about what she knows of her brother."

"Something just doesn't jive, Denny." Viñals got up and paced the office deliberating. "Let's assume that KGB Officer Pavel Volkova recruited an American student to betray his country, for whatever reason, and sabotage the space shuttle and kill American astronauts. Wouldn't anyone connected to such a heinous act want it to remain forever hushed up? Why would Volkova stir things up?"

Special Agent Rowles refilled his cup then shut off the machine. "Pavel Volkova would obviously want it to remain a secret. So would Mr. Lasky but he is long dead so he could care less. Let's see, the present Russian government is on the verge of unprecedented economic growth and will likely become a member of the European Union and also become the number three or four trading partner with the United States within a few years. This evidence would certainly throw some obstacles in the path. Therefore, the Russians would want the activities of their soviet ghosts to stay secret. And, the United States has enough on its plate right now. If the American government didn't know their shuttle was sabotaged or, worse yet, covered it up, it would impair the credibility of its intelligence community, NASA, you name it.

The administration doesn't need that type of sideshow while they are hunting down maniacs in Afghanistan."

"See what I mean?" Viñals said.

"I see that if your conjecture is correct, then everyone involved would want this to remain buried. So, why has Volkova reappeared? Why does he take risks to make sure that something that everyone would want to remain secret, stays secret?"

"Perhaps because he believes that if the truth is ever known, he will be made the scapegoat to salvage any damage it causes to United States-Russian relations. The Russians will claim that he was a rogue and he'll be placed on trial for his crimes or summarily executed, most likely the latter."

"He told you that?" Rowles asked.

"Not directly, but that may be his motivation."

"Then the next issue is whether someone else, besides the operatives, knew what Volkova knew; and, if so, what their motivations are."

"The Russian mob might know."

Rowles replied, "The Russian mob is a boogey man that gets blamed for every malfeasance over there, but I can't discount that thought. They might use the information to blackmail the Russian government, and even the American government. Perhaps Volkova got wind of that and decided to make sure that every bridge was, in fact, burned."

"Something else doesn't fit," Viñals continued. "The Russians have been hiding soviet bodies since 1991, so why haven't they killed Volkova already?"

Rowles thought about that for a moment and replied. "The Soviets were much better at keeping secrets than we were. First of all, they didn't have multiple intelligence organizations all competing against one another like we do. It's easier to compartmentalize when only one agency is working on a project. And, second, they didn't have a free press up their ass.

"A plan to destroy the space shuttle could have originated and remained secret among fewer than five people, and they could all be dead by now except Volkova. So, it's very likely that if this were an approved operation, no one in the present Russian government even knows about it.

"Alternatively, Volkova could have done this completely on his own. If he had any indication, after the fact, that his bosses weren't happy with what had happened then he would just have kept his mouth shut."

Viñals asked, "Why would he act alone?"

"You don't know what his tactics were in Central America. Pavel Volkova is an evil man and is capable of indescribable mayhem. He may have thought to bring the news of his success to Moscow like a dog bringing a bone to his master and looking for a reward, or...he may have done it just for his own edification or amusement."

"But wasn't Lasky trying to accomplish the same thing, and that was state sponsored?" Viñals asked.

"There's no evidence of that except what we learned from you and the investigations that followed. If successful, your recruits could never have destroyed the space shuttle. At best, they would have caused very expensive damage to the pad and support systems leading to lengthy delays and repairs, that's about it. Besides..."

Rowles stopped. "Besides...?" Viñals pressed him.

"Besides...blowing up the space shuttle with a teacher on board would have started World War III, for Christ's sake. Unlike our new enemies, the soviets weren't fucking nuts."

"I suppose we have a riddle on our hands, then," Viñals said. "Volkova expects me to produce some more intelligence for him. Thanks for getting me the info on the Mustang; I made the phone call to the insurance company in New Jersey like you suggested."

Viñals handed the special agent Laura Smith's credit card billing statements he received at the pancake house and told him how Volkova had obtained them. "He expects something back from me."

Rowles looked at it. "Okay, I'll see what I can do. When does Volkova want to hear back from you on this?" Rowles said, tucking the envelope away.

"ASAP, brother."

Rowles stepped close to Viñals, held the Cuban's upper arm with one hand and shoved his index finger firmly in his chest for emphasis. "Raoul, I want to nail this guy. By the time Garcia connected all of the dots, the bastard was long gone. Even if he stayed, we couldn't prove jack shit. Get closer to him."

Viñals nodded affirmatively at the special agent, then walked him to the door and unlocked it. "I'll call you tomorrow around lunch time. Keep your phone on." Rowles said, moving out the door.

Viñals relocked the door, walked back to his desk and dialed home. "Hello *mamasita*, papa is on his way home…no, she isn't here…no, she left hours ago…honest, I've been working."

Chapter 23

Early Sunday morning, January 19. 2003
Interstate 40

It was an effort to get back into the car and start a fifteen hour road trip after their brief sojourn in Lexington. Dan and Laura stopped before getting back on the interstate and Laura paid for the gas, coming out of the convenience store with more goodies for the trip. She repacked the cooler with barbeque pork sandwiches and other treats from her old hometown. She insisted on buying Dan a Moon Pie and Royal Crown Cola, true Southern delicacies, for when he got the munchies during the night.

Six hours later, the Volunteer State was behind them and Dan was headed for the northern suburbs of Fulton County, Georgia. He broke down and ate the Moon Pie at one in the morning and regretted not having another one. Laura stayed awake for the first two hours, going through Ken's belongings in the back seat. She did a cursory look at everything then went back looking for any significance in the remaining potpourri of her brother's abbreviated existence.

The box from his job contained some technical drawings made on course graph paper and other entries written on paper pads; but the barn was not climate controlled like a modern storage facility and the paper had aged as a result - sheets of paper easily separated from the pad. There were also the normal supplies and junk found in every desk in America: paper clips, half-used note pads, scissors, ruler, correcting fluid, really short pencils, pens that no longer worked, chewing gum and a roll of breath mints long since fused together by the Tennessee heat. A framed photograph of a young woman, posed in a way to suggest intimacy, was protected from damage by in an inter-office envelope wrapped around it but the rubber bands around that had long since decayed. Laura studied the picture and commented that his girlfriend seemed a little older than Ken.

She continued combing through the pile and spent some time studying Ken's papers and byproducts of his high school years. Laura had many of the same teachers and Dan heard all about their idiosyncratic behaviors. There weren't many artifacts after high school since Ken never lived at home again upon entering college. Laura also found some things that belonged to her since she had moved into Ken's bigger room. She reread, for the first time in twenty years, a love letter from the nerdiest boy in her class, who went on to become a multimillionaire personal injury lawyer in Memphis. She kept that discovery to herself.

After putting everything away, she placed both boxes on the front seat, turned off the dome light and fell asleep on her make shift bed on the back seat.

Dan channel surfed along the AM and FM bands looking for programs that would make the drive more tolerable. He kept thinking back, however, to Laura on the bearskin rug and the lovemaking later on in the shower. He was reflecting on that once again as Atlanta neared. An opossum feasting on some carrion in his lane made him swerve.

"What happened?" Laura said, raising her head.

"Nothing; go back to sleep."

Dan was listening to an all night talk show whose supernatural genre he found bizarrely interesting in the middle of the night. He was following the dialogue between the host and a priest discussing an allegedly real exorcism on a New Mexican Indian reservation when he heard Laura moving around restlessly.

"What *are* you listening to?" she asked after a loud yawn.

"Something to keep me awake," he replied.

"Well, I'm ready to drive for a few hours. Why don't you pull over?" she said leaning between the front bucket seats and messaging Dan's shoulders and neck.

"I think I have another hour left in me, but I'll pull over at the next rest area if you need to stop."

Laura said she was fine and moved the boxes to the back and then wiggled her way to the front seat. Dan pinched her ass as it went by.

"Hey, watch that mister," she kidded.

They listened to the priest tell the host how he was accompanied by a psychiatrist and two layman during the Catholic rite lasting several hours and that the local diocese had an audio and video record of the ordeal. The radio program eventually was lost to static.

"Do you believe that?" Laura asked Dan while looking for another station.

"I'm not sure. The priest sounded pretty convincing, though."

"Aren't you Catholic?" She asked, finding a country music station.

"I try to be," he replied. "You're not going to make me listen to this are you?"

She pressed the button to change stations and found Dell Shannon singing about his little runaway. "I thought Catholics believed in exorcisms?"

"I've never personally heard a priest talk about one. I think it's a matter of individual belief. Although..." He stopped talking for a moment, and then started singing...*Run Run Run Run Runaway.*

"Yes." she prompted him to continue.

"I believe that there is such a thing as pure evil and it can possess people. I'm just not sure it makes you puke pea soup," Dan said, referring to the classic movie.

"What about pure love?"

"Sure baby, remember the bear?" he answered, lightly squeezing her left leg just above the knee.

"I don't know why I like men." She took his hand off her leg and put it on his lap. "Here, you'll need this from now on."

"Okay...pure love...yes, I believe in pure love, too. Parents, most parents anyway, have pure love for their children, especially when they're infants. That love is total and absolutely unconditional. Mother Teresa was pure love."

She opened the vents some more and raised the heat, then reached behind to take a soda from the cooler. "Want one?" He replied that he did, she opened a second can and placed it in the cup holder.

"How did you get your second Purple Heart?" she asked.

He looked over at her and made eye contact in the reflected lights of the oncoming traffic. "You really want to know?"

She nodded.

"Okay, then…no shit, this really happened."

Laura laughed and lowered the oldies music.

"I made my second combat jump with the 82nd Airborne Division. I was a platoon sergeant in the 1st Battalion of the 504th Parachute Infantry Regiment.

Laura asked, "The 82nd is in North Carolina, right?"

"Fort Bragg, Home of the Airborne," he replied.

"When did you leave the Rangers?"

"That's another war story in itself. Hard as it is to believe, some people don't like me."

"I think we can put Detective Leonard on that list."

"See what I mean? There I was, helping his police department and he gets territorial with me. Do you remember the plane crash that killed all of those soldiers from the 101st Airborne Division in Gander, Newfoundland?"

Laura thought for a moment. "Not really."

"You're not alone. Just about everyone has forgotten, except the next of kin. In early December of 1985, almost two hundred and fifty soldiers in the 3rd Battalion of the 502nd Infantry were flying home in time for Christmas after serving six months in the Sinai. A half a year away from their families, patrolling the desert to keep the Israelis and Egyptians from killing each other and they were on their way home for the holidays. Their plane landed in Gander to refuel but the weather iced up the wings, the plane was overloaded and they crashed on take off. There were no survivors. It was horrible.

"Afterwards, the army had to reconstitute the battalion and a memorandum was sent requesting non-commissioned officers to join as cadre during the rebuilding of that unit. The army didn't want rangers to volunteer because we were so elite, but my chain of command made an exception for me. I was with the 101st for about twelve months but wanted to get back on jump status so I requested a transfer to the 82nd Airborne.

"The eighty deuce…it was a high speed unit but not quite as fast as the rangers. For the first time in my army career, I actually took some time off and enjoyed a few weekends. In the rangers, I was just one among many, but in the 82nd, folks took notice of the bronze star on my jump wings denoting a combat jump, my Combat Infantryman Badge and my Ranger Regiment patch on the right sleeve. It was lordly being the only veteran in an airborne unit who actually had made a combat jump, and I played the role to the hilt. The odds, I thought, were heavily against having to make another combat jump in my lifetime and I was happy about that.

"That changed in December of 1989. Manuel Noriega was getting out of control down in Panama. We wanted him out of power and there was a coup attempt that failed so he was on the edge. Noriega couldn't trust the Panamanian Defense Forces any more. He formed his own army made up of thugs, officially known as Dignity Battalions but we called them Dingbats.

"By December, things were totally bonkers down there with the dingbats overtly threatening American citizens and even murdering a Marine Corps lieutenant. We knew we would be going down there but we didn't think it would be by parachute. First of all, we had a big military presence there and secondly, one of our battalions from the 82nd previously deployed there to bulk up the firepower already in country. If we had to go too, we figured it would be another Grenada deal. The rangers would be the ones jumping in to secure the airfield for us and we would land in our airplanes.

"Not so. We got alerted for Operation Just Cause on December 19th for a combat jump onto Torrijos International Airport the next day. I mean, holy shit, what are the chances of this happening. The only two major airborne operations since World War Two and I'm in the lead assault battalion on both.

"You've got the luck of the Irish," Laura remarked.

"True. I met you."

"That was really sweet, considering you're in the middle of a war story."

Dan laughed and took a swig of his cola.

"The weather at Fort Bragg on December 19th was unbelievably cold and wet. We went through our alert, same drill as the rangers, and we were trucked over to green ramp at Pope Air Force Base. It rained constantly and then the temperature dropped, turning to freezing rain. Remember that we're jumping into Panama, so everyone is wearing jungle fatigues and nobody has warm weather gear. We loaded onto the C-141 Starlifters, the big four engine jets, but they had to be deiced first and so it took a lot longer to load than anticipated. By the time we got on the big ugly mothers, everyone was soaked to the bone.

"Our wet rucksacks hanging down below the reserve parachutes were twice as heavy not to mention all of the other gear we were wearing: helmet, web gear, parachutes and weapons. Men needed help getting to their feet and they waddled onto the aircraft like pregnant women going to the hospital to give birth. On top of all that, we were soaked and freezing. I lost feeling in my toes and fingers and thought it would be funny being a frost bite casualty on the drop zone in tropical Panama.

"Sounds humorous to me," Laura said.

"Gallows humor. Once we finally got airborne, it wasn't too bad, not much different than a training exercise. But, I had been shivering uncontrollably for at least two hours and was so damn exhausted I just wanted to get to the drop zone, secure the airfield and get some sleep. I actually fell asleep on the way down.

"About two hours before drop time, the air force crew woke us up and we all started rigging our gear and getting ready. I was the left door jumpmaster which meant I would be the last one out on that side. As we made our final approach, me and the right door jumpmaster started shouting our commands. We stood up, hooked up our static line to the anchor cable that would deploy our chutes when we jumped, checked equipment and got ready. The air force crew opened the jump doors; the tropical air whipped through the airplane as I started the last pre jump inspection by holding onto the doorframes with my hands and hanging outside the aircraft which was flying at one hundred and twenty five knots, a little over stall speed."

"Why did you have to hang outside?"

"Primarily, to check for damage to the aircraft by flak that might slice a static line in half or otherwise harm a jumper exiting the aircraft and to make sure that there are no trailing airplanes flying beneath us. Then, we look for the drop zone and make the final decision to unload the airplane whether or not the pilot throws on the green light. We had a hung jumper during Grenada. Not sure what happened, but they had to pull the guy back in the airplane.

"Well, we came back in and we were about ready to jump when we started taking small arms fire. There were tracers coming up and I could see heavy ground fire through the open door when the C-141 pilot was ordered to abort the jump; he banked hard to make a racetrack."

"A racetrack?"

"An oval, we would fly back around hoping we could jump without getting shot at the next time. The racetrack took about twenty minutes and guys were just falling down with all the weight they were carrying. Most of the men in my stick were on their knees holding on to their static lines with both hands just to stay upright. Finally, the men started shouting: let's go goddamn it…let's fucking jump…we gotta get out of here.

"The pilot brought us back on azimuth for the jump run and we repeated the pre-jump routine. Finally, I pointed at the number one jumper and yelled 'Stand by!' Ten seconds later, the green light came on and yelled 'Go!' By that point I was so fatigued, cramped and miserable. After the last man on my door jumped, I just moved and stepped out of the jet into the night sky like you would wander into your bathroom after waking up in the middle of the night to pee."

"Were you shot at on the way down?"

"No, the ground combat had moved away from the airport but I landed hard on the runway. My butt landed on something hard and I discovered a bruise there that stayed with me for a month.

"Our company was given a portion of the airport to secure, I forget which end now, but we assembled on our company's colors…"

"What's that?"

"Each company, on a night jump, designates a primary and alternate man to put up a pole with chemical lights, chem lights, the plastic things you bend and they stay lit for about eight hours. Our company had two green lights with a red light in the middle. We looked for our lights, assembled, and then moved off to our objective.

"On the edge of the airport, there was elephant grass; that stuff grows in Vietnam, too, and I remember those vets talking about firefights there where nobody ever saw who the heck they were even shooting at. My platoon was moving through a patch of elephant grass and all hell broke loose. I'm not sure who fired first, but we ran into elements of the PDF trying to evade and escape from the airport. Those guys had M-16s, too, so it wasn't like Grenada when you could differentiate the sound of AK-47s.

"I yelled for my lead squad leader to hold his position and get his men on line; then I turned to get my trail squad leaders to bring their men up so I could get the whole unit on line and start moving in bounding over watch. That's when one squad moves and the others provide cover fire and they keep alternating until you get to where you're going. Anyway, I took about three steps back when I was hit from behind."

"What happened?"

"I got hit by an M-16 round, I assume from the PDF, since I had gotten all of my men in front of me pointing towards the enemy. Sergeant Chris Canney, my trail squad leader actually tripped over me while bringing his men up. It was pitch black, explosions were constantly degrading our night vision, and the elephant grass was about ten feet high.

"I guess I was knocked out because I don't remember him falling on me. He woke me up and took off my rucksack and performed first aid. The bullet went in at an angle right behind my left shoulder blade and passed upward to here." Dan indicted the front part of his left shoulder.

"Sergeant Canney said that there wasn't an exit wound but he could feel the bullet under the skin. The round had gone through my rucksack, passed through a spare uniform that was tightly rolled, an MRE, and a map case so the velocity slowed considerably or else it would have done a lot more damage. But, I was bleeding pretty badly and it hurt like hell; I couldn't move my left arm without being hit by tremendous pain.

"Canney ordered two men to bring me back through the elephant grass and to the company command post that was still on the drop zone. I must have passed out from the pain or just exhaustion, but the next thing I recall is waking up in one of the airport terminal buildings that had been transformed into a hospital, sort of. I was on the first floor, prisoners of war were on the second and the morgue was on the third floor. The doctors felt that I was stable enough to be flown back to the States for surgery and I was medevaced within a few hours.

"How are your wounds now?" Laura asked.

"My leg is fine but my shoulder still hurts occasionally, especially when it gets cold out or I overuse it at the gym or playing basketball with the guys at work. I was in rehab for a little over four months and had a profile from having to do push-ups for a year.

"When it hurts and I feel sorry for myself, I remember the 82nd troopers and the other Americans who died that day."

Dan wanted to say more but focused on the road instead.

Laura stroked the back of his neck.

She felt his tension ease and he said, "So that's why I became a military cop when my enlistment was up. After my first combat jump, I was lightly wounded within forty-eight hours, after my second combat jump, I was moderately wounded within two hours. I figured God had some kind of crazy algorithm warning me that the next combat jump would be my last."

Laura took Dan's hand that was resting on the console, clasped it in hers and watched the road and traffic signs go by. After a few songs had played on the radio, she said, "Dan?"

"Yes."

"Do you have a girlfriend, or someone waiting for you back home, who thinks you're fishing right now?"

Dan laughed, "No. Why are you asking me that?"

"If you can use the word 'algorithm' correctly in a sentence, I think you can figure it out."

Chapter 24

Sunday morning
Going to Cocoa Beach

Leaving Katenka in the motel room, Volkova drove towards Cocoa Beach. It was still early but he was anxious for information. The Cuban had always been resourceful for Lasky but Volkova was not a trusting man. He made a mental note to verify the sources used by the Cuban; maybe he could use them directly. The Russian found his cell phone and tapped in Viñals number.

"Hola!"

"What do you have for me?" Volkova asked.

"*Buenas dias* to you, too. It's still rather early, my friend." He paused, but quickly realized there was no humor at the other end. "I will get you more information later but for right now, we have her using her credit card at a motel in Islamorada and for gas and food purchases along Interstate 75." Viñals said, repeating Rowles information to him a few hours earlier.

"What times were the cards used?"

"The motel swipe was Friday and the other purchases were yesterday." Viñals gave him the address for the motel and gas stations.

Volkova made some quick notes with a felt marker on the palm of his hand. "Are you sure of these transactions?"

"I can not vouch for the accuracy of what I am telling you, although my sources have very good track records," he said as a matter of fact.

"You are, of course, correct. What sense do you make of someone paying for a motel room and then traveling in the opposite direction?" Volkova queried.

"I can't help you with that one."

Volkova paused.

"My friend, let me help," Viñals offered, remembering Denny Rowles's finger in his chest.

"How can you do more to help me?" the Russian asked, knowing he already had a list.

"Well, first of all, I could have taken care of the Gainesville location for you."

"You wouldn't know what to look for," Volkova replied.

"You could have told me; don't you think it was too risky?" the Cuban said referring to the fire reported on the news.

"He had plenty of mafia friends that will lead the investigation elsewhere. But, maybe you *can* further help me. Tell your secretary to manage the office. Leave now and head for Cocoa Beach. I'll call you later and let you know where to meet me," Volkova ended the call, and turned to speculate about Laura's route.

Chapter 25

Sunday morning
Still on the road

Dan spotted a sign for the next rest area informing him that he needed to hold his bladder for another twenty minutes; he told Laura he wouldn't be able to make it. Pulling over and stopping near a wood line, he got out and used the trees as cover to relieve himself. Dan then reconfigured the load by placing all of the boxes in the trunk, putting the metal box containing Laura's family records on the floor behind the passenger seat. He made a bed in the backseat and lay down.

Laura found a country western station, putting Dan quickly to sleep. He dreamed for the first time in many years about being a paratrooper again-one of those disturbing nightmares where he was always forgetting something. He boarded a C-130 only to realize he was barefoot. Then he ran off the plane, put on his boots, got back on and discovered that he wasn't wearing a helmet. This went on for a while until something jarred him awake and he dozed off again to dream about something more pleasant.

An hour after first light, BMNT as he remembered from the military for Beginning of Morning Nautical Twilight, the sun was shining through the leafless trees and directly into his face. He tried to stave off consciousness by putting Laura's sweatshirt over his head; it worked for only another ten minutes.

"Where are we?" he said, slowly rising to a sitting position.

"We're about twenty miles from the Florida line. I pulled over for about a half hour to gas, wash up and get some coffee. How're you feeling?"

"Not bad, considering I ache all over," he retorted.

"Do you want me to pull over?" Laura asked.

"No, let's wait until we're in Florida."

"I bought you a coffee when I stopped in case you woke up but its cold now."

Dan cleaned up the back seat area gathering up articles of clothing, paper wrappers and a horse blanket that Laura bought in Lexington. He chose to stay there for the brief time it would take to reach Florida and he picked up the metal box to move into the front seat to give him more room.

"Mind if I look in here?" he asked, changing his mind.

She turned her head and saw what he was referring to. "No, go ahead."

He opened the box and looked through some papers.

"Some neat stuff, here." He said. "Here's the deed from when you're grandparents bought the farm in 1938 for forty five hundred dollars. The grantor is a bank so the farm was probably foreclosed during the depression. Here's your Dad's discharge certificate from the army."

"He was in the Korean War. His old uniform and medals went up in smoke."

Dan pulled more papers out. "Here's your birth certificate, it says 1962."

"Liar, my birth certificate is in my house. I needed it when I enlisted." She laughed.

"Okay, you got me. Here's your parent's marriage certificate and your mother's birth certificate. How old was she when you were born?"

"Fifty two." She laughed again. "Stop trying. I'll tell you on our next date, maybe."

"So, you're now admitting that we dated," he cross-examined.

"Yes."

"What date are we on now?"

"I would maintain that this is still a continuation of our first date."

"You always sleep with guys on the first date?" he asked.

"Come here for a second." He moved forward expecting the smack she gave him. "What else is in the box?"

He read through some more old papers then pulled out a stenographer's note pad and flipped through it. Several photographs fell out and he put them to the side. "Did you ever keep a diary?"

"No, why?" Laura replied.

"This seems to be a diary or a journal from ..." he checked the pages, "October 2, 1985 until January 10, 1986."

"Let me see it." She turned to look and Dan passed it to her so she wouldn't swerve off the road. Laura held it with one hand and glanced down at the pad while driving. "This is Ken's handwriting." She looked up. "There's the welcome center," she said sliding the convertible towards the exit.

*****

Laura ran off to the restroom wanting to get back and read as soon as possible. Dan threw their garbage into a trash receptacle and looked at the large map mounted near the vending machines, calculating the time to Laura's home.

Spotting her coming out of the building he felt happy…young, too, he realized, for the first time in a very long while. She got in, leaned over and gave Dan a quick kiss that caught him by surprise. "Ready," she said.

She put the box on the floor in front of her. "Here are the pictures - there are three." She looked through the box. "No more pads, though."

Dan attempted to look as well, but there was heavy traffic keeping his attention on the road.

"Two are with Ken and the girl in the framed picture…his girlfriend. And one just of her. Nothing written on the back."

Laura placed the photos back in the metal container. "Let's read his diary."

"You read it to yourself and then let me know if you want to share it."

She nodded and started to read. Dan glanced over after a few minutes, sensing that she was uncomfortable. She hadn't read much before she flipped back to the previous page to reread Ken's words.

"I think I want to share this with you," Laura said going through the pages again.

"It starts on October 2, 1985, and there are only nine entries. The last one is dated about three weeks before he died. He refers to things that happened previously; I suppose he was writing it chronologically hoping to get caught up and then maybe he would continue it as a diary. Who knows?" Laura started to read out loud.

October 2, 1985, 2:30 a.m., Briggs City, Utah

I have decided to keep a journal of my life with Katenka Tiverzin and the struggles we have gone through to maintain our relationship. Someday, when we have children and grandchildren, I believe they will be proud of what we did in these times of turmoil. Writing is difficult for me as I am working over one hundred hours a week and travel often, but I will write when I can. I know that some people, maybe most in this country, will question what I have done, but I have acted not only from my conscious but also for my love of Katenka and for world peace. What I have done would certainly put me in jail for a long time if caught, but I do not intend to get caught.

Because of her love for me, Katenka is also at risk from her own government. However, in the final analysis, I do not blame her country because it is only reacting to the actions of this present administration; so, I believe they have a lesser moral culpability.

I first met Katenka towards the end of my post graduate work just after I received a full time employment offer to work building rockets. I called my old friend Mickey O'Connor to tell him about my new job. Katenka and I owe a debt of gratitude to Mickey for introducing us. Mickey O'Connor is a real radical Irishman. He is completely insane but has always been a good friend. In college, Mickey supported the IRA, PLO, SLA, FALN, etc., and dragged me to many of his rallies, protest marches and sit-ins. Any group against the establishment, he was for. He called me a few days after I gave him my good news to say that his friend, Katenka, was attending the same school as me and I should meet her. Mickey told me that Katenka was a huge disappointment to him because she was not a very good communist and always took the American side when they argued. He liked her anyway but I suppose it was largely due to the fact that she's beautiful, talented, smart, funny, etc.

So, I looked her up and we soon started dating; that was almost two years ago. As our relationship grew, I learned more about her struggles. She confided in me that life for her family in the Soviet Union was very hard and that she would prefer to stay here, if she could. Her family can trace its roots back to relatives of the Romanovs, the last tsar's family, and so they have always been under suspicion. She has extended family in France who escaped Russia in 1917 and smuggled out a number of treasures that were invested in many profitable ventures over the years. When I first met her, she was an exchange student from the Soviet Union studying American Art & Dance, both at the undergraduate and then graduate level. Katenka graduated a few months after me but was allowed to stay in the United States through a cultural exchange program. She was able to find suitable employment with a theater group near my new employer and we have been inseparable except for my business travels, which are often, to the Kennedy Space Center where I'm on the team that assembles the SRBs. Before meeting me, Katenka planned on becoming a university professor when she returned home and perhaps run a dance studio for young girls, as well, since she is also a ballerina.

The first Christmas after my graduation, we were living together and it was difficult making ends meet. Katenka's Christmas gift to me was repayment of my student loans. She told me that she had been in contact with her second cousins in Paris and they sent her some of her family's money. Apparently, this money had been held in trust for all of these years. I protested strongly but she argued with me saying that the money could never be sent to her family in the Soviet Union and I was the closest family she had. She said that if I felt guilty, I could make arrangements to repay her and I said that I would.

I asked Katenka if it would it be easier to stay in the United States if we were married and she replied that it would help. She said that she would only marry me if I truly loved her and I said that I did.

Laura stopped reading and looked over at Dan.

"Is that it?" he asked.

"That's the end of the first entry." She closed the book and then shut her eyes to rest for a few moments.

"It's hard to picture my brother on his own, as an adult, with these thoughts and feelings. I can only remember him as my big goofy brother who teased me a lot. The whole time he was at home, before going away to college, he never even dated. It's strange reading his words about being in love."

Dan reached over and held her hand. "It's like discovering a new part of him. He only knew you as a bratty kid. Do you think he could ever imagine you in the air force and working towards your doctoral degree? I bet he would be very proud of you, now. Let's hear the next entry."

Laura took a sip of her soda and opened the steno pad.

October 10, 1985, 11:30 p.m., Briggs City, Utah

Katenka told me last Christmas about the threats made to her family. Katenka said that her parents were told that if she did not return within the next six months, then her family would be punished. They could be relocated to a one room flat, also they could lose their jobs, and the gulag was mentioned. I had no idea such things still existed. Katenka said that there is a crisis all over the Soviet Union because of America's military build up since Reagan took office. I still can't believe an actor, who co-starred with a monkey, is the president. Her two younger brothers tested very high on intelligence tests and are expected to go to the university but her mother was told that they would be drafted and sent to Afghanistan as infantrymen - human mine detectors the local commissar joked - if Katenka did not return.

She said Pravda and other papers all report that America is going to weaponize space. The only reason to place weapons in space is to have a first strike capability par excellence, and I must agree. We have enough missiles in silos and on submarines and bombs in the goddamn air force to destroy her country several times over. I just do not understand what we are doing. The Soviet government believes that Reagan will use the space shuttle to deploy lasers in space to destroy soviet missiles on their launch pads and deploy nuclear weapons in space for a first strike option. I know that is beyond our capability now, but I certainly hear talk that this is where we're headed.

I feel very angry that my education is being used to support this militarism. We have peacefully coexisted with soviet communists since their revolution, even being their allies against the Nazis. Now, it's obvious that

Reagan wants to start a war. I had hoped that my education and work in this company would be used to further space exploration and discovery, not to put a fucking H-bomb in orbit. She also mentioned her family's fear of the two hundred megatons we have targeted on Leningrad. Our country's policies have directly impacted my life and the life of the woman I love.

"That's it for the second entry," Laura said.

"I guess that answers the question about how he would feel about you being in the air force," Dan looked over and couldn't help grinning.

She looked over at Dan. She wanted to respond but knew he was correct.

"I can't believe this is my brother. He came home for a week during the summer of 1985 and he never mentioned any of this." She looked out the window for a while and repeated her disbelief.

"I know this is troubling for you but we have to keep one thing in mind," Dan said.

"What's that?"

"What does all this have to do with that Russian professor?" Dan asked. He put his hand on Laura's knee and said, "Hey, there is some good news in this - at least we know that your brother and the professor weren't gay for each other."

"Good one, Dan," she didn't laugh. "Let's see what the ending holds before we jump to that conclusion. With what I'm learning, the professor may have been a drag queen named Katenka."

October 15, 1985, 1:45 p.m., Briggs City, Utah

Katenka told me on New Year's Day of 1985 that she and her family were in serious trouble. Her government found out about the transfer of money from France and she said that she was contacted by the consulate's office to explain how and why she received the money. The Soviet government has subsidized her education here and they are very upset that she had that much money available to her. She has been accused of defrauding the government and Katenka said that they would certainly harass her family over this and may bring criminal charges against them as well. I told her that I would give her back all of the money if that would make the problem go away. I suggested that I could go to my mother since her home is paid for: she could get a mortgage and I would make the payments. I certainly have a secure future and could manage those payments. Katenka said that she wanted to go back home and be with her family but I did my best to dissuade her. She finally agreed to stay here and we would work out a solution together. Love will always find a way.

"That's it for October 15th. What do you think?" Laura asked.

"I'm not sure, yet. I keep thinking ahead as you're reading to see the connection between Ken and the dead professor. Maybe the professor is related to Katenka or knows about her family's connection to wealth. Detective Leonard said that the professor was probably connected to the Russian mafia, right?"

"I don't believe those were his exact words, but that was the impression."

"Perhaps he was just looking for her and knew that your brother was close to her."

"How would he know that?"

"That's what Leonard should be able to tell you. If that's the case, then maybe he was just looking for Katenka's money through some clue left behind by Ken."

"Why would he kill himself?" Laura asked.

"Because he didn't get the money. He may have been desperate and your tenuous link to Katenka's wealth may have been his last hope."

"Maybe. Are you ready for the next one? It looks short."

October 25, 1985, 11:45 p.m., Briggs City, Utah-

Around mid January 1985, Katenka told me that she'd met a consular official in Salt Lake City. He wanted to see her again to confirm the facts of the money transfer. She said that he didn't believe that she'd used all of the money for my loans and he wanted proof. Katenka asked me if I would meet him at our trailer and I, of course, agreed. I gathered up the proof of what my student loans were and the letters I received stating that they were paid off.

In the days leading up to the appointment with the consular official, his name is Peter Kola, I noticed Katenka becoming more and more nervous. She became short and irritable whenever I told her everything would be all right. The day before Mr. Kola came to our place, she confided in me that she had been under pressure to talk to me about my job.

When I asked her what my job had to do with anything, she said that her government was interested in anything to do with the shuttle. If the Soviet Union could keep up with America's massive military build up then the policy of mutually assured destruction would still be viable. Hard to believe, but in 1985, staying with M.A.D. is one of the sanest things I have heard lately. Katenka said that Mr. Kola would offer her and her family a deal if I were willing to help them.

"That's the end of that entry." She flipped the pad closed. "I'm not sure I want to know any more."

"You said that you never met this woman." Dan asked.

"He never brought her to Lexington, so we never met her. Like I said before, at the service in Utah, her name came up only once or twice and we all assumed she was too heartbroken to come. Do you think it's strange that she never tried to contact me or my mother?"

"I think your brother Ken is writing new definitions for strange."

"Thanks a lot."

"Who knows where she is, she may have gone back home and married someone else. As for why Ken never spoke of her, well, let's see…your family is from the Bible belt, and you said your mom was a church lady, right?'

Laura nodded.

"How do you think your mother would have accepted her son shacking up with a commie heathen?"

"I think she would have been more upset about the shacking up part then her being a Soviet citizen. My mother could convert a rabbi."

"I think your brother had a lot on his plate. He worked for and earned very difficult degrees. He landed a challenging job. He was in love with a woman who he thought would be leaving him forever to go back home where she would be politically persecuted. This stuff was written at a time when we were at the height of the cold war and there was no end in sight. He must have thought, rightly so at the time, that if she went back to the U.S.S.R., he would never see her again. Also, he was probably keeping their relationship a secret or making up some cover story because I'm sure his employer would not appreciate someone with his security access banging a commie.

"Add to the list that the geo-political views he picked up in college weren't exactly shared by the folks at the plant and in Lexington. He probably just didn't want the extra burden of having to explain his personal life and defend his political views with his family.

"Let's see if it gets any worse. Read the next entry," Dan said.

Chapter 26

Sunday afternoon
Orlando

Raoul Viñals hated to miss the Chamber of Commerce luncheon scheduled for that afternoon; it was an opportunity to network and eat free food. The chamber was honoring the president of a local mortgage company that the Cuban did a lot of business with; not only did he share the lender's points, under the table, but he shared one of their loan officers, Ana Marie, under the sheets. She left a very horny message for Viñals saying to stick around after the lunch. Viñals had just reserved a room in the hotel hosting the luncheon when he received Volkova's invitation to meet him.

Passing by the hotel on the way to meet the Russian, he spotted Ana Marie's car. He hit the dashboard with his fist, pissed off at the lost encounter. He fiddled with the radio buttons, going through the entire spectrum and not finding anything he liked. Popping in a CD, he listened for a few minutes before turning the sound all the way down in frustration.

Viñals called Special Agent Rowles using the cell phone controls on his steering wheel. Even the FBI had computers answering their calls, he muttered to himself, pressing zero to talk with an operator. Rowles got on the line and told him he would call back in five minutes.

"Good afternoon, Raoul. How's it hanging?" The special agent asked calling back from a private line.

"It's hanging very low; you have no idea what I'm missing out on."

"I can only imagine. Did you pass along the information?"

"I did and he wants more," Viñals said, changing lanes and checking out a young girl whom he was passing on the right.

"You can relay to him that her card was used again outside of Atlanta early this morning." Rowles gave him the time it was swiped and the location of the gas station.

Viñals wrote down the information. "Is that it?" he asked.

"For now. What else do you have for me?"

"I'm going to the beach," the Cuban said.

"What are you talking about?"

"Pavel wants me to meet him at Cocoa Beach."

"Where in Cocoa Beach?"

"I don't know. I offered to assist him like you asked and he immediately wanted my ass on the road to meet with him. If I knew what his answer would be, believe me bro, I would have said no to your request."

"I appreciate it, Raoul. You don't have any of my phone numbers on your speed dial or anything like that, do you?"

"No, Denny, but I got your wife's picture in my wallet." Viñals made a kissing sound.

"Good, keep her happy so I can play more golf."

Viñals laughed, and then said seriously, "Just how did Volkova get back in the country and why don't you guys just pick him up?"

"Did I miss reading that you got promoted to the Senate Oversight Committee?" Rowles asked sarcastically.

"No, my friend, I just want to know."

"Honestly . . ." Rowles started.

"That would be a first," the Cuban finished.

"Honestly," Rowles continued, "we don't know how he got in the country. Now that he's here, I believe it's more important to see what he's up to rather than enforce our immigration policy."

"What immigration policy? *Gracias Dios.*" Viñals laughed. "Denny, what's the story with the air force sergeant checking into the motel and then heading north? Where is she going?"

"I'm not entirely sure myself, but I can't give out any more information for you to share with Volkova. Tell him the credit cards arc a dead end. For Christ's sake, she's an American soldier and I'm putting her life in jeopardy."

"Is anyone from the FBI watching her, I hope?" Viñals asked.

"No," Rowles replied.

"You of all people know what kind of man we're dealing with."

"What can I tell you? The Bureau's focus is on other pressing national security issues right now, my friend. We *are* the counter-intelligence task force for Florida, maybe the southeastern United States. Don't worry about Sergeant Smith; I plan on talking to her, soon. I'm heading to the Cocoa Beach area myself to meet with Detective Leonard who's working the Bera case."

Viñals cleared the heavy Orlando traffic and pushed his Lexus up to eighty. "Denny, you *are* working this case…officially?"

"I have your back covered if that's what you're talking about."

"I know you have my back covered. But who's watching *your* back?" Viñals asked, slowing down as his radar detector spoke to him.

Rowles voice lowered over the phone. "I promised Garcia I would get this asshole if he ever showed up again, and I'm not going to bust him because he doesn't have a valid passport or entry visa. Garcy spent the last eight years of his career working those student cases and it was his investigation that tied together a half dozen somewhat dissimilar crimes and apparent suicides and identified Volkova as the architect of a Soviet operation being run on our campuses. He was the only one to see a pattern when every case had been marked unsolved or suicide. Not only did Volkova steal millions, maybe billions, of dollars from us, he killed Americans. I don't care how fucked up their politics were. Their mothers and fathers sent these kids to college and he manipulated their little mush minds then whacked them after they delivered the goods."

"Is it worth your career for Garcia, he's been dead for five years?" Viñals replied.

"It's not for him, now. It's for me. *I* made the promise. *I* want him. If I take him now, I have absolutely no evidence that would hold up in court against him. Volkova worked over ten universities using various names and disguises. I probably couldn't even prove he was here back then. You need to find out what happened between him and Smith. Then, you're going to wear a wire for me."

"We need to talk about that some more, bro."

"Call me when you can, Raoul, and be careful." Rowles said and hung up.

Viñals cursed, tapping the off button to kill the dial tone. He took the exit for Highway 520, called his secretary at home forgetting what she was saying as he thought more of wearing a wire.

Chapter 27

Sunday afternoon
Still on the road

Laura took a break from reading her brother's journal to check her messages at home and to call her unit. Dan wanted to hear more but decided not to press her until she resumed reading on her own. He kept his thoughts about her brother to himself.

Dan Gill had held the line against communism in the Republic of Korea, fought a battle against communism on the island of Grenada and served most of his military career prepared to fight more communists, if necessary. But he had never given much thought to the subject of communism itself. Perhaps it is a fairer system in theory, he thought, but it doesn't work in the real world and its practical application created regimes that he viewed for himself across the 38th parallel. In Grenada his unit had been welcomed as liberators and the medical students had kissed the ground when they'd deplaned in America. Dan had always felt that communism was flawed but held no particular passion about being an instrument in its demise.

He thought of Ken and Laura being so at odds with one another: Laura, serving her country and Ken seeming to believe that America was at fault for everything. Yet, they grew up in the same household with the same parents, the same neighbors, and the same teachers. Dan was upset enough when his brother became an Oakland Raiders fan, he couldn't imagine having Ken as a brother and listening to his political tripe over Thanksgiving dinner.

Something else bothered Dan as he tried to visualize what her brother was like back then. He'd only seen a few pictures of Ken as an adult, but it was very apparent that Laura had all of the looks in her family. When Dan first saw Katenka's photograph, he almost remarked that she was absolutely stunning but held that thought in check surmising that Laura would not appreciate his approval to that degree.

As a sergeant, Dan had counseled many young soldiers who wanted to marry the girl of their dreams. Whenever a pretty girl matched up with an ugly GI, he knew something wasn't kosher. Often he discovered that the young lady would also be working on immigration and naturalization issues. He always advised against marriage but rare was the soldier who heeded his recommendation.

"Ready for some more?" Laura asked, picking up the journal.

"Sure, go ahead," Dan said looking over at her.

Laura settled back into her seat opening up her brother's note pad.

November 1, 1985, 10:30 p.m., Briggs City, Utah-

I met Mr. Kola for the first time on January 18, 1985. I was nervous about this meeting because of my own pre conceived prejudice about what I thought a communist official would look and act like. I was pleasantly surprised by his gregariousness. He gave Katenka and me a big Russian hug and kissed me on both cheeks. That was a first for me-being kissed by a man! He said that despite the circumstances, Katenka was a comrade and he was going to help her out the best that he could. He insisted that I call him Peter.

He brought some rich dark coffee wrapped in tissue paper and asked if Katenka would put on a pot. He also took a bottle of Russian vodka and beluga caviar from his attaché case.. The vodka was exceptional but I'll pass on the caviar if ever offered again.

Peter brought some news for Katenka from home. He'd grown up near her part of town and they chatted about old times switching from English to Russian when they got hung up on a word. Finally, he said that we needed to talk business. Peter said that he understood about the money. Apparently, under French law, if money in trust isn't paid out at some point, it will revert to the government. Therefore, it only made sense for Katenka's relatives to send her the money.

I showed him my student loan documents evidencing the amounts I owed and the final pay off letters and he confirmed that those amounts were roughly equivalent to what Katenka received.

He asked Katenka if she knew that she would be receiving that money when she accepted her exchange student appointment and Katenka replied no.

Peter apologized profusely but said that he was bearing bad news from Moscow. He could intercede on Katenka's behalf and prevent any criminal charges against her or her family. But, she had to go back home within the week. Peter took flight schedules out of his brief case. Back home, she and her family would have to make restitution and Katenka would never be given another visa to leave the country.

Katenka started to cry and then I did, too. Peter stepped outside to give us some privacy and later knocked and came back in.

I offered to make the full restitution and explained about mom's house and the mortgage she could take out but Peter said that it would be unacceptable for a third party to intervene under Soviet law.

Peter's eyes started to tear up as well as he looked at me and Katenka. He said that he knew we were in love but it was his crazy government that was to blame. They are extremely fearful of America and the arms build up. He cited Reagan's 'evil empire' speech. I said that I actually agree that his country should be afraid of us. Our nation has been out of control since 1980 and we are marching to the sound of war drums. For fun, practically, we taunt the Libyans so we can shoot their planes down over the Mediterranean and we pat ourselves on the back for invading Grenada where we slaughtered their policemen just to test our new weapons.

Laura stopped reading and looked over at Dan who was just shaking his head in amazement.

"He's your brother," he finally replied to her gaze.

She continued.

He asked me how much I knew about the soviet space program and I admitted that I knew a great deal. He confided in me that because of the arms build up, their space program had suffered tremendously. He asked me if I were involved with Star Wars, the Strategic Defense Initiative, and I said that I was to the extent that the shuttle would eventually be putting the proposed components into orbit.

We then talked about the space shuttle program, the orbiter, the SRBs and all of the components and compared them to the shuttle that the Soviets tried to launch. He admitted that they had many problems and I told Peter that our program is riddled with problems as well. I told him about how concerned my bosses were about the O-rings on the SRBs and the tiles that keep falling off the orbiter.

Peter then came over and sat with me and Katenka on our small couch. He spoke softly saying that he had been asked by his superiors to ask me something. Peter apologized in advance and said that he would leave if I asked him to and he would never try to see me again. I asked him what he wanted to say and he said that there may be a way for Katenka to stay in the United States, permanently. After a few years, her family could even join her.

Katenka reached over and held my hand tightly as Peter asked if I could help stop the lunacy in the world by slowing down the arms build up. I said that I agreed in principal with that objective but what could I do specifically.

Peter asked me what would happen if the shuttle stopped flying due to mechanical problems and I replied that it would completely halt our space program since we had abandoned every other lift vehicle in favor of the shuttle. I asked him what he had in mind when he said 'stopped flying'.

He said that if enough component parts failed and grounded the shuttle time after time, then friends in Congress, who also wanted peace, would stop budgeting money for the program. It would take America years to replace the shuttle with another system and it would certainly stop the Star Wars program in its tracks. By then, Reagan would be out of office and a new era of peace might dawn.

Peter said that it was important that no one be hurt because of the Soviet Union's respect for America. He said that he looked forward to the day when astronauts and cosmonauts could fly together in peace and I agreed with that sentiment.

He needed an answer to bring back that day and I must admit that it was an easy decision to make. Looking at the plane schedules on our coffee table, I realized that in a week, I would never see Katenka again unless I agreed.

"My brother agreed to sabotage the space shuttle," Laura said haltingly, putting the note pad down on her lap.

Dan absorbed that statement, thought for a moment and said, "Despite that revelation, we still need to link Ken to the professor. I still think Bera may have been looking for Katenka's money." He wanted to give Laura an alternative explanation for her own sake.

"Come on, Dan. Katenka was a Soviet agent and they set my brother up."

"It doesn't sound like she had to try very hard."

"You're right. And, if she was an agent, then her story is total BS."

"But," Dan said, "did the professor know that? Maybe they ran a similar scam on him and mentioned your brother somehow."

"I don't know what to think, except..." She trailed off.

Dan looked over. "Except?"

"Except that I don't like the man who wrote in this pad and I prefer Ken the way I remember him. Now, I will never have nice memories of him without knowing about this...shit." She smacked the pad against her knee.

Laura wanted to clear her thoughts so she turned up the volume on the radio, choosing an all news station for the weather forecast. She changed the subject. "The unit stays busy with a shuttle in orbit. We constantly track the weather worldwide in case of an emergency and the orbiter has to land at the Cape or any of the other contingency landing strips. Maybe you can watch it land as well."

"Sounds great. I'd love to see that."

Laura picked up and flipped through the pages of the pad. "Another short entry."

November 15, 1985, 2:20 a.m., Briggs City, Utah-

Peter came back to our trailer five days later. True to his word, he had staved off Katenka's departure and showed us a letter from his office extending her cultural exchange by three months. Katenka and I felt like we were just released from a long prison sentence. Peter wanted to know how I could help delay our space flight program and I explained to him what I had planned. He laughed and slapped my back saying that I was too smart for him, so I drew some diagrams for him that made it easier to understand.

Peter did not like my first two suggestions because he felt that an investigation might conclude that the components were deliberately damaged. I agreed that in order to degrade those parts, intentional damage might be revealed by an experienced investigator. He was afraid that I was taking too many risks and he was worried for my safety.

He suggested the O-rings that I had mentioned the last time he was here. Peter thought that since we were already experiencing some problems with that component then its failure would raise less suspicion. I told him that on one launch, an O-ring had almost burned completely through and it scared the hell out of everyone. Perhaps if that happened again, I said, and news of it got out, then we could ground the shuttle indefinitely.

Designers had been working on a solution of the O-ring deficiencies but an easy fix wasn't on the horizon. I explained that I could generate some conditions where debris could damage an O-ring during assembly. Because of the other problems we have not seating the joints during launch, it would be possible for the primary and secondary O-rings to practically vaporize during the ascent. In that case, no evidence of tampering would even exist. Aluminum oxide residue from the propellant would form where the seals had been and create a new seal that should hold for the duration of the SRB's two minute flight. Unless there was massive wind shear that really buckled the SRB segments, the orbiter would be safe and later we could discover the problem and make it public. A complete vaporization of the rocket segment seals should ground the program for 24 to 36 months, I speculated.

Peter liked this idea and I sketched out some more diagrams for him. I told him that I could accomplish the degradation as early as my next visit to the space center. He told me to wait before I did anything.

He gave me another bottle of Vodka but no caviar. He must have read my mind

Chapter 28

Sunday afternoon
Kennedy Space Center

Pavel Volkova called Viñals and told him to meet him at the Kennedy Space Center Museum parking lot. He told him where to park and that he was to wait there. On the way to the space center himself, the Russian drove by Laura's house, noting her pick-up truck and Camaro still parked in the driveway. He also spotted three newspapers that had been tossed onto her lawn just off the driveway. An airman advised him that Sergeant Smith was on leave but wouldn't give any other details when he called posing as her insurance agent and stating that he needed to contact her immediately because her automobile policy had lapsed.

Viñals drove into the parking lot, under Volkova's observation, and looked for the lot signs where he had been directed to park. The former KGB agent had noted the cars that had entered the area for the past hour and was satisfied that they were not federal agents. He waited another twenty minutes before pulling up to the Cuban, who was listening to salsa and smoking a hand rolled cigar from his hometown.

They both got out and greeted each other by their real names. Volkova started walking slowly towards the museum's collection of rockets and space vehicles.

"A little close to the scene of the crime, aren't we, Pavel?" Viñals asked.

"Crime? I was no criminal. Do you have any more information for me?" The Russian was annoyed.

"One more piece of the puzzle: Laura Smith stopped for gasoline and snacks at this place in Georgia." Viñals handed him a piece of paper that Volkova glanced at and placed in his pocket. "Unfortunately, my hacker friend was not able to secure the time that she was there. Also, I will not be able to get any more information for you on her credit cards."

"Why not?"

"Because my friend's boss almost caught him and is now very watchful. I can't afford to lose him and in a few weeks, things will settle down and he will continue to provide information."

"I can not wait a few more weeks but…we have to accept what is handed to us and adapt." Volkova said. They walked in silence until they reached the massive Saturn Five rocket on display along side the Redstone, Atlas and other missiles used to carry American astronauts into space.

"This was their most successful rocket, Raoul; the Saturn Five worked magnificently every single time. It is strange that they did not keep producing it as a backup orbital delivery system to their shuttle. The Americans are so extravagant: Russians know how to stay with something that works. I have a task for you, my friend."

"What is it?"

"I know it has been a while since you have worked in the field, but I need for you to do a break in for me. I can't afford to be seen or caught and the house may be under watch, although I do not believe that it is."

The Russian gave the details to Viñals as they walked towards the entrance of the museum. Viñals repeated everything that was told to him and didn't ask any questions as he received his instructions. They stopped near the large reflecting stone memorial honoring the astronauts killed in the line of duty and rested against the handrails along the walkway adjacent to it. Volkova read each of their names aloud, softly to himself. Viñals had turned to look at the tourists milling around, especially the younger ladies, but his mind was thinking of a way to contact Rowles before carrying out his task.

"Raoul, you don't want to know why I am asking you this favor?" Volkova asked.

"I have learned that you will tell me what I need to know," Viñals answered.

"True, but you have lived in America for a long time. I thought perhaps their curiosity would have rubbed off on you by now."

"It has. But it is wasteful to ask a question when the answer is already known."

"And, what is the answer, Raoul?"

Viñals turned around to face the memorial and pointed to the section containing the names of the seven astronauts who perished aboard Challenger. "The answer is that you are responsible for that engraving."

Pavel Volkova looked up to where Viñals had pointed and reflected a moment. "Not directly, Raoul. But…I wrote the script."

"A script that you do not want screen credit for."

Volkova nodded affirmatively and walked towards the museum entrance with Viñals alongside.

"I am going to become a tourist while you become a criminal," Volkova said taking out his wallet as they approached the ticket area. "Call me when you are clear of the area and I will let you know where to meet me later." He shook Viñals hand and wished him luck.

Chapter 29

Sunday, late afternoon
Nearing Laura's home

Dan returned to the highway after a quick pit stop, merged into traffic then placed his breakfast meal on the dashboard for quick access while Laura studied the photographs of Ken with his girlfriend.

"Let's end the suspense," Laura said, retrieving Ken's writings.

December 1, 1985, 3:15 a.m., Cape Canaveral, Florida

A few weeks after we agreed that the O- rings would be the best way to slow down the space program, Peter came by with some schematics for me to review. They were done, I believe, by soviet engineers who experienced similar problems with their shuttle program. I was able to achieve what I wanted to do the following week at the space center. Since then, Katenka and I have enjoyed our life together with no further pressures and no more visits from Peter.

I have been working at the assembly building at Cape Canaveral for the past week but will be going home tomorrow. I believe that the next launch, or possibly the one beyond, should result in what we are hoping for. The O-ring that I selected was on an SRB that had some faulty wiring in the ignition sequence and was pulled off the line. Quite frankly, I'm not sure which STS mission it will be used for after the electricians re-certify it.

The situation between the United States and the Soviet Union is probably the worst it has been since the Cuban Missile Crisis. I can't help but laugh out loud when I watch Reagan on television anymore. Last month, at the Geneva Summit, our warmongering president said that he only wanted peace. I don't understand how the American people can be so fooled by this man. He claims that an agreement has been reached to reduce ballistic missiles by fifty percent and the ultimate goal is total elimination of these abominable weapons. If that is true, then why are we spending billions on Star Wars to defeat missiles that won't be around anymore? Right before Thanksgiving, Peter Kola came through once again and was able to extend Katenka's cultural exchange visa. He can only do it in three-month increments and during the weeks preceding each expiration, Kaneka and I are nervous nellies. We managed a short vacation together and I asked her to marry me and she agreed. We have kept it a secret since my employer would screw with my security clearance. I barely mention Katenka to 'the guys' at work and we rarely go out in public. We plan to get a 'quickie' marriage in Las Vegas sometime during the spring. If the shuttle program is grounded, then I should have some available time for a honeymoon.

I had an idea before coming out to Florida this time. There is certainly a risk to the crew with what I have done. I believe that in the alternative, I could just go public with the deficiencies in the seal designs and I can also speculate as to assembly defects. If I keep the pressure up, they will have to take apart the SRBs for inspection. This should cause the lengthy delay in the flight schedule that we are trying to achieve without the danger of a major malfunction. Of course, being a whistleblower, I will also be looking for a new job, as well!

I ran my idea by Katenka and she said that she didn't understand any of what I was saying but that she would call Peter Kola while I'm in Florida.

"It sounds like he was getting a little weak kneed," Dan said. "Maybe he overestimated the safety of a launch when all of the big rubber washers get vaporized."

"Dan," Laura started, and then reflected on her thoughts. She began again, "I really am ashamed by this."

"Why? You didn't plan to sabotage the space shuttle so there's no reason for you to be ashamed." He added, "Embarrassed would be a better word. Humiliated might apply, too."

"Are you using Gill family therapy on me?"

"No. Gill family therapy involves fists and a lot of cursing. Look, if he were my brother, I would be humiliated that my family name would be associated with this...let's face it, if this ever becomes public, you are going to be on every news show, every talk show, you know the media hype that you'll be subjected to. You will become a household name right up there with Monica or OJ. Even if you go on and become the first woman to be awarded the Medal of Honor for bravery under fire, you will always be connected to this." Dan reached over and tapped Ken's note pad.

He focused back on the road then picked up the pad and said, "Until the day you die, this is *your* legacy, too. This will be regurgitated in *your* obituary." He tossed it back on her lap. Dan readjusted his posture and pushed his sunglasses up to rest on his forehead. He looked over at Laura who was re-reading her brother's last entry. "Ordinarily, I don't like to tell people who I care for how I feel about them. That's a Gill family tradition that goes back many generations. Also, we really just met and I don't want to blow any future with you by sounding over-the-top, but...I have come to care for you a great deal in the short time we have been together."

Laura took Dan's hand. "Gee Dan, you sound just like a Hallmark card," she replied, ghosting a smile knowing he was sincere.

"What I'm trying to say is that I don't want anything bad to happen to you, your career, and all of your future plans. And . . ."

"And, what?" She squeezed his hand a bit.

"And I would like to be a part of your future plans."

"You are so sweet when you're not a wise ass."

"Well, let's hear what the rat bastard has to say next," Dan said and Laura nodded her head in agreement.

December 15, 1985, 1:30 a.m. Briggs City, Utah-

Katenka fell asleep a little while ago and I am trying to keep this journal up-to-date. I am traveling back to Florida tomorrow, although we are supposed to receive heavy snow. In any event, I will fly out when the weather clears.

When I returned home from Florida earlier this month, Katenka said that she had run my idea of going public prior to the next launch with Peter and he'd agreed that it would be a good idea, a much safer alternative. Peter had suggested that I wait so that he could contact the public relations firm that his embassy and consulate office use and they can review my statement beforehand so that I will sound more polished. Public speaking is not my forte and I would not want the message hampered because the messenger, me, can sound like a dolt at times. Yesterday, Katenka said that she received an urgent call at work from Peter and he needed to meet us today at a secluded spot. Katenka suggested our hiking area. We drove out there in her old Opel and she said that she didn't want to sound melodramatic but I needed to keep a watch behind us to make sure we weren't being followed. I made a lot of jokes along the way spotting and calling out the names of 007's villains in the other cars.

We arrived at our spot and Peter showed up about an hour later. He had gotten lost and had to stop several times for directions he told us. Some secret agent he would make. He was very upset because he said that he recently received some photographs at the consulate and he showed them to us. They were photos of him and Katenka outside of the theater where she worked and also photos of them in front of our trailer. Peter said that no note attended the photographs and he was not sure of the motivation. We all brainstormed the issue. Katenka and Peter both believed it was the FBI tailing Peter or Katenka or both of them. He said that the FBI Counter-Intelligence Unit routinely followed Soviet citizens. I wonder if the American public knows how we treat our guests. I suggested that it could also be a private investigator hired by my company because we do have clearances and they might be verifying information that I gave them when I was hired.

In any event, it is very obvious that someone is interested in Katenka and Peter and because of the photograph taken outside our home, I must be factored in as well. Peter thought that it would be unwise for me to go public knowing that the FBI, most likely, had been watching us. They would use my relationship with Katenka and her acquaintance with Peter to discredit me. Peter said that the FBI would accuse him of being a spy and he would have to immediately leave the country. Without his support, we could forget about Katenka staying in the United States.

Although I would prefer to go public immediately, I now think that my message would become lost in the propaganda campaign that would be waged against me by my government.

Katenka just woke up and invited me to bed. Until next time…

"Do you think he banged her?" Dan asked looking over at Laura.

"Dan, for God's sake." She sounded annoyed.

"What? It's a logical response to your brother's last sentence."

"Logical for a man…I think that may be an oxymoron," she observed closing the note pad.

"I'm just using my male crudeness to figure out what your brother was up to because getting laid seemed pretty important to him."

"What do you mean by that?"

"What do I mean? Katenka was probably the first girl he ever laid and she kept dangling that trim right in his face to keep him on course."

"That's a little vulgar, don't you think?" Laura replied defensively.

"So is trying to blow up the space shuttle."

"He didn't try to blow it up, he tried to . . ." she articulated in the air with her hands.

"Yeah? Try finishing that explanation on *Oprah*."

Laura put her hands down, looked out the window and slouched down in her seat putting her knees against the dashboard. The late morning sun was heating up the car and Laura said to pull over and let the top down.

"There's one last entry," she said after Dan pulled back on the highway. "Before I read it, what do you think happened to my brother?"

Dan merged back into the fast lane and waved in the rear view mirror to the trucker he cut off. "I think, in all probability, your brother adopted political views in college that left him… open to persuasion. He was obviously a very bright and talented man and people who would like to do harm to our country observed his career path. If I may be blunt…"

"More blunt than saying Katenka hung trim in his face?"

"I actually thought of using another word back then but…I'm sorry. Anyway, if I may be blunt, your brother was friggin' homely."

"What! He was cute."

"Are you kidding me? His ears stuck out so far he could gain altitude on a strong breeze. And he parted his hair on the wrong side, like Adolf Hitler. What's up with that?"

"My brother had…little boy cuteness," she defended her shared gene pool.

"Who did he take to his senior prom?"

"He didn't go."

"Aha!" Dan exclaimed.

"That doesn't mean anything. I didn't go to my senior prom, either."

"Why didn't you go?"

"Because three guys asked me and I couldn't decide right away. When I finally did, they all had other dates."

"I don't think that was Ken's problem. And besides, Katenka was a hottie."

"A hottie?"

"Very much so."

"Is that your type?"

"You're my type."

"Forget about it."

Dan said. "Look, when it comes to male-female relations, I'm considered an expert."

"By whom? Your ex-wife?"

"I think we're having our first spat, but anyway, by a lot of people. My former marital condition happens to give me a lot of perspective. When it comes to male and female relations, water always reaches its own level." Dan said profoundly.

"What does that mean?"

"Meaning…in the ordinary course of things, good looking women wind up with strong, handsome, athletic, smart and witty guys…look at us," he said with a smile and waited for the response he had hoped for. She finally conceded. "Anyway, when you have a situation where the woman is young and beautiful and the man is old and bald then there must be an X factor: usually the X factor is money. Here, you have your brother, a boyishly cute albeit ugly man, and a woman who could be a centerfold. What is the X factor?"

Laura leaned back in her seat and enjoyed the warm sun on her face. She finally replied, "She was a Soviet agent and played Ken like a fiddle."

"Possibly," Dan replied in a tone reminding Laura of his investigative background.

"What else could it be?"

"Another possible alternative is that the X factor was that she wanted to stay in the United States and marrying your brother was the way to do that."

"Then why not just marry him right away?"

"Maybe it would have screwed with his security clearance at work. He said that himself."

"But what about this whole journal...the schematics...the photographs." She fingered through the pages.

"Let's consider the range of possible, though not probable, scenarios. What if your brother just took the pictures himself and this journal is sort of like...a working novel, or screenplay. Was your brother into science fiction or mysteries?"

"I don't know. I guess he was sort of geeky when it came to science fiction. I don't know about mysteries, though."

"What if his notes ever became public, resulting in your brother forever being pilloried as the saboteur of the space shuttle? And the real truth is that he fantasized this story with its theme having a genesis in some defects in the shuttle that he was aware of because of his job?"

Laura looked over at Dan. "What chances do you give as *that* being the truth?"

"Slim to none, but absent corroboration, it is never - the - less a reasonable possibility. The truth died with your brother."

"What about Professor Bera's involvement?"

"It died with him, too."

"Maybe the last entry will help us find the truth." Laura picked up her brother's note pad from the floor and flipped it open.

*****

"Look at this, the last entry is from Lexington," Laura said showing the page to Dan.

"Let's hear it," he said.

Laura waited for Dan to finish passing a line of trucks before beginning.

January 10, 1986, 2:15 p.m., Lexington, Tennessee

Well, I guess I should have called my mom before making this surprise visit. There were terrible snow storms out west delaying flights so I decided to rent a car and drive to mom's house from the Cape. I planned on surprising her and Laura since I haven't seen them since last summer. I waited for eight hours before realizing that something was askew. I went out to the mailbox and saw that mom had placed a note saying to hold her mail. I called Aunt Michelle in Michigan and spoke with my cousin Tara. She said mom was up there visiting but was out shopping with my aunt. Tara said that Laura was on a class field trip to Washington, D.C.

Laura stopped reading. "Now I remember. My mom told me he had stopped by but I had completely forgotten." She paused. "Within three weeks of this entry, we were planning his funeral arrangements." She reflected for a moment while Dan passed slower traffic to his left.

We chatted for a while and I told her to have my mom call as soon as she got back. I will probably leave in an hour because there is a Memphis to Salt Lake City flight through Chicago that I can catch tonight. I was planning on staying at least a couple of days but I'd rather be with Katenka than alone in my old bedroom. I feel so utterly removed from my mother's house as if another person, not me, grew up here. I find myself looking at old familiar items in this house as if I were walking through a museum viewing relics. There is a sense of time and distance forever separating me from the home of my youth.

I wanted to speak to mom about Katenka. Mom should know that I am very much in love and I do want her blessing. But I can not tolerate any criticism which I do expect. I doubt if a blessing will come from my mother without the requisite lecture and I don't know if I can remain respectful if mom starts in about Katenka. I think mom would be jealous of her.

Laura stopped reading. "My brother was a little shit."

It took Dan a moment to differentiate Laura's sentiment from what she had been reading. He looked over and lowered his head so that he could see her above his sunglasses.

"He was..." Laura continued after realizing Dan was looking at her, "he was ready to ask my mom to mortgage the friggin' farm for that slut but he wouldn't want her advice about love and marriage. Mom was never the same after he died and it ultimately led to her last sickness and he only thought of her as a damn bank."

Dan thought to add a word or two of comfort but realized that she would smack anything that moved or spoke in her immediate vicinity.

She continued reading.

The next launch is scheduled for later this month. There is more public relations hype with this flight than any other launch since I started work. With the teacher going up in space and all of the publicity surrounding this flight, now would have been a perfect opportunity for me to spill the beans, as it were.

All I can do, all we can do, is sit tight and wait. I can't believe the morons at NASA stating how safe space travel is nowadays. They must know that we send these shuttles into orbit each and every time on a wing and a prayer.

I have thought long and hard about what Peter Kola has done for Katenka and me. He is right about the course of action I have taken. If I did go public, I would ultimately wind up being the loser. My fiancée would be teaching ballet to four year old girls in Leningrad and I would be unemployable. This way, my role will essentially remain anonymous and Katenka will remain in the United States and become my wife. Her family will be permitted to emigrate. Space flights will become safer and dedicated towards peaceful enterprises once that idiot is out of the White House. When I consider what I have done, I just can not see it as anything but a win-win scenario for everybody.

When I am old and gray, maybe I will tell the truth about what I did on the assembly line. I am certain that history will treat me fairly.

After a lengthy pause, Dan asked, "Is that it?"

Laura didn't answer at first as she re-read her brother's final words. She put Ken's note pad into the glove compartment then cleaned up the wrappers from Dan's breakfast.

Dan asked again. "Was that it?"

"Yup, history will treat him fairly, alright."

"What do you want to do?"

"Eat a big lunch then sleep on a mattress," she replied lazily.

"I meant, what are you going to do about your brother's notes?"

She brought her feet up underneath her and looked at the citrus orchards going by. "I don't know. I would like to just shred the damn thing up and make believe it never existed. But, it does exist and it has historical value, if it's true. I'm not sure if I am up to releasing it now. I don't think I want to share this with Detective Leonard."

"For all intents and purposes, it was a pretty big fluke that you even found it. You can still plausibly deny knowledge of its existence and later on, when you are ready, you can say you just found it when you finally move your stuff from storage. By the way, how do you think his note book wound up at the Kurke's barn?"

"Good question. I thought maybe it was in the box I got from his co-worker and maybe my mother re-packed things but that wouldn't make sense. Mom got sick pretty fast that spring and never recovered and besides, I think going through his belongings would have been too painful. I think that in his rush to catch the flight from Memphis, he may have just left it behind at the kitchen table, or wherever it was in the house that he wrote the last entry."

"So your mother must have placed it in the box with all of your family's records. Why didn't she just call your brother and mail it to him?"

Laura thought about that. Her mind thought back to her mother's kitchen. Laura's mother returned home from Michigan a few hours before she came home from her class trip. In her mind Laura could see her mother picking up the note pad and then becoming fretful when the photographs fell to the floor. She would see that the pictures were of strangers and then her mom would have opened the pad to see who it belonged to.

Laura Smith remembered the way her mother was and she smiled as the memories returned. Although not a true daughter of the South, Laura always thought of her mother as a petite and genteel antebellum dame. Her mother must have spotted the notebook when she came home from her trip then opened it looking for some evidence of ownership. She would have immediately recognized Ken's handwriting. When Ken first went away to college, and practically all the way through graduate school, he always called home on Sunday, collect at mother's insistence, and he never failed to send birthday and holiday cards, usually with a long letter and pictures inside. The diminished communication with her son must have been hurtful and Laura knew that her mother, despite her respectful disposition, continued to read her boy's words.

"She read what Ken wrote, that's why." Laura said. "She may not have understood everything but she would have understood the last entry about her and it would have hurt her deeply. Also, she certainly understood how changed her son had become. Mom probably put it off to the side with the intent of talking to Ken about it but he died. I reckon at some point she just put it in the metal box."

"Do you think she knew he may have been responsible for Challenger?" Dan asked.

"She probably believed he was. His death was very hard on her as a child's death always is but…there was something more. Knowing my mother, she would have assumed the responsibility of Ken's actions, citing his crimes as her failure as a mother. That's how she was. I don't think she wanted to live with the guilt. My God, the damn television kept showing Challenger blowing up every night on the news for months and my mother *knew*. That bastard killed our mother as sure as he killed the shuttle crew."

After driving a few miles Dan said, "Laura, I'm not convinced, beyond a reasonable doubt anyway, that your brother was responsible."

"You still think he was writing a story for Hollywood?"

"Like I said before, that *is* a possibility. But, even if he sabotaged the O-ring during assembly, he wasn't sure where that damaged seal was going. He said he didn't know which STS mission would be using the SRB he…sabotaged. Also, Captain Dave told us that everyone knew that the seals were the weak link and he certainly has concluded that it was an accident along with NASA and every sane person in America.

"During my collegiate years…while studying for my associate degree in criminal justice…" Dan feigned seriousness and waited for Laura's faint smile then continued, "we had a lawyer teach us about the elements comprising each felony crime. I remember his lecture about the subject of intent. If you died of a stroke right now and I didn't know it…"

"You would have to be pretty stupid not to notice that I stroked out two feet from you."

"True, but criminals are generally stupid people. Anyway, let's pretend that you died and I didn't know it. Now, I want to kill you because you pissed me off."

"By dying?"

"No, before you died."

"What did I do?"

"That doesn't matter."

"It does to me."

"You're dead, remember. Alright, I wanted to stay with you until I go back to Jersey and you said that I couldn't and that I should have a nice life. That pissed me off, but then you stroked out. Okay?"

"Okay," she said, absorbing his scenario.

"So, I pull out a gun, hold it to your temple and blow your brains out."

"Do you often have these anger issues with women?"

"Lots o' laughs. The point is that although I intended to kill you, I didn't because you were already dead. I can not be convicted of murder but I can be convicted of attempted murder because I possessed, at the time of pulling the trigger, the *mens rea*...

"The men's what?"

"*Mens rea* – it's Latin for guilty mind."

"You learned all of that in community college."

"Yes, on the days I was awake. So, I could be convicted of the attempted crime because I wanted to kill you but I could not be convicted of murder, because you were already dead when I shot you. Therefore, Ken's notes only prove, if true, that he attempted to bring about a certain consequence. There is enough evidence, according to Captain Dave, that the shuttle was destroyed by accident. At least, that's what everyone has concluded. The O-rings could have failed before Ken's act of sabotage had any role to play in the disaster."

"Well, I suppose you're correct if we were in a courtroom. But, this isn't a trial and public opinion will indict, put to trial and convict Ken."

"I know that. I only mean to present it for you to think about. *You* don't have to convict him. He's your brother and you're allowed to give him the benefit of the doubt."

Laura was tired of sitting in a car and wanted to jump out and run until she dropped. Or dive into a lake and swim until exhaustion overcame her.

"Another two hours and we'll be at the house. You can just drop me off." She waited for him to look at her and said, "Have a nice life."

Dan reached over and pinched her behind the left knee before she could move out of the way. "Okay, you can stay for lunch."

Chapter 30

Sunday afternoon
Laura's home

The Russian was correct, Viñals thought as he considered their conversation back at the space center, it had been a long time since he worked in the field. Volkova had given him Laura Smith's address along with several Polaroid photographs he had taken during his last drive by her house. The former KGB officer gave Viñals information on traffic patterns in the area and observations made concerning Laura's neighbors but respected the Cuban's ability and said nothing on the matter of entry. Volkova never appreciated micro management from Moscow and wasn't going to instruct a field agent, albeit a rusty one, on how to break into a house.

Cruising slowly to the pending crime scene, Viñals mulled over renting a white van and buying work clothes to resemble a cable or telephone repair man. However, his experience dictated that he should just go with the simplest plan. Studying the snapshots at red lights, he noted that the front door had windows along both sides. He could tactically park in her driveway, backing in rear first, so that any nosey neighbors would only be able to describe the car but not give a license number; Florida requiring only a tail plate. The windows along the side were about four inches by eight inches and he could punch the one closest to the locks with a gloved hand making little noise. The only issue remaining was whether the lock had a handle on the inside that he could simply turn. If not, he was prepared to pick the lock although he was never particularly good at that covert skill. He hoped that there wasn't an alarm system.

The actual burglary shouldn't take very long, he guessed. Sitting just off the Intracoastal Waterway, there wouldn't be a basement to rummage through and he gathered that the attic was just a crawl space. Sergeant Smith was a senior air force sergeant and Viñals knew that her home would not only be immaculate, but highly organized. She probably had a spare bedroom turned into a home office with all of her personal files, photographs, old love letters and whatever else of value she kept over the years tucked away in storage boxes ready for the move to her next permanent duty station.

The delay would come after he located what was most personal to Laura Smith and then sifting through those effects to find the items Volkova wanted. He needed anything pertaining to her brother. *Anything*. The last thing the Russian gave him before leaving was an old picture of Kenneth Smith. Also, he was to leave no evidence of what was searched for or taken. The broken window would be a clue that some malfeasance occurred, but if he placed all of her belongings away where he found them, she might not notice missing pictures and letters from her dead brother until well into her retirement. Viñals thought of providing some cover to his operation by leaving her television and stereo equipment on the floor but decided against it. The local *policia* might want to investigate more fully and ask around to see what the neighbors may have seen. With just the broken glass, her doors locked and nothing apparently stolen, they certainly won't waste man hours.

After leaving Volkova, Viñals tried several times to call Rowles. But all he got was the Special Agent's voice mail. He contemplated leaving a message for the receptionist to tell Agent Rowles that the confidential informant/field operative working on the agent's unauthorized mission involving the illegal tracking of an American citizen needed a return phone call, ASAP. Cursing at his friend while the voice mail prompted him, he left a more professional message. This was no way for Denny to be watching his back, he muttered.

As Viñals approached Laura's neighborhood, he reached into the back behind the passenger seat and grabbed his straw hat with tropical flowers and parrots along the band and placed in on his head; he adjusted his sunglasses and then checked himself in the rear view mirror. He took a hand rolled cigar out of his alligator skin four cigar holder, stuck it in his mouth but left it unlit for the duration of the mission. Once on Laura's street, he obeyed the fifteen-mile per hour posted speed, pulled slightly ahead of her house then backed into the driveway as if he had done so a hundred times before. Without looking around to see if anyone was watching, Viñals walked up to her front door, rang the bell with his right hand while shielding his left hand with his body. He punched in the window with one quick jab using the sound of a passing car to shield the noise he made. The glass fell on to the Spanish tile floor in the foyer but made no sound that could travel next door or across the street. He undid the doorknob lock then felt the lock above...grateful that it was a simple handle - he quickly turned it. The Cuban opened the door and acted like he was greeting the woman of the house to anyone observing. Hopefully, a busybody wouldn't observe long enough to notice the broken window.

Once inside, he checked to make sure there wasn't an alarm system. The front window did not have the tell tale metal strip along the inside seam suggesting that the house was wired but he wanted to rule out the possibility so that the local cops didn't roll up on him while he was going through the sergeant's underwear drawer. Had there been an alarm, Viñals had decided that the mission would be aborted.

The house was as neat as he surmised and he swept through the rooms taking stock of the interior layout first. The master bedroom closet contained a panel in the ceiling providing access to the crawl space. The Cuban slid her uniforms and civilian dresses to one side, got a chair from the spare bedroom and looked into the attic confirming that nothing was there. He placed everything back as neatly as he had found it. Her bedroom appeared ordinary and he hurriedly checked the rest of her closet, chest of drawers and night stand for anything relevant.

Raoul Viñals then went to the spare bedroom that she had made into an office; no surprise there. There was a futon, some chairs and a computer on a sleek metal desk with file drawers. The third bedroom had been converted into a home gym containing a treadmill, weight bench, and all of her sporting equipment including a twenty seven speed road bicycle, a cross country bicycle, tennis rackets, racquetball equipment, scuba gear and ski equipment both downhill and cross country. In the gym room, Viñals picked up a photograph of Laura on a beach standing next to a plastic sea kayak wearing a bikini bottom, wet suit top piece and a ripped belly in between. She was smiling and ringing her wet hair when the picture was taken. The Cuban nodded his head in approval, wishing he could be in her home under more inviting circumstances.

He went back to the spare bedroom and checked the closet. "Bingo," he said aloud taking the cigar from his mouth. She had cardboard boxes lined along the bottom shelf and a row of shoe boxes on the top shelf. Viñals pulled out the first box; and found it contained technical manuals and course materials from a non commissioned officer professional leadership course she had attended years earlier. Unfortunately, her organizational skills did not include labeling the outside of the boxes, he groused. It took the Cuban forty-five minutes to go through all of the boxes and repack them in order. He took a break walking over to the window to make sure that a SWAT team wasn't getting into position.

The first seven shoe boxes contained shoes, and then he hit pay dirt. The first box not containing shoes had memorabilia from her elementary and high school days. There were old date books, little stuffed toys, notes that had probably been passed back and forth to a friend in class and pictures cut from magazines that had long ago lost any significance but were kept in storage none – the - less. The next two boxes contained her childhood birthday cards along with Christmas, get well, congratulations and other cards. Viñals found about a dozen cards from her brother and placed them off to the side. How these could possibly be relevant he had no idea; but he was determined to bring Volkova some proof of his escapade.

The next several containers held nothing of significance but then he came across three shoe boxes filled with old photos, some even in black and white. He brought his find over to the futon and settled himself in keeping the photograph of Ken given to him by the Russian off to the side for quick reference. It took a little over a half hour, but Viñals found over three dozen pictures of Ken from his baby pictures that his mother wrote on the back of to his graduation photograph from high school. There were only four pictures showing him as an adult.

The Cuban placed the photos on top of the greeting cards then placed everything back in the closet. He went over to her computer desk, turned it on, and then went through her desk and files as the machine came to life. Sergeant Smith's computer files were as organized as the rest of her belongings and she had a folder marked 'personal correspondence' that he perused. He was reading a letter that she had sent contesting the amount of cable television bill because of a five day failure of service when his cell phone vibrated.

"Yeah?" Viñals answered.

"It's me," Special Agent Denny Rowles said.

"Where you been, *hermano?*"

"Sorry Raoul, I was stuck. The Department of Justice called me on a case we're working on and I was in conference for over five hours. I tried to check on you during breaks but couldn't get a damn signal and I wasn't about to use a land line."

"I hope you can make my bail."

"Why? Where are you now?"

Viñals walked over to the master bedroom window to check the street and spotted some clothing that Laura had laundered but not yet put away. "I'm looking at Laura Smith's panties right now, *mi amigo,*" he said, picking up her underwear.

"What does that mean?" Rowles asked.

"At my friend's insistence, I am in her bedroom rummaging around looking for ghosts."

"Is Smith there?" Rowles asked excitedly but barely raising his voice.

"No, she's in Atlanta, remember?"

"Get out, now!" Rowles said, knowing that she wasn't.

"What's going on?"

"Now!" Rowles yelled.

Chapter 31

Sunday late afternoon
Nearing Laura's home

Laura took over the driving, wanting to concentrate on something other than her brother: she forced herself to think about Dan and what he had said about wanting to stay with her and she *did* want him to stay - for a while anyway. The past few days were most definitely the strangest in her life, she reflected, shaking her head. Chilled by the realization that Professor Bera was obviously interested in Ken, she decided that he would have approached her ultimately, and probably with a gun. Laura thought how serendipitous it was to have had Dan around when Bera chose his time to appear. She also appreciated having him by her side during the journey back through her past and for his companionship and insight. There was only one other man she knew who would have been an equal partner these past few days but he was separating from his wife and Laura wanted some distance from that situation.

It really was time to settle down, she thought. Dan could be the right man for her but he would have to be willing to work with her as she pursued her military then post military career. Then again, maybe being a *hausfrau* in New Jersey would be fulfilling. Laura smiled at the passing thought, knowing she would never allow it-she would rather be a *hausfrau* in Colorado Springs after giving her morning lecture to the Corps of Cadets at the Air Force Academy. The oft mentioned proverbial biological clock was ticking, however, and she did want children. She snuck a stare over at Dan to imagine what their kids might look like.

The best friend Laura ever had in the service got out during the mid nineties, taking advantage of a generous post cold war reduction in force early-out bonus. Kim Sullivan left the service, invested in and worked for a dot com company earning two point five million dollars-on paper. Unfortunately, she hadn't bailed out when everyone else did and now worked as an office administrator for a group of cardiologists in her New Hampshire hometown. Kim, her husband Matt and baby Jaime had visited Laura last Thanksgiving, staying for the long weekend. Matt had offered to baby sit so the two of them could go for a girl's night out. Listening to her friend talk about her husband and daughter, Laura had become morose watching the singles displaying their wares on the dance floor-she knew that too much time had slipped away. She had recognized that something terribly important was missing in her life and a sense of panic had swept over her.

The next few days might make a big difference in my life, she thought as she made the final turn onto her street.

"That's odd," Laura said.

"What's odd?" Dan replied, sitting up straight after his nap.

"It looked like that car came out of my driveway but I can't tell for sure from here."

"What car?"

"The one coming our way and making a right turn up ahead."

Dan watched the Lexus roll through the stop sign and make the turn. His cop mind recorded the make, model and color of the car and a general description of the lone occupant. Unfortunately, the driver's hat and sunglasses would limit any useful identification. When their car came to a stop for the same sign, the Lexus was too far away to read its license tag or even tell what state issued it. Laura drove up to her house and pulled into the driveway. Dan got out walking over to retrieve her newspapers and mail at the curbside as Laura went to the front door.

Dan was pulling envelopes and Chinese take-out flyers from her mailbox when he heard Laura yell his name.

Before he could reply she yelled again, "Come here!" Dan raced over to where she was standing but noticed the broken pane before she said anything further.

"Don't touch the doorknob." He said. "Do you have an alarm system?"

"No."

"Okay. Unlock the door and try to open it using only the key to push. There may be prints on the doorknob or door itself," Dan said, pointing, and then examining the window frame where the glass had been.

Laura unlocked the top bolt then the doorknob lock and opened the door as Dan had instructed.

"Be careful; there's glass here." She said going in first.

"Let's check the whole house together and see if anything is missing." Dan believed that even if the house were broken into, it was vacant now; but if he was wrong, he didn't want Laura to discover otherwise by herself. She started creeping through the foyer towards the kitchen like a mime imitating a burglary.

"I think we can just walk normally," Dan suggested.

"What if he's still here?" she asked still crouching low.

"That's why I'm with you. You know, if Detective Leonard were here he would ask you how you know it's a man."

"I think he would only bust your chops, not mine."

"True."

Laura took her aluminum baseball bat from the hall closet where she left it after last week's softball game and followed Dan as he took the lead through the whole house. He checked every closet, behind the shower curtains, under the bed and every conceivable place where an adult might hide.

"Well, there's no one here. Why don't you check on where you keep your valuables and I'll go unload the car."

"I don't keep cash lying around but I do have a lot of mom's and my grandmother's jewelry."

He carried in the boxes from Tennessee and their personal bags and left them by the stairs then went back out to clean up the car. He carried in a bag of trash and left it near her kitchen wastebasket, not having spotted her outside garbage can.

Laura came down and met him in the kitchen where he had already helped himself to a bottle of light beer.

"Everything all present or accounted for?" Dan asked.

"Seems to be. I'm not sure if I should call the police," Laura said, taking his drink. "I just want a sip; I'm too tired. Let's eat a big lunch then sleep until tomorrow morning."

Dan proffered the menus he brought in and she suggested they order. Laura took a pencil from a kitchen drawer and began to study the choices, then circled her choices.

"You should call the police to make a report even though nothing is apparently missing. You may discover something gone later on and then you'll be able to make a claim through your insurance."

Laura nodded her head at Dan's suggestion while she studied the menu. "I guess I've been very lucky this weekend to hook up with a former cop who is now an insurance investigator. That's good advice."

"Good advice, but not great advice."

"What would be great advice?"

"That we carry your stereo set, television and computer to the trunk of my car and then call the cops."

"Have you given that advice often?"

"Circle the General Tso chicken, hot and spicy soup and beef on a stick for me," Dan replied. She continued to wait for an answer and he finally answered no, his back turned towards her shielding his face.

Laura circled Dan's selections and called in the order. Dan drifted into the living room and sat in her leather chair, turning on the news. He kicked off his shoes and put his feet up on the chair's matching ottoman.

"Thirty minutes for delivery. Don't fall asleep, that chair does me in every time," Laura said, coming into the room. She took a seat on the couch and they watched the coverage about a kidnapping in Montana until a commercial break.

"What are your plans, Dan?" she asked during the third commercial.

"For today, for the rest of my vacation or for the rest of my life?" he muttered, slowly falling victim to the chair's comfort.

"Let's start with today."

"Well, I was hoping that a beautiful woman I know named Laura something or other would let me stay here until tomorrow. Then…" he stopped when the news came back on; uncomfortable, he was grateful for the respite.

"Then?" Laura finally prompted.

Dan used the remote to lower the volume and turning towards Laura, he said "Then, I would be hard pressed to want to leave you."

Laura considered Dan's statement. "Did you ever see your parents kiss?" she asked.

"No PDA allowed in the Gill household…Public Display of Affection."

"I know what PDA is…Dan, tell me how you feel about me."

"That's an unfair question to ask a man who hasn't slept or eaten decently in three days."

"True. But you're sober at least."

He moved over to sit next to Laura and put his arm around her. She cuddled closer in response, laying her head on his chest and closing her eyes. "I'm very happy I met you." he said kissing her forehead. They drifted off into sleep until the doorbell startled them. Dan jumped up and went for the door, fumbling in his pocket for money. The deliveryman placed the food down, spotted Dan's twenty and started making change.

"Is that your name?" Dan asked pointing to the man's name tag that said Lee Wong.

"Yes, sir?"

"Are you married?"

"Yes, sir." he replied looking for more change.

"Remember, two Wongs don't make a wight." He heard Laura groan behind him while Mr. Wong ignored him. "Just give me two bucks back." Dan said, taking two singles and saying good-bye.

"How many times have you used that one?" she asked as Dan closed the door and she followed him into the kitchen.

"Every chance I get since I first saw *What's up Tiger Lily?"*

Laura took several plates, bowls and utensils from her cupboard placing them on the table next to Dan.

"Put a little of everything on a plate for me. I'm going to call my unit real quick." She said leaving the kitchen. Dan made up two plates.

Laura came back barefooted wearing her gray air force sweats.

"Everything is good at the base," she said, starting to eat. In between bites of shrimp fried rice she said, "I had a message from Detective Leonard. He said to call him immediately and that it was very important."

"That's the same message every detective in the world leaves. Let's enjoy lunch first."

Laura nodded in agreement, pouring more noodles onto her plate.

Chapter 32

Later that afternoon
Outside of Laura's home

The Russian waited for his phone call in the Kennedy Space Center visitor's parking lot. A sizeable crowd still milled around and he felt comfortable amongst them. He walked over to the reflecting pond by the astronaut's memorial and smoked a cigarette.

His cell phone rang to the tune of *Yankee Doodle Dandy*; he smiled, confirmed it was her number, and answered.

"*Da?*"

"I'm still here but your friend is gone," Katenka replied.

"Where are you?"

"I'm parked two car lengths away down a side street and I have Smith's house in plain sight."

"You are not conspicuous, I trust?"

"When you said it could be a while, I decided to rent a minivan with tinted windows. My presence is unnoticed."

"Good girl. What happened?"

"I got into position about an hour before Señor Viñals arrived. He is very good. He was in the house before I even got my binoculars out of the case."

"How long was he inside?"

"About an hour and a half, and he was very lucky he didn't get caught."

"Why is that?" The former KGB officer perked up.

"Because, after he left the house, Smith and her boyfriend drove up."

"How soon afterwards?"

"Minutes."

"Interesting. How did Viñals appear when he left?"

"What do you mean?"

"Describe how he left," Volkova instructed.

Katenka paused. "I would say that when he arrived, he acted deliberately and when he left he acted hurriedly."

"Very good observation, my star pupil. Was there anyone in the house with him?"

"I wouldn't know. Smith's car and pick-up were there as you said they would be but no other cars. I spotted Viñals a few times through the windows but no one else."

"How many times did you see him in the house?" he asked.

"I saw him twice at the main window on the second floor and a few times through the first floor windows."

"What was he doing when you saw him?"

"Downstairs, I saw him moving around like he was checking out the house and upstairs - I think he was checking the street."

"That's it?"

"I believe so." She paused. "Pavel, don't you think this was a risky move for him to be in the house?"

"It was not supposed to be a high risk venture. I was led to believe that your old lover's sister was out of state."

"Pavel, love had nothing to do with it. Do I need to remind you of that again, tonight?"

The Russian enjoyed her aggressiveness. "Yes, I would like to be reminded. Unfortunately, I need for you to watch the house a little longer."

"But Pavel, I need to eat and wash up," she pleaded in her way that Volkova found hard to deny.

"Do what you must, then get back into position. I need the house watched. I will probably have to confront her myself but the boyfriend, or whoever he is, presents a wildcard factor. I have to call my friend now. Call me later when you're set up again. *Dosvedanya.*"

He knew Viñals had been absent from field duty for quite some time and so he had placed Katenka in a position to help him if needed. But the close call was too much of a coincidence and Pavel Volkova did not believe in coincidences. Obviously, Viñals relied on his own intelligence sources that placed Smith in Georgia or else he would not have broken into her house; the Cuban would have to explain himself later.

Pavel Volkova walked towards his car and the next rendezvous with Raoul Viñals.

Chapter 33

Sunday, early evening
Laura's home

"The report will be ready in five days," rookie cop Mila Alicea told Laura turning to and walking back to her patrol car.

Laura watched the police officer as she took off her Smokey the Bear hat and settle into the patrol car. Laura closed the front door and went back into the kitchen where Dan had remained.

"She said that she thought someone may have been knocking on the window and it just broke or perhaps it was a burglar that got spooked by something. She suggested that I ask my neighbors if they saw anything suspicious over the weekend. Aren't detectives supposed to do that?"

"There was nothing stolen so they're not going to waste time investigating a broken window. Besides, Leonard will be here soon: maybe I can ask him to canvas the block," Dan said, then let out a long loud yawn.

Laura went into the living and brought her mother's metal storage box into the dining room and placed it on a chair. She took out all the contents except Ken's materials and laid them across the table.

Dan came in and started perusing some of the old papers.

"He doesn't know we went to Tennessee. What do you think I should tell him?"

Dan walked around the table, looked in the box and picked out the photographs. "Tell him we went to Tennessee and this is all you could find," he said, motioning over the table. "Unless you're ready for prime time." he turned Katenka's picture towards Laura.

The door bell rang. Laura looked over at Dan, but he offered no further advice. She walked around to where he was standing and took her brother's papers and photos but said nothing. She went to the front door through the kitchen, placing her burden in the utensil drawer.

Laura let the detective in and invited him into the living room. Dan met them in the hallway and introduced himself again - committed to being courteous.

"I remember," Leonard said.

The detective was wearing a camel hair sport jacket with maroon pants, tan shirt and regimental tie that were all coordinated. His shield was prominently displayed on his belt but his holstered Glock was hidden. Dan thought he looked a little too good and felt the effort was for Laura. No wedding band, he noticed.

"I saw a cop," Leonard said.

"She was here for that," Laura said pointing back to the missing window and telling the detective what had happened.

Leonard went back towards the front door, inspected the area and then followed Laura into the living room. "I have some information to give you concerning what happened last Friday that you may find… disturbing." He pulled out his notes as Laura motioned him towards the couch. The detective sat down with Laura beside him: Dan moved the recliner so he could face them.

"I think I gave you most of the preliminary information that we had as of Saturday. The man who approached you was Vasily Bera, an economics professor at the university."

"Right," Laura confirmed. "You said that he had a picture of me in the car and that he may have been…" she looked at Dan.

Dan pushed the recliner back. "Connected," he finished.

"Dan had some questions about the photograph of me and if there were any fingerprints on the gun," Laura said.

"What questions do you have about the photograph?" Leonard asked looking over at Dan who was smooshing up a pillow trying to get a good fit behind his head.

"Do you know where it was taken?"

"No, but that's a good question," Leonard conceded.

"Thank you."

"We believe it was taken at a distance but it was enhanced and cropped to show only your face," Leonard said, looking back at Laura.

"What was I wearing?"

"Don't know. It was cropped pretty tight."

"How was my hair?" Laura asked.

"You were wearing it up."

"Then I must have been at work. I always wear it up for work but if I'm outside, I wear a cover…a hat, it's my uniform."

"What about on the way to or from work?" Leonard asked.

Laura thought for a moment. "When I stop for gas, I might run into the store for a bottled water without wearing my hat."

"Well, I'm not sure that it's important to know where the photograph was taken. What is important is that someone felt it necessary to take a photograph for identification purposes.

"That makes sense," Dan interjected. "Were there any prints on the gun?"

"No," Leonard replied.

"None at all or none you could use?" Dan raised his head from the pillow for the answer.

Detective Leonard looked down at his notes then at Laura. "The gun was clean. No prints anywhere on the gun or on the cartridges in the cylinder."

"What does that mean?" Laura asked.

After a moment, the detective turned towards Dan. "That means it probably wasn't a suicide," Dan answered.

"But there was no one else around," she said.

"We don't know that," Dan said, resting back again and closing his eyes. "After I chased him off, several minutes passed before we heard the gunshot. Then, I crept up to the edge of the building and looked around before spotting the body. I got to the body first before people started coming out from the restaurant."

Leonard wrote down what Dan was telling him.

"Do you know anything more about the professor?" Dan asked.

"I met with Special Agent Dennis Rowles who is with the FBI. It appears that the professor had his hand in a lot of nefarious matters. Most of his family is still in Russia, although he had a wife who lived here for a while. He was known as quite the lady's man at one time and had the moniker 'The Caspian Charmer' among some of his colleagues. Hard to believe that with the way he looked last Friday. Anyway, about seven years ago, he started a consulting business and acted as an interface for American companies based in Florida and the southeast which wanted to do business in the former Soviet Union. According to Special Agent Rowles, his bank accounts showed a lot of transactions although he could not identify a single customer that ever called Bera's office. Apparently, his company was a shell and used to launder money from the Russian mafia in Brooklyn but beginning to get a big foothold in Florida.

"The Gainesville PD told me that they busted some local gambling operations, mostly college football and basketball games, where his name came up but nobody could finger him directly."

"How in the world can I be involved with this man?" Laura asked.

"That's why I make the big civil service bucks," the detective replied.

"When did the professor come to the United States?" Dan asked.

"His passport states 1993."

"Anytime before?"

"Not that we know about."

Laura said. "My brother died in 1986, seven years before the professor even came here. Why do *you* think he was interested in Kenneth?"

Dan caught Laura's attention and showed with his expression that he was proud of her question that targeted the answer they had been seeking.

Detective Leonard flipped his notepad closed and leaned back on the couch. "That's the sixty four thousand dollar question, isn't it? I have two working theories, however. The first one is a simple case of mistaken identity. But didn't you tell me over the phone that Bera called you by name?"

"I did tell you that. I believe he did call me by name. He said, 'Are you Laura Smith?'"

"Did he mention your brother by name?"

Laura gazed at the detective for a moment, contorted her face briefly in thought and said, "No, he asked about my brother's papers but said 'brother' not 'Ken'."

"It could be a case of mistaken identity, but not likely. My other theory is that Vasily Bera was put up to approaching you by someone else. He was certainly blackmailable. For some reason, probably because he failed to get what he was after, he was killed to shut him up."

Dan saw Laura's face turn white as she absorbed the detective's theory and said, "Detective Leonard, Laura and I just came back from her hometown in Tennessee."

"Really?"

"Yeah, we just got back a few hours ago. Everything she has left of her family that has any possible relevance is over in those boxes by the stairs and on her dining room table," Dan said pointing out the boxes.

"I wanted to know if there was something in my brother's past that could help your investigation and ease my mind about what happened on Friday," Laura said, getting up and opening the boxes for the detective. She explained about her brother's death and her mother's death and then the house burning down when she was at her first duty assignment in Alaska. Leonard went through some of the belongings, then followed Laura into the dining room and looked at the papers she had spread out.

"Is there anything else in storage?"

"Nothing that pertains to my brother," she answered truthfully and then described what was left at the barn. Leonard asked for the mailing address and phone number for the Kurke's and Laura gave it to him.

"Detective, have you worked any theories about any relationship between Ken's former employment and the Russian professor?" Dan asked.

"I know that Ken Smith worked at one of the assembly plants for the space shuttle, but he was only there for about a year before he died. I did find it curious that he died in an explosion. However, I called the local police over the weekend and this morning I spoke with Greg Zimmerman, who handled the case. He's retired now but remembered that it was a propane tank leak and no foul play was evidenced. Is there anything you can think of that might help?"

Laura looked at Dan and then towards the kitchen but Dan's grimace made her reconsider. She said instead, "This surprised me." Laura picked up the framed photograph of Katenka. "I think this was his girlfriend but I know very little about her. She didn't come to the funeral and Ken never brought her home to meet us. I think she might be Russian."

Leonard studied the picture. "She's quite a looker. Why do you think she might be Russian?"

"After Ken died, I met several of his co-workers who brought us his stuff from work. I think one of them made a comment about her. I didn't pay much attention at the time since I was very upset and my mother was inconsolable. But, I've been thinking about it and I believe that one of Ken's co-worker said she may have been a Russian exchange student; he thought maybe her visa had expired and she went back to Russia - actually, he said 'Soviet Union'."

"Do you know the name of the man who told you this?"

"He introduced himself at the time, but I don't remember," Laura fibbed some more.

"Do you remember the girlfriend's name?"

Dan interjected just as Laura was about to speak, "Laura said that she remembered writing the name down back then because she wanted to get in touch with her. She believes it may be in one of those boxes. We can get the name to you if she finds it."

"Okay," Leonard said, turning to look at Laura, who smiled and nodded her head in concurrence. "Can I have this picture for a few days?" he asked.

"Sure. I would like it back, though," Laura said.

"Absolutely. I want to run it through our computer to see if it matches anyone in the data base. It probably won't, though, since our d-base is only about five years old. I'm sure she doesn't look the same and if she is Russian, she probably weighs in at over three hundred pounds by now," Leonard chuckled.

"Something else you should know," Leonard said, changing the mood. "The professor's house caught fire on Sunday and burned to the ground. I didn't find out until this morning."

"Was it arson?" Dan asked.

"Probably. I spoke with the arson investigator and he ruled it a suspicious fire. The investigator was going back to the house today. The fire appears to have started in the home office and spread quickly from there. I'm going to Gainesville tomorrow to speak with him and also to find out anything else I can on Bera."

"Did he live alone?" Laura asked.

"We think so."

"I think your second theory is looking more probable," Dan said.

"What should I do?" Laura asked.

"An excellent question but…I don't have an answer for you." Detective Leonard stared at the floor. "It certainly appears that someone today is very interested in your brother, who died over seventeen years ago. And whoever is interested in your brother blackmailed or otherwise motivated Bera for him to find out what you might know or what you might possess. When Bera failed, largely thanks to Mr. Gill, here, the person who blackmailed the professor killed him and then burned his house down presuming maybe there was some evidence linking the killer to Bera. So, I would say that someone very dangerous is still interested in what you know or what you possess concerning your brother."

"And?" Laura asked.

"And, I'm a detective, not a bodyguard and you don't live or work in my jurisdiction. Do you own a gun?"

"Yes, I have my father's old revolver upstairs somewhere."

"Then I would keep it handy."

"I don't even have bullets for it."

"Buy some." Leonard started walking towards the front door. "How long will you be in town?" he asked Dan.

"I fly back home on Sunday."

"Where are you staying until then?"

Laura opened the door, pausing until everyone felt sufficiently uncomfortable, she offered, "With me."

Leonard shook hands and said he would be in touch after his visit to Gainesville. Laura thanked him and Dan wryly observed as she gave him a brief embrace.

"I never got hugged when I was a cop," Dan said after she closed the door.

"You're leaving Sunday and I have a lunatic stalking me. I need him to watch my six." She said

"Believe me…he's well aware of your six."

"Let's go," she said stepping over to the foyer table and tossing Dan his car keys.

"Where are we going?"

"To buy bullets."

Chapter 34

Sunday, early evening
Merritt Island, Florida

Raoul Viñals turned into the parking lot of a Thai restaurant near Merritt's Island but waited several minutes before walking in. He reflected on what the Russian had told him just an hour before: that he was appreciative of Viñals's effort but that what was pilfered from the sergeant's home was of dubious value. He had told the Cuban to be ready to assist again if need be. Volkova had added that he might only need Viñals for the next few days or so and then they could both go back into anonymity. The debriefing had been a little too thorough, Viñals thought. The Russian had been particularly interested in whether he had used his cell phone in Smith's house. Viñals had explained that he had just called his office to check on things. He'd offered the cell phone for inspection. Having known what to expect, he had cleared his call log and he had, in fact, called his office once out of the house.

Viñals was also troubled by the questions concerning whether or not he had seen Laura Smith. He had replied that he had not, but Volkova insistently asked a series of questions concerning why he had decided to leave the house when he did. Viñals had told Volkova that he assumed Smith was in Georgia and so he had plenty of time; he had not planned on leaving at any particular time. He simply said that he had left when he finished. The Cuban surmised that Volkova had knowledge of a close call and he was sending a message to him that he was being watched.

Inside the restaurant, the dim lighting accented by dust covered sconces that projected a yellowish light upward caused the Cuban to wait near the entrance for his eyes to adjust. He stood under a bamboo arch decorated with artificial ivy. As his vision improved, he saw that that a plastic jungle of potted plants shielded him from the table area. The reception counter was empty but a little Vietnamese woman approached him.

"You order take out?" The hostess/waitress asked.

"No, I'm supposed to meet a friend here."

"Oh, FBI man. He wait for you back there." She led him to Rowles's table near the kitchen door that was partly hidden by a rice paper room divider decorated with panda bears.

Rowles was sipping clear broth and Viñals saw that he was almost finished with a bottle of Thai beer. The woman gave Viñals a menu but he handed it back to her.

"One of those beers and some very hot pad Thai."

"Very hot," she said, nodding and heading off towards the kitchen.

"She called you 'FBI man'," Viñals said dryly.

"She spotted my badge."

"Why didn't you say you were with INS or something?"

Rowles finished off his beer. "My dad fought in the Pacific during World War II, my uncle was in Korea and I was in on the tail end of Vietnam. You can't pull the wool over these guys."

"You realize you just commingled about a half dozen Asian cultures," the Cuban noted.

"Don't worry, we've never been here before and we'll never be back. As long as we weren't followed, then it doesn't matter what mama san knows."

The woman came back just as Rowles was referring to her as mama san and she smiled broadly; Rowles gave her his empty bottle and ordered another beer in Vietnamese. They waited until she brought the beer before talking.

"Why are we here, bro? I told you that Volkova may be watching me," Viñals said.

"I'll take my chances."

"No, you're taking *my* chances. Why was I almost busted in the house?"

"Because I didn't tell you that she and her boyfriend were on the way back to Florida."

"And, why didn't you tell me that?"

"Because you didn't have a need to know; because I didn't want that information passed on to Volkova and because I didn't think you would be robbing her house."

"I didn't rob her house."

"Did you take anything?"

Viñals let the question hang as he took a bite of his rice noodles. "I took some bullshit Christmas cards and pictures."

"Then you robbed her." Rowles started in on his dinner. "Why did you take Christmas cards?"

In between visits from the hostess/waitress, Viñals explained what Volkova wanted and how he had broken into the house. He reported he had brought the Russian the only articles that he could find that related to the air force sergeant's brother.

"He knows she's back at home."

"How does he know that?" the special agent asked.

"Because it was obvious from his debriefing that I barely got out in time. Either he was following me or someone else was. He wanted to let me know that. Was all the information you gave me about her credit cards totally made up?"

"What I gave you was accurate." He looked at Viñals, who knew that he had been given some, but certainly not all, of the information Rowles had about Laura Smith's movements. He continued, "What else does Pavel Volkova want from you?"

Viñals washed down the spicy noodles with his beer and waited for his mouth to cool down. "He wants me on stand-by for the next few days."

"What a coincidence: so do I."

"You know, I do have a business to take care of."

"So do I, it's called the United States of America."

"You do?" the Cuban asked sardonically.

"What does that mean?'

"That means that I think you're flying totally solo and I'm flying blind."

"I might be flying solo but you're on instruments."

"What are you doing, Denny? You know how dangerous Volkova is."

"You know how dangerous I am. I'm going to nail that sick Russian bastard."

Viñals leaned forward, closing the distance between them across the small table. "Nail him as in bring him to trial following a lawful arrest?"

The special agent considered the question, not knowing the answer himself. "Maybe. I need to talk to Smith and see if she'll help me."

"And if she doesn't?"

"Then you'll arrange a meeting between me and Volkova."

"You mean I'll arrange an ambush."

"That's right."

Viñals took a break from eating to let his mouth cool. He watched Rowles expertly use his chopsticks and said, "You know, it would be even money on who is ambushing whom."

Rowles acknowledged that proposition with a wink. "Where does Volkova go from here?"

"I'm not sure. What are you thinking?"

The FBI special agent settled back, looking upward, and watching the dust covered ceiling fan slowly revolve. He spoke quietly after some reflection. "He had Bera attempt to get information from her and that failed. He had you get information and that will prove inconsequential. At some point, he has to make a run at her again if he is trying to save his own skin as you have theorized. What's puzzling me is that you say he is in fear that his involvement with her brother will be discovered. Yet no one else seems to be interested in Sergeant Smith and she obviously doesn't have a clue about what happened so long ago. There has to be some other motive driving the train, here. I don't think Volkova is in danger from anybody - I think he is warped enough to just be looking for souvenirs. But it is going to end one way or the other…very soon. The next time Volkova meets you, I'll pick him up. If he resists, I'll kill him. If he is dead or exposed for what he did, then Sergeant Smith should no longer be at risk by Volkova."

"Her house may be under surveillance by him."

"That's okay: I'm coordinating with Detective Leonard who is working the Bera case. Bera had ties to matters that the bureau is interested in. It would not be suspicious for me to visit her."

Mama san brought another beer for Viñals and laughed at him for not being able to take the heat. He fanned his mouth for a few seconds for her amusement.

Denny Rowles watched Viñals entertain mama san and then commented when she moved off, "You're living the Life of Riley, my friend. You're an American citizen, an entrepreneur, set up by the U.S. government, making good bucks. You've banged every secretary and receptionist who ever worked for you, none of whom have ever filed a sexual harassment claim, and, every so often, you get to play a secret agent. What else were you going to do today?"

For the first time since leaving the Orlando area, Viñals thought of Ana Marie waiting for him, wearing her push up bra and thong underwear under her business suit. He just shook his head as he imagined the missed opportunity.

Rowles instructed Viñals to stay available and explained that he was heading over to Smith's house. The special agent let the Cuban leave first and watched from behind the front blinds to see if anyone followed Viñals out of the driveway: satisfied that it was clear, he left.

Chapter 35

Sunday night
Laura's home

Dan wanted to make love to Laura again and thought of all the different pleasurable possibilities that might unfold over the next several days. He assumed she was interested as well but tried never to jump to any conclusions when women were involved. By the time they arrived back at her house from Wal-Mart, however, they were so exhausted that sleep came to them during the six o'clock local news.

Neither one heard the doorbell nor the knock on the door. Finally, Laura jumped to her feet when she heard someone yelling through the missing window by the front door. She turned to wake up Dan but he was already shooting upwards. Laura waited for Dan to awaken fully and then they walked to the door together.

"Who is it?" she yelled from the hallway.

"FBI. My name is Special Agent Dennis Rowles."

It was dark outside but her motion detector light was on and the man, his badge and identification were clearly visible. She looked over at Dan who shrugged his shoulders and followed her to the door.

"Can I help you?" Laura opened the door, standing firmly in the entrance way, on alert since Detective Leonard's visit and thinking of the bag of bullets left on her kitchen table. She was hesitant about letting a stranger into her house, even one flashing a federal badge.

"I'm investigating an incident that occurred this past Saturday that you were involved in concerning a man named Vasily Bera."

"I was there, too," Dan said, moving next to Laura.

"Right, Detective Leonard told me. You're Mr. Gill?"

"Uh huh. Why are the feds involved with a local matter?" Dan asked.

"Because the FBI was monitoring some of Mr. Bera's activities and I would like to discuss the incident with the only two eyewitnesses who last saw him alive."

Laura motioned for Special Agent Rowles to enter and she and Dan stepped aside. "We are really tired Agent..."

"Rowles."

"Agent Rowles, couldn't you call me first. I already met with Detective Leonard this afternoon and with the local police because of that." She pointed to the missing window but didn't offer any details.

"We are following many aspects of this incident and I happened to be in the area. If this is terribly inconvenient, then I can come back." Rowles had no concern of having to oblige such a request because he knew that no one in his twenty plus year career had ever asked him to leave their home once they invited him in.

"It's like *deju vu* all over again," Dan uttered, sitting down.

"Pardon me?" Rowles asked.

"Yogi Bera...nothing, we just went through all of this a few hours ago."

"Well, Detective Leonard and I are investigating different aspects of this case. He is concerned about the circumstances of Vasily Bera's death and I am concerned about his goings-on when he was alive. Chiefly, I want to know why he sought you out on Saturday." He sat back and waited for an answer that didn't come.

Finally Dan said, "It seems that Detective Leonard was concerned about that, as well." Between Dan and Laura, they told the FBI special agent the same story given to Corey Leonard. Laura thought of offering to make a pot of coffee but reconsidered; she just wanted the interview to end and to go back to sleep. She had to be awake at oh five hundred and she started calculating how little sleep she had had since Saturday morning.

"I assume that Detective Leonard told you that Vasily Bera was involved with the Russian immigrant mafia."

"He did. But maybe you can tell me what that has to do with me... or my brother." Laura asked.

"Well, I believe it has to do with your brother and what you may know of your brother's activities."

Dan perked up, leaned forward and said before Laura could respond. "Agent Rowles, with all due respect, Laura and I are both a little tired of this and perhaps it's time that you give us some information. As you must know, we only met last week. Neither one of us knows who Professor Bera is…or was. Laura's brother died a long time ago, well before the fall of the Soviet Union and well before Russian immigrants came to our shores in large numbers. So, we find it highly unlikely that there is any link to Kenneth Smith and the Russian mob. In any event, Laura and I went back to her hometown in Tennessee over the weekend and gathered up every item, relevant or not, that belonged to her brother and that has been in storage since 1986. We have shared that information with Detective Leonard. Now, we are a little tired of hearing about the Russian mob. For Christ's sake, we just came back from buying ammunition so Laura can protect herself and we want the truth."

Rowles sat back absorbing Dan's tirade and looked around the room. "When was your window broken?" he finally said changing the subject to let the tension subside.

"I don't know," Laura answered. "We discovered it this afternoon when we got back from Tennessee. I called the police and they took a report. I checked the house and nothing is missing. The cop didn't think much of it."

"Ever been broken into before?"

"No. Neither have any of my neighbors."

"Well, the timing is certainly suspicious." Rowles gave no indication that he was recently eating Thai noodles and drinking Tiger beer with Laura's purloiner.

"Look," Rowles said, "I do have information to share with you. If it is true, then your brother was involved in activities that were… treacherous. I need to know what you might know because others are certainly after the same information. However, my investigation comes from sources that are highly classified and I must protect those sources. Therefore, if I share information with you…and you Dan…it must remain highly classified. You can't tell anyone, even Detective Leonard, for now. Laura, you are on active duty and can appreciate the nature of a secret. Dan, I know you are retired army, so I know the same goes for you as well."

"Well, before you share state secrets with us, I need to hit the head," Dan replied.

"Me, too," Laura said and added, "Why don't we move into the kitchen and I'll make some coffee." She decided that sleep didn't matter.

Rowles stood up and noted that Dan went upstairs while Laura used the bathroom off the kitchen. No opportunity for getting stories together. The special agent perused the contents spread out on the table while he waited. Dan joined Rowles at the dining room table while Laura worked in the kitchen.

"This is what we brought back; there are some more boxes over by the stairs and some belongings left in Tennessee. Whatever we found that concerned Ken, we brought here."

Special Agent Rowles picked up various papers and looked into the boxes by the staircase while Dan went into the kitchen. Laura looked at him then at the drawer containing her brother's belongings, but Dan quickly shook his head no and softly mouthed *not yet*.

"Coffee is on," Laura said.

Rowles walked into the kitchen. "I guess the best place to start is at the beginning."

The special agent told Laura and Dan about his prior posting as a counter-intelligence agent within the bureau and his old partner's hunt for the campus bear. He told them about KGB Officer Pavel Volkova and his recruitment of university students to deliver secrets that his country wanted and also told of his Central and South American days serving the Soviet Union's mission to bolster pro-communist regimes and foster pro-communist insurgents.

The coffee machine's ready light popped on and Laura brought the carafe over to the kitchen table along with some mugs, cream and sugar. They all sat down and fixed their own cups.

"Is Pavel Volkova in the Russian mob now?" Dan asked.

"That, I don't know. But I do know that..." He paused for effect to let them know that this was the big secret. "Pavel Volkova put

Vasily Bera up to approaching you last Friday and that Bera is certainly connected to the Russian mafia."

"Maybe a mutual mob connection is how Volkova found Bera to use as a...tool, but how is her brother involved?" Dan asked.

"I believe it goes back to Volkova's campus bear days. I believe that your brother was one of his recruits."

Laura shook her head and glanced at Dan who gave her a *keep mum* grimace. Laura said, "You said that Volkova was primarily interested in pharmaceutical research. My brother had nothing to do with that. You know his background."

"That's true. But, Kenneth may have been...what we call...a target of opportunity. Perhaps someone who worked with Volkova came across this bright young rocket scientist who was well placed in the industry and had a history of radical behavior."

"Radical behavior?" Laura responded with shock; only Dan knew what a good actress she had become.

"Of course, I have no evidence of that. Perhaps he belonged to some leftist organizations or had friends that leaned that way. It could be that he was blackmailed for some reason we will never know. I did uncover that Ken's student loans were paid in full shortly after graduation from grad school. He would not have been able to achieve that on his earnings. Do you know if he came into some money around that time? Maybe a family member passed away and you and Ken were in the will?"

"No. My mom had equity in the house, but he died before I sold off the property; my mother died in 1986 and I was the executrix of her estate. None of her money went to Ken before he died. At least I didn't see any evidence of that from her accounts."

"Well, you see why the bells and whistles are going off. Unfortunately, your brother's death was a long time ago. Detective Leonard told me that he spoke with the arson investigator in Utah when your brother died. Among the other facts of the case, the investigator also noted that your brother was quite a loner."

"I guess that's true," Laura agreed.

"That also fits the profile of someone who might betray their country. I am trying to connect the dots, here. I have a known former soviet agent who recruited university students and is now seeking information about your brother. I also know that Ken came into quite a bit of money before his death and that he was a loner."

Rowles summary hung in the air. Dan said, after taking a sip from his mug, "He wasn't exactly a loner."

"What does that mean?"

Laura took over. "We think he may have had a Russian girlfriend." She then went on to tell Rowles about the photograph that she had given to Detective Leonard.

"That's another dot to connect," Rowles replied making a note.

Dan watched the special agent focus on his writing, then glanced at Laura who remained expressionless. "Why now? What is the pattern here? Why would Volkova care now about what Laura might know? Obviously, she doesn't know anything or, if she did, she has kept silent about it." He had some more questions but Rowles began to answer.

"The pattern indicates that he is trying to sterilize his past. From our campus bear investigations, we never found any proof. Special Agent Garcia actually stumbled upon Volkova when he realized that all of the victims became close friends, within months of their deaths, with a man who was always described the same way by friends and associates of the victim. Maybe some proof was left behind that Volkova wants to keep for himself or destroy."

"Why now?" Laura asked.

"Maybe this has been the first opportunity to get back into the United States, despite the fact that we let illegals and terrorists cross our borders everyday." Rowles frowned.

"Why risk all of this exposure when no evidence has ever surfaced since Ken's death? Why not let sleeping dogs lie?" Dan asked.

"That . . .is a question I find difficult as well."

"You must have a theory."

"I have a very loose theory. I believe that Volkova is now being blackmailed and wants to destroy any evidence that there might be."

"Who would want to blackmail him?" Laura asked.

"Maybe a reformer, someone who wants to bring Pavel Volkova to trial for their own reasons. Perhaps a pro-American politician over there who wants to show how evil their country's past was and that they are truly changed. For example, if a former soviet official offered proof about what happened to our MIAs during the Korean War and the

Vietnam War I think he or she would be warmly received in America. That person would become famous and could write their own check - book deal, movie deal, lecture circuit, you name it. Same thing goes for anyone who could offer proof that the former soviet government tried to sabotage our space program. Alternatively, perhaps the Russian mafia wants the information to blackmail its own government. Congress may not want to expand business relations with Russia or let it into NATO so quickly if there's proof that they're still hiding things from us."

They all finished their coffee but only Rowles helped himself to a refill. Dan got up and walked over to the kitchen drawer where Laura had stashed Ken's notebook and leaned back against it. He said, "Agent Rowles, assuming that there is a connection between Ken Smith and Pavel Volkova, how does that rise to the level of affecting relations between the United States and Russian now? I think if Americans knew about the drug cases, they would care less. We both spied on each other and tried to rip off what we could. All is fair in love and cold war, right?"

"Your cynicism is probably correct. But . . " Rowles trailed off and warmed his hands around his mug.

"But what?" Laura asked.

"I think the ultimate dot that will be connected is that your brother, through Volkova pulling the strings, destroyed the space shuttle Challenger."

There it was, hanging out there as heavy as the aroma of the freshly brewed French Roast. What Laura feared to be the truth was expressed by an FBI agent sipping his drink as casually as an office worker on a ten minute break.

"I think Americans might get pissed off about that," Rowles continued. "Pissed off at the Russians for what they did; pissed off at the Russians for covering it up all of these years; pissed off at our own government for letting it happen and pissed off at our own government for either covering it up or being too inept to discover what had happened. In any event, someone may be well placed to be handsomely rewarded for keeping Americans from becoming so pissed off."

"You think my brother had something to do with the Challenger disaster?"

"Yes. His job certainly gave him the opportunity and the Volkova connection provides a possible motive."

"My brother was an all American guy," Laura protested, wishing it were true.

"So was Alger Hiss," Rowles responded quickly.

"Okay," Dan cut in, "Laura was a few years behind her brother and wasn't close to him at all once he left home. As much as you love your brother," he spoke to her directly, "you didn't know him very well. So, let's just keep all possibilities on the table.

"Agent Rowles, like I've said before, Laura and I just met but it seems much longer…"

"Thanks a lot!" Laura interjected.

"What I meant was . . .since the shooting, we have lived this event a thousand times over. Laura just doesn't know anything that will help you. What is she supposed to do? Leonard tells her to arm herself and you are saying that a former KGB officer is here illegally and may soon be in contact with her. Why aren't you doing something to catch Volkova or to protect Laura?"

"First of all, I'm here." Rowles didn't say it was unofficially. "Unfortunately, most of our resources are focused on fighting terrorism and there's insufficient evidence to link Volkova to your brother and Challenger. The bureau doesn't have the means to protect you. However, I am working on getting Volkova arrested. I second Detective Leonard's advice that you stay armed. Keep your gun with you at all times. Whether its registered or not, if you have to use it, I'll get you out of any trouble.

"It would help her accuracy if you told her what Volkova looks like," Dan suggested.

Rowles stated that it didn't matter since the Russian was adept at changing his looks but gave an overall description of size. He added, "he speaks perfect English. Be on guard. I want to get this son of a bitch real soon. If I find out where he is I will call you. I'll call Detective Leonard later because I want to see the photograph of the girlfriend and run it through the bureau's counter-intelligence files. Here's my card."

Special Agent Rowles's impression from the interview was that Laura Smith would help him get the Russian. He needed to wait for Volkova's next communication to Viñals and then he could lay the ground work. He thought of going on the record by letting the Miami office know what he was up to. But he knew what had happened to Garcia when he had tried to pursue what he knew. There was insufficient evidence and so why go public with a story about soviet agents working American schools and whacking college kids; they had made Special Agent Garcia look like a fool for his efforts - a conspiracy nut. What would the bosses think if the space shuttle were mentioned, he ruminated, may as well mention the Kennedy assassination while I'm at it - he decided to keep the investigation…*unofficial.* Rowles pulled out his card and wrote on the back. "That's my personal cell phone number. I answer it twenty-four hours a day." He handed it to Laura and got up, thanking her for the information and coffee.

Laura walked him to the door and gave him her contact numbers by the door.

"When are you going to fix this?" Rowles asked pointing to the missing window.

"I was going to put plastic wrap over it tonight then go to the hardware store tomorrow," Dan replied.

"Good. I'll call you if anything comes up." Rowles said and walked down the driveway.

Laura watched the special agent get into his car and drive off. Dan returned to the front door with plastic wrap, scissors and tape from the kitchen. She watched him make the temporary repairs.

"Explain to me why we didn't tell the FBI special agent everything we know," she demanded.

"You can call him back right now if you want," Dan said, taking measurements of the window frame.

"My life is in danger and the FBI knows that my brother probably blew up the space shuttle. Why should I keep this secret now?"

"For the same reasons you had before. Your life will be forever changed by this revelation. Do you want that?"

"Not really," she concluded with a sigh and sat down on the hallway floor, leaning her back against the door.

"Rowles sounds like he has a handle on things. If the FBI catches Volkova, they'll try him on those college cases and your brother's involvement may never come up." Dan cut out a rectangle from the plastic wrap, but it caught up on his fingers and clung to itself ruining his first attempt; following a flurry of curses he started over again. "Besides, if you gave Rowles what you have, how would that change anything for you? They still don't have the manpower to protect you. We would still be here right now trying to fix this damn window."

"That's easy for you to say. You're going home and away from here and I have a Russian mad man stalking me. What do you suggest I do?"

Dan finished taping the plastic and checked it over.

"According to Rowles, I suppose that even if Volkova is arrested, you will always be on someone's list to see if you have any information concerning your brother if the FBI theory is accurate. I guess I would want to know if your brother really could have damaged the shuttle from the evidence we have in the kitchen."

"What are you getting at?"

"Maybe we should find out from an expert whether or not your brother really could have sabotaged the shuttle. If he really could have and you believe that he is responsible, then maybe you want to continue to sit on the evidence, or destroy it or do whatever you want with it knowing that your life will be forever changed by its release. The choice is yours.

"On the other hand, if your brother was not in a position to sabotage the shuttle…maybe he thought he was but in reality he couldn't. Perhaps he thought more of his abilities than he should have. Then, it might make it easier for you to hand over what you have. You will know that your brother may have been a traitor…may have been a loser…may have been a total nut job…"

"I get the point."

"But he wasn't responsible for killing seven astronauts and destroying Challenger. Let me bring what we have down to Captain Dave. I'm sure he could give us a fairly accurate and honest opinion."

"When?"

"I'll leave in the morning. Wake me up early with you."

"I'm going, too."

"What about your inspection?"

"I'll call Ben tonight and ask for emergency leave. He can't say no." She smiled.

Dan returned to the kitchen to place his repair tools back in the drawers where he had found them while Laura went upstairs to use the phone. He wondered if Ben would replace him as her protector once he boarded his Jersey bound jet. He realized that he was quite jealous at the thought.

Chapter 36

Monday, early morning, January 20. 2003
Outside of Laura's home

Katenka Tiverzin returned to her parking spot and barely got comfortable before Special Agent Dennis Rowles walked up to Laura Smith's front door. She called Volkova to give him the update and reported that the black Ford had U.S. Government tags and that Rowles had flashed some kind of identification for Smith when she opened the door. Pavel Volkova knew it wouldn't be too long before the feds were involved, but he was hoping for more time. He planned on a little more breathing room, considering that the federal law enforcement agencies were busy harassing eighty year old women boarding airplanes and chasing down bad information from Guantanamo.

The former dancer kept herself occupied listening to Faulkner on tape and doing isometric stretches within the confines of the minivan. Dutifully, she took several pictures of Rowles when he left about an hour later including a straight-on face shot hoping that the ambient street light was sufficient. Katenka waited for Rowles to drive off and then followed suit to attend to some personal business: Volkova told her to use the bathroom, get something to eat and begged her to return to her surveillance for the night. Just one more night, he promised. The former KGB officer said that he would take over and tail them in the morning and that she could then go back to the motel room that he had rented nearby and take a well deserved sleep on a comfortable mattress.

Volkova wanted to know when Smith's pesky boyfriend would be leaving. He assumed that they would be together constantly while he was in town. Since Dan Gill had a rental car, Laura Smith probably would not drive him to the airport. The Russian was looking to confront her as soon as Gill left alone, with luggage, in his Mustang. Even if Laura Smith were juggling boyfriends, there would have to be some down time when Gill went home, unless she was as horny as Katenka. In any event, he needed to find out what she might know within the next two days. He had promised his new friends that there was, in fact, a smoking gun and he had also promised them a timetable for delivery. After all, they had their schedule to keep, too.

After driving back to Laura's neighborhood, she found the same parking space and pulled over. Knowing that Laura was in the military and would probably rise early, Katenka set the alarm on her cell phone for six in the morning. It would still be dark but not for much longer at that hour. Despite not drinking anything the night before, Katenka's bladder woke her up at five o'clock. She saw that the lights were on in the Smith house, the front door was open and the trunk to the convertible was up. *"Shit"* she muttered.

She called Volkova, certain that her call would wake him up but he sounded alert. He reminded her to follow only if the pair left together. They did and Katenka tagged behind the convertible from a safe distance of two blocks until it turned into Patrick Air Force Base where she couldn't gain access. She found a parking spot across from the base entrance; she was sure that she would spot the convertible on the way out but wasn't sure if there was any other way to leave the base. Volkova was not able to enlighten her when she called.

Smith was not in uniform so the Russian thought that their stay on base would be brief. There were much better places to go in Florida, he told Katenka. Twenty minutes later, she spotted the convertible leaving the base and head south. Katenka almost lost them as she caught two unsynchronized red lights but then to her relief spotted the car at a gas station.

Without any hesitation, she pulled in and stopped just across from her targets – the boyfriend was pumping gas and Smith was inside shopping. Not knowing how long the trip might be, Katenka decided to top off her tank. As Katenka slid her credit card through and selected the grade, she observed Gill. Although she had slept all night in her car, Katenka, wearing white stretch pants and a light, almost a summer weight, sweater that fit snugly around her athletic frame, made heads turn at the pumping plaza. With her hair pulled back in a pony tail and wrap around shades hiding some age she stood with her back to her target. Gill finished gassing up first. Katenka spotted him checking her out from the reflection of the minivan's tinted windows; she turned abruptly and smiled causing him to look away, embarrassed, just as his woman was returning to the car.

Katenka knew it wasn't smart to draw attention to herself, but there were times when she could not resist flirtation - being on the hunt again rekindled old emotions. Katenka Tiverzin enjoyed seducing men and admitted to Volkova that she enjoyed the best sex when there was danger present. She felt a thrill of victory when a young target selected by Volkova would fall in love with her. After she carnally satisfied these men by fulfilling their any want, they were ready to sell out their employers, their families, their country and even their souls - if she had that power. Perhaps she did, she had believed at times. Katenka thought that had Volkova chosen other methods for *this* mission, she would have had Gill in her power ready to betray his girlfriend or anything else, for that matter. Katenka Tiverzin knew that the moment she felt Dan's eyes on her ass.

Katenka followed the convertible south on the local roads, then over the Intracoastal Waterway westward until both vehicles turned southbound. She called Volkova.

"*Da.*"

"I am southbound on ninety-five. What next?"

"Stay on them. I will try to intercept you."

"Intercept me? Where?"

"I'm almost at Orlando. I had a hunch that the boyfriend would probably stay through the week and that they might go off somewhere. I wanted to be near an airport. There's a flight to Miami that I can be on in thirty minutes and I'll rent a car from there. I suspect they will enjoy the beaches in Dade or Broward County or head out toward the keys."

"I hope we can enjoy those same beaches ourselves."

"We will soon enjoy beaches elsewhere."

"That sounds very enchanting, if not mysterious. What beaches have you in mind?"

"None around here. I will call you from the airport. Please do not lose contact with Smith."

"I won't. I have good distance between us."

"Good. *Dosvedanya.*"

Volkova next called Viñals to make sure that he was already at the airport purchasing their tickets.

Chapter 37

Monday morning
Interstate 95

Laura checked the handgun again and placed it back into the glove compartment, shaking her head at the incredulous turn her life had taken. The revolver held six rounds of either .357 Magnum or .38 Special. Dan recommended that she buy thirty eight specials since there would be less of a kick when she unloaded on the Russian. He wanted as many rounds as possible to strike home. The revolver was an older model her father bought during the seventies when a rash of burglaries erupted in their part of town. As far as Laura knew, it was only used once when the old man had taken the family out behind the house and they all took turns shooting at soda cans on a mound of dirt. Mr. Smith instructed every one on how to use the revolver, feeling that the curiosity would be gone if he let the kids take some shots with it. Afterwards, he kept it in such a safe place it wasn't found until Laura did an inventory of the house after her mother's death. The break-ins apparently subsided and he kept the gun in an old dresser up in the attic, unloaded, with no ammunition anywhere in the house.

Laura remembered the recoil bringing the gun back to within inches of her face. Her dad had helped her fire the remaining shots in the cylinder and she had no desire to pick up a handgun again. In the air force, Laura qualified on her assigned weapon annually. Over the course of her career, she qualified on the M-16A1, M-16A2, Colt .45 caliber automatic and the M9 Beretta nine millimeter automatic. The latter she liked the best because it was very smooth to fire. The forty-five scared the hell out of her.

Dan watched her check the revolver again but didn't say anything. He knew she was careful even though he had to remind her that the only safety on that model was her trigger finger.

"When you were in with...Ben...I called Captain Dave. I told him we wanted to go out tonight for whatever was running."

"What did he say?"

"He thinks we're nuts, and so does Mrs. Harwood, for bolting like we did. I told them you had to get back to the base because of an emergency."

"A weather squadron emergency?" she laughed.

"They seemed to buy it."

"You still think it's odd that I call my commanding officer by his first name?" Laura asked.

"Not as odd as keeping a picture of the two of you in your living room."

"You noticed that, huh?"

"It's kind of hard to miss - it's set off like a shrine."

"It is not!" She slapped him on the right thigh. "It's one of many photographs that have special meaning for me."

"Do you ever have anyone over the house you work with? What do they say about you dating your CO?"

"I rarely have guests; when I do expect someone from work to come over I put the frame in the closet. And, we are not dating."

"The picture did look old. Good ole Ben didn't have any gray."

"The photo was taken at his cousin's wedding right before we both deployed for the Gulf War. At the time, he wasn't my commanding officer. I've known Ben since my first assignment in Alaska and we have served together off and on ever since."

"Isn't he married?"

"He's separated."

"Kids?"

"A boy and a girl. Sean is eight and Erin is six."

"Good Spanish names."

"His wife was a Murray."

"Why are they separated?"

"I don't know…but I suspect that his wife blames me."

Dan turned the radio off. "This I gotta hear."

Laura, uncomfortable with the conversation, turned the radio back on but then lowered the volume.

"Why do men always think that the woman they fall in love with has never been involved with a man before?"

"And we're talking about whom, now?" Dan asked.

"You…asshole."

"Asshole? What did I do?"

"You started this with your nasty tone when you said Ben's name."

"I would describe it as more of a probing tone. I'm just trying to figure out what the deal is with the two of you."

"There is no *deal* between the two of us…anymore."

"See!" Dan pointed at her like a prosecutor in a closing argument. "That's what I mean. There's this hint of something going on between the two of you and I admit that I am curious."

"You're jealous," she replied.

"I'm perplexed."

"Were you forthcoming about your relationships?"

"I told you about my ex-wife."

"I mean now. Are you going home to someone that's been pining away for you?"

"The only person waiting for me in Jersey is my boss, Rawlins, who will go over every voucher I submit with a fine toothed comb."

"Well, why isn't there anyone? Am I missing something here?"

Dan laughed, bringing up a little of the coffee he had just swallowed. "Thanks a lot," he said, wiping his chin with a paper napkin. "I last dated, seriously I guess, over six months ago. At my age, every woman I meet is either divorced with kids and exuding distrust for all mankind or has never been married; and let's face it, if they've never been married, there's got to be a reason. The last relationship I had was with a full blooded Italian girl and its over. Every date was like a psychoanalyst session; I couldn't take it any more. How did we wind up talking about me? You were going to tell me about you and Ben."

"I don't believe I was," she replied, looking out the passenger window but feeling his eyes still on her. "Okay," she said, turning to him and getting comfortable in her seat.

"Ben and I met in Alaska on our first duty assignment. I was an E-2 and Ben was a shave tail straight from the academy. Ben was in the weather unit and I was in the personnel section of an early warning radar unit so we weren't in the same chain of command. It was my first time away from home, I had no family to speak of and I was very lonely. I volunteered to be the chaplain's assistant and that's where I met Ben. He was also a volunteer chaplain's assistant. So every Sunday, we helped convert the community center into an interfaith chapel and we also helped the chaplain arrange Bible studies and things like that. I found a lot of strength doing that because it helped fill the void. I really missed my mother and Ken and I had a hard time adjusting.

"As it turned out, Ben and I had a lot in common. He came from a rural place in Maine and lost his only brother in Vietnam, as he told you. So, with both of us losing brothers, we talked a lot and bonded. He was a bit of a loner and not too many people were in his peer group that he could talk to at such a small base.

"We were both pretty naïve, actually, when it came to having a relationship. We decided that we should try dating but even though we weren't in the same chain of command, it would have hurt his career. So we made plans to meet away, far away, from the base on weekends when we weren't on duty.

"After seeing each other for about eight months, I told him that I thought I was pregnant." Laura looked over to watch Dan's reaction but he kept looking ahead. "I went to a clinic off base and the gynecologist confirmed that I was six weeks pregnant. I told Ben and he suggested that we meet with the chaplain for guidance.

"He said that if we we're in love then we should get married. It was more important for Ben to be a good father and husband than to become a general. We were both due for some leave since we had been in Alaska for almost a year at that point; Ben suggested that we go to Las Vegas since neither one of us had ever been there before and it was in the desert - we were both getting a little tired of the arctic.

"Ben and I took two weeks of leave and flew on separate flights, meeting in Las Vegas. After about four days, Ben asked me to marry him and I said yes. That night, we went to one of those hokey wedding chapels and got married. We promised to have the chaplain perform a religious ceremony when we got back to Alaska."

"So, why aren't you Missus Ochoa, today?"

"Well, during the start of our second week of leave, we rented a car and drove out to the Grand Canyon. We stayed at a lodge the night we got there and planned on hiking down to the Colorado River the next day and sleeping under the stars and hiking back up the following day. Ben had called ahead and made reservations for a campsite. We tried to do the mule ride but you have to reserve that about a year in advance.

"So, there we were, hiking down the Grand Canyon and about two hours into it I doubled over in pain. It took a long time for it to pass and when it did I just wanted to get the hell out of there. Ben helped me walk and it took us the rest of the day to make it back to the lodge. The next morning we drove back to Las Vegas but I was still in pain from the day before. Ben took me to the emergency room and a physician's assistant examined me, told me that I probably had a miscarriage and that I should follow up with my gynecologist. When I got back to Alaska, that's exactly what my gynecologist said."

"But, what about you're marriage?"

"Since there wasn't a baby anymore, we decided that we would just sort of forget the Vegas wedding. The chaplain was Catholic and I was afraid he would think that I got an abortion but he never said anything about it. He just wanted to make sure that I was healthy and alright.

"About a month after we got back from Vegas, Ben received transfer orders to Germany. He still had almost a year to go in Alaska but there was a shortage of officers with his specialty in West Germany, at least that's what he told me. I'm still not sure that he didn't arrange to get the hell out of there."

"When did you see him again?" Dan asked.

"We wrote to each other a lot at first and then it dwindled to the occasional holiday cards after about a year. I saw him again at Patrick Air Force Base in early 1990 when I was transferred there from Japan. That's when I found out that he just got engaged but he said he wasn't sure about going through with the wedding after seeing me again. Since I was assigned to the same base as Ben it made seeing him very difficult. We managed some time off together for his cousin's wedding. His engagement wasn't known to the family yet so there was no explaining why I was there instead of his fiancée. That weekend, he asked me if

I still loved him and if I would marry him, re-marry him technically, if he broke off his engagement. I was sort of perturbed about his engagement and didn't give him an answer right away. My feeling was that he had to break it off first before I committed to anything.

"When we got back to Patrick, Iraq had invaded Kuwait and within two weeks I was at an air base in Saudi Arabia on a forward deployment team to set up a personnel system for the thousands of airmen expected to be deployed. I was in Saudi Arabia for the next ten months. I heard that Ben was also in country but never ran into him. After the war, I found out that Ben got married before he deployed…right after he found out he was going to be a daddy. Bad timing all the way around, I guess.

"Needless to say, I was quite annoyed. Our paths crossed several times over the next few years and we stayed friendly, but then, eighteen months ago, I was assigned to his unit. He was the executive officer at the time but took command about six months ago. When I was first assigned, we went out to dinner, in Orlando, to clear the air and make sure that we could work together.

"Anyway, about the time he took command, he moved out of his home and into bachelor officer quarters. We've gone out a few times, very covertly as you can imagine, but he hasn't told me why his marriage is breaking up. I believe he is too much of a gentleman to say anything negative about the mother of his children.

"We went away for a weekend about a month ago and he said that he wanted to marry me when his divorce becomes final and he leaves his command in a few months.

She waited for Dan's response and he finally took his eyes off the road. Noting a sense of unease in him, she reached over and took his hand.

"I told him no. I didn't want him, or anyone, on the rebound. I told him that he should work on reconciliation if he still had love for his wife and especially for the kids. I told him that I didn't want to be a home wrecker and that's how his children would always view me."

"Do you love him?"

Laura nodded her head *yes* and said, "I always will. He was the first man I ever loved and I will always love him. He has done nothing to make me not feel that way. I would like to think that I will always be there for him if he needed me and he will always be there for me. We have been through a lot together. However, I realized that I am not in love with him. I can't be in love with someone who is married and has two beautiful kids who are going through hell because mommy and daddy can't work things out.

"So, you have no reason to be jealous, for now. I'll let you know if I change my mind and decide to marry Ben."

"What does his wife look like? Maybe we can have a double ceremony."

"Ugly as hell."

"Really?"

"No, she's beautiful and a frigging size four."

Laura turned the radio volume back up. She looked in the fast food bag from the stop they'd made an hour ago and finished off the potato patty.

"What did you tell Ben? You were in with him for a while."

"I basically told him what we told Detective Leonard and Special Agent Rowles. I left out the detail about Ken's notebook. I told him that they both said that I need to stay low and be prepared to defend myself and that Rowles was fixing to arrest Volkova."

"What did he say?"

"He was flabbergasted. He said that I could take up to thirty days leave if I needed and he offered his parent's place in Maine if I wanted to hide out there."

"What about me?"

"He said you could go too, if you wanted."

"He's a hell of a guy. What did he really say?"

"Ben said that he thought you were a nice guy but that I shouldn't jump into any relationship too fast. He asked me to give him some time."

"What did you say?"

"I said okay."

"Okay?"

"Look Dan, what happened in Tennessee would not have happened if I didn't feel strongly for you. But, you're going back home this weekend and I have a career to finish out here and I have plans for a second career. If you want me then *you* have to figure out how we're going to make this work."

"What does that mean?"

"That means I love you but I'm not moving to New Jersey anytime soon."

Dan let the 'I love you' fly out the convertible. "What's wrong with New Jersey?"

"I could start now…how much time until we get to Islamorada?" She looked over but Dan wasn't smiling. "Dan, I'm not going to leave my home to finish my career at McGuire Air Force Base. And, when I retire, I'm not even sure what university I want to attend. You said that you're not happy with your job and you would like to go to school for something."

"I said that when I was trying to impress you. For Christ's sake, you have plans to teach at the Air Force Academy and I'm chasing down automobile fraud claims. I wanted you to think I was capable of doing something else."

"I think that you can do whatever you set your mind to. If nothing else, you can chase down fraud claims in Florida. We have plenty. I don't care what you do as long as you're happy doing it. You've done enough in the army to earn just sitting on your butt until you croak, if that's what you want. Look, I don't want to fight. But, the fact of the matter is that I don't know if we have something here we can build on or whether these past few days have just been a huge adrenaline rush with a little romance thrown in for good measure. I know that I haven't felt this way about someone in a long time. But, we both know that long distance romances don't work."

Dan digested what she said, reaching over after a few minutes to rub her leg so she would know he wasn't upset. It was a lot to think about. He knew she was right. Long distance romances didn't work but he didn't want to quit his job and sell the farm only to realize that their relationship couldn't survive when they weren't being chased by a rogue KGB officer. Despite the danger, he enjoyed the thrill of the circumstances and he suspected Laura did as well. Maybe that was something to build on.

Chapter 38

Monday late morning
Orlando

The airport terminal wasn't as crowded as it was on the weekends when the vacationers came and went, making Viñals feel exposed. He knew that Volkova, out of the country for so long, probably lacked the resources to go after Laura Smith and spy on his crazy Cuban as well but the Russian could be pretty damned inventive when he wanted to be. Viñals tipped off Special Agent Rowles when Volkova summoned him to the airport but after he was in the terminal, the Russian called him again to make reservations for two round trippers to Miami International for the next available flight.

Raoul Viñals believed that Volkova was already in the terminal and didn't want to raise any suspicions. He complied with his orders and then headed towards the nearest men's room, hoping for good signal strength on his cell phone.

"Denny, I can't talk. I'm on the crapper at Orlando Airport."

"What are you doing there?" Special Agent Rowles asked.

"Take a guess…I'm on South Atlantic Air flight 1035 leaving here and arriving in Miami at one thirty. Got that?"

"Yeah." Rowles repeated the information back for corroboration.

"I'll be with Mr. V."

"Understood. Where are you headed after you land?"

"Beats the hell out of me, bro. I'm just doing what I'm told."

"Okay. Look Raoul, I've got a meeting with my boss in fifteen minutes that I can't get out of and my cell will be off. Leave a message as soon as you find out where you're going and I'll be there. Make sure you delete your calls to me on your cell phone."

"No shit, bro. I would feel a little better if you were available 24/7. You know what I mean?"

"Yes, I do. I'm taking the son of a bitch down today."

"I hope you have back up, Denny?" Viñals heard people enter the bathroom and he ended the call quickly punching in the sequence of commands to delete his last call from the call log feature.

The Cuban found a seat outside of the security area and waited for the Russian. He watched the other passengers submit to the inspections, laughing at the process. He learned enough from the Central Intelligence Agency and the *Komiter Gosudarstevennoi Bezopanosti* to bring aboard, undetected, a variety of substances that would bring down an airliner. The only hitch being that he had to be willing to die in the process. At least the masses believed something was being done for their safety, he smiled as he looked back at his newspaper. Halfway through the sports page, Volkova sat down next to him.

"Good afternoon, comrade," the Russian said, grabbing the front page.

"I was afraid you might miss the flight. They should start boarding us soon. What's going on?" Viñals handed the Russian his ticket and they headed towards the security check area.

"My friend and her boyfriend are heading south. I figure they are either going to the Miami area or the keys," the Russian said.

"Obviously, you have at least one other person working for you. Is that person with Laura Smith now?"

Pavel Volkova nodded his head.

"What are we doing, Pavel?" Viñals asked.

"I have a deadline, my friend. I know for a fact that Smith's brother kept a journal that I was never able to locate after he died. I need to know if she has that journal or knew about what was written."

"And how do you plan on ascertaining that knowledge?"

"That's where you come in, *mi amigo.*"

Chapter 39

Monday early afternoon
Islamorada

Laura dropped Dan off at Heike Harwood's motel office to get a room while she went to a quick mart to get supplies for their time on the boat. She selected light beer, soda, snacks and egg salad sandwiches wrapped in clear plastic - they looked terrible but would taste great on the boat, she hoped. Getting back to the motel, she spotted an open door to the same room Dan had had on Saturday and pulled up. Dan heard the Mustang roll over the crushed coral surface and came outside to help with their bags.

"How's Eva Braun today?" Laura asked.

"In fighting form…she asked about you. Mrs. Harwood was very happy that we only rented one room. She said you seemed head over heels in love with me."

"She said that, huh?" Laura laughed as they started walking towards the ice machine. Dan opened up the plastic bag and admired her collection of snacks.

"Well, Captain Dave should be at the dock in about an hour. We should meet him there when he gets back and tell him that we just want to get out on the water as soon as possible."

"We can still fish, too, if you want," Laura said.

"We'll see if he's available for a charter tomorrow but for now, I just want to pick his brains so you can decide what you want to do. Let's check in with Leonard and Rowles."

Back in the room, Dan placed the cooler on the floor by the front door and unpacked his sweatshirt and long pants from his bag then fished around looking for his cigar case - packed with four Limited Edition Partagas he'd gotten from a friend who went to Montreal to watch the Mets get clobbered.

The front door was still opened and he leaned against the frame, taking in the Florida Bay view from across the parking lot. The temperature was in the low eighties and he thought of the snow mounds outside his front door waiting for him back home. The palm trees were gently swaying and he hoped the wind would die off completely once they were on the water. Hibiscus and oleander bushes were growing naturally on the edge of the motel's property that, in Jersey, could only survive as indoor plants. Not a bad place to retire…maybe Dave Sisk could use a mate, he thought.

Dan looked back to say something to Laura but saw that she was lying down on the bed. Her sunglasses were still on and he couldn't tell if her eyes were on him, elsewhere or just closed. She had on khaki shorts that came down mid thigh and a cotton shirt. Not the sexiest garb in the world but they looked great on her. He surveyed her prone body.

"Are you sleeping?" Dan asked.

"Not any more," she replied then added, "You have something in mind?"

Laura turned on her side towards Dan with her hands around the pillow - he took in her curves. She unbuttoned her shirt; Dan closed the door and went to her.

*****

Dan and Laura spotted Captain Dave putting gas into the skiff; his morning charter clients had already packed their equipment and were gone. Not a lot of fish, Dan thought, eyeing the clean looking dockside filet table. They walked towards the boats with Dan carrying the cooler and Laura holding a plastic bag with a change of warmer clothing inside along with Ken's notebook, photos and the schematics.

"Ahoy there," Dan yelled over the music coming from the boat.

"Howdy," Captain Dave said, turning around. "Hope you two will pay me to actually go out fishing this time." He lowered the music of *Jefferson Airplane.*

Laura squeezed Dan's hand indicating that it was his duty to explain what they wanted.

"What's running?"

"Everything. The question is what's being caught?"

"How were they hitting this afternoon?" Dan asked.

"They weren't. I had an unhappy father and son team. Someday, hopefully, they'll realize the fun was just fishing together."

"What are your thoughts for tonight?" Dan said, looking into the boat while Laura watched a minnow school swimming along side the dock.

"The bonefish just aren't hitting yet so I thought we could fish over by the bridge and the channels and try to bring in some snappers with live bait. How's that sound to you folks?"

Laura looked back at Dan who was looking at the captain's other boat. "Well, Laura and I were hoping to just go out for a little boat ride…with you."

"Sounds romantic. I'm sure the wife won't mind. Should I put on something a little sexier for you two or do you like me the way I am?" Captain Dave asked, wiping the grease from the fuel can's nozzle onto his tee shirt stained with fish blood and bait.

"That's not what we had in mind. I'll tell you what; let's just head out to your fishing hole. Are we taking the big boat?"

"Yup. Put your stuff on board. I need to go to the little boy's room, and then we'll shove off."

Captain Dave returned carrying two fishing poles with spinning reels and a bucket of bait - live fish and small crabs. The three hundred pounder was pure ballet maneuvering his way from the dock to the boat. Laura shot a quick look of concern to Dan when the boat rolled precipitously with the added weight. He started the big Johnsons and let the engine idle as he placed his bait into the on-board bait containers. He pointed towards Laura's feet and Dan complied with the non verbal order and dumped his Styrofoam cooler's contents into the boat's cooler then ran back towards the office area to leave his behind. When he got back, Captain Dave had cast off the stern rope and yelled to Dan to get the bow line.

"It'll be about forty minutes...get comfortable," Captain Dave yelled above the engine noise as he pointed the twenty-five footer out towards the narrow channel cut into the coral. Dan grabbed two beers and took Laura up front to sit on the small seat in front of the center console. Laura brought the plastic bag with her and put on a faded blue Air Force Academy sweatshirt that Dan figured probably came from Ben but kept that deduction to himself.

"I guess we're heading to that bridge," Dan shouted to Laura over the sound of the engines running at full throttle.

The wind died down to practically nothing and the boat cut the glassy surface of the water. The sun was about an hour from setting with about another forty minutes of twilight to follow. A weather front was moving along the western sky that would hide the sun but promising a great hue of colors at sunset. Dan thought of the old saying 'red sky at night sailor's delight, red sky at morning, sailor take warning.' He smiled, hoping for some delight of a personal nature later on.

Laura had her left arm through the plastic bag's handles and held on to Dan's hand. They both leaned back enjoying the ride and each other's nearness. Dan thought back to an hour ago and went over the words in his head again. It had been a long time since he'd said that he loved anyone. His preferred method was to suppress any urge to express emotion and when faced with a woman saying that she loved him, his response would be 'me, too' or his favorite 'right back at ya'. The 'right back at ya' was accompanied by a quick little point of the index finger.

The steady pitch of the engine and vibration of the boat moving through the water lulled them both to sleep. Dan was firmly grasping his beer but Laura wasn't, and Captain Dave reached around, took it from her and placed it in the cup holder on his console. A half hour later, he tooted the horn quickly, waking them up.

"We're here," the captain said as he throttled down the engines.

"Where's my beer?" Laura said looking around hoping she hadn't spilled it all over the deck.

"Here," Captain Dave handed it to her.

Dan and Laura moved back to the stern and watched the captain maneuver closer to the bridge supports. He knew a spot off the second support from the main span that was deeper than the surrounding area. Most boaters looked for the ridge line along the channel but Captain Dave's spot was created by the dredging when the bridge was built. The fishing hole was a near circle with a diameter of about two hundred feet that sloped down to almost fifty feet in the center. He drove the boat so it faced the current and dropped anchor. This way, his clients could fish from the stern into the hole. With live bait and the lights from the bridge, they were guaranteed fish - better than going to the supermarket.

"Ready to catch some fish?" the captain shouted from the bow.

"Captain, we have something we want to show you," Dan started.

Captain Dave moved back to his chair and swiveled it around to look at them.

"I've seen my share of live sex shows in Juarez, kids," the captain said, folding his arms and studying his shipmates.

Laura chuckled nervously and eyed for Dan to continue.

"Captain, before we start fishing, let's have a beer and smoke one of these." He took the cigars from his windbreaker pocket.

"Cuban?" Captain Dave asked.

"Straight from Canada." He cut his and lit it up then offered the cutter and matches to the captain, who did the same. Laura played waitress and opened up three beers from the cooler.

"Nice and smooth," the captain said taking a deep pull. "Now, what's up with you two?"

Dan began by telling the skipper about Vasily Bera and bringing him current through the meetings the day before with Detective Leonard and Special Agent Rowles, touching briefly on Pavel Volkova.

"Now you know as much as the county investigator and the Federal Bureau of Investigation but not as much as we do," Dan said then paused. "When we went to Tennessee, we came across a journal written by Laura's brother Ken. Only three or four people in the world know about this journal."

"We think," Laura added.

"That's right, we think," Dan agreed.

"And what is so...special...about this journal?"

"Dan and I both suspect that my brother was responsible for sabotaging Challenger."

"Challenger! The space shuttle?"

"Yes," Laura replied, taking out her brother's journal from the plastic bag. "There aren't a lot of entries and he had neat handwriting so it's easy to read. I'll get you another beer when you're ready."

"No thanks, I've got to drive this boat." The skipper took the book from Laura. He got as comfortable as his large frame would allow in his seat, shifting his legs from the deck to the rungs on the marine chair. He flipped back, re-reading a few passages.

Fifteen minutes later, his cigar had died out but he was still holding it.

Laura opened three more beers and handed them out, collecting the empties in return. Dan set up his rod with a double hook rig. He started setting up Laura's rod when the captain handed the journal back to Laura.

"What do you think?" Laura asked.

"I think your brother was a very strange man, I'm sorry to say."

"Well, Dan pretty much agrees with your assessment. I just want *you* to know that the man who wrote this is not the person I knew as my brother. But, I have come to accept that he changed significantly since leaving the farm, so to speak."

Dan added, "It appears that Ken was probably used by a soviet agent; two actually. One agent, we were told by the FBI, was a former KGB officer Pavel Volkova. He used Katenka Tiverzin to bait Ken. Ken was so pussy-whipped I think he would have shot gunned his own family if she asked him to."

Captain Dave looked over at Laura who responded, "I would have been offended by that appraisal a couple of days ago, but he's right."

Laura told the skipper about what they learned of Pavel Volkova, his so-called campus bear days, ending by telling him that both the detective investigating Vasily Bera's death and the FBI told her to remain armed until Volkova was apprehended. She opened her bag to show Captain Dave her handgun.

"I want Volkova arrested and put on trial for the killings he did as the campus bear. According to Special Agent Rowles, the aerospace industry was not his forte and I hope my brother's involvement with him never sees the light of day. I don't want the attention it will draw to me."

"Let sleeping dogs lie," the skipper offered.

"Exactly," Laura replied.

"Then why are you on my boat showing me this stuff?"

"Because . . ." Dan started, "if she gives this notebook over to the authorities, it will change her life. If Volkova isn't arrested soon, I think she is going to have to turn it over since it may contain some investigative relevance that will help law enforcement. Also, if they know for a fact that there is a connection between Ken and Volkova and Challenger then maybe they will offer protection for Laura until Volkova is caught. But, before she makes the decision to turn it over..."

"I want to know if my brother really could have destroyed the space shuttle or if these notes are just some warped fantasy he was living out." Laura said.

"Show Captain Dave the drawings," Dan said. Laura retrieved them from her bag and handed them over.

Captain Dave looked at them for a moment and handed them back.

"What are they drawings of?" Laura asked.

"O-rings." Captain Dave relit his cigar. "Specifically, the depth of a cut or an abrasion that would trigger a seal failure...but...not enough to be readily apparent."

Captain Dave could sense Laura's countenance turn to ash despite her shades and the glow of the setting sun cast on her. "Look, those drawings don't prove anything." the skipper said. "We all plan for disaster. Those drawings are probably in the nature of quality assurance for the factory assembly team. In other words, if a worker finds a defect with a seal then they will know if it is a defect within tolerance or if the seal needs to be rejected. As far as the journal, I guess we don't know if its evidence of criminal intent, an attempt at a spy novel or a man with a psychiatric disorder - I'm very familiar with the latter."

"Captain," Dan said, "I would agree with you but we're not existing in a vacuum here and bringing you something that we just stumbled across. There is a real dead body that once answered to the name of Vasily Bera and there is a real former KGB officer interested in Laura's brother. Now, we can probably exclude any theory that Ken was a struggling author, although I agree with you that he was nuts, although not clinically. The real issue is whether or not he would have been capable of really sabotaging the shuttle or was he just running a scam back on Katenka, even keeping a journal that he probably knew that she read when he was asleep or away. Maybe he was saying more than he could actually deliver to satisfy what was being asked of him.

Captain Dave handed his empty bottle to Laura, said no to another, and puffed life back into his cigar.

"After you folks left on Saturday, I went through a lot of what happened back in eighty-six in my head. It wasn't fun," the skipper said.

"I'm sorry about that," Laura said and Dan nodded his head in sympathy.

"Anyway, I went through some old junk I have at home and I found my old company newsletters. I looked for the article about your brother's death. It just said that he was only with the company for eighteen months or so and a little about what he did and his educational background. There was a picture of him in the company jumpsuit wearing a safety helmet and goggles down on the factory floor with some co-workers.

"Your brother was on the quality inspection team for the manufacture and assembly of the O-rings and rocket segments. The team usually has several members and as a rule, no one person is supposed to have sole access to any critical stage of manufacture or assembly for obvious security reasons. However, people call in sick or go on vacations and so the team size may be reduced. Furthermore, someone might have to run to the bathroom or become engaged in a conversation. In any event, it would not surprise me that he could have an opportunity for mischief."

"What kind of mischief?" Dan asked.

"Anything to damage a seal. He could have pierced it with something sharp and thin. He may have put some kind of slow working corrosive on it. The key to being a good saboteur is to not be apparent…or inpatient. Apparently, your brother's friends were satisfied that something was in the works and they weren't very anxious about the exact timing.

"Based on what you folks are telling me about the KGB and the FBI, I have to assume something very real took place back then. Also from what you have shown me and my knowledge of what your brother's access was at the time, I would find him guilty.

"There you have it." Laura took off her glasses and looked over at Dan. Her eyes began to water as he embraced her, still holding the fishing pole he was rigging, which he awkwardly handed off to the skipper.

More of an emotional spasm than an all out cry, Laura recovered quickly and asked Captain Dave what he would do if he were in her shoes.

"If I were in your shoes, I'd have mighty painful feet," he said hoping she would laugh, and then he turned his attention back to the question.

"I suppose I'm in the same situation as you two now that you've shown and told me everything. I reckon that I could call the *New York Times* tonight and they'd have a reporter at my door tomorrow. But, what would that accomplish?"

Laura sat back down and Captain Dave handed the fishing pole back to Dan. They all took a moment to watch the sunset while Dan and the skipper puffed on their stogies.

"The O-rings failed and that is the cause of the Challenger explosion," Captain Dave continued. "We had a systemic problem and we were trying to rectify it. If your brother did help the O-ring failure along, then it was pure genius to sabotage a component that we all believed would ultimately fail. I suppose that's what plausible deniability is all about. Anyway, your brother is dead and he can't be cross-examined or placed on a lie detector machine. The drawings don't tell me jack shit about anything.

"I guess we have to consider what the moral thing is to do. And then the issue is one of a cost benefit analysis. Obviously, revealing this information would put you in a terrible position. Almost like being the sister of Benedict Arnold. But, do you owe it to the country, to yourself, and especially the family of the Challenger crew to make public what you believe in your heart happened all those years ago?

"As far as cost-benefit goes, if this information were to be made public, would it help prevent something similar from happening again?

Is there something in our manufacturing and assembly process that could be modified as a result of learning how it was once penetrated and in so doing, then maybe a similar scenario being played out right now…could be prevented? The release of this information would cost you dearly, but look at what you may be accomplishing."

Laura looked out over the water and up at the traffic on the overland highway bridge.

"It would have been a lot easier if you just said that I should toss this bag overboard," Laura said. "What do you think, Dan?"

"Well, Captain Dave is a smart guy. For crying out loud, he really is a rocket scientist. But, I don't know. After 9/11, I hope our country doesn't need what's in that bag to prevent any more acts of that magnitude. I think we know from the journal that your brother had a motive and from the skipper's knowledge, Ken had the opportunity, as well. But, you can't convict a dead man. Since he is dead, then we will never know the truth and so why put the families through all of that pain once again? Sometimes, suppressing the truth is the best thing to do. My roomie in Korea, Jeff Morris, was killed when his jeep flipped over and he rolled three hundred feet down a mountain just south of the DMZ. My squad leader told me to gather up his effects and the company clerk would send everything to his next of kin. Well, his next of kin was his pregnant wife whom he married just before going overseas. When I went through Jeff's stuff, he had about twenty letters from his old girlfriend who wanted him to dump his wife when he got back to the states. She sent him a lot of great nudie photos of herself, too. The son of a bitch never shared them with me. Anyway, I took those letters and photos to our company communications sergeant, who kept a burn pit outside of his office to destroy classified documents and codes, and we burned everything right there. Now, technically… legally, I was supposed to pack up the man's personal belongings for his wife who became the owner of *all* his property the moment he died. Did I do the right thing?"

"Sure you did, but I'm not sure that we are comparing apples to apples eh, Dan?" Captain Dave said.

"I think we are. The issue is whether there is morality in suppressing the truth as opposed to telling the truth. With respect to Laura's brother, we don't even know what the truth is, or was…nobody does now but God. And, going public with what she has will provide only dubious value to the present investigation of Professor Bera's death. I think Laura should sit on it at least until we know if Special Agent Rowles is successful in getting Pavel Volkova. And, if he is, then I think she should throw that crap overboard. On the other hand, if you're concerned about its historic value then maybe she can provide in her Last Will and Testament that it not be revealed until twenty years after her death. If the situation turns out that Volkova gets arrested and will walk without the evidence that's in that bag, then Laura must hand it over. Until that time, I say let sleeping dogs lie."

"What if *I* go public with what you've told me?" Captain Dave asked. He gauged their reactions, then laughed. "Don't worry, that's all I need. I go public with no proof, you deny everything, and my long history of psychotherapy will be dragged out again. Besides, I don't want the black helicopters buzzing my house anymore."

"Anymore?" Laura asked.

Chapter 40

Monday early afternoon
South of Miami

The flight from Orlando to Miami took less time than it did for Raoul Viñals to get the rental car and fight his way out to the interstate. Volkova made several calls on his cell phone but Viñals couldn't hear what he was saying. He was obviously coordinating some activity slipping between English and French; the former KGB officer did not brief him in on what was being planned and he knew not to press. What really concerned the Cuban was whether or not his brief messages to Denny Rowles were sufficient enough for the special agent to provide support for what was coming. He began to understand how his uncle felt at the Bay of Pigs waiting for President Kennedy's unrequited promise of overwhelming naval air power.

Viñals was able to duck into the men's room at Miami International to check in with Rowles. He left a message saying that he had landed and was going to get a rental. At least, his friend would know he wasn't taking a connecting flight to some other destination. An hour out of the airport, Volkova suggested that they get food and Viñals got off another quick call to say they were southbound and heading towards the keys.

"Here you go my friend, the finest food in Florida," the Russian joked, handing him a burger cooked only God knew when and kept warm by a heat lamp.

"*Gracias*. I just got my cholesterol to below three hundred."

The Cuban exited the parking lot and followed signs for Highway One south. He started to eat the cheeseburger.

"Why do you remain loyal to the cause, Raoul?" Pavel Volkova asked.

"Pardon me?"

"After all this time in America, why do you risk your comfortable lifestyle serving my needs when I call you? Why not call the *federales* and be done with me? You can go into the witness protection program and live a nice little life somewhere."

Viñals finished chewing and took a sip of his milkshake. "Honestly, I don't know. Maybe I should." He looked over at the Russian who was looking out the passenger window. "Do you really want an answer?"

The Russian turned to face him. "Sure, we have a long trip together. Let's chat."

Raoul Viñals had been in tight situations before and this didn't even come close to the butt puckering moments he had had working as a double agent. Yet, he was concerned over the Russian's inquiry and the fact that he probably had been observed during the burglary. Maybe he was seen at the Thai restaurant as well. In any event, he was driving the car and if Volkova tried to do anything Viñals knew it wouldn't be while he was cruising at eighty miles per hour. He took another bite of his burger and played to his old comrade.

"Maybe I do this for the same reason aging ball players attempt a comeback. I guess I miss the game."

"Is it only a game for you?"

"I'm too old to be an idealist anymore. But, I do believe the Americans need to be taken down a few notches. I don't want to hurt Americans - or anyone for that matter - anymore. However, the Americans have no concept of what is going on in the world. Most of them can't even find the countries they attack on the map. Like they say, war is God's way of teaching Americans geography. Yet, they seem to succeed everywhere they go. Quite frankly, I don't understand it. They are the modern day Romans and we are the barbarians from the hinterlands of their empire.

"But, when you look past their foreign policy and their ridiculous movies and music, they are genuinely nice people. Let's face it, Pavel, have you ever heard a Russian or Cuban ever say 'may I help you' and not expect payment? Have you ever dealt with the Germans?"

They both laughed.

"I try not to humanize my enemy," Volkova offered after a while.

"You haven't lived among them. What was the term they called the American and British soldiers who went native during their fight against Japan? I think it was called 'going Asiatic.' I'm not saying that I have gone completely native but I am saying that I don't hate the American people anymore. In fact, many Americans feel the same way I do about their own government."

"What if I told you that I wanted an American dead?" Volkova asked.

Viñals thought about the Russian's question and took another sip of his shake. "Twenty years ago, I would have said where and when. Now, I need to know why. I won't rule out doing it; it just better be for a damn good reason."

The Cuban saw Pavel Volkova nod his head in agreement.

"Where are we going, Pavel?"

To Hell, of course, he thought but ignored the question. Noticing the long silence he answered, "Quite frankly, at this particular time, I'm not sure. My guess would be one of the keys, probably Key West."

"Why Key West?"

"Because we're following Laura Smith and Dan Gill, a couple who want to have a good time together until Mr. Gill returns home. His office voice mail says he will be back at work on Monday."

"I don't see us following anyone."

"*We* aren't. I have more fish in my net than you, Raoul Viñals," the Russian said abrasively, hoping to coax a response but the Cuban remained focused.

"Are you serious about killing someone?"

"I do not know if it will come to that," the Russian answered.

"Laura Smith?"

Pavel Volkova shook his head, "No, I need information from her. But she may need to see her boyfriend die to convince her that I am serious."

Viñals wanted to pull over, get out of the car and run for it but knew he couldn't. He crumpled up the burger wrapper and tossed it in the back seat. "What information, Pavel?"

The Russian knew that Viñals would need that information since he was going to be the lead interrogator. "Remember our conversation at the pancake place? Well, I know for a fact that her brother kept a journal during the time I was working him. My partner kept track of what he was writing and, if discovered, it could lead to the arrest of my partner and my partner could involve me if properly…interrogated.

"It was the only mission where we used her real name because our cover for her exactly matched her real credentials as an exchange dance student. I determined that he was not revealing any information to third parties at the time and his journal entries were a source of confirmation of his activities for us so…we let him keep his note book. The stupid little shit kept it with him at all times but when he…died… we couldn't find the goddamn thing anywhere."

"It seems to me that it is probably long forgotten," Viñals offered.

"Maybe, but if it exists, I want it."

"Why, Pavel?"

"That I can't tell you."

"I must know why if you expect me to kill someone."

The Russian thought about Viñals' inquiry. "Ken Smith's ramblings are a continuing threat to my old partner and me...a lingering headache," Volkova laughed. "However, if I am captured, I will gladly talk my way to freedom. I will start by naming the Cubans on my retainer."

"Then why shouldn't I just call the FBI when we stop and dime you out first?"

"Because you don't know who my partner is. Because you don't know how many people will be upset that you turned into a rat. Because you don't want to live looking over your shoulder for the rest of your life. And, because…" he paused.

"I'm listening."

"Because you like me Raoul Viñals, and because this is…fun."

The Russian slapped the Cuban on the shoulder. "Let's have some fun." Volkova took out two cigars that he had purchased back at the convenience/food store and turned the radio dial until he found a salsa station, turning up the volume and looking at Viñals until the Cuban accepted the cheap Honduran and smiled.

Chapter 41

Monday early evening
Islamorada

Katenka drove back to Heike Harwood's motel and found a spot at the far side of the parking lot near the dumpsters that were enclosed by a cyclone fence. Her cell phone rang; she grabbed for it, not realizing it had fallen from the passenger seat when she pulled into the parking lot; she got out of the car, opened the passenger side door and searched for it. Checking the 'missed call' feature, she punched in the numbers.

"*Da,*" Pavel Volkova answered. "Where the hell were you?" He said harshly.

"Here, my love. My phone rolled off the seat and I couldn't find it. Don't worry. When will you be here?"

"In a few minutes. Are you sure they are not there?"

"Yes." Katenka ended the call upset with Volkova's tone. She had thoroughly briefed him on two prior calls within the past ninety minutes and felt he was too paranoid at times. His management style, learned in the Red Army and finessed by the KGB, annoyed her adopted American sensibilities.

Katenka Tiverzin had followed her prey right to the motel earlier in the day and watched as Dan and Laura had moved their belongings into the room. Afterwards, she had followed them down to the marina and waited until the boat pulled out. Katenka had grabbed one of Captain Dave's flyers from the shack and called the number to inquire about night fishing, and Mrs. Sisk had informed her that evening charters ended at eight o'clock. She had watched the boat as it headed out of the narrow channel, made a turn to the west and disappeared out of sight, knowing that she and Volkova would have several hours until their return.

She was listening to Igor Stravinsky's *Rite of Spring* on a station that offered classical music along with fishing and tidal reports. Her mind drifted back to her first recital just as Volkova pulled into the parking lot and backed into the space next to hers. Katenka observed the driver and could not remember ever meeting him before. This should be interesting, she thought.

Volkova motioned for her to open up the minivan's sliding door and he and Viñals got in.

"Raoul Viñals, may I introduce Katenka Tiverzin," Volkova said, recalling his protocol lessons as a young lieutenant.

Katenka turned her body to sit sideways along the driver's seat and extended her hand.

Viñals brought her hand up to kiss it and Volkova rolled his eyes at the gesture.

"Latin lovers," the Russian grumbled.

Katenka took her hand away then reached over the seat giving Pavel Volkova a kiss on the cheek. "Jealous?"

"Always," he replied blankly.

"Raoul, Katenka and I go back a long way. Just a little bit longer than the two of us do actually. She's been following Laura Smith and her boyfriend for the past several days and ended up in this motel this afternoon."

"Where are they now?" Viñals asked.

"On a boat…fishing. They should be back within the hour."

"What do you want me to do?" the Cuban asked and the Russian explained.

*****

The twenty-five footer motored gently towards the dock and Captain Dave used the engines to slowly turn the boat around so that the stern was facing his shack. Dan had packed up everything including the red snappers and the lone grouper that he had cleaned on the way in, placing the fillets in plastic baggies. As soon as the boat throttled down, Dan jumped off to retrieve his Styrofoam cooler and Laura helped the skipper with the lines.

"Well, this was certainly the most interesting charter I ever had," Captain Dave said as Dan and Laura transferred their fish and drinks to their cooler. "I suppose if I don't read about this in the funny papers then you folks will have decided to remain mum."

"You think I should go public?" Laura asked. Captain Dave slowly nodded his head *yes.*

"I understand. I still am not decided but I'm not doing anything until I speak with the FBI again."

Dan shook the skipper's hand, promised that he would be back next year. He put his tip in the captain's shirt pocket. Captain Dave offered his hand to Laura but she gave him a hug instead.

"You gonna be back next year, too?" he asked.

"With him?" he pointed with her thumb. "Maybe. If not, I'll come back anyway."

Laura grabbed the bag with her brother's effects and took Dan's hand to walk back to the car while Captain Dave started to hose fish guts off the back and side of his boat.

Chapter 42

Monday evening
Sisk's Marina, Islamorada

Special Agent Dennis Rowles was getting concerned that he had not heard from Raoul Viñals since early afternoon. He had been calling Laura Smith's home and cell phone numbers but he wasn't getting an answer. Finally, he called her unit and spoke to her commanding officer, Lieutenant Colonel Ben Ochoa, who told him, grudgingly, that she was headed towards Islamorada for a few days; he gave the FBI man the phone number for Harwood's motel. She was following the FBI's advice to stay low, Ochoa said, and then commanded Special Agent Rowles to take care of his sergeant.

Rowles called in a favor to a FBI buddy who ran down Laura's credit card again learning that she had used it at a convenience store on Islamorada. He then manufactured an excuse to leave his office early. Although he wasn't in panic mode yet, he was troubled by the lack of communication with Smith and Viñals. His plan was very loose: he hoped to secure the area where she was and then wait for Viñals to call so he could set up an ambush for the Russian. If he didn't hear from his Cuban friend, he would have to bring her into protective custody and trust that his superiors would give him the resources to go after the campus bear.

He went to the convenience store where Laura had purchased her snacks and spoke with the clerk who was born and raised on the key. He remembered Laura and told Rowles that the pretty blond was going fishing that night over at Sisk's Marina. Rowles tried Laura's cell phone again but got her voicemail. He left another message.

Special Agent Dennis Rowles drove over to Sisk's Marina, parking next to the only other vehicle in the lot. The only activity was a big man stowing away cleaning supplies in a bin underneath the sole working light on the dock.

"Good fishing today?" Rowles asked, not wanting to the startle the fat man with *Stop! FBI!*

"Pretty fair. Do you want set up a charter?" Captain Dave asked.

"I wish I could." Rowles took out his identification and showed it to the captain. "My name is Special Agent Dennis Rowles and I need to locate a young lady by the name of Laura Smith. I understand she may have been fishing with you tonight?"

"What did she do wrong?" Captain Dave asked. Laura's story fresh in his mind, he knew who Rowles was but didn't want to let on…just yet. The skipper also wondered whether or not the man before him could be the campus bear. He remembered telling his therapist once that you are not really paranoid if everyone *really is* out to get you.

"Nothing. She's a witness in an on-going investigation and I need to contact her."

"Well, she was here with her fella but they left about thirty minutes ago."

"Dan Gill?"

"The one and only."

"You know him well?"

"He's a regular. Been fishing with me for five years. Great tipper and refers his friends. I won't testify against him," Captain Dave said to test the government's humor.

"No need to," Rowles said matter-of-factly. The government failed. "Do you know where they're staying?"

"I sure do. I'm going there in a few minutes. You can follow me."

"Where would that be?"

"Heike Harwood's place. I owe the old dame some cash, she sent me two charters last week. This is a dog-eat-dog business, too many skippers and too few tourists.

*****

Dan wanted to take a shower with Laura but she felt too grungy from the fish smell. Dan took a walk to the ice machine and filled up his cooler. He'd only kept a few of the filets, letting Captain Dave keep the rest, and thought that he would buy one of those cheap Hibachi grills in the morning. He saw Ms. Harwood getting ready to leave for the evening and observed her instruct her night time clerk like a sergeant giving orders to a sentry. Dan smiled, happy for her and the life she had.

Laura was out of the shower wrapped in an undersized motel towel - barely covering the goodies above and below. She was leaning forward drying her hair with another towel and when she did, there wasn't much left for the imagination. She caught Dan looking at her and closed the bathroom door with her foot.

Dan turned on the television news and opened a bottle of beer for himself. Laura's cell phone was next to the remote control and he picked it up. When the hair dryer stopped he knocked on the bathroom door.

"Your phone says you have four messages and two are urgent." He was met with silence for a few minutes and then the door opened. Laura had on a pair of sweatpants and a tee shirt.

"Take a shower. You stink," she said.

"I'll take that as a compliment for my fishing skills."

"I caught more fish than you."

"But mine were bigger."

"No, they weren't." She tossed him the towel she was still holding.

"Laura, you gotta work with me, here. I do have a male ego, you know."

Laura turned down the volume on the television and moved around the room until she found the best signal on her cell phone then retrieved her messages. The first was from Special Agent Rowles who left the code for urgent but his message sounded routine. The next two were from her unit. The acting non commissioned officer in charge of her section was in a panic getting ready for the inspection and Colonel Ochoa just had a conversation with him. "Jacked him up" was the actual term used when he couldn't produce the personnel activity logs fast enough. The last message was again from Rowles and it did sound urgent. Laura decided to wait for Dan to get out of the shower before calling so that she could use the speaker function and not have to repeat everything.

Dan broke into Springsteen's *Thunder Road* and Laura unmuted the television. Between the two competing sounds, she didn't hear the knock on the door at first. The singing was still going strong and her first thought was that a neighbor was complaining about the noise. Laura didn't think about daddy's gun until after she opened the door.

For a moment, Laura wanted to run back towards the bathroom but she quickly dismissed the flight option of the 'fight or flight' psychological reaction to danger. Instead, she stood at the door ready to punch the stranger in the throat and kick him in the balls on his way down.

"Yes?" Laura said.

"May I come in?" the Cuban asked.

"Pardon me? Do I know you?"

"No, but I know you. I know that a crazy Russian bastard wants to speak with you."

"Who the hell are you?" Laura raised her voice wanting to project authority and not the fear that was swelling up in her belly. Friggin' Dan was now singing *Born in the U.S.A.*

"I know that you are here with your friend, Mr. Gill, who I assume is the crooner in your shower. He is much larger than me and could kill me if he wanted to. I am not here to hurt you. In fact, I am unarmed and I assume that you probably have some weapons at your disposal." Viñals raised his arms and turned around. Laura thought that he could have a weapon in an ankle holster but the Cuban, after doing his pirouette, hiked up each pant leg.

"Please, your life may be in danger and I know that my life certainly is," Viñals said and added. "Laura, the Russian sent me here. My life is in danger, too. The FBI can't protect you from this man or else I wouldn't be standing here right now. If the Russian wanted you dead or hurt, you wouldn't be standing here now, either. He wants information…truthful information…and full disclosure of what you may know of certain events. That's it. Then he will be out of your life, forever."

Laura stepped back.

"Come in and stand by the door…leave the door open." She backed up to the bathroom door and pushed it open.

"Dan! I need you out here…now!"

"Baby, that's what I've been waiting to hear!" The shower shut off and Laura saw the man at the door smile. She grabbed the small gym bag that held the magnum and unzipped the bag for quick access.

Dan slid the shower door back not realizing Laura was right there.

"What's up?" he asked and noticed that she had the weapon bag in her hand.

"We have a visitor, put your pants on."

"What?" Dan stepped out of the shower quickly losing any excitement he had over the expectations running around in his head. He hurriedly toweled off putting on the same trousers that he had been wearing before; opening the door to the bathroom more fully, he saw the Cuban standing there.

"Who the hell are you?" Dan said, walking up to him with Laura hanging back ready to draw out her revolver.

"My name is unimportant. I was sent by Peter Kola."

Raoul Viñals watched as the color ran from Dan's face and he looked back at Laura.

"Who?" Dan demanded but their demeanor had betrayed their knowledge.

"I believe you know who I am referring to. And, if I am correct in that belief, you know what kind of a situation we are all in."

"How are *you* involved?" Laura said, taking the gun from the bag and holding it with two hands as she did with her nine millimeter Beretta automatic on the qualification range.

"As a young man, I was very passionate about my belief in the supremacy of the socialist state over the capitalist system. I did many things back then that I am now ashamed of and sorry for. However, my old boss could care less about my redemption as he is not…shall we say a 'God fearing man.' He looked me up and I either comply with his demands or wind up as one of the many *disparos*."

"Did you know my brother?" Laura brought her weapon level to the Cuban's chest but controlled her emotion.

"I knew of him but didn't know him. Peter Kola used him like he used me and others."

Viñals stopped upon hearing movement outside. He turned so that he could look out the door. Dan then heard footfalls on the crushed coral, too, and then, sounds of heavy bags being dropped. Laura moved up to stand by Dan.

"What's the commotion? Who else is with you?" Dan said reaching for and taking Laura's gun.

"I don't know," the Cuban said, turning his head towards Dan and Laura. "Honest."

A loud shot rang out and a moment later, another. From inside the room Dan could not discern where the reports had come from. They sounded like they had come from across the parking lot but a two story stucco building stood there and very well could have echoed the gunshots.

"*Stoppen Sie, was Sie tun!*"

"That's Mrs. Harwood!" Dan shouted to Laura.

The Cuban bolted from the room.

Dan moved to the front door, shutting off the light and holding his free hand back to keep Laura at arm's length. "Shut off the TV and the bathroom light."

He peered around the edge of the door towards the motel office. He saw the old German *frau* walking towards some objects in the parking lot. His attention was distracted by two vehicles which started up towards his left and backed up over the curb into the neighboring property's parking lot before driving over the sidewalk to the Overland Highway. Laura came back and stood behind Dan.

"I think our guest . . .and his friends…took off. Let's go see about Mrs. Harwood."

Finding their shoes, they sprinted towards the old lady who was now standing over the objects.

They stopped running when it became obvious that the objects were bodies. Laura fell in behind Dan and Dan stopped a few feet from Mrs. Harwood who was holding a Lugar. The night clerk turned on the parking lot lights from inside the office and Dan immediately recognized the bodies.

"Holy shit," Dan blurted out, clutching the revolver to his mouth.

"What is it?" Laura tried to come around but Dan turned to stop her. "What?"

She grabbed Dan's arms and looked around.

"Oh my God! Oh my God!" She wanted to see if they were alive. The head wounds had already leaked a voluminous amount of blood from each body, but she bent down anyway.

"Laura, they're dead. Don't disturb the area."

The Lugar dropped to the ground and Dan rushed to Mrs. Harwood, embracing her before she dropped, too. He and Laura helped her walk towards the lobby, sitting her down outside on a concrete bench near the front door.

"He kilt *der Capitain,*" she finally said.

"Who killed Captain Dave?" Dan asked.

"*Ich nicht fershta.* Poor Dave." She started crying. Dan told the night clerk to bring some water but the old lady shouted at her to get the schnapps instead. The clerk returned with the bottle and some paper cups.

After tossing back one shot and sipping another, Mrs. Harwood said, "Dave calt me und said he vas bringing me some money so I vas vaiting for him. I saw him valking vit dat man. He must have valked over from the marina instead of driving. He said he vas trying to lose veight. I bring my Lugar ven I carry cash home.

"Den a man came up from over der und shoots dem. Dat man sees me und her." The old lady trembled and pointed to her clerk. "Vitnesses. I take out my Lugar und go to de door. Boom. I shoot und his eyes get dis big," she demonstrated after finishing her schnapps and pouring a third.

"Den he runs to de cars parked over der und I shoot again. I hit der son of bitch in de leg, I dink."

"Mrs. Harwood, the other man is an FBI agent. His name is Dennis Rowles."

"I don't know him," the old lady responded.

"Dan, I'm going to be sick." Laura said and went to the side of the building.

Dan stood up and took a long swig from the bottle. "Did you call 911?" Dan asked the clerk.

"No," she gasped. "I'll do it now."

Dan grabbed her arm. "Don't call yet."

Laura came back, her face white. Dan offered the schnapps and she drank from the bottle.

"What happened?" Laura asked.

"I think that our house guest had back up and they knew who Special Agent Rowles was. Rowles must have been looking for us all day and tracked us to Captain Dave. Captain Dave was bringing him here. Wrong place at the wrong time.

"Mrs. Harwood, that FBI man over there was supposed to be protecting Laura from a former KGB officer who wants to hurt her. I can't get into the whole story now so please just trust me. Right before the shooting, a man was at our door who said he was sent by that KGB officer. I have to get Laura out of here now. I don't have time to explain all this to the locals. Please wait five minutes before calling 911."

Mrs. Harwood looked up. "I trust you, Danny boy," she said simply.

Dan took out the card from his wallet that Detective Leonard had given to him. "Take this. You are free to tell the local cops everything I told you. Tell them that we will be in touch with this detective when we feel that we are safe. He bent over and kissed the old lady on the forehead. *"Got mit uns,"* he said softly and she smiled, remembering her father in uniform, that phrase emblazoned on his belt buckle.

Dan and Laura started back towards their room.

"Danny," Mrs. Harwood said and he turned back, "Take dis." She handed him her father's 1935 P-08 Parabellum Lugar Automatic, he was awarded upon commission in the Waffen Schutzstaffel.

"I can't take that: you need to give it to the police."

"Fuck the *polizei*. They always give my customers tickets and dey never come when you need dem. You dink KGB was here?"

Dan nodded *yes.*

"Den I got him. The *polizei* don't need to know dat and you need anuder gun to protect your *freulein.*"

Dan took the gun. "I really shouldn't but I wouldn't mind the extra firepower. Tell the police the truth and tell them that I have the gun.

Dan was going to kiss her on the forehead again but she stopped him.

"Danny boy, you kill that *Russische* son of a bitch vit my Lugar."

"Yes, ma'am."

He turned and sprinted back to the room with Laura.

"Laura, just throw all of our crap in the car; I need to check something out."

"What?" she asked but Dan had already moved away.

Dan went into the middle of the parking lot and realized suddenly that the other guests were looking out of their windows but no one had come out to see what was going on. He guessed that they were waiting for the safety of the police lights to appear. He bent down over a spot that he correctly guessed was blood.

The old lady did hit someone, he thought. He followed the blood trail to where the cars were parked and concluded that it wasn't an arterial wound - too bad. Dan faulted himself for not getting the tag numbers but then realized there wouldn't be tags on the front of the cars anyway.

He turned and saw that Laura had thrown their bags in the convertible's back seat and was closing the room door. He jogged back over.

She tossed him a clean shirt to put on. "What did you find?"

"Someone got shot. There's a blood trail." He pointed. "And we know it wasn't our house guest. It's not a bad wound from what I could tell. Maybe even a graze. Let's go." They got in the car and he pulled out, passing near the bodies outside of the motel office. Mrs. Harwood had gone inside and they watched her pick up the phone and hold out five fingers as they passed slowly by the dead men. Laura mouthed a thank you to Mrs. Harwood as Dan gave the bodies of Captain Dave Sisk and Special Agent Dennis Rowles a wide berth driving over some small bushes on the side of the parking lot. Laura watched Dan make a sign of the cross; she formed a silent prayer as well.

"Where are we going?"

"West," Dan replied.

"There's only so far west we can go, you know."

"I realize that, but both cars turned east. And we can assume there are at least three people. Both cars were moving before our houseguest could have gotten to them. I presume he jumped in one of them."

"Then what?"

"We find a patrol base and call in artillery."

"Where are we?" Laura asked.

"What?"

"I said…where are we?"

"Islamorada, why?"

"I wanted to make sure you didn't think we were in Grenada or Panama."

"Very funny. Rangers put their patrol bases in the most ungodly spots they can find. Someplace that is inaccessible and where you can see an enemy coming from a long way off. We need to find a patrol base. Special Agent Rowles is dead. That leaves Detective Leonard as our only connection to safety. He is our artillery. We need to contact him and let him know. He can work with all of the folks in the FBI who were working with Rowles on this matter. We don't have time to form a new relationship with Rowles's partner or whoever else the FBI puts on this case."

Dan pointed to a sign that indicated Key West was seventy-five miles away. He took the Lugar from the floor board, placed what he guessed was the safety selector switch on, and wedged the gun between his seat and the center console.

"I screwed up," Laura said.

"How's that?"

"I had a message from Agent Rowles. If I didn't forget to bring my phone on the boat, this would not have happened."

"Hey," Dan reached over for Laura's hand. "That's total crap. With everything they told us, the best that the FBI and the police could do was to tell you to protect yourself. Well, you did. We're alive and Rowles is dead and he walked Captain Dave into an ambush, not you."

Dan realized that he was driving almost twenty miles over the speed limit; he braked to five miles under and set the cruise control. At the next light, he raised the top on the convertible and they continued in silence.

Chapter 43

Monday night
Towards lands end

Halfway across Seven Mile Bridge between Marathon and Ohio Key, Laura lost herself in thought gazing out over the black water and the remnants of an earlier bridge linking the two isles. She jumped when she felt the phone vibrate a moment before it rang. Dan looked over at her and she showed him the illuminated window with the caller identification indicating that it was from Detective Corey Leonard.

"Not bad; it only took him an hour." Dan remarked.

"Hello," Laura answered

Dan listened as Laura explained current events to Detective Leonard. He thought she would start with the shootings and then work back but she kept to chronological order. Her non-commissioned officer training was evident and she laid the whole scenario out as if she were recalling log entries from a duty shift.

"I can't…no, I won't tell you," Laura said. She paused. "Because, the FBI couldn't protect me and neither can you. What? Call me when you're done."

Laura ended the call.

"What happened?" Dan asked.

"He got a phone call from the police on Islamorada. Good ol' Mrs. Harwood kept her word. He wanted to know where we are and where we're going."

"Excellent questions."

"Dan, where are we going?"

The question remained unanswered because Dan was uncertain as well. He finally admitted so.

The phone rang again and Laura quickly answered.

"Detective Leonard?" she asked.

"No."

"Who is this?" She asked, taking the phone from her ear but the caller identification only said 'blocked.'

"I am your friend from the motel. Our conversation before was cut short."

Laura put the phone down on her lap and covered the mouthpiece. She jabbed Dan in the side to get his attention.

"It's the guy from the motel," she whispered.

Dan looked at her for a moment. "Find out what he wants," he said.

Laura switched on the speaker phone. "How did you get my cell phone number?" she demanded.

"As they say in the movies, ve have our vays," then added, "I was in your room while you were fishing. Your phone was lying right on top of the dresser and your phone number is taped to the backside."

"Are you responsible for murdering Agent Rowles and Captain Dave?"

"No. I wasn't even sure Rowles was coming and I certainly didn't think he would show up with your fishing buddy. That was entirely a non-scripted event. So, we should not let that unfortunate occurrence side track us from the reason I paid you and Mr. Gill a visit this evening."

"And, what reason was that? To kill us?"

"No, I could have killed you both simply by lying in wait at your room. Mr. Kola wants to know what information you have. That is it. You will never hear from him or me again."

"Look, shit bird," Dan started.

"Good evening Mr. Gill. My name is Raoul."

"Okay, Raoul. You know a lot about us. So then you will know that I just met Laura last week so I don't know jack about what her brother did almost twenty years ago. You know that Ken Smith lived away from home since Laura was in grade school and then he died. If

Ken Smith had some big secret, Laura doesn't know about it. She told that to Detective Leonard and she told that to the FBI."

"I believe that she may know more," Raoul answered.

"And why is that?" Dan demanded.

"Because Ken Smith kept a journal and spoke of Mr. Kola."

Laura looked over at Dan and he placed a finger to his lips.

"Ken Smith may have kept a journal, but his sister does not have it. We went to Tennessee and brought back everything that ever belonged to her brother that survived his trailer blowing up and her mother's house burning down. It is all in Laura's house now. Why don't you go break in there as well and check it out for yourself."

"Then why were the two of you in such a rush to consult with Doctor David Sisk? I googled him and discovered that he used to work with Ken Smith?"

"Because, I'm on vacation, shit bird, and Doctor Sisk is Captain Dave to me. I've been fishing with him for a long time. Ask him yourself…oh yeah…he's dead, now."

"I want the journal," Raoul said coldly.

"You can't have what we don't possess. If Laura had it then why wouldn't she have just handed it over to the cops or the FBI?

After a long silence, Raoul said, "That is probably true. But Mr. Kola would like to look into Laura Smith's eyes when she says that. If he believes her, then that will be the end of it."

"We'll consider it. What's your number? We'll be in touch," Dan said but Raoul had hung up before he could finish.

"Shitbird?" Laura asked pressing the button on her phone to end the call.

"What can I say? When I get mad, stuff from the old neighborhood bubbles up into my brain and comes out my mouth. I was moments away from cursing in Italian and Yiddish."

"What next?"

"We should probably check to see if we are being followed. I'll pull in at the next open convenience store. We need to wait for Leonard to call back. Maybe we can arrange with the FBI a time and place for Peter Kola to look into your eyes."

"Use me as bait?" Laura asked.

"Appropriate metaphor for where we are, but yes. You need for this guy to be caught. Now. Even if you hand over your brother's effects to the FBI or Detective Leonard, this guy…Peter Kola…Pavel Volkova…whatever name he is going by, will still want to know from you what it was that you handed over. He will want to know what evidence there is against him. This is analogous to organized crime cases. The mob always wants to know what the witness will testify to at trial. Either you will have to go into a protection program or we nail the Russian bastard."

On Big Pine Key, Dan turned off the Overland Highway into the parking lot of a twenty-four hour market, driving around the building and stopping on the far side from west bound traffic.

"All I remember is a white minivan and dark colored sedan, maybe a Ford Taurus, from the motel. But, they may have friends in other cars," Dan said. He cleared the Lugar, pulling out the clip and counting six remaining rounds. He chambered a round then tucked the gun into the small of his back.

"Why don't you take care of business first and I'll keep a lookout?" Laura asked.

She watched Dan get out of the car, adjusting the gun as he walked towards the entrance. It wasn't obvious that he had it hidden under his shirt but if he kept adjusting it inside the store, she thought, the clerk would surly become suspicious. Laura took her father's revolver from the bag lying on the floor between her legs and placed it back again feeling comfortable that she could access it very quickly if need be.

Laura checked her cell phone to make sure that she hadn't accidentally turn it off when she spotted a blue Ford sedan slow down as it passed in front of the store. She made mental notes to herself…no passengers…male driver…white or Hispanic…when the cell phone rang. She was momentarily startled but quickly regained composure seeing that it was Detective Leonard calling back.

"Hello." She said.

"What the hell are you two up to?" Detective Leonard yelled.

"Fuck you," Laura replied, surprising herself with language she never used. She looked up and saw Dan coming back. He gave her a 'thumbs up' for her last comment not having any idea who she was talking to. "Hold on, I'm with Dan and I'm putting you on speaker."

"Look detective, I'm following your advice and Agent Rowles's advice by laying low and protecting myself. I'm sure you know Agent Rowles is dead," Laura finished.

"I've been informed. I've also been informed that you and Gill were involved in the shooting and fled the scene. Guests at the motel saw Mr. Gill attempt to give the murder weapon to the little old lady that runs the place."

"Detective Leonard," Dan took the phone and filled in the detective on everything Special Agent Rowles said was top secret. He continued, "I would suggest that you tell the locals to gumshoe the crime scene a little more. I am in possession of a German Lugar that the little old lady used to shoot the person who killed Special Agent Rowles and Dave Sisk. She hit someone because there is a blood trail in the parking lot. She gave me the gun so I could protect Laura.

"At least three individuals were involved and they came to the motel in two vehicles, a white Chrysler minivan and a dark colored Ford sedan. I think it was a Taurus. A man visited me and Laura in our room to ask about her brother and was with us when one of his friends, probably the Russian, Volkova-by the way, he is also know as Peter Kola-shot Rowles and Sisk. Heike Harwood, the little old lady who was once an expert with a *panzerfaust,* fired one round from her Lugar at the assassin who was coming at her and would have killed her and her clerk to eliminate witnesses if she didn't get the drop on him first. She fired the second round as he fled. That round struck home. I watched the man from our room get into the minivan as both cars exited the parking lot and turned east on the Overland Highway.

"We are now at an undisclosed location waiting for help." Dan handed the phone back to Laura and took off the lid of his coffee cup to add cream.

"You should have stayed at the scene to tell that to the police," Detective Leonard answered.

"Where do you think Laura and I would be if we started telling them about an ex-KGB officer who is chasing us because Laura's brother had something to do…maybe…with the Challenger explosion? I'll tell you. We would be at the psych ward receiving Thorazin intravenously right now. We gave your card to Mrs. Harwood and she came through, right?"

"Okay. Tell me where you are."

"No way," Laura retorted.

"You can't hide forever."

"We can hide for now," Dan said. "Look, detective, call the FBI and find out who else was working this case with Agent Dennis Rowles. The man who was in our room identified himself as Raoul. Who knows what his real name is. He has called us since the shooting and wants to set up a meeting with Laura and Volkova. We think you and the FBI should be there as well."

"What you are doing is very dangerous. I can call the local police of whatever town you are in and they can protect you."

"For how long? Until the next shift change? Get your ass in gear and call the FBI." Dan motioned to Laura to end the call and she complied.

"Are you sure he's not right?" Laura asked.

"No. But we think there are only three of them. One of them is wounded and we are both armed and will see them coming. I think our chances are fair."

Dan handed Laura a coffee. "Do you need to use the facilities? Otherwise, we should keep moving."

She said that she did but described the car she spotted to Dan before getting out of the car. He took the Lugar from behind his back and wedged it between his seat and the center console.

As an infantryman and then as a cop, Dan liked the night. It was a good time to be on the offensive. The hours between two and four were the best time to catch someone with their pants down. There is something about that two hour stretch, he thought, that made it very difficult to stay alert, stay focused and stay awake. Dan knew that he and Laura were now the hunted and they were vulnerable. They were both very tired and running from events they couldn't control. It was time to hole up in a safe place and turn the proverbial shoe around. Dan took out his Florida road map, scanning the chain of keys westward from Big Pine Key; he knew that they would soon be running out of road.

Chapter 44

Monday night
On the Overland Highway

By the time the police arrived, Mrs. Harwood and her evening desk clerk had finished the bottle of schnapps and were significantly through a bottle of bourbon brought over by the clerk's boyfriend. Neither Mrs. Harwood nor her employee, or any of their guests, gave useful information about the cars that had left the parking lot after the shootings; the former two because of alcohol and the latter due to the natural desire to remain uninvolved.

Katenka Tiverzin drove the minivan eastward looking for an all night drug store while Pavel Volkova dressed his leg wound, technically an ass wound, in the back seat with towels from Katenka's gym bag. The Lugar's nine millimeter round had struck his left cheek at an angle going from the crack outwards and approximately a quarter inch down at its deepest cut. He knew it wasn't life threatening unless the sweaty towels infected the gash. Volkova lay on his right side and compressed the wound with his left hand. His pants and underwear were pulled down and he hoped that he wouldn't be pulled over by the cops and forced to make his final stand in this condition. The Russian felt that the bleeding was slowing down but would open again as he removed the cloth that was congealing into the wound.

Pavel Volkova trained his students well, he thought. In pain, he didn't think to stop at several locations to get first aid supplies. The police would obviously canvas the keys for a gunshot victim and

Katenka instinctively knew to keep a low profile. It took her almost to Key Largo, but she was able to purchase large compresses, tape, anti-biotic creams and other first aid supplies along with several days' worth of groceries mixed in at each stop. In time, she knew, the police would figure it out; but by then she was hoping to be on a beach somewhere as promised by her old lover.

At the last drug store, Katenka properly dressed Volkova's wound and offered him left over pain killers from a recent visit with the orthodontist and anti-biotic pills from last winter's sinus infection. She drove another few miles before disposing of the bloody rags and other evidence at a fast food restaurant's dumpster.

She knew Volkova was more upset about letting himself get shot then he was about the actual wound and she avoided starting any conversation with him. Katenka knew the difference between being a good soldier and being a good lover. Now, she had to be a soldier and get her comrade to safety without upsetting him even more. Although he would never admit it, she knew that he was also in shock and so she had to keep him warm and not raise his stress level any more than it already was.

Volkova told her to turn around, keep moving and wait for Viñals' call. They couldn't afford to stop where they might arouse a nosy person's antenna. Well after midnight, Katenka's cell phone jumped to life.

"Yes? " Katenka answered, looking back at Volkova, who had shifted himself to a seated position favoring his right side. She handed the phone to him, saying that it was Raoul.

"Where the hell are you?" Volkova demanded.

"I'm on Cudjoe Key. Where are you?"

"Where are they?" Volkova asked, ignoring the Cuban's query.

"I don't know," he reported quickly, wanting to get past telling the Russian the bad news. Surprisingly, Viñals thought, Pavel Volkova did not go ballistic at the unfavorable report. "How bad is your wound?" he asked.

"Not to worry. Where did you last see them?"

"On Seven Mile Bridge. There was no traffic so I had to hang back. I thought I spotted them at a convenience store on Big Pine Key but when I circled back their car was gone. One of the employees from the store was taking out the garbage and told me that their car headed west but I never caught up to it. I was driving ten miles over the speed limit and didn't want to risk going any faster. What do you want me to do?"

"My bet is that their best hiding spot is to disappear into a crowd. Go to Key West and stay near Duval Street. Keep an eye out for their vehicle on the way and we will do the same from where we are."

"I'm sorry, my friend, for failing," Raoul said, sounding sincere.

"*Mi amigo*, all battle plans change after the first shot is fired; however, our mission remains the same. We will find another way to achieve success. We know that they are between my location and Key West. Call them and maybe they will be foolish enough to tip their hand." Volkova ended the call handing the phone to Katenka and lying back down.

The Campus Bear watched the landscape go by and thought about the merits of what he was doing. Was it wise to come out after all these years he questioned himself as the pain pills began to take effect. Certainly, the payoff would be tremendous if he could show some tangible evidence of what he once accomplished for Mother Russia.

*****

Dan pulled off the roadway on Stock Island into the parking lot of a bait shop and parked behind the trash dumpsters so that the car wasn't visible from the Overland Highway. On the edge of a golf course across the highway, homeless men huddled around a small fire blazing in a garbage barrel and listened to a tinny sounding boom box radio. Dan thought that when they left, he would leave the car unlocked so they could vandalize it. The homeless men wouldn't be very helpful to the police in describing the occupants if they were guilty of stealing stuff from the car.

Laura wasn't very comfortable with Dan's plan but agreed none – the - less. They would call for a taxi to take them to Key West and abandon the rental car. The convertible was too obvious and they could get another rental at the Key West Airport.

"Let's carry our stuff over there." Dan pointed to a spot a hundred feet away. If the taxi driver asks anything, we'll just say we were hitching and our ride dropped us off here. I don't want the driver to remember the car."

Laura called information and got the number to a local taxi company. The dispatcher said that a cab would pick them up in about thirty minutes.

The taxi picked them up right on schedule and to Dan's satisfaction, the driver appeared half stoned and content listening to a warbled Best of the Grateful Dead cassette tape from a portable player perched on the dashboard. Dan told him to head straight for the Hyatt and upon arrival he left a reasonable and forgettable tip and took his own bags from the trunk.

"Where now?" Laura asked.

"Not the Hyatt. Our driver may not remember where he dropped us off but the dispatcher will. Let's head towards Duval Street. We can get a drink and figure out our options."

Dan and Laura had repacked everything while waiting for the taxi and only took a small backpack that Dan wore and Laura's bag. Dan moved the Lugar to his front and put on his windbreaker to better conceal it. Laura kept her pistol in the unzipped bag, hidden under a shirt. There was a cruise ship at the municipal dock and Duval Street was still crowded despite the late hour. They stopped in at one of Hemingway's favorite bars looking no different than the hundreds of tourists roaming the streets of Margaritaville.

Laura had her cell phone on the bar when it started bouncing. The caller identification feature did not display the caller's number. Although the band was apparently through for the evening and getting drunk at the other end of the bar, the juke box was on. Dan did not want the caller to place them in a bar. He grabbed the phone and ran outside onto the street and away from the music.

He pressed the answer button but kept the phone tight against his side until the noise level from the bar dropped to an indistinguishable level.

"Hello," Dan finally answered.

"*Buenos noches.* You were being rude to me before with your insulting name calling," Viñals said.

"It was rude of you to kill my friend, shitbird."

"I did not kill anyone and you promised not to call me that if I told you my name. It is Raoul Viñals."

"Like hell it is."

"It is my real Christian name."

"Christian…don't tell me, you're a born again commie?"

"If you want the truth, I am. Except for my libido, I am a good man."

"Did we suddenly become old friends?"

"No, Mr. Gill, but I was hoping we might become new friends."

"Why's that?"

"You know who Special Agent Dennis Rowles was, do you not?" the Cuban asked.

"Yes. You had him killed."

"No, I did not. He and I were friends."

Dan found a spot where he could continue talking away from the noise of the saloon while still keeping an eye on the entrance. He wasn't sure who he was looking for but felt certain he would know it when he saw it.

"Look sh…look Raoul…stop the bull and talk to me. We will be meeting the FBI shortly and your time is quickly running out. Unless you have a boat or an airplane, you won't be driving back to Miami. The police already have road blocks set up."

"Now, it is time for *you* to stop the games. No one at the FBI has any idea of what Rowles was up to. We were sort of…moonlighting. I will tell you that in my career, I have worked for Special Agent Rowles and Peter Kola."

"Pavel Volkova," Dan interjected.

"Yes. Now my federal protector is gone and I am up the creek, as they say. I know you will not believe me, but if you and your girlfriend meet Mister Volkova, in a public place, I think that we can put this all behind us. And, if there is a journal and other documents, then please…just give it over and we can all move on."

Dan digested what was being offered. "I find it hard to believe that Agent Rowles acted alone."

"I did not say he acted alone. I said he acted with me," Viñals corrected.

"In any event, I will take what you said under advisement. Call me in one…make that two hours… and I'll tell you what we're going to do."

Dan ended the call and walked back to Laura thinking she needed to call Detective Leonard and find out the truth about Special Agent Rowles. If the FBI wasn't already sending a task force down to protect them, then maybe Raoul Viñals just might be telling the truth.

*****

Reentering the saloon, Dan realized the lights inside had come on, indicating that the bar was closing soon - probably within the next half hour. The juke box volume was down and he looked around searching for anyone unusual. Of course, in Key West, he had to redefine what 'unusual' meant. He sat back down, noting that two more drinks had appeared.

"Raoul wants us to meet with him and Volkova in a public place." Dan said, sitting down and taking a sip.

"Let's finish our drinks, call Detective Leonard and set it up," Laura replied.

Dan stopped sipping his drink, finishing it quickly instead and placing the glass back on the bar. He waved off the bartender, who was ready to make another Jack Daniels and Coke, despite the fact they had already announced 'last call.'

"Ay, there's the rub," Dan said.

"Pardon me?" Laura asked.

"*Hamlet.* It's all I remember from high school literature. According to…our new friend, Raoul…who claims to be a double agent who was working with Special Agent Rowles, he said that Rowles was free-lancing this case and not to expect much help from the FBI."

Laura digested what she heard. "Still, an FBI agent was gunned down. Stuff will hit the fan and they will certainly react and try to catch the killer, or killers, even if he wasn't working on an official matter. Now that he has been murdered, they will say it was official so they don't look like idiots."

"That's probably true, but it may take some time. I think we should go someplace that is secure for the next day or two."

"What did you have in mind?"

"Let's get out of here first," Dan said, getting off the stool. He readjusted the Lugar and felt reasonably confident that they would be safe for at least the next day.

Chapter 45

Tuesday early morning, January 21, 2003
On the Keys

Katenka drove through the night while Pavel Volkova fought off exhaustion. She knew that the police might have an all points bulletin out on them and she drove just under the speed limit anxiously looking for police lights ahead which would indicate a check point. Twice she saw flashing blue lights and nonchalantly pulled off the road to observe. On each occasion, it appeared to be a routine stop for speeding or some other violation of the Florida motor vehicle law and she continued her westward trek.

Crossing a small bridge, her phone buzzed making Volkova spasm. She answered in a whisper hoping he would not be disturbed. It was Raoul checking in, sounding very excited; Katenka started to query him when Volkova took the phone away.

"What is it?" Volkova demanded, wincing in pain.

Katenka Tiverzin tracked the conversation, speculating as to Raoul's end, as she watched the roadway ahead. Her lover seemed pleased and was readjusting his position in the back seat so he could sit up the best he could. The Russian ended the call, dropping the phone on the passenger seat and leaning against the back of the driver's seat.

"Good news, my love. Raoul spotted Laura Smith and Dan Gill on Duval Street in Key West about a half ago and he's been following them. They are at a marina now checking out flyers for scuba diving and fishing. If they go out on a boat, then we will have time to get there and set up a reception for when they return. We will find out where they are staying and I will have Raoul put an end to this soon."

"What do you mean when you say...*put an end to this*?" Katenka asked.

"That depends on how foolishly they act. If Laura Smith gives me her brother's journal and the schematics that I gave that idiot then she may live. Otherwise, if she denies any knowledge of it, she will not be so fortunate. In any event, Raoul will probably have to dispatch Mr. Gill at the onset of our interrogation to convince Sergeant Smith that I am not a patient man." He paused. "We need to pull over so I can use a restroom and to change my dressing again."

Katenka thought about what her involvement might be but dared not ask Pavel Volkova. He had never required that she be directly involved in that aspect of his business. Sure, she had led people to their deaths. She had left locks unlocked and arranged the time and place of meetings where her *assignments* would never leave breathing. But, she had never been in the same room or played a physical role in killing, or even hurting, anyone.

Now, with her lover nursing a gunshot wound and only Raoul available, she wondered how the two of them would be able to corral two healthy and strong individuals who weren't very keen on being taken. She knew that she would have to play a more active role. She wasn't looking forward to it. Up until now, she had been enjoying her decadent American lifestyle. The past few days had been fun, a memory, she thought, of playing spy. Katenka Tiverzin, forever in her mind the aspiring ballerina, felt useful...and youthful once again. But now, the play-acting was coming to an end. Soon, she feared, her lifestyle might be taking a turn for the worse. On the lamb in some third world hell hole or, worse, back in Russia. But, what were her choices? She weighed them in her mind glancing up as the sky changed hue.

Katenka slid off the roadway into a fast food restaurant parking lot. Pavel Volkova checked his pants to make sure that blood was not coming through and managed to walk, albeit slowly, with a slight hitch that was barely perceptible. She remained in the car and watched him enter the restaurant and walk back towards the bathroom. Katenka moved her hand up to the gear shift, wishing for the nerve to reverse her vehicle, and her life, and drive towards the red streaked morning sky.

*****

Dan and Laura left the saloon and found an all night drug store on the main drag that was stocked with everything they needed. Laura wasn't thrilled with Dan's idea but, while walking the emptying streets, she acknowledged that it wasn't a bad plan. Dan bought a bigger knapsack and filled it with bottled water, tinned snacks, suntan lotion, heavy beach towels that he intended to use as blankets, if necessary, and toiletries. He struck up a conversation with the night manager of the store while Laura waited outside, glancing up and down the emptying street for any signs of imminent danger.

The first boat leaving for the Dry Tortugas National Park left the dock at seven in the morning and Dan planned for both of them to be on it. About seventy miles due west of Key West, it was a perfect patrol base. A cluster of seven coral reefs, with an eighteenth century federal fort situated on the largest key, it was only accessible by boat or seaplane and so they would be able to see who was coming. Nothing like pre Civil War defenses to fall back on in the twenty-first century, he mused. Dan planned on at least one overnight but wanted to avoid that if possible. He was relying on the FBI getting its act together and, once on the boat, he would tell Raoul where he and Laura were going.

The ball would then be in the Russian's court. If Pavel Volkova came to them then the FBI should be able to get him. There were only so many ways into or out of the Dry Tortugas - or the Florida Keys for that matter. If he couldn't be caught here then he and Laura might as well make plans to relocate to White Bread, Iowa, with the federal witness protection program.

The crew for the boat arrived at six and the ticket office opened thirty minutes later. Dan bought two tickets and he and Laura waited at the dock near the gangway so they could check out all of the passengers as they boarded the vessel. Laura called Detective Leonard twice and called again once they got situated on the dock but all she got was his voicemail each time - so much for 24/7 availability.

Fifteen minutes before the boat pulled out, Detective Corey Leonard called back.

"Where have you been?" Laura demanded.

"Traveling and on hold with the FBI." Leonard answered.

"Hold on, I'm going to put the speaker on but we're walking over to a more private area." Laura and Dan left the dock area, keeping the boarding passengers in sight as they walked to a picnic table outside of a restaurant that wouldn't be open for another few hours.

"Detective, it's me, Dan Gill. Did you speak with Agent Rowles's partner or his boss yet?" he asked, looking at Laura. They were testing Raoul's information.

"Not yet."

"Why not?" Laura asked.

"They weren't available," Detective Leonard replied.

"I find it hard to believe that the FBI was not available to speak with the lead detective working a homicide case of their murdered field agent," Dan said.

"Believe me folks, I found it hard to believe as well. Where are you?"

Laura looked at Dan and he nodded affirmatively. "We're in Key West about to get on a boat for Fort Jefferson."

"What!" Leonard's voice carried far from the little speaker. "Where the hell is Fort Jefferson?" He asked, tone subsiding.

"It's on the Dry Tortugas. You know, off Key West," Laura answered.

"Do you think this is a good time to be sight seeing?" the detective asked sarcastically.

"Detective Leonard, we got a call from Raoul a few hours ago, the man who confronted us in our room last night. He told us that he was also working for Special Agent Rowles and that Rowles was working this matter…unofficially. Is that true?" Gill asked.

"Beats the hell out of me, but it sure explains the stone wall put up by the bureau. Four hours ago, I woke up my chief and asked him to call the local and Miami FBI field offices. They wouldn't tell him anything. He told me to head down towards Islamorada to coordinate with the locals and so I'm on my way there now. Tell me again why you two are going to Fort…where the hell are you two going?"

"We're going to Fort Jefferson on the Dry Tortugas because it's a pretty remote place. The trip should take about three hours. Raoul wants us to meet Pavel Volkova in a public place and this is it. He can meet us out there and we figured that it would give you and the feds enough time to catch him en route," Laura explained.

"Actually, under the circumstances, it's not a bad idea if he goes for it - I doubt that he will. Anyway, at least I won't have to worry about you two for the next few hours. I'll be in Islamorada in about two or three hours. I spoke with the chief detective working the case there and she said that the feds have called her and she's expecting an FBI team from Miami to arrive about the same time I do. She said that she was a little surprised at how long it took for the feds to respond to one of their own being killed.

"If Raoul or Volkova or whoever calls you before I do, don't tell them where you're going. Let's get our trap primed and ready before we invite the bastards in," Leonard added.

"Detective," Dan said picking up the phone, "so far, Laura and I don't have much of a reason to trust a whole lot of people right now. But we do trust you. If we can get this guy out in the open, *you* have to take him out. This may be our only chance. If he gets away, then Laura will be looking over her shoulder until the day she dies. If the FBI obstructs you, will you promise us that you will come anyway?"

"I'll be there."

Dan clicked off the phone and surveyed the passengers getting aboard the vessel and felt comfortable, a gut feeling anyway, that none were former Soviet agents in disguise. One of the mates yelled down to them saying that the boat would be shoving off in five minutes. They both boarded and Dan waited by the gang plank until the young girl from the ticket booth took it away.

The boat navigated through Key West harbor heading due south towards Sand Key then making a sharp turn to the west. Dan and Laura went to the upper deck and found a spot to spread out their beach towels and get comfortable. By the time the Sand Key buoy passed off their port side, Dan and Laura were fast asleep, each realizing that they might never feel as safe again.

Chapter 46

Tuesday morning
Key West

"Man, you must be crazy," Nat Butler said, leaning back in the boat's fighting chair.

"I can assure you that I am as sane as a man can be in my line of work." Raoul Viñals replied, stepping onto the boat from the dock. All of the boats in the little fishing marina had left with their charters except for Nat Butler and the "At Your Service," his thirty one foot Pursuit boat powered by twin 7.4 liter gas mercruisers. The Cuban guessed that the skipper might be willing to take on an odd ball charter since he wasn't going to make money sitting on his ass.

"What's your line of work?"

"Real estate," Viñals replied.

Nat Butler eyed the man who was now sitting on the edge of his boat. "Tell me again what you want to do."

"I want you to take me to the Dry Tortugas."

"And back," Nat Butler said and added, "and how long do you intend to stay there?"

"Not long."

"What's in your bag?" The skipper pointed towards the dock.

"Snorkel and fins."

"I can't afford to sit out there while you snorkel."

"You won't have to. I just need for you to drop me off a few hundred yards from the key and then you can turn around and go home."

Nat Butler slowly swiveled the chair from side to side as he considered the offer. "Real estate, huh?"

Raoul Viñals nodded his head in the affirmative and slowly smiled.

"I charge eight hundred for a half day charter. This trip will take me all day plus you'll want me to keep my mouth shut…so that will cost as well. Let's call it twenty five hundred even."

"I know that you charge five hundred for a half day charter and would do this trip for less than one thousand dollars but it's not worth it to me to haggle with you this morning." Viñals pulled out a roll of bills from his front pocket and counted out twenty five one hundred dollar bills and handed them to the skipper. The Cuban turned to get his bag but was cut off by the fast moving young boat captain.

"I'll get your bag, man. I'm working for you now."

Chapter 47

Tuesday late morning
Gulf of Mexico

Laura and Dan rolled over in their slumber, pulling their new beach blankets over their heads as protection from the morning sun. Dan woke, not realizing where he was at first. Sweat was pouring from his face as he watched the azure sea slide past him between the bottom rung of the side railing and the deck. Mesmerized watching the flying fish sailing just off the water through his half closed eyes, he dozed off again until the loudspeaker came to life a few feet over his head.

"Good Morning! We will be arriving at the Dry Tortugas National Park in approximately ninety minutes." The young girl's voice was chipper - too chipper, Dan moaned. Laura pulled her blanket up and wrapped it tightly around her head to shut out the monologue which ensued. Dan surrendered, sat up, and moved over to some benches away from the speakers.

"The Dry Tortugas were discovered in the year 1513 by the explorer Ponce de Leon. The word *tortugas* means turtles in Spanish and he originally called the island chain *Las Tortugas* for all of the sea turtles that his men caught and ate there. Later, they used the word 'dry' as a warning to other sailors that the keys lacked fresh water. As you all probably know, the word 'key' comes from the Spanish word *cayo* which means island."

Dan, now fully awake, enjoyed watching Laura fight off the narration by intermittently turning over and readjusting the towel around her head. She missed the history of the Spanish treasure fleet that encountered a hurricane in 1622 en route to Spain from Havana and sank, stranding some survivors on the Dry Tortugas and nearby Marquesas Keys. He thought she was going to finally get up during the plight of the H.M.S. Tyger that shipwrecked on Garden Key in 1741, the key on which Fort Jefferson is built, but she only moved away from the speaker and jammed herself against the railing and a life boat.

He went down to the galley and bought a coffee and Danish. When he returned to his bench, he spotted Laura sitting up wearing the blank stare reminiscent of suspects after a long interrogation. She finally got up, soaking wet with perspiration, and walked over to Dan as the young voice finished her history lesson with the story of Fort Jefferson's conversion to a prison and its most famous inmate, Doctor Samuel Mudd, the physician who treated John Wilkes Booth's broken leg after he assassinated President Lincoln. She concluded by saying that Doctor Mudd was eventually pardoned for saving the lives of fellow inmates and prison staff during a yellow fever epidemic.

"Could they find someone with a more annoying voice?" Laura asked rhetorically, taking Dan's coffee.

"I guess we'll find out soon. There'll be a brief history of wildlife at the Dry Tortugas starting in ten minutes."

Laura sat back, tried to get as comfortable as she could on the wooden bench, and let the breeze dry her off. She remembered her two piece bathing suit that she had on underneath and removed her shirt. Dan watched her walk over to their bags, draping the wet shirt over his backpack. She then took off her khaki shorts and placed them over her bag. She rummaged around in the bag to get her bottle of suntan lotion and returned to where she was sitting. He watched her apply the lotion remembering what she felt like back at the motel. "Do my back."

"You know, we may not get a signal out there. That could be a serious flaw in our plan." Dan said, spreading the cream over her back and neck.

"*Our* plan? Do you have a signal now?" she asked.

"Low. Where's your phone?"

"Over there - we won't be able to hear the ring," she said, getting up to retrieve it. "No messages but I have decent signal strength."

"Well, our friend...Raoul...should be calling back any time now." Dan stood up to get more coffee just as Laura's phone rang. She held up the phone showing him the 'blocked' identification message.

"Hello," she answered.

"Hello, Laura, Raoul here. Where are you now?" The Cuban asked as the skipper of 'At Your Service' navigated out of Key West Harbor and slammed the throttle forward after passing the last *no wake* sign.

Laura whispered into Dan's ear Raoul's query and he took the phone.

"At sea. Where are you?" Dan asked then whispered to Laura that Raoul was on a boat. They both began to scan the eastern horizon.

"My location should not be a concern to you at the moment."

"Wait one." Dan said, lapsing into military radio procedure talk. "Look," he said to Laura, "despite what Leonard said, I'm going to tell him where we're going. It sounds like he is on a boat but I don't want to tip our hand to that. He will probably assume that we can figure that out by the engine turning thirty knots in the background. He must have been trailing us but knew we would spot him if he tried to get on this ferry."

Dan turned his attention back to the cell phone. "Raoul, Laura and I are on the way to Fort Jefferson on the Dry Tortugas. We'll be there in about one hour. We will catch the last ferry out at three o'clock this afternoon. Before we head back to Key West, we will contact the FBI to meet us at the dock there. Your boy, Pavel Volkova, can meet us at Fort Jefferson for his face to face meeting, in public, and right next to the park police folks. If he's not convinced that we know nothing *or* we feel we're still in danger...then we blow the whistle. If that means I go into witness protection and Laura is transferred to the armed forces weather channel in Afghanistan, then so be it."

Dan knew that if he ever saw either the Cuban or Volkova again, he would kill them without a moment's hesitation. Never – the - less, he looked at Laura: she indicated her approval of the plan he had just offered and they waited for the Cuban's response.

"You are being unreasonable with your schedule," Raoul Viñals finally answered. "My friend is no where near Key West and so he can not possibly get to Fort Jefferson by three o'clock."

"That is *your* problem, not mine. I need your cell phone number or a number that I can contact you since I may be losing my signal shortly. I assume there will be a phone on the island that I can use to contact you."

"What boat are you on?" Raoul asked knowing the answer; Dan told him. Raoul ended the conversation, quickly calling the Russian with the hope that this nonsense would soon be over so he could return to his real estate deals and his accommodating fat secretary.

*****

Dan wanted to kick himself for not buying a pair of binoculars while he'd had the chance on Key West. Despite the effectiveness of his polarized sunglasses, the tropical sun made viewing the horizon, off the water, a difficult task even after just a few minutes of scanning. Dan spotted a decent pair of binoculars attached to a kid's backpack, along with a Florida wildlife handbook, but he suppressed the larceny in his heart and went back to his unaided search pattern.

Staring at the horizon and knowing Raoul Viñals was out there, Dan hoped the background noise he heard on the phone was from a boat engine and not the prop of a seaplane. He wanted to be the first to set foot on the Dry Tortugas so he could better manage the day's affairs. Dan Gill had seized the offensive and the momentum was with him, or so he kept trying to convince himself. Walking into a trap would seriously jeopardize his order of battle. He didn't think that they would be summarily executed, especially in plain view of a hundred or so tourists, but the possibility remained. It wouldn't take much, he thought. Raoul could get close enough popping them both in the head with hollow point ammunition, the preferred round for the *one shot, one kill* aficionado. If Raoul had a seaplane at his disposal, he would be able to get back to the plane and be airborne before the pilot realized what was going on. From the Dry Tortugas, he could take the plane to Cuba, flying it himself or hijacking the pilot, unless the pilot was in on it too.

Laura came back from the bow and told him that Fort Jefferson was in view. It appeared first as a burr along the flat sea but grew in size until the red brick federal fort was recognizable. Dan confided to Laura what his concerns were about Raoul arriving first and so they decided to be the last tourists off the boat hoping to spot the enemy before he spotted them. Laura thought that she should go alone, as bait, to see if Raoul, or his friends, appeared, but Dan vetoed the plan, citing the long established military doctrine of massing the force. They each had a handgun and could, presumably, fight their way out of an ambush. Otherwise, if Laura were overwhelmed and taken hostage, both weapons would be useless. Better to go down fighting than bargaining, Dan said and Laura nodded without comment.

Laura just finished putting her dried out shorts and shirt back on when her phone rang.

"Hello," she answered.

Dan continued to watch the approaching dock as the boat navigated the last several hundred yards between Garden Key and Bush Key, passing the remains of the north side coaling dock. He noted that no seaplanes were run up on the beach across from the harbor light and only a half dozen boats were docked at the pier. He had been watching two objects off the stern and saw that one was a ferry sized vessel and the other was a private boat. Before he could ask Laura who was calling she was already putting the phone back on her belt clip.

"It was Detective Leonard. He's on the way," she said.

"On the way…where?"

"Here," Laura answered.

"By boat? He wasn't even at Islamorada a few hours ago."

"He has a pilot friend on Marathon Key. He bagged meeting the locals and the FBI and decided to come straight here. He said that the FBI was still giving him the run-around. Detective Leonard wants to be with us while his boss coordinates with the feds. He thinks that Raoul may have been telling the truth, at least with respect to Agent Rowles. He said that he has never seen the feds go into the bunker like they are now."

"When does he think he'll get here?" Dan asked.

"Not long. His friend flies a twin beech for a jump club. He's going to fly Detective Leonard to Key West and then he'll take a seaplane here. He said his friend might be able to get his hands on a seaplane in Marathon. If so, he'll fly straight out here from there."

"That's it?" Dan asked.

"Yeah, his friend, the pilot, was calling him back and he had to go. I gave him your love."

"Thanks. He's not a bad guy…for a detective."

"Jealous?" Laura said, turning to look at Dan.

"Of a detective? No." Dan turned around to watch the boats closing off the stern.

"What's wrong with detectives?"

Dan turned to watch the approaching pier to look for anything unusual, like a former KGB officer setting up a machine gun. He finally replied, "Detectives think they're smarter than everyone else on the police force so my first move, as a cop, was to always get under their skin as fast as possible and throw them off balance. Otherwise, they'd run roughshod over the uniform guys giving orders like they were in our chain of command.

Dan put on his back pack, heading towards the starboard side of the boat since that angle gave them the best view of the rapidly approaching fort.

Chapter 48

Tuesday, late morning
Key West

With the engine off, the tropical sun quickly heated the minivan. Katenka lowered the window and eventually opened the side doors instead of starting up the motor and running the air conditioning. She and Pavel Volkova looked no different than the other tourists waiting for the fun to begin in America's paradise. Katenka had already paid the pilot directly and now they were just waiting for him to finish fueling the seaplane and signal for them to come out to the dock and get in the aircraft. Volkova decided that it was better to wait in the vehicle since he could avoid idle chit chat with the aviator. Also, he was afraid of re-opening his wound when he stepped off the dock into the plane. He didn't want to sit in the confining cockpit seat bleeding while the pilot jerked around with his pre flight checklist.

Volkova knew that the Cuban had come through again; arranging transportation to Fort Jefferson, Raoul Viñals proved he was as resourceful as ever. Just out of Key West harbor, the Cuban had asked Nat Butler for the telephone number of the seaplane charter airline that flew tourists out to the Dry Tortugas and other points of interests. Butler's ex-brother-in-law, but still his best friend, was a pilot with the company. Bernie Lorenzetti was booked; but, after he found out that he would be paid five grand in cash, explained to the young newlyweds from Illinois how his seaplane suddenly developed severe hydraulic leaks in the flaps and an unexplained loss of manifold pressure; they asked for a return of their deposit money and Bernie happily obliged.

"Let me have your phone, please, "Volkova asked Katenka politely, then added. "Leave me alone, now. I have some work to do."

She handed her phone to the Russian and walked over to an ice cream shop that was just opening up; she bought a double scoop pistachio cone. Her diet had been shot to pieces over the past few days and she reckoned that she would not have such luxuries in the near future…so…what the hell. She saw that Pavel Volkova was no longer on the phone and headed back to the car.

"Who did you call?" She asked but he did not answer. Sitting down, she gazed blankly toward the dock. "Are we not in this together?" she asked bleakly.

"We are…very much so." the Russian replied getting out of the car to stand erect. He winced, momentarily, but seemed otherwise unaffected by his recent encounter with the Lugar.

"Well then, who did you call?" Katenka asked, again knowing that he was in a mood that invited a repeated question. She saw him smile as he took some small steps, anticipating the pain, in the direction of the dock.

"You do not need to know that, yet. Just know that I will not allow us to be trapped."

She saw that old look on his face that shone through as he was about to go in for the kill. The aging KGB officer had lines in his face and graying hair, but the eyes had not changed. And, the look was still…frightening.

Katenka Tiverzin remembered when she first saw that countenance, the face of a hunter, when she left the graduate student Volkova had set her up with on one of her first assignments in the new world. The promising young man with a Ph.D. in organic chemistry was naked and exhausted, lying spent on the dirty motel bed where Katenka, then Sophie, fucked him for three and a half hours. She got up, satisfied that her faux lover was fast asleep and left the room, brushing past Pavel Volkova as he was going in. She saw that look, for a moment, as he reached inside for his silenced automatic. Her heels clip clopped on the concrete steps as she went downstairs into the parking lot, not hearing the muffled reports from behind the closed door. She waited while Volkova left behind cocaine and other evidence for the police to discover; the local cops quickly concluded that the promising young man's drug habit left him in a place where he shouldn't have been - part of the overall profile of a man who also stole from his employer to feed his desires. Katenka realized that she probably had had that look, too, because she had felt like a lioness that night. Though, she thought, she didn't feel like a predator now.

"When will you tell me why we are going to such lengths and taking such risks over something so long ago forgotten? Who is blackmailing you?" she said, locking up the car.

"I can't tell you but I need some tangible proof, other than my own story telling, of what we once accomplished for Mother Russia."

"For whom do you need this proof?" Katenka asked, catching up to Volkova and holding his arm in hers.

"For the true believers still left."

She knew that he would not tell her, at least not now. Sometimes he gave her the complete truth, sometimes he didn't, and sometimes, she knew, he gave her nothing but horseshit, probably for her own protection, she realized. Anyway, all she could do now was to go along for the ride. The seaplane pilot waved them over.

*****

The warbling voice on the salt bleached public address system announced that the ferry would be leaving for Key West at three o'clock and that if passengers missed the boat they would either have to camp out until the next day or swim. Dan checked his watch, noting that they would have just under six hours. He then continued scanning the key from the upper deck, finally going down the stairwell to meet Laura at the gangway after he was satisfied that Raoul and company probably had not beaten them to the key. He suggested that they do a quick three hundred and sixty degree sweep of the fort to rule out any suspicious persons or activities and then stake out the dock area from a safe spot, preferably near the park ranger office.

Dan noted that most of the passengers from the boat gathered near a blond, thirty something female park ranger who was commencing a tour. A young couple had run over to the campsite area to stake their claim to a spot they deemed the best.

They entered the fort, walking over a bridge that crossed the sea water moat. They found their way up to the rampart so they could walk along the perimeter and simultaneously scan both the open sea and the fort's interior. Dan noted some singles and couples walking along the rampart and terreplein: all-in-all, he estimated about fifty people on the key. Nearby Bush Key was open for the bird watchers but it looked barren of people.

"Some place, huh?" Laura said

Dan slowed his pace. "Yeah," he said stopping. "I didn't realize the fort would be so big." He gazed into the interior of the six sided structure for several minutes.

"Look, let's go back to the pier. We won't be able to canvass this whole structure before those boats arrive," he said pointing. "Let's check those out…see who gets off…then we'll finish our reconnaissance."

*****

"Are you sure of your time?" Raoul Viñals asked the skipper.

"Sure enough, we're definitely faster than that big ol' ferry boat but they did have a ninety minute jump on us." Nat Butler shouted over his boat's engines.

"I don't need to beat them," the Cuban yelled back and added, "and you will approach from the right direction?"

"I'll do my best. The waters are very shallow outside of the channel and I don't want the park rangers taking an interest in my boat being where it's not supposed to be." Nat Butler lit another cigarette, letting a smile spread across his face as he again felt the lump of cash in his cargo pocket.

Chapter 49

Tuesday, late morning
Dry Tortugas

"What's wrong with this spot?" Laura asked.

"Nothing, but I have a better idea," Dan said, getting up from the concrete and wood bench partially hidden from the pier by a row of hedges. He grabbed Laura's hand and walked back to the ferry. He remembered that their boat, docked at the outermost slip, would provide an excellent vantage to view any other vessels coming into the adjacent slips. Dan also recalled that they would be able to make that surveillance from the air conditioned galley while sipping a cold drink and eating a sandwich.

The first boat through the narrow channel was the smaller of the two. He saw one person driving it from the interior console but couldn't spot any passengers.

"Here," Laura said coming over from the snack bar. "Enjoy your four dollar grilled cheese sandwich." She sat down next to him and sipped her iced tea. "What do you think?" She asked.

"Don't know," he tried to keep his eyes focused on the approaching boat but the glare of the water made it difficult. He thought about stealing the binoculars he'd spied earlier if given another opportunity.

"Looks like a family," Laura said as a woman and two children, a boy and girl, twins, around seven or eight years old, came up on deck and took seats on the front of the boat while daddy maneuvered the last several hundred feet to dock.

The boat pulled in to one of the smaller slips fifty feet from where Dan and Laura had established their stake out. The little boy helped tether the boat to the mooring cleats while the man shut down the engines then headed off towards the fort.

"Well, I suggest that we don't open fire on them," Dan finally said. "What did you get me to drink?"

"Iced tea. Drink it before all of the ice melts." Laura slid the drink over. The air conditioning was turned off to save diesel fuel and the air in the galley area turned squalid from the heat of the tropical sun and working stove. Laura said. "Let's check out the next boat from up top."

Laura got up and Dan attempted to move across the vinyl covered plastic seat to follow but realized he was momentarily stuck. He grimaced as he unglued himself, then grabbed their belongings and followed Laura to the top deck.

"I think this is worse," Dan said. The deck reflected the sun's heat and without the wind, it made standing there for any length of time unbearable. They moved downstairs and forward towards the bow and found a spot that was shaded by the upper deck's overhang. By the time they set up, the larger vessel was in the channel.

*****

"Are you sure about this? Nat Butler asked, steering his boat so it was facing the southwestern side of Fort Jefferson. The deterioration of the fort was clear. From the boat, the pock marked exterior walls of Fort Jefferson made it look like it had been under siege; but, it was just the effect of the rusting of the reinforcing iron work that had swelled over the centuries pushing the red bricks out and into the waiting sea. The fort did not have a combat record except for a few scattered cannon shots at passing Confederate privateers and blockade runners.

"Yes, my friend. Are *you* certain that I won't be run over by a rogue propeller?" the Cuban asked.

"Pretty sure. About twenty yards off my bow you'll hit the reef. Boaters know it's there. I can't guarantee you that some knucklehead with a wave runner won't plow you over, though."

"Fair enough." Viñals lowered himself into the water and pushed back from the stern, going under water and reappearing after a few seconds blowing water through his snorkel.

Butler handed Viñals his waterproof bag and the Cuban attached it to a short piece of rope. The bag was heavy and most of it was hidden underwater like an iceberg.

"I'll stick around until you hit the reef. I'll try to distract anyone I see coming near," Butler said, lighting up another smoke.

"*Gracias mi amigo*. I trust that you will also protect my confidentiality in this matter, as well," Viñals said.

"You bet." Butler grinned, slapping the bulge in his pocket. "Good luck."

The Cuban made it to the reef, surfacing only once. From the reef he would fit in with the other tourists. The Cuban knew that he would need a lot of luck in the coming hours.

*****

The second boat was a ferry, much smaller than the one Dan and Laura took. Dan went on board and after searching the vessel and looking over all of the passengers and crew he walked down the gangplank and met Laura. Eighteen people got off and none looked like Raoul Viñals or otherwise looked suspicious Gill surmised.

"Satisfied?" Laura asked.

"Yup."

"Okay, let's finish our reconnoiter of the fort," Dan said, taking Laura's bag and his back pack.

"You go up to the rampart and walk the perimeter and I'll stay down here to check out all of ground level nooks and crannies," Dan suggested, already heading towards the inner walkway that connected the first level gun sallies and magazines.

"You want to split up…divide the force? Not a good idea," Laura responded.

Dan realized she was right. "Good point, tactically speaking…not bad for being in the air force," he said coming back and following her up the moss covered brick steps.

*****

"How much longer until we get there?" Pavel Volkova asked the pilot.

"At this altitude, we should see Fort Jefferson in about twenty minutes; I should be landing in about thirty." Bernie Lorenzetti had dropped the sea plane until they were flying fifty feet off the deck. Bernie had flown his share of unorthodox flights in South Florida over the past two decades. From smuggling cocaine to hauling Cuban refugees, he had done it all. If the cash was right, he was airborne, no questions asked. Something was very peculiar about the couple in his cockpit, but what the hell. They want to fly low, for five thousand dollars he'd fly low.

"I have to pop up to get some altitude before landing. You know, look around and make sure we don't run into a partially submerged log. That would ruin your honeymoon in a hurry."

"I understand," Volkova replied, looking out the window. He took Katenka's cell phone from his shirt pocket and made a call. By the time the pilot noticed the conversation, the Russian was already handing the phone back to Katenka. Volkova then gazed out towards the horizon. It would be hard to maintain the element of surprise under these circumstances, he thought. Flying to an island where he was expected. He thought of that silly American television show with the midget yelling *De plane, boss, de plane!* If they landed under the eyes of Laura Smith and her boyfriend on the pier, then he would have to play it straight. Raoul had already briefed him that she had not seemed to react to the name Peter Kola back at the motel on Islamorada. But, he wanted to see her reaction for himself. Get a feel for whether she was telling the truth and then get the hell out of Dodge

The Russian knew he was coming to the end game with Sergeant Smith. He would like to get her brother's journal and especially the technical drawings that had been given to him. The soviet space shuttle was practically a carbon copy of the Rockwell design. He had given young Ken Smith the drawings to show how he should damage the O-rings. It was clearly an oversight on his part, Volkova realized afterwards, that the special paper used for the drawings could be traced back to the Ukrainian company that made the graph paper books. That oversight would be useful now in proving his claim.

Katenka Tiverzin was supposed to gather those loose ends up but she never could find where her fiancée put them. She and Volkova searched the home, his office, and his mother's home in Tennessee. No luck. If Pavel Volkova could get his hands on those papers now, and if they were in relatively good shape, DNA analysis would prove that at one time, Kenneth Smith had his hands on a soviet plan to sabotage the space shuttle and it did, in fact, fail as indicated in those drawings. Volkova had old love letters that Ken Smith had given to Katenka and so his DNA would be on those envelopes - sealed with a kiss.

For the longest time, the Russian worried that somebody, CIA, FBI, DIA...had to know what had really happened. But, no one had come after him. In time, he came to accept that his mission was a complete success. He had destroyed the American space shuttle, crippled the enemy's ability to deploy a space based weapon system against his country by grounding the entire shuttle fleet for years, and made the whole event look like an accident. Wherever Ken's journal and those drawings had gone, maybe they were gone forever. But if he *could* get his hands on them...the Russian knew that he could change the world.

Pavel Volkova's wound began to irritate him as Katenka's pain pills started to wear off. In his misery he rued his country's recent history. For Christ's sake, he muttered aloud and then continued with his thoughts, who knew that his country would fall apart. How could communism fail he contemplated. Our leaders were greedy and didn't have the balls to go against the Americans he grudgingly admitted to himself. The Americans lost almost sixty thousand men over three decades of fighting in Vietnam before withdrawing; they brought the war right to the front door of the Soviet Union and Red China. The lazy, decadent Americans had more will than our supposedly iron fisted premiers who couldn't even win a war against the goat-buggering Afghanis armed with bolt action rifles and living right on our border. Sure, the Americans eventually gave them Stinger missiles but you don't win wars with helicopters. You win wars with infantry having the will to fight backed by a nation with the will to win. The bitterness swelled inside Pavel Volkova. He loved his country, the Union of Soviet Socialist Republics, and was loyal still to the ideals espoused by its founding fathers: Marx, Engels and Lenin.

Now, Russia had let its former Warsaw Pact allies join NATO. Before long, Russia will be in NATO as well, the Russian groaned audibly in the noisy cockpit. Pavel Volkova believed that the Russian people were being led down the wrong path by leaders who only wanted western goods and wealth. Sure, the old commissars were scumbags. They enjoyed their *dachas* while Muscovites lived ten to a room. But they provided the necessities of life and a well ordered society. Russians want…no, they *need* the iron hand. Volkova gripped the arm of the seat tighter as he felt a brief stabbing pain down his leg. Look at the crime now in Russia's cities - organized crime, youth gangs, hooligans, the black market…all far worse now than ever before, he knew for a fact. The widening gap between the rich and the poor that will never be closed because Russians don't know how to become middle class - they never had a middle class and they don't desire one, Volkova firmly believed.

The former KGB officer was incensed, incredulous in fact, that the Russian government sought unprecedented cooperation with the West. For God's sake, the Russian atheist lamented, he read in the London papers that the Russian army would even be switching to NATO compatible military systems - the Red Army marching past the Kremlin carrying M-16s: Volkova was getting a migraine.

Enough was enough. Pavel Volkova decided that he would not be thrown into the ash heap of history, as that fool Ronald Reagan had repeated ad nauseam about communism. Whole nations still believed as he did and he could disrupt Russia's assimilation by the West, or at least slow it down, as he had the American space program. All he needed was to find some tangible proof that could be used to retard these new friendships. Proof that would make America suspect their old enemy and thereby…would help his new friends.

"Okay, I have to go a little higher, now," Bernie Lorenzetti said and imperceptibly pulled back on the wheel.

Pavel Volkova reached into his small bag and pulled out ten thousand dollars. He would need to speak further with Mr. Lorenzetti.

*****

"Hello," Laura answered on the second ring, realizing she was out of breath from excitement.

Dan took her bag, setting it down and stepping closer to her. He gestured to put the call on speaker.

"Hold on. Can you hear me?" she asked, holding the phone between them.

"Yes, my friends, loud and clear. How are you two holding up?" Raoul Viñals asked.

"Just great. Yourself?" Laura replied.

"Wonderful. Are we ready to do business?"

Dan checked his watch. "The boat pulls out at three and the FBI will be at Key West when we get there. Let's get this over with. When is Volkova going to meet us?"

"Well, like I said before, you're really giving us a tight schedule to work with. Mr. Volkova would like to know if we could extend this..."

"Tough tits, Raoul. It's now or never," Dan said, looking to Laura for approval: she nodded in the affirmative. He took out a cigarette from a pack he'd purchased the night before and kept hidden from Laura.

"He assumed that would be your position and he is attempting to meet your demands. Laura..."

Laura waited for him to continue but was met with silence. "*Yes?*" she finally replied.

"Are you a bird watcher?" Viñals asked.

"Excuse me?"

"Are you a bird watcher? Do you know about birds?" the Cuban reiterated.

"Get to the point, shitbird," Dan said, lighting up.

"Oh, Mister Gill, I thought we had worked past that. I was only asking because I wanted to know what type of birds those are."

"What birds?" Laura asked.

"The four blackbirds off to your left...on the rampart wall."

They both looked over and spotted the winged foursome. Dan reached behind for the Lugar but stopped short of pulling it out when he saw the family with the twins from the boat approaching. The young boy was walking too close to the edge and his mother just yelled at him. Laura crouched down and realized she had zippered her bag and could not immediately access her daddy's revolver. She calmly unzipped the bag, placing it over her shoulder: her free hand found the gun and she pulled back the hammer with her thumb.

"Calm down, we're not going to have a shoot out on Fort Jefferson in front of fifty witnesses. When this day is done, I just want to get on with my life…as do you." they heard Raoul say as Laura clicked on the speaker phone button.

Dan looked around, but didn't see anyone on a cell phone. Viñals had to be within line of sight, close enough to see those friggin' birds.

"Okay, so now what?" Dan asked.

"I need for you to come to me: I will be going to the far western interior wall near the officer's quarters."

"No, you will come to us near the park ranger's building," Laura demanded.

"I understand your fear, but I really don't want anyone overhearing what we are talking about. I will call Mr. Volkova and we can all listen together on the speaker phone. He is on a boat trying to get here before you leave. He wants me to see you and judge whether you are telling him the truth in case he doesn't get here. I am walking out and you should be able to see me…right about…now."

Laura saw him first and nudged Dan. Raoul Viñals came out from under an overhang wall about a hundred yards away. He walked towards them, raising his hands slowly then bringing them down and tipping his hat. He was wearing sandals, shorts, and a Hawaiian shirt, carrying nothing except his phone.

"Take your shirt off," Dan said.

"That demand would be more welcomed if it came from your partner."

Dan and Laura watched as Viñals walked about ten more steps, then took off his shirt and did a slow three sixty. He stepped over to a civil war era cannon and rested against it.

"Nice try Raoul, step away from the cannon," Dan ordered.

"Do you think I have hidden a weapon in the barrel already?" the Cuban laughed.

"You never know. Take twenty steps towards the interior of the fort and I will meet you there."

Viñals wanted them both inside the fort but knew he wouldn't win this battle so he didn't bother to spend any more energy on the effort. He hoped he had already accomplished what he had set out to do.

"Move over there." Dan directed to Laura, pointing to the convergence of two of the fort's six sides, one of which abutted the sea and had a brick wall along the walkway that would protect Laura from any interior line of fire. "Cover me from there. I don't intend on talking with Viñals down there. I'll grab him by the arm and escort him towards the ranger office. You start moving there as well once we get going. We still need to keep an eye on who's arriving."

"We are deviating from our plan," Laura barked. "Let's get back to the pier and wait in the open. I need to contact Detective Leonard and find out what's going on. How do we know Raoul didn't bring anyone else or that Volkova isn't already here?"'

"I would bet my pension that Volkova was shot last night. I think Raoul followed us out here without Volkova. You're right, though, others could be with him. That's why I want you to cover me and I will take him to where we want to be. I presume he is unarmed at this point: if I stay with him then he will remain unarmed."

"No, we stick together. Tell him to start walking towards the front gate. We will meet him there and then go to the ranger station."

Dan acknowledged that Laura was right again. He winked at her. Trying to keep his eye on Raoul while surveying the entire landscape, sector by sector, he said. "Start walking towards the front gate." He took one last drag from his cigarette and tossed it away.

"Mr. Gill, please listen to me."

"Start walking." He ended the phone call and stared down at the Cuban until he turned and started walking slowly in the direction commanded.

Chapter 50

Tuesday Afternoon
Dry Tortugas

The fort was designed to repel ship borne invaders and protect America's burgeoning trade lanes in the Caribbean. It was brick and mortar proof that the United States of America meant business and provided teeth to the words of the Monroe Doctrine to keep the European weasels out of America's hen house. Unlike the harbor forts built along the eastern seaboard, the designers of Fort Jefferson did not think an amphibious invasion likely due to the limited approaches guarded by treacherous coral reefs. Therefore, the interior was wide open to allow rapid shifting of defenders from one wall to another to man the massive ship crippling cannons. Modern military planners would say that it had good interior lines of communication. That worked out nicely for Dan and Laura since they could view the entire interior from the front gate, precluding any surprises from that approach, where they would meet Raoul Viñals again.

"It is a pleasure to see you both again," the Cuban said, offering his hand to Laura. "Hopefully, there will be no further unpleasantness."

"Keep moving," Dan said, taking a step between the two.

"Where to?" Viñals said, taking a few more steps and stopping.

Laura kept her focus on the fort and Dan motioned to the nearest picnic table by the campsites. The picnic area was close enough to the park ranger station and pier, the former army ranger concluded. Dan followed a few steps behind Raoul Viñals, checking out the campsite area: glancing over towards the ferry, he spotted a white object coming off the stern: he abruptly halted.

Laura stopped behind him.

"What are we waiting for?" she asked.

"What's that?" Dan said, pointing towards the ferry just as the object moved out from behind the boat and they could hear its engine. "Son of a bitch!" Dan growled. "When did that get here?"

"I think he's taking off," Laura said, as they watched the seaplane navigating past the moored sailboats. It stopped briefly, changing its azimuth. The plane started moving at full throttle for a few seconds before the increased noise of the propeller reached shore.

"Was it here before?" Laura asked.

"I don't think so. Maybe it's Leonard. We should have heard it coming in, though," Dan said, lighting up another cigarette. "But we were too busy dealing with him." He started walking toward the picnic table where the Cuban was waiting. Laura followed checking her signal strength and looking for a message from the detective.

Dan motioned for Viñals to sit down and told him to keep his hands on the table. They stood opposite him and Laura turned to keep her eye on the fort and the pier.

"Who was on the seaplane?" Dan demanded.

"How should I know?" The Cuban answered.

"How did you get here?"

"By boat."

"Which boat?" Dan said, looking out towards the dock and then towards the moored sail boats.

"It's gone."

"Where is it now?"

"Half way to Key West, I presume."

"If you knew we were coming here, why not just take the ferry with us? Laura asked, turning to face him.

"Mr. Volkova wanted me to follow you and I did. I lost you two on the way to Key West. By luck, I found you walking on Duval Street and tracked you. I called Mr. Volkova once I realized you were getting on the ferry to come here."

"You could have come aboard before we left." Laura responded.

"I was waiting to be instructed. By the time I got him on the phone, the ferry had pulled out. I had to search for another way to get here. I spotted a lone fishing boat at the fishing boat marina. The skipper was willing to drive me out here, one way, for a lot of money."

"Again, if you got here before us, why not meet us at the dock?" Dan said.

"I don't believe that I arrived before you. You two seem to think that I am making the decisions here. Pavel Volkova is a deranged man who will kill me as easily as he would kill you two. He lives in a fantasy world where we are still fighting the cold war. Unfortunately, he re-entered this country and knew where to find me. I am confident that if you give him what he wants or he is convinced that you have no idea of what he is talking about, then he will leave us all alone. Well, he will leave you two alone, I made a deal with this devil years ago and my obligation, I fear, is life long. Trust me, I want to live a long time."

"Where is Volkova now?" Dan asked.

"He's trying to get a boat the same way I did. I recommended a seaplane but they were all booked. He called me an hour ago and said that he found a boat but the skipper just needed to get the owner's permission and, I assume, work out a financial arrangement."

"Let us assume that he doesn't make it. What does he want?" Dan said.

Laura stepped closer to the table but maintained her field of vision towards the pier. While still inside the fort, Dan had moved the Lugar from the small of his back and had tucked it into his front waistband. He had to adjust the barrel now that he was sitting down since it was pointing to a part of his anatomy that he wanted to protect and he forgot whether the safety was on or off.

"What are you packing there?" Viñals asked.

"Don't worry about that. What does Volkova want?" Dan said.

"You must realize that he never gives me the full story. However, I am to understand that Laura's brother kept a notebook…a journal… and that he also had some technical drawings given to him by Mr. Volkova."

"You mean Mr. Kola." Laura said.

"Of course…one and the same."

"How does Volkova know whether or not there was a journal?" Laura asked.

"Because Kenneth Smith's fiancée, Katenka Tiverzin, observed him writing in the journal and she reported what he wrote to her boss, Peter Kola...Pavel Volkova. Also, I am to understand, the technical drawings can be traced somehow to the former Soviet Union and so Mr. Volkova would like all of that evidence back."

"Did they kill my brother?" Laura said coming towards the table and moving her hand inside of the gun bag.

"Yes." The quick and candid admission surprised her. Viñals continued, "From what Mr. Volkova told me on the drive down to Islamorada, your brother thought for sure that the O-ring defect would be discovered during preflight. At worst, he thought that the flight could safely be aborted. As the January launch date approached, he had notions of going public to say how dangerous the shuttle system was and that it should be grounded indefinitely. In any event, he didn't expect the explosion. The death of the seven astronauts and especially of that civilian astronaut, the school teacher, troubled him deeply. He was overcome with remorse and wanted to turn himself in. Pretty Katenka urged him to think about it. After soothing his despair, she called her boss to tell him that the jig was up. Your brother was killed before his trailer exploded."

"Who killed him?" Laura demanded. Her anger overwhelmed her and she moved into Dan's position. He got up to maintain surveillance taking a few steps away from Laura and Viñals.

"A prosecutor would say that they both did - it was a conspiracy. But the fatal blow came from Volkova. He crushed your brother's skull in after Katenka fed him Valium with bourbon chasers. Ken never knew what hit him; he was asleep when it happened. They moved his body to the kitchen, and after the explosion, it appeared as if the blast had knocked him against the door frame. Pavel Volkova should have let the body burn so that there would be even less evidence for the investigators, but Volkova's older brother was burned alive in his T-55 tank during the '68 invasion of Czechoslovakia, burning flesh is a phobia that I know he has.

"Before blowing the place up, they searched all over for the journal and the drawings. In time, they also checked out his office and your mother's house. In case your brother had a hiding spot that they couldn't find, they burned your mother's house down, too."

Laura reached over and struck the Cuban across the face with her open hand. She wanted to pistol whip him but was able to control herself and not bring the revolver from its hiding place. Dan stepped back, putting a hand on her shoulder.

"Please accept my apology for the cold narration but I had nothing to do with what happened to your brother. However, I deserve a lot more than a slap for the things I have done." Raoul Viñals leaned back and checked his wine colored mouth. Blood was on his hand and was forming again over his lower lip. Laura put her hand back in the bag, took out a bandana that she had bought the night before, and tossed it in front of him. The Cuban opened it up and wiped his hand and face.

After a few minutes, Dan asked, "After all these years, why now?"

"Perhaps he can tell you if he gets here," Viñals answered.

"Give us your best guess," Laura said.

"The Chinese," the Cuban answered without hesitation.

"Excuse me?" Laura said, understanding the words but wanting to hear it again. Before he could respond, the phone in Viñals pocket rang. He looked at Laura before moving to answer it.

"Go ahead," she said.

*****

Katenka had no idea that Dan had ever seen a photograph of her. In any event, she had pumped gas right next to him and he had given no clue that he knew who she was - even as she felt his eyes canvass her. And no way was he able to see her in the minivan at the motel the night before.

A natural introvert, Katenka had to force herself to converse with others. She spotted the campers and waited for one of the women to use the public restroom. There, she struck up a conversation with her and by the time they headed towards campsite number three, they looked like two old buddies. At least, they looked so to Dan.

Dan heard the taller woman say, "See you later, there're my friends," as she stepped from the pathway towards Laura.

"Relax, don't move," Katenka commanded as she straddled the bench next to Laura, grabbing the arm that had access to the magnum.

Dan lunged towards the table.

"Stop!" Viñals ordered. "She is with Mr. Volkova and he is here."

Katenka slid a .32 caliber semi-automatic pistol from her waist and pressed it against Laura's side as she moved even closer to her. The former ballerina pressed her muscular thigh against the small of Laura's back pushing her tight against the picnic table. Laura quickly realized that she would not be able to get out of the way of the little automatic. Options ran through her head, but none that wouldn't leave a bullet blasting through her abdomen. She watched as the Cuban reached under the table and took her bag.

"Pavel Volkova will see you now, Mr. Gill."

Dan stepped around quickly, wanting to get to the Cuban's side of the picnic table without provoking Katenka into gunfire. Standing behind Viñals he pulled out the Lugar and the Cuban felt the metal on his bare back. Dan grabbed Laura's bag and tossed it over towards the base of a young palm tree.

"Let me have the phone," Dan said and the Cuban handed it over.

"Where?" Dan said into the phone but only heard silence. "He hung up, get him back." Dan put the phone on the table in front of Viñals.

"He won't answer it now. He wants you to go inside the fort and over towards Doctor Mudd's cell."

"What for?"

"I really don't know," the Cuban answered.

"I'm not leaving Laura."

"You two no longer have choices to make. Volkova landed in that seaplane and it's probably flying ovals waiting to pick him up. According to the man who brought me out here, the pilot is quite a mercenary. If you do not comply, Laura dies."

Raoul Viñals waited for them to digest that prophesy, and continued. "Look at her." He gestured towards Katenka who had not taken her eyes off Laura since moving up against her. "She knows her life is over if she doesn't do what Pavel Volkova orders her to do. If you do not comply, she will put two or three quick rounds into your girlfriend and then empty the magazine in our direction. It really doesn't matter if she hits me trying to get you. The seaplane will come back and take Volkova and her out of here.

*****

Dan ran the permutations. It just didn't work out in their favor. Maybe if he had a few weeks and a Cray computer, a correct solution could be worked out. For now, no matter how he figured things, leaving Laura alone was just too dangerous. He looked towards the eastern sea and spotted the sun glare off the cockpit window as the plane turned and began its descent. No one else noticed, he observed, but eventually the aircraft engine noise would become apparent. Dan prayed it wasn't the same airplane that just took off.

"I'm not going," Dan said

"Like I said, there are no more choices to be made," Raoul replied, pivoting his legs over the bench seat so that his back was to the picnic table.

"Then we all go. Let's start walking," Dan said.

Raoul stood up briefly, and then sat down on the table with his feet on the bench seat, turning to look at Katenka, who offered no opinion.

Dan glanced around and took note that the nearest tourists were some distance away. He took aim with the Lugar at the Cuban's temple.

"You shoot me, she shoots your girlfriend, and then, I suppose there will be a Mexican standoff," Raoul said.

Dan took a quick step, grabbed Laura's bag and took out the magnum, leveling it at Katenka. He knew that a sudden head shot would immediately paralyze the woman, rendering her trigger finger useless. But he just couldn't take the chance, he decided. A belly wound this far from an emergency room would make survival pretty dicey for Laura.

"Certainly Mr. Volkova did not plan on your obstinacy," the Cuban said.

"He should have consulted with my ex-wife," Dan said. "I'm sure that after all these years and all of the spy shit we've had to put up with for the past week, Volkova doesn't want a shoot out in a federal park with no great means of escape. "Now, if I go alone, I risk having you two take Laura with you to a boat or that seaplane that just left. Also, I risk being shot in the head in one of those cells in the fort. So, Laura and I will meet Volkova together."

Raoul did not want to make the next decision and was saved by Volkova's impatience. His cell phone rang: he looked at Dan, who indicated that he could answer it.

"They are still here," the Cuban said. He explained the situation, listened, then folded the phone and put it away in his pants pocket.

"Let's go," Raoul Viñals said, and then added, "All together. Katenka; put your gun away, it is no longer needed."

Katenka slid back along the seat concealing the automatic between her legs, ready to bring it back into Laura's side if need be. She was afraid that the younger woman would try to retaliate and wasn't about to be slapped around; she had not permitted that for quite a long time. Laura got up from the table and walked over to Dan, picking up her bag and taking back her father's gun. She slung the bag over her shoulder, keeping her right hand, and the gun, hidden.

"Let's go," Dan said and they all headed towards the fort. At the entrance, he looked back and eyed a seaplane on the water. For some reason, the wind direction perhaps, no noise reached them.

Chapter 51

Tuesday afternoon
Fort Jefferson

The magazine wells and lower cannonade positions had been converted into prison cells during the Civil War as soon as it had become apparent that the Confederate Navy was in no position to dictate terms in the Gulf of Mexico and the French and British navies would mind their own business. Excellent cells they made, too, for punishing traitors to the Union, from both the North and the South. Dark and dank with daylight penetrating only from a small slit in the brick work for the cannons, the cells presented a breeding ground for infectious diseases and hopelessness.

The foursome did not look outwardly unusual, but Park Ranger Debbie Hammer took note of their stuttered walking. Eyeing Dan Gill covering his stomach with one hand, she assumed he was still fighting the effects of being sea sick. Hammer watched them enter the fort and made a mental note to check on them later, to see if the man was still ill, just as a young boy came up from behind and asked her about a shark he thought had seen in the moat.

Raoul Viñals led them past the cell that once held Doctor Samuel Mudd and halted fifty yards beyond. "He's in there." The Cuban pointed.

Dan looked into the musty enclave that held one of the fort's interior cisterns used to collect rain water. It was dark. He looked back, took out his Lugar, and entered. Laura followed keeping her back to his and pulling her magnum from the bag. Before their eyes could adjust they heard the Russian for the first time.

"The weaponry is truly unnecessary at this point."

Dan and Laura both turned to the voice, raising their firearms as they did. Pavel Volkova was seated in the corner near where they entered so that he could silhouette whoever else came into the cavern - like area with the minimal light that was available.

"Then why did your psycho girlfriend stick a gun in my ribs ten minutes ago," Laura demanded keeping her revolver pointed at Volkova's head.

"Because it was apparent that you two were armed and I didn't know if you would shoot first before my friend, Raoul, could tell you what I wanted. Mr. Gill, you may frisk me if you want: I believe you are well trained in that area. Katenka?"

"Yes." She replied.

"Please come inside and hand Sergeant Smith your weapon; bring Raoul with you."

Despite Dan's pledge to himself that he would kill the Russian on sight, he found he just wasn't capable of cold blooded murder. The former cop took up the Russian's offer and gave him a little bit more than a Fourth Amendment approved pat down. The Russian was sitting on a folding camp stool and Dan inspected its underside and the framing as well. He spotted a black bag nearby, and tossed that towards the entrance well away from Volkova's reach. He looked at Laura, who was now holding two guns while Katenka and Raoul moved inside.

"I want them sitting down on that far wall and facing away from you," Dan ordered.

"Come now, Mr. Gill. There are three guns in this room and you two have them all. Let's be civil about this, shall we?"

"Okay, they can face us, but I want them sitting down over there," he said, pointing. "And I want them apart."

They all waited while Katenka and Raoul moved to their assigned spots. Dan took Katenka's automatic from Laura, pulled out the clip, checked if a round had been chambered, then reinserted the magazine and placed the little gun in his back pocket.

"Why shouldn't I just kill you right now for what you did to my brother?" Laura said, aiming the magnum directly at the Russian's head.

Dan decided to keep a closer eye on Laura than the Russian, fearing that she would pull the trigger. Feeling that he had the situation under control, he placed his hand on her firing arm and after a moment, she lowered her weapon.

Dan raised the Lugar at Volkova. "Don't think I won't shoot you in a heartbeat, either. But I'm not as personally involved and I'm willing to hear what you have to say."

Pavel Volkova did not flinch as either weapon, in turn, was pointed at him. He was a man who had experienced the threat of death many times before and these two were...well...they were rank amateurs he thought.

"First let me say that what is done is done. What you believe, Sergeant Smith, even if it is the truth, can not be proven in your courts of law. So, by killing me, you will achieve great moral satisfaction but your career will be over and you will spend a great deal of your life in prison. We are here purely for business reasons - you Americans should understand that best of all." The Russian adjusted his position on the tiny campstool.

"Enough of the bullshit. Let's hear what you want," Dan said lowering the Lugar so that his aim was now at the Russian's heart...a center mass shot was an odds on favorite over a head shot any day.

"Do you know what my relationship was with your brother?"

"I'm going to shoot the son of a bitch right now," Laura said raising her weapon again.

"Enough with the history lesson, Ivan; your buddy over there," Dan pointed his gun at Raoul, "filled us in. Put the gun down, Laura". He placed his hand back on her shooting arm. "We think we know all that we ever want to know about Ken Smith, you, and that whore over there," Dan said. "Now what do you want from us?"

Volkova could hear Katenka shifting her position; he knew her temper was up and so he motioned with his hand for her to be still. He said to Laura, "I want the journal that Ken Smith kept during the last few months of his life and I want the technical drawings that were given to him...by me."

"What?" Laura faked and prepared to raise up the magnum again. "Why would you want my brother's diary?"

"It doesn't matter to you. Do you have them?" the Russian asked pointedly, keeping his eyes focused on Laura. He waited while she hesitated and then the Russian clapped loudly. "You *do* have them; I can see it in your eyes. Hand over what you have and we all leave this dungeon right now and go our separate ways."

Dan looked over at Laura and said, "You're right; we do have them…but not here."

"On this key?" The Russian shot back.

"Yes."

"Then go get them and come back."

"Not until we know why," Laura said.

"You Americans with your having to know why," the Russian said caustically.

"That's right, we Americans want to know why. And I'm still pondering whether I should feel morally satisfied in killing you. It may be worth a few years in prison. Dan, you'll wait for me, right?"

"Actually, with all of the evidence from the restaurant shooting to last night, I think the feds would let us off scott free as long as we promise not to go on the Larry King Show."

Pavel Volkova absorbed Dan and Laura's last statements and studied their body language. They were scared and she was pissed off as well. The American sergeant might just plug him, he realized.

"I am a communist," the Russian declared. "I believe in communism as fanatically as the Christians believe in Christ as their true lord and savior. Like Christianity, true communism is a faith, a secular faith, which requires apostolic work. I am required to defend my faith and spread its teachings."

"I guess you missed the whole Berlin Wall coming down thing," Dan interjected.

The Russian thought back to the days when he was a master interrogator in the concrete basement of Lubyanka Prison in Moscow. He enjoyed a sudden vision of shoving an electric cattle prod into Mr. Gill's rectum.

"Mr. Gill, what political party do you affiliate yourself with?" The Russian asked.

"None of your business pal."

"Fair enough, I assume you are both Christians."

"What's your point?" Laura asked.

"What if a man took over your government? A man that you detested from a political party that wanted to change the whole fabric of your society. And..."

"We survived Clinton," Dan said.

"I am serious, Mr. Gill. And your religion was outlawed, as well. Just because this new government took over and was accepted by the world community, would you just sit back and accept it? Or would you still bubble underneath with your patriotism and your faith and fight back?

"Communism was an article of faith for over seventy years in my country. Communists stopped the Great War and won the Patriotic War. By smashing petty nationalism, ethnicity and religion, communism was able to unify all the republics into our former union. Look how Tito was able to control all of the fractious peoples in Yugoslavia and look at what a mess everything is today in that region.

"I believe that the very future of mankind lies in the expansion of communism. We must dedicate ourselves to the good of the state over everything else. When we abandon our self interest, our ethnic pride and our religion, then we can recognize that the good of all humanity will be our only priority.

"Like you, Mr. Gill...and you, Sergeant Smith...I fought for my country, the Union of Soviet Socialist Republics. I have lost family and many good comrades in our struggles. You must understand how bitter I feel over the betrayal that has occurred in my country..."

"Take a breath Ivan; you're swinging after the bell." Dan said keeping his aim.

Pavel Volkova appeared to relax. Looking around the enclosure, he continued to kill time. "Only a few real communists are left and only one communist nation that can rival America - Red China. I want to help them. I think Americans would rather deal with the hard line Chinese communists who mean what they say and are thoroughly pragmatic than with the two-faced politicians running the show now in my country. I want to ruin Russian-American relations and foster Sino-American relations...for the time being. The Chinese are about to put astronauts into orbit and they have other plans. They want to cause...disharmony...between America and Russia. They want hard evidence about my efforts to destroy your space shuttle to bring to the United Nations and to the World Court. As the American opinion of Russia declines, the Chinese will do a full court press to bolster Sino-American relations. They need a space partner to get them to the moon."

"Wouldn't you be exposing yourself to some legal difficulties?" Dan asked.

"No. My full amnesty deal will be worked out first and I will be set up with my own private island in the South China Sea."

Laura glanced over at Katenka, hoping for a reason to shoot, but the ballerina sat quietly with her legs crossed in a modified yoga position. Dan took a step back to keep the entrance in his peripheral vision.

"After you testify, you will have no more value. Why would the Chinese continue with that arrangement?" Laura asked.

"Because I have other secrets that may be as valuable."

"So, let me get this straight," Dan said. "You want *us* to help *you* and that help...ultimately, will hurt the United States."

"No. Ultimately, the United States will have the scales dropped from its eyes and see what type of people they are dealing with in Russia. Without American or western help, the Russian economy will not be able to survive and the people...ah, the people, who never really wanted freedom anyway, will demand a return of the communists."

"So, you would have us return to the cold war?" Laura said.

"Wouldn't you rather be there now yourself? Let's be honest with each other. Russians and Americans struggled to sell their ideologies throughout the world. While we did indeed have the megatons and throw weights aimed at each, we all knew that the missiles would never fly and the bombers would never be ordered past fail safe. Instead, we jointly ruled the world...perhaps...arguably, saner than any one ever acknowledged at the time. We contained our disagreements to the hinterlands...Vietnam, Afghanistan, Angola. You take Somalia, we take Ethiopia, or was it the other way around?

"We had the Arabs scurrying around, begging for our favor, so they could buy our arms to kill each other; the Europeans pissed their pants like frightened little school girls and ran to Uncle Sam every time we rolled out our armored divisions for a little field exercise; the Chinese and all the nations in Asia kept to themselves for the most part. Wasn't that preferable to the chaos that exists now?

"Besides, China doesn't want to be a global superpower ; they just want to be the baddest kid on their block. If the old USSR can not be revived, then the next superpower will be the radical Islamists aided by the anarchists you see protesting every international trade meeting. Those people don't think rationally and they certainly don't give a rat's ass about who dies in their maniacal suicide attacks.

"You and I both know that the day is coming when one of those lunatics will detonate a nuclear device instead of just crashing airplanes into buildings. They will think nothing of killing hundreds of thousands or even millions of people if given the opportunity. Maybe America has the will now, but eventually the rest of the world will give in to whatever demands they set. And if they ever get to control all of the oil and gas spigots, America will have no allies left in its war on terrorism. The Europeans…the whole world…would rather fold than fight any day. This asymmetrical warfare will bring America to its knees despite your overwhelming military power.

"We all thought, naively so, that in the market place of ideas, either capitalism or communism would win out and humankind would go on from there. What we didn't realize was that the titanic struggle between our nations kept the world in balance. With the collapse of my country, capitalism did not win out; chaos did.

"I am sorry for what happened to your brother, I truly am," Pavel Volkova lied. "But in my mind, he and I were both soldiers and he died a soldier's death.

The Russian hoped that he was easing her hatred and hoped for a quick delivery of the journal and drawings. He even thought of letting them live; but it was a very brief thought.

Laura checked the big magnum, not recalling when she had pulled the hammer back, and thought about what the Russian had said. "We can't return to a two superpower world. The cat is out of the bag. Even if your countrymen haven't grasped the real meaning of freedom yet, they still will not go back to a system where a privileged few enjoy the goodies while the rest wait three hours in a queue for something to eat and then four hours for the toilet paper.

"Sure, there is instability, unrest and fear now; but in time, the Islamic world will see the truth just like your people have. Just like the people who lived under the thumb of Hitler, Tojo, and Mussolini, who saw their dictators' lies washed away by the truth. The Muslim people will see that their hatred has been mixed up in a cauldron and served to them by their monarchies and religious oligarchies to hide the fact that a very few are reaping the wealth of their oilfields. Some day, the House of Saud will fall harder than the Berlin Wall and the three hundred royal cousins spreading the hatred over there will be thrown into the ash heap of history along with your piece of shit Vladimir Illych Lenin.

Leveling her weapon at the Russian's head and taking a step towards the entrance, Laura said, "I have my brother's journal and the drawings you gave him and I will make them public because the truth will always conquer ignorance and hatred."

"Laura, wait…" Dan reached out and touched her on the back. "Let's just all simmer down." Dan pointed his Lugar briefly at Raoul and Katenka making them sit back down. He checked the doorway and took aim again at the Russian. "It still doesn't make sense, Laura. I never heard anything about the Chinese going to the moon. He's running a scam on us just like he did to your brother."

Laura thought for a moment. "The Chinese don't even have a reliable orbital space system and the United States certainly has not expressed interest in returning to the moon anytime soon. Dan's right."

*****

The Russian laughed and decided they would, after all, have to die. Might as well tell them the truth while he waited, he thought.

"The Chinese are working, concurrently, on two top secret endeavors. The first is a world class space program and the second is nuclear fusion technology. The Chinese have developed space delivery rockets - the Long March 2F Carrier Rocket can boost their piloted space capsule into orbit. Their capsule, the *Shenzhou*, meaning 'magic vessel' is based on the Russian *Soyuz*, but it's much better. In 1996, the Chinese and Russians entered into a space cooperation agreement and Chinese astronauts, taikonauts, have been routinely training at the Star

City cosmonaut training center. Also, Red China's lobbying efforts in America during the '90s paid off handsomely as your government allowed the sale and transfer of technology that significantly improved their satellite communications and rocket guidance abilities.

"The Chinese had the opportunity to look at American technology and Russian technology side by side and decided that they would be immeasurably better off if they had America as a space partner, for now, rather than Russia."

"What about the fusion research?" Laura asked.

"Helium-3," Pavel Volkova answered, getting blank responses that he expected. He continued, "Helium-3 is nature's second most abundant element, behind hydrogen, and can be used to generate electricity that would be radiation and pollution free. H-3 is spread through space from our sun, all suns in fact, but here on earth, our atmosphere keeps most of it out. Your Apollo astronauts were pivotal in discovering its presence on the moon in the rocks they brought back. Because the moon has little atmosphere, it acts like a receiver, trapping H-3 in its rocks and in its soil. Approximately twenty tons of H-3 can provide the United States with electrical energy for one year - absolutely clean energy. One ton of it would have a value of approximately seven *billion* dollars. Therefore, going back to the moon to mine H-3 would be profitable.

"Only the Chinese have a plan to go to the moon *and* build fusion energy facilities on earth. Intelligence agencies have speculated about their capability. I am here to tell you that they will be sending H-3 back to earth within ten years. The Chinese will have the only operating space program that can achieve routine lunar missions and they will have the only fusion energy power plants on earth that will, eventually, turn the middle east oil producing nations into third world slums once again.

"The Chinese want to hurt the Russian space program since they are the only nation with rockets and capsules that can theoretically compete with them. Even America could not easily duplicate its Apollo program. You don't even have capsules on the drawing board anymore. By making the Russians a pariah in the world community, the Chinese hope to retard their space program sufficiently enough so they can not play catch-up any time soon. While my countrymen are busy defending what they did in 1986, the Chinese will be rolling out their moon shot booster rockets."

"Why would you want to hurt *your* country?" Dan asked.

Volkova laughed. "The Chinese have their objectives and I have mine. Like I said before, making Russia the bad guy again will enable the Russian communists to ferment anti-western prejudice and retake control. The Russian people will see that the West does not trust them and does not want them in their community. They are already weary of the capitalist experiment - the rich get richer and the poor get to vote for one slob over another. The Russians are ready for a change. We were not fools for letting the Chinese use Star City and for our information swapping. Soon the hard-liners will return to the Kremlin and we will also have a lunar base mining H-3. Within ten years, the two greatest communist powers that ever existed will have the exclusive control of the safest and cleanest form of energy known to mankind. Meanwhile, Americans and their western partners will be jerking each other off in the International Space Station studying tse tse fly mating habits in zero gravity.

Dan noticed a shadow in the entrance. He spotted the movement in his peripheral vision. His first thought was that it couldn't be real… but it was.

He prayed that the former SS Officer's handgun still worked as he took a side step, aimed, and…while pulling the trigger, he saw the flash from the muzzle that was aimed at him. The gunman at the entrance fired a silenced round but the Lugar's report reverberated in the small enclosure, deafening everybody. Dan felt moistness at first under his left arm and then noticed everybody moving around him; he saw the gunman outside go down a moment before he hit the ground hard.

Laura spotted Raoul getting up and dashing towards Dan as she spun around sensing the cat-like stealth of Katenka nearly upon her. Sergeant Smith had fired her service sidearm more times on the range than she could remember and always shot expertly. But this wasn't a practice range with pop up plastic targets; she was taking aim at a human being. She brought the magnum to bear at Katenka thinking she would stop in her tracks but the gun did not dispel Pavel Volkova's ace student. The old lakeside snapshot came into her mind and she saw young Kenny teasing his kid sister again. Sergeant Laura Smith fired two quick shots, center mass, at the approaching woman.

Laura did not have time to comprehend what she had just done as Dan and Raoul struggled for the Lugar. The flashes temporarily blinded her in the dark room but she knew Dan needed help. Just as she began to move towards him, the former KGB officer tackled her. She went down hard hitting her head against the brick wall and hearing another gunshot as she collapsed to the ground.

Laura's sense of time had dissipated but she soon realized only a moment had passed. Pavel Volkova had pulled her up by her pony tail and he shoved her daddy's gun into her back. Her head was aching from the impact with the wall and from being pulled to her feet by her hair. Then she felt the pain in her legs, hips and lower back and slumped, but the Russian kept her standing by pushing her back against the wall. Laura saw the Russian's mouth moving as he yelled at her but she only heard the ringing from the gun shots.

Finally, he shouted the words directly into her ear. He wanted to know where the documents where.

"I don't know!" She yelled back, not intending to yell but she was nearly deaf. "He hid them somewhere in the fort," Laura said, pointing to Dan. "Dan!" She tried to break loose but was slammed back against the wall. The last shot she heard was Dan shooting Raoul. The Cuban was now sitting back against the wall where he had been before, but now he was clutching a bleeding belly wound. Dan was on his stomach, motionless.

Pavel Volkova saw that Katenka was not moving either. The rounds had knocked her against the wall where she had fallen in a heap, revealing the exit wounds in her back. The Russian looked at Viñals struggle with his gunshot wound, then aimed at the Cuban's head and fired once.

*****

Eighteen years as a park police officer and Debbie Hammer had never taken her gun from the holster except on a pistol range. She trembled as she lifted the heavy piece out now and took aim. She couldn't understand why he wasn't responding. "Stop, or I *will shoot* you!" She was screaming now. She had the man's head placed right above the orange painted front sight of her service revolver. Hammer heard the gunshots and didn't know what had gone on inside the cell but knew this was some type of hostage situation taking place right before her eyes. The young woman was bleeding from the back of her head and she could see the man holding a gun at her waist. The park ranger couldn't believe he was pulling her around by the hair like a rag doll.

Volkova turned and saw Hammer for the first time. He could see she was shouting but couldn't hear the words as the multiple pistol shots had deafened him as well. The Russian didn't think any more about it; he lowered Laura's gun and fired the remaining rounds at Officer Hammer. He then bent down and grabbed the gunman's Colt XM-177E1 he was still alive, although quite near death, but the young Haitian wouldn't release it.

"*Au revoir*" Volkova jerked the carbine from him.

The dying Haitian was Felip Laurier whose twin brother Andrě worked with Volkova organizing resistance against U.S. Marines on their home island. Once their identities were known and wanted posters went up they rafted to Miami and set up a carpet cleaning business in the Haitian community. They responded eagerly to Volkova's call to escape their boredom.

Volkova was hoping Andrě would not fuck up like his brother. He should be down at the dock calling in Lorenzetti's seaplane. Volkova thought to also take Hammer's gun but before he could turn around, he heard a shot and instantly felt the pain: he couldn't believe it, shot in the ass again, this time on the other cheek.

Hammer collapsed. Her last thought was of the bullet proof vest she had hanging back at the office. Volkova limped over with Laura in tow and kicked Hammer's radio from her hand and took her gun. He then moved along the wall toward the fort's entrance, still pulling Laura along. He heard the prop of a seaplane beyond the walls and jerked on Laura's hair. "You have until the time we reach the seaplane beach to tell me where your brother's effects are or you die, too."

*****

Detective Leonard reached the fort by seaplane, with no back up and no plan other than to keep his chief informed. Seeing no signal strength on his cell phone, he went to the ranger station and gave a quick description of Laura and Dan to Park Ranger Stacey Shewler who told him that she thought she'd spotted a couple matching those descriptions around by the campsites. He told her to arrange a conference call with his chief and with the coast guard about getting some assistance while he looked for his subjects. Ranger Shewler was startled but Detective Leonard told her to just do it and that his chief would explain everything to the coast guard. He scribbled down his boss's number and raced off to the campsite area.

The first shots that were fired in the cell were muffled and not easily discernible from other parts of the fort. Detective Leonard was talking to some campers when he heard them. His gut feeling told him there was a firefight going on but he couldn't tell from what direction the sounds came. Instead of running back to cross the moat into the fort's interior, he ran the opposite way thinking there was quicker access. That was his first mistake.

*****

"See that, Sergeant Smith?" Pavel Volkova asked, as they crossed over and turned left towards the beach pointing to the moored seaplanes. They had had a wide avenue with no obstacles from the moment they had started moving. Every tourist in sight had run for cover and still remained hidden with only the occasional head appearing above a trash receptacle or corner to see if it was safe to come out - it wasn't. Park Ranger Shewler was in the office and on the phone, having just connected Leonard's boss to the coast guard when she heard the shots that killed her partner. Shewler ventured into the fort, but backed out once she saw Volkova, carrying a gun, moving towards the main gate and pulling a woman along by her hair. The park ranger shouted towards the dock for people to stay on their boats and ran back to the office to call for help.

Volkova's seaplane came to life and the pilot was throwing off his mooring line. The engine's noise echoed off the brick work making normal conversation impossible.

"Is the coast clear, Andrě?" Volkova shouted to the Haitian guarding the beach.

"All the way, boss mon." He pulled out a sister to the weapon his brother had died clutching and pulled back the charging handle to slide the first of thirty rounds into the assault rifle.

"Now or never." The former KGB officer punched Laura in the stomach, dropping her to her knees; he brought the park ranger's revolver to her head.

"Watchit boss!" Andrě yelled, taking aim in Volkova's direction.

The Russian, feeling weak with the loss of blood from his new wound and his reopened old wound, tried to move out of the way but fell over Laura in the process. He heard the XM-177E1 spit out its military 5.56x45 millimeter rounds and heard them breaking the sound barrier inches over his head.

*****

The first several rounds went wild and Detective Leonard scrabbled for cover but found none on the drawbridge. He heard the shots hit the two hundred year old bricks behind him and he suddenly felt pain in the back of his head. A ricochet round or piece of brick had struck him, he thought. He touched the wetness on the back of his head. Firing at the machine gunner without taking aim, he crawled back to the entry way. The detective saw several rounds hit the ground fountaining sand and coral just yards, then inches, from his head. He thought of getting up and running when three shots slammed into him in quick succession, all in the upper body, rolling him over several times. He heard one last loud shot fired from right over his head.

Leonard couldn't move at first, and then realized he couldn't draw full breaths either. He managed to crawl the few feet to the fort's wall and pulled himself into a sitting position. The detective looked down and started to unbutton his shirt, then pulled open the Velcro on his Kevlar vest. He had huge welts forming on his sternum and on each side of his chest. At least three ribs were broken along with internal bruising, he guessed. Looking over, he saw Dan Gill blood soaked and on his knees, a few feet away.

*****

Laura felt like she was losing consciousness again as fort and sea began to whirl together. She heard Pavel Volkova's last threat as the ringing noise began to abate and felt the pain from the unexpected kick. She realized she was lying on the ground with the Russian on top of her trying to avoid bullets. Gunfire was all around her but all she could think of was moving the rock that she was lying on. She pushed her hand under the small of her back and felt a pistol grip.

*****

Gill slowly got to his feet again and stumbled over to where Leonard had propped himself up.

"You okay?" Dan muttered.

"Hell no. How about you?"

"I think I'll live if I can stop the bleeding. I don't think anything important got hit."

"Where's the shooter now?"

"Over there." Dan pointed to the downed Haitian.

Dan spotted Laura getting up on her knees then fighting to stand up as the seaplane roared away from the beach. Dan tried to stand, going to one knee first, but fell back down. He crawled closer to Leonard and fought to get into a seated position resting his back against the fort. They watched Laura stepping painfully towards them.

She fell on her knees next to Dan then held on to his face, kissing him.

"I thought you were dead," she said.

"So did I," he said brushing her hair and looking for the source of the blood.

"Leave it. I'm okay. Let's get your wound under control." She helped him lie back on the ground, took out a bandana from her back pocket, and applied direct pressure to the wound. She felt around for an exit wound but there wasn't one. She paused, turning her head to watch as the seaplane throttled its engine to full power and sped across the narrow band of water between Garden and Bush Keys. Laura reapplied pressure as they all watched the plane gain altitude then bank sharply southward and descend so that it was flying only meters high off the waves. It quickly disappeared into the glare of the sun on the water.

Laura kept the pressure on and beckoned to nearby tourists to come over and help. No one moved.

Leonard was able to stand up briefly but sat right back down, having lost his breath again. "Sit tight, detective," Laura commanded.

"Volkova hobbled to the seaplane as fast as he could once he saw that I had this," she nodded to the ranger's weapon she placed on the ground. "He was definitely going to kill me if he hadn't been distracted by you, detective."

"To protect and serve," Leonard laughed, giddy that he wasn't dead.

"The gun must have fallen out of his hand when we both fell. Maybe I should have taken some shots his way but I didn't feel comfortable doing that. Lots of people on the nearby boats and I figured my aim would be off."

Park Ranger Shewler ran over with her first aid bag and within minutes, crew members from the ferries and some private boaters were bringing first aid supplies to them as well. Laura was relieved of treating Dan and a young mate from one of the ferries treated her head lacerations.

"I held the phone out the window when I heard the machinegun fire; I think the coast guard figured out what was going on. They're sending everything they got. They said that a navy frigate is nearby and is launching its helicopter with a doctor and corpsmen on board. It should be here within thirty minutes."

Dan pushed away his first aider. "Get them on the horn again and tell them to splash…shoot down…that seaplane that took off."

"Who's on it?" Shewler asked.

"I can't explain everything now. Just do it!" He grunted, and fell back against the wall.

*****

A small crowd finally formed around them and Dan concluded that the all clear signal had somehow been spread around the fort.

"I notified the coast guard about the seaplane," Shewler said out of breath from running back and forth from the ranger station.

"What did they say?" Laura asked.

"They said that they can't shoot down what they don't see and they didn't think you had the authority to make them go weapons hot – whatever that meant." Park Ranger Shewler took a knee.

Laura looked at her name tag. "Stacey, your partner is dead."

"I figured that when she wouldn't answer the radio. I'm going there now." The ranger got up and started into the fort.

"There are three other bodies there as well," Laura said.

"Take some first aid supplies; one is still alive," Dan said.

Half a dozen people with first aid kits followed Ranger Shewler. Laura looked over at Dan. "Who?"

"That crazy Cuban. Volkova's shot only grazed the top of his head. He was still ticking when I left. He made me promise him that I would kill Volkova."

*****

Detective Leonard, Sergeant Smith and Dan Gill sat in silence as they waited for the chopper. Laura's head had been bandaged and ice bags brought over from the ferries had been placed on Leonard's wounds. Only Dan still required active help to keep pressure on the gunshot wound. The navy helicopter could be faintly heard approaching over the water. Shewler came back to tell them she was going to bring the chopper right inside the fort and she started clearing the area of people.

"Dan, where *is* Ken's stuff? It's not in the backpack." Laura whispered.

"It's not here," Dan struggled to say.

Laura turned to give him a long stare. "What? Where is it?"

"I Fedexed it this morning. Remember the drug store we went to last night? I gave the clerk a hundred bucks and he said he would take care of it this morning when his shift ended."

"You trusted some kid working the night shift?"

"He seemed honest enough."

"Where did you send it?" Laura asked louder as the chopper approached.

"It's a secret." Dan struggled to laugh then passed out.

"Where did you send it?" Laura was shouting now as the chopper made its landing, kicking up sand and loose debris on the ground.

Chapter 52

Friday, January 31, 2003
Cape Canaveral

All of the Fort Jefferson wounded were taken to a hospital on the keys where Dan underwent surgery to remove the 5.56 millimeter round that had imbedded itself in muscle, after skimming his shoulder blade. Viñals required much more time in the operating room. Detective Leonard and Laura were kept overnight for observation, Leonard in the cardiac intensive care unit since his heart was bruised. Upon discharge, Leonard's chief escorted him and Laura to Miami where they were debriefed by the FBI.

Raoul Viñals and Dan Gill briefly shared some time together in the post operative ward. They watched the evening news together as a spokeswoman for the United States Attorney's office in Miami gave a briefing about the Haitian drug smuggling deal gone bad on the Dry Tortugas. "The first time in almost three hundred years that the tiny keys had heard the sound of pirate's muskets," the tall blonde read from a prepared statement. The dead woman was still unidentified but believed to be an innocent tourist. Raoul and Dan discovered they were innocent and unnamed tourists as well.

That evening, while they were still in the same ward, they were visited by a man claiming to be from the FBI counter-intelligence section assigned to South Florida Homeland Security Department. Yeah, right, Dan thought.

He pulled no punches. He asked for the nurse on duty to step outside and then told Viñals to keep his mouth shut or he would be on the next flight to Havana gift wrapped for Uncle Fidel. He told Dan that he could kiss his military pension good-bye and to expect an IRS audit every year until he died if he didn't shut up as well. Dan didn't mind keeping mum…for the time being anyway.

In any event, the message was delivered…and received. Laura called every other hour but they didn't speak of what transpired over the open lines. Raoul was moved the next morning. The nurse told Dan he was being air lifted to Miami since his internal wounds were still bleeding and his temperature had spiked. They had better facilities there, he was assured. That was the last he saw of the Cuban.

"My wife will never believe this. Damn, my girlfriends will never believe this either. They'll all think I was cheating on them. They may as well send me back to Cuba." Dan remembered Viñals last conversation with him. He still wasn't sure whose side he was really on but the swarthy little prick had grown on him.

The hospital arranged for medical transportation to Laura's house on Friday afternoon. Dan was accosted by reporters while being manhandled into the medical transport van. He confirmed that he was on vacation and visiting the Dry Tortugas - just like the spokeswoman had said. He threw in a plug for Knight's Insurance but that wound up on the cutting room floor.

Not knowing what time Dan would be discharged, Laura left the back door unlocked. With the shuttle landing scheduled for the next morning, her squadron was in crisis mode, monitoring storms tracking down from Canada and a bizarrely shifting jet stream that could affect the landing. She insisted on returning to duty right away and kept to her story, the same one reported on the news with only her commanding officer knowing otherwise. Dan called her from the house when he arrived, but by the time she drove home, he was fast asleep. She woke him up at six in the morning to ask him if he wanted to watch the shuttle land. She also arranged to have another guest join them.

Chapter 53

Saturday morning, February 1, 2003
Cape Canaveral

"Did you keep the bullet? Over." Colonel Ben Ochoa asked Dan over the military radio in the Humvee.

"No sir, no souvenirs. Over." Dan replied, looking at Laura who was driving them to a viewing area to watch the shuttle land.

"Well, enjoy the show and don't forget to come by and see me before you leave town. Out."

"Why? So he can put a bullet into me, too?" he asked Laura.

She laughed, "No, he really does like you. I guess he figures that if he's lost me forever, then you're an acceptable second." She reached around and turned the volume of the radio down as she wasn't expecting any more transmissions. "I think it's finally safe to tell me where you sent Ken's stuff?" She asked.

"It's safe and sound in New Jersey."

"What? You didn't send it home, did you? It's already gone if you did."

"You must think I'm an idiot. I sent it to John Gotti."

"John Gotti…the gangster."

"No, he's dead. John Gotti, the lawyer."

"What's the difference?"

The laugh hurt his shoulder. "John Gotti is an ambulance chaser in Newark. I took a statement at his office before coming down here and the address came to my mind when I was at the drug store. I called him from a pay phone in the hospital and he has it. They have a safe in their office and that's where it is right now."

Dan moved in his seat to relieve the pressure he was feeling from the wound. "This has been some vacation for firsts. First time I've seen a shuttle launch and a shuttle land; first time I got to kill people with a German pistol from World War Two; first time I…no…second time I got to bang a broad in Tennessee…"

"What!"

"Okay, first time in *Lexington*, Tennessee." He smiled, knowing she wouldn't hit a man still patched together with surgical staples. "Just kidding."

The Humvee offered a pretty smooth ride and was big enough for Dan to stretch out comfortably. "When will we get there?"

"About fifteen minutes. The shuttle should be landing about forty-five minutes after that."

"How are you holding up?" Dan said after they had driven several blocks.

"Alright, I reckon."

"Feel copasetic about sending Katenka to ballerina Valhalla?"

"I have absolutely no remorse about killing that…bitch. When I start to feel some sorrow, I just think of how she manipulated and killed my brother. I just wish I didn't have to keep it a secret. It blows the government's whole cover up if one of the innocent tourists put two rounds into another innocent tourist."

"How did they threaten you?" Dan asked.

"Bull crap about national security and that I am subject to the Uniform Code of Military Justice and we are considered to be in wartime. You?"

"Worse, my pension and the IRS sword of Damocles"

They entered the secured area of Cape Canaveral and Laura had to stop at several checkpoints. She had Dan's temporary security information and had to show it each time.

"Where do you think Pavel Volkova is now?" Laura asked.

"Probably in Cuba. I saw a little news story about a seaplane crash sixty miles south of Key West. I'm sure that was staged to kill off the pilot. Volkova is drinking rum and Coke on some beach now, I would guess. We ruined his plans for now. He will probably wait for things to settle down and then move on."

"Do you think we'll run into him again?" Laura asked.

"As long as Ken's writings need to remain a secret…they have value. The day it appears on the front page of the '*The New York Times*' is the day we stop worrying about it ever again."

"What do you think we should do?"

"Laura, you've asked me that all along and all I've managed to do is get us in more trouble. What you told Volkova back at Fort Jefferson is dead on. The truth shall set us free."

"I think I already came to that conclusion but I wanted to hear it from you. I have over sixty days accumulated leave. I think that I'll take thirty days leave and go with you to New Jersey. We'll pick up my brother's stuff. Then, we'll decide how to release it."

"Then what?" Dan asked.

"I guess that depends on whether I get court-martialed. You'll wait for me, right?"

*****

They parked in a handicapped spot and Laura helped Dan to the viewing area. She spotted Detective Leonard there with his wife and two young boys. Corey Leonard waved back and immediately grimaced in pain.

"Go up with him and I'll be with you guys in a few minutes. I need to check back with my unit."

"He's married with kids?"

"I told you that he wasn't after me."

Dan walked over to the grandstand and Detective Leonard introduced Dan to his wife and kids as *the man who saved daddy's life*.

Mrs. Leonard poured Dan some coffee from a thermos and offered him a thick homemade BLT sandwich.

"Hey detective…" Dan said moving closer to Leonard.

"Corey, please."

"Corey, I'm sorry about giving you such a hard time early on in the investigation. You're a stand-up guy."

"Yeah, you were a bit of a jerk, weren't you?" Leonard laughed. "Laura told me you were a bad ass airborne ranger in your day."

"Excuse me? This is *still* my day. I saved your ass, didn't I?"

"Okay ranger, don't hit me. What outfit were you with?"

"I was with the 75th Ranger Regiment and the 82nd Airborne Division."

Detective Leonard took a doughnut from his wife's picnic basket. "Ever hear of the triple nickel? It was an airborne outfit in World War Two."

"No. Why?"

"My grandfather was in it."

"Really?" After a moment Dan asked, "The army was still segregated back then, wasn't it? I mean…well…I never heard of black paratroopers in World War II."

"Oh yeah, grandpappy was in the first black parachute company that was later expanded into the 555th Airborne Battalion…Colored."

"I never knew that."

"Not too many people do. The war ended before they could fight but they were sent out west and became smoke jumpers: you know, putting out forest fires. They practically invented all of the techniques used today."

"What are we going to do about the mess we're in?" Dan said to the detective once he saw that his wife and kids were preoccupied waiting for the landing

"I don't know; I was read the riot act at work. They knew that I put an application in for the FBI a few years ago and promised me all kinds of goodies if I just play ball. They offered me an appointment as an FBI Special Agent with assignment at Quantico…lots of TDY…temporary duty to increase my base pay. My wife is a paralegal and they offered her a job up there at twice what she's getting now."

Dan told him that he and Laura were going public despite the threats made to keep quiet - Volkova was just too dangerous to worry about for the rest of their lives.

"You compromise once; you compromise your whole life, my friend. Your grandfather was treated like a second class citizen in his day, yet he volunteered for the toughest job in the United States Army to fight the Nazis. What would he do?"

"That's not fair, Dan."

"I know, below the belt."

Dan watched Detective Leonard's tight lipped mouth grow into a grin.

"Okay, I'll support whatever you two decide to do. Let's face it, I don't know what happened in 1986 but I will certainly confirm the results of my investigation into the death of Professor Bera and confirm what really happened at Fort Jefferson. Screw it, I'm civil service."

Laura arrived just as they were shaking hands.

"So what's up with you two?" Leonard asked.

"I told him you're going to spend some time with me up in New Jersey," Dan answered and then told her what Detective Leonard had offered.

"What happens afterwards?" Leonard asked.

"Don't know. Hopefully, I can return to my job and finish my twenty," Laura answered.

"And you?" he said to Dan.

"Well, I was thinking of going back to school to earn a degree."

"Check out the college man. Degree in what?" Leonard asked.

"Don't know, yet. Maybe criminal justice."

"Where at?" The detective asked.

Dan looked at Laura. "Don't know that either. I'm thinking around the Cape Canaveral area, though."

"Well, our department just posted some openings; you should look into it. I'm sure my referral will kill your chances, though." Leonard laughed, and then winced with pain.

Laura smiled. "Let me call HQ: there should have been an announcement by now that the shuttle is coming into visual range." Laura checked her watch and stepped down the bleacher steps and over to her Humvee.

Detective Leonard's older son, Curtis, had let Dan borrow a pair of binoculars and he scanned the approach azimuth but saw nothing.

"Dan!" Laura shouted and then motioned for him to come down. He handed the field glasses back to Curtis and struggled with the pain as he descended the bleacher steps.

"What's up?"

"I need to get back to headquarters, ASAP. You should leave now. Ask Corey to drop you off at my house."

Laura sounded like a sergeant again and Dan understood her request to be an order.

"What's up?"

"Columbia won't landing today…we lost contact over Texas. . . " Laura couldn't finish; lowering her head to shield her emotion from the nearby civilians she disappeared into the Humvee, heading back to her unit.

Dedication

On January 28, 1986, I was serving in the 504th Parachute Infantry Regiment of the 82nd Airborne Division at Fort Bragg, North Carolina. Upon learning of the explosion of the space shuttle *Challenger*, the Headquarters Company Charge of Quarters NCO hunted up a small television set and placed it on his desk. Throughout the morning we speculated if the Soviets had somehow sabotaged the shuttle and what that would mean for our unit. A wise enlisted man spoke up and said that even if it were sabotaged, it would be covered up. We would not risk World War III for seven astronauts.

It was with much hesitation that I began this novel because I felt that by writing a work of fiction stemming from the loss of *Challenger* that I would be trivializing that event. Words can not convey the respect in my heart for the crew of STS-51L.

"The crew of the space shuttle Challenger honored us by the manner in which they lived their lives. We will never forget them, nor the last time we saw them, this morning, as they prepared for the journey and waved goodbye and 'slipped the surly bonds of earth' to 'touch the face of God'" President Ronald W. Reagan, January 28, 1986.

Mike Smith	Dick Scobee	Ron McNair
Ellison Onizuka	Greg Jarvis	Judith Resnick
	Christa McAuliffe	